SPARKS SHOWERED FROM THE *FOXBAT*'S WHEELS AS VIKTOR STOOD ON THE BRAKE PEDALS....

An instant later they smashed into the barrier. It wrapped around their tandem cockpits like the churning arms of an octopus. The *Foxbat* shrieked as the webbing pulled hard against the metallic surfaces of the fuselage and controls, but the needle-nosed cockpit and sharp-edged wings gouged the trapping like a grizzly making a fight for its life.

Viktor's eyes were wide open, fixed on the bow edge of the flight deck that was still moving ominously toward them. He had to take the chance. He had to get himself and Nadia out of the plane before it tore free of the barrier and darted over the bow to the waiting sea. Keying his intercom, he shouted to Nadia: "Brace yourself! We're bailing out!"

Also by
Robert J. Szilagye and Stanley C. Monroe

THE TRIDENT TRAGEDY

MEDITERRANEAN MANEUVER

Robert J. Szilagye
&
Stanley C. Monroe

A DELL BOOK

Published by
Dell Publishing Co., Inc.
1 Dag Hammarskjold Plaza
New York, New York 10017

Copyright © 1984 by Robert J. Szilagye and Stanley C. Monroe

All rights reserved. No part of this book may be reproduced or transmitted in any form or by any means, electronic or mechanical, including photocopying, recording, or by any information storage and retrieval system, without the written permission of the Publisher, except where permitted by law.

Dell ® TM 681510, Dell Publishing Co., Inc.

ISBN: 0-440-15560-6

Printed in the United States of America
First printing—May 1984

*In loving memory of
Helen M. Gerken-Monroe*

We gratefully acknowledge Paul McCarthy for devoting himself to this novel as its editor. His skill, his patience, and his loyalty to the story were an immense contribution to its completion.

PROLOGUE

If he had a smidgen of guilt at first, it wasn't because of the Party, Yuri Velinkov reflected as he looked out the kitchen window of his six-room guesthouse and made a sour face at the third snowstorm to blanket his native city of Kiev since the month of January had begun. He might have felt uneasy about spying on the two young Soviet Air Force MIG pilots that had now made their fourth secret romantic rendezvous at his guesthouse in the past two months, but there was no feeling of guilt left in his sixty-year-old disappointed heart about the Party. His days of illusion were long over. He need not swallow any more lies or be victimized by any more party corruption. He had eyes.

The Party had been responsible for the hideous milk and bread lines, and the rotten meat that the butcher shops offered at inflated prices because of shortages. Of course there were food shortages. He had eyes. The Party was growing more bullets, tanks, ships, and planes instead of more food. And what food was available was being hoarded to sell to the rich for a better price or to give to corrupt party leaders in return for privileges and favors. Even a blind man could see that.

Yuri knew it was the Party who no longer had eyes. Not for the poor, or the old, or the sick. It could not see his wife, Yekaterina, suffering from arthritis and rheumatism. It could not see her in her armchair by the potbellied stove in the front room all winter long, trying to ease her aches and pains. It could not see how age and the cold compounded the short-windedness that a Nazi sniper's bullet had brought into his life by ripping out one of his lungs while he'd been defending some part of Mother Russia he had not seen since. The Party had no eyes to approve his and Yekaterina's request to relocate to a warmer part of Russia before one winter closed Yekaterina's eyes for all time . . . maybe his eyes, too.

The Party was preoccupied with nurturing the newest of new Soviet man. Just as it had nurtured his son, Petr, during the

Nikita Khrushchev era, when his son'd frozen to death defending Mother Russia from an invasion of the "Dark Force of the West" that never came. The Party had spent more rubles on Petr's bullets than on clothes to keep him warm. For the war that never came.

Now, as another brutal winter was at hand to renew his and Yekaterina's suffering, Yuri decided he didn't care about Mother Russia anymore either. All he had left now was apathy for the Party and pity for the two young pilots. He had eyes. He knew why the young lovers avoided patronizing the more convenient and more luxurious hotels in the heart of the city. The city had a host of additional KGB agents walking the streets to watch the horde of new military personnel that had arrived at the air force base near Kiev along with the Party's newest Foxbats. Because his guest house was well out of town in an intimate country setting, it offered privacy from the watchful eyes of the KGB. The privacy earned him an extra five rubles each time the young couple made their overnight stay, just to keep their romantic rendezvous the secret it obviously needed to be.

Yuri Velinkov had eyes. And he had a friend who had opened his eyes for him. His friend and neighbor, Comrade Ivan Trotsky, had opened his eyes when he'd shown Yuri how much milk, bread, and fresh meat were available for the right amount of money. Ever since their friendship had begun, around the time the Party's new Foxbats had come to Kiev, Ivan Trotsky had brought an end to milk, bread, and meat lines for him and Yekaterina. And when that friendship began, Yuri pledged his loyalty to Ivan Trotsky—his loyalty to the Party was no more.

Ivan made sense. Ivan shared his bitterness about the Party. With Ivan he could safely voice his dissent without fear of being reported to the local Party leaders, or worse than that, the KGB. It was a liberty that had brought some laughter into his life and he recalled having Ivan in hysterics one night when after drinking much vodka with Ivan he had commented to Ivan that Soviet ideology bordered on idiocy. He and Ivan had laughed for a long time about that, then they'd sunk into an alarmed silence, realizing it was not a laughing matter that their homeland was under the leadership of idiots.

Yuri had eyes. Now that he was on intimate terms with Ivan, he knew that the friendship they shared had been no accident. He knew Ivan had planned it that way. Ivan had cunningly filled his eyes with the unattainable. Then Ivan wittingly filled his ears with the unthinkable. Now Ivan was going to generously fill his pockets with the unbelievable. Tonight Ivan was going to pay him a thousand rubles for finding the young faces of his special guesthouse patrons among a collection of photographs that Ivan was to get from his other secret friends. And Ivan promised him there would be many more rubles to come if Ivan's secret friends liked the faces he picked out for them. He didn't quite understand what meaning his two young patrons held for Ivan, but he was too old to care anymore.

Yuri returned his thoughts to the kitchen table and anxiously watched as his wife spooned up the last morsel of soup that had been their supper. Predictably, Yekaterina would go right to bed after supper without encouragement, but Yuri's anxiety had him restless and made him hurry her along anyway. As soon as she had returned her spoon to the bowl for the last time, he got right up from his seat and began clearing off the table. "Now that you have eaten, go to bed, old woman. Sleep will give you strength."

Yekaterina toyed with her disarrayed snow-white hair for another moment as she watched her husband doing the work she was no longer able to do. Then after drawing her frayed robe closer around her frail frame, she muttered, "You should eat more soup, Yuri. You are getting too thin. With all the work you do for both of us, you need your strength more than I need mine."

"Who is taking care of whom, old woman?" Yuri returned playfully. "I will take more soup later if it will make you sleep better," he added. "Now, let me help you up and I will come along and tuck you into bed."

Yekaterina accepted Yuri's affectionate support as she strained to get up from her chair. "I feel the long sleep is near," she said with a faint groan. "Soon you will not have the burden of this old woman anymore."

"When that time comes, I will rush right out and get a beautiful young girl to take your place," Yuri teased, but Yekaterina's comment about dying had disturbed him. "Until then, this old man will continue to enjoy pampering his Yekaterina."

"Who could blame you for wanting a pretty young woman?" Yekaterina went on as she shuffled toward their bedroom on the first floor in the rear of the guesthouse.

"I could blame me," Yuri returned, steadying Yekaterina through each painful step she took. "Young women have no experience. An old woman, like aged wine, has a refinement that offers excellence. Now keep your voice down, you will awaken our guests."

"If you think those two young people are sleeping, Yuri, then you are an old man."

"Of course I am an old man," Yuri said as he strained to help Yekaterina into bed. He tucked the covers around her bony body, then kissed her lightly on the cheek. "And you are an old woman. Soon I will take you away from this cold place and the warmth of the sun will shine on you all year long to return you to good health. Then . . . we will go dancing together. For now, get plenty of rest so you will be in the mood for dancing when that time comes." After another light kiss on the cheek, he switched off the bedroom lamp and went out to the front room.

Yuri paused to listen at the bottom of the wooden staircase that led up to his six guestrooms. With his guesthouse relying mostly on summer trade, five of the rooms had been absent of the sounds of life since the winter season had begun. The other room, which the two young officers had always chosen over the past month, released no sounds of sleep, as Yekaterina had predicted. Instead, unmistakable sounds of passion were seeping out into the quiet hall. The sounds were not new to Yuri, just unlived for long years. His ears were still sensitive to the urgency in the young couple's lovemaking. He thought it hinted of a necessity to be free of restraint.

Yuri left the staircase and moved over to the hall closet to get his greatcoat and fur cap. He wondered as he slung the heavy calf-length coat over his rounded shoulders why the young couple's lovemaking was of such interest to Ivan? Why they were afraid their lovemaking would be discovered by the KGB? Why it hinted of urgency and restraint? He placed his fur cap securely over his thinning gray hair, deciding it was none of his business. Ivan had made it quite clear to him that he was only to report on the behavior of the young officers, not evaluate it. He stepped out into the driving snowstorm and closed and locked the door, then began his trudge through the ankle-deep drifts toward Ivan's neighboring farmhouse.

Ivan Trotsky's huge rounded body ballooned his satin robe as he gazed out the glass window of his front door in anticipation of his late-night visitor. He squinted from behind herringbone glasses as the stunted figure of his friend Yuri Velinkov emerged from frenzied snowflakes and stumbled through the deep drifts toward him. Ensuring that Yuri's visit would not awaken his wife, Ivan had the front door opened before Yuri could ring the doorbell. His breath turned to vapor as he called out softly, "Keep your voice down, I do not want to awaken Raya."

Billows of vapor rose from Yuri's mouth but he was too winded to even whisper, much less speak, as he rushed inside to Ivan's toast-warm, spacious living room. With rose-red cheeks and watery eyes that released a stream of tears down his nearly frozen face, Yuri passed a moment hyperventilating to catch his breath before he could finally speak. Then, with a tone of anxiety that was edged with wheezing sounds, he asked, "Did you get the photos, Ivan?"

Ivan nodded as he closed the front door quietly. "The young ones? They have come again?" he asked with raised eyebrows that were thick and graying to match the few strands of fine hair that were oddly styled across the front of his otherwise totally bald head.

"For the fourth time," Yuri replied through short breaths. "I am sure they will make another romantic rendezvous at my guesthouse next weekend. And the weekend after as well."

"You are quite sure they do not suspect anything? You have done or said nothing that might suggest you were monitoring their visits?"

"Nothing. And if you had heard the sounds coming from their room, you would be as convinced as I am that they are dependably in love."

"The pattern of their visits suggests they come to your guesthouse each time they are granted overnight passes from their air base. I hope we can depend on the continuation of that military procedure long enough to bring their identities to the attention of my colleagues, with time to spare for further steps to be taken," Ivan commented firmly.

"Depend upon love, Comrade," Yuri offered. "Continuation of the passes will follow. I was in the army, you were not. I know what can be done in the military when there is a strong enough necessity. They will keep coming as long as there is vodka to offer a barracks officer in exchange for passes."

Ivan nodded in agreement. "Come quietly to the basement, Yuri. I have a multitude of dossiers for you to search through. When you find the faces of your guesthouse patrons among the photos, the thousand rubles I promised you will be yours."

Over an hour passed as the dossiers stacked at his left were examined one by one and added to the steadily growing stack at his right. Yuri finally stopped at a photo of a female junior flight lieutenant. Handing the dossier across the table to Ivan's waiting hands, he said excitedly, "That is the woman! The photo does not do her beauty justice, but it is she!"

Ivan studied the photo carefully, committing it to memory, then began digesting the lines of information contained in her dossier. Seeing something of particular concern, his thick eyebrows raised to express his delight. "Interesting," he commented.

"Her beauty?" Yuri questioned naïvely.

"Her being a married woman," Ivan returned coolly. "If they *are* meeting in secrecy as you suggest, Comrade, then we can safely assume it is not her husband she is sharing your guesthouse room with."

"Infidelity!"

"Precisely," Ivan replied as he refilled his and Yuri's glasses with vodka. "That would give the most apparent explanation for keeping their meetings from the watchful eyes of the KGB."

"Does that make her well worth the thousand rubles you will pay me?"

Ivan raised his glass and gestured for Yuri to do the same. Then touching rims in toast, he said, "She may be worth ten times that if my associates find the combination of marriage and secrecy useful to them."

Yuri wanted to ask what Ivan's associates would do to the young couple, but his mind was occupied with thoughts of what he could do with the ten thousand rubles Ivan suggested he might also earn. It was an unheard of sum of money to his poor ears and had him envisioning a place where the sun always shone for him and Yekaterina to spend the rest of their lives in. He was sure some of the rubles could be put into the greedy hands of his local party leader and entice him to hurry the approval of his request to relocate to such a warm place. "Do you know who the woman's husband is?" he asked anxiously.

"No, Comrade," Ivan lied. The dossier did mention the woman's husband in full detail on the page that followed her photograph, which Ivan knew Yuri had not bothered to study. She was Soviet Junior Flight Lieutenant Nadia Potgornev. The dossier noted that her husband was Major Joseph Potgornev, an adjutant to Soviet Army General Dhorkinov. The dossier also stated that her husband was stationed in East Berlin at present. That meant it couldn't be Major Potgornev that Nadia Potgornev was entertaining at Yuri's guesthouse. He could just guess what Major Potgornev might do to the man taking his customary place in bed beside his wife if he ever found out.

The news was explosive to Ivan. "Go on searching for the man, Yuri," he urged. "Find her lover and make it a matched set of photographs."

"Will there be another thousand rubles for his face when I find him as well?" Yuri asked.

"Do not seek all your rubles at once, Yuri. There will be more for you to earn on another night."

When Yuri did come to the familiar face of his male patron, the photo stared back at him hauntingly with two gray eyes that seemed boyishly innocent and had him remembering his son, Petr. Like Petr, the man had yellow hair and handsome features that were sure to get notice from the most beautiful women. But unlike Petr, who had been rather short and quite frail, this man possessed a powerful body that stood over six feet tall and suggested he might be with the Soviet Olympics instead of the Soviet Air Force. The man's size had frightened him the first time he'd come to his guesthouse. It frightened him more now that he had been secretly spying on him.

Ivan noticed Yuri lingering over one photograph. "Is it he, Yuri?" he asked anxiously.

Yuri handed Ivan the photo he had been studying for long moments. "Yes, Ivan . . . it is he," he said softly. His voice was edged with worry.

"You have done well, Yuri," Ivan said, then handed Yuri an envelope.

Yuri slipped the envelope into his shirt pocket, then responding to Ivan's gesture for another toast, he raised his glass of vodka and touched the rim of Ivan's glass. After a healthy swallow he asked, "Will the young officers get into any trouble, Ivan? Will your friends do them any harm?"

"Do not fret, Comrade," Ivan returned with a smile. "Without their knowing it, you have probably done them a great service. Now be sure to keep this to yourself. I will be in touch with you soon."

PART ONE

CHAPTER ONE

Mondays stunk. No, on second thought they sucked. Every goddamn one of 'em. That's what Matthew Ferris decided he thought of Mondays as he drove his half-paid-for 1979 Buick Regal along the snow-covered Baltimore–Washington Expressway at six thirty in the morning. Today was Monday and he weighed it as a case in point. Today he was supposed to hop aboard the *Wings of Man* and flee to sunny Waikiki Beach for two weeks of badly needed rest and relaxation, with a dash of recreation thrown in, so he could wash his brains out now that his second marriage in twelve years had ended. His airline tickets were stuck behind his visor, his golf clubs and luggage were in his trunk, and tucked loosely into his trousers under his hooded parka was the short-sleeve, floral-print Hawaiian shirt he planned to be wearing when he arrived in Waikiki, just so he'd look like he'd been there all his life. Mondays.

Ferris had worn the Hawaiian shirt, with its flashy swirls of bright red and yellow, just in case he still got to go to Waikiki, but he knew deep in his heart that Monday had killed that for him. His boss, Hal Banks, had called him at five thirty in the morning and told him to hop over to CIA headquarters in Washington on the double. There hadn't even been a hint of flexibility in Hal's voice, so he was sure it was going to be aloha Waikiki. The good-bye version.

Mondays. They were dependably woeful, Ferris thought as he shivered in the heatless car and eyed the worn wiper blades slaving to remove the ice and snow from his windshield. He jiggled the heater switch for the tenth time since he had left his modest duplex house in Baltimore, just in case it might somehow defy Monday and turn on. It didn't. Instead, the switch broke off in his hand. The car was the only thing he had left now that his first wife, Kathy, had possession of his ranch house in Virginia, and his second wife, Cynthia, had just won ownership of the duplex in Baltimore. But it seemed to him that Kath and Cyn hadn't been satisfied with the houses and their stiff alimony payments. They had obviously gotten a witch doctor to put a curse on his car, and in all probability they each had voodoo dolls that looked like him, which they religiously stuck pins into every goddamn Monday.

Marriage, Ferris mused as he thought about the whopping divorce settlement Cynthia had her "snake in the grass" attorney squeeze him for. He could still remember when they were first married, how Cynthia used to complain that his first wife, Kathy, was sucking him dry with her huge settlement. Now Cyn had become a vampire, too, and she had learned from Kath, who in his opinion was an expert at bloodsucking. Kathy and Cynthia really had him wondering which he hated more, marriage . . . or Mondays.

Ferris turned off the expressway heading for downtown Washington, thinking as he did that he was sure of one thing. He was glad he'd never had any kids with either Kathy or Cynthia. If he had, he'd have bet anything they all would have been Monday babies. "Kids," he muttered when he turned off the exit ramp and got onto Pennsylvania Avenue. Wives he could get rid of, though the process was costly. But kids would have been like Mondays for him. They would have kept boomeranging into his life with woeful results.

Ferris studied his face in the rearview mirror as a traffic light brought him to a stop on Pennsylvania. "Look at you," he muttered in disgust. He thought about how Kathy used to admire his hair, say it was toast brown. And Kath used to say his eyes were bedroom blue. By the time he'd married Cynthia, Cyn was excusing his graying hair by saying it was peppered and distinguished-looking. But Cyn thought his eyes were more barroom bloodshot than bedroom blue. Now he thought his hair always looked like it was in a goddamn snowstorm, the way it had turned completely gray. Silver gray was the best he could say about his hair now. And his bedroom-blue eyes always looked like they were ready for bed. They were always puffed up and had deep, permanent rings around them.

Ferris reached across the front seat for the fur cap he'd brought back from his last assignment, in Pakistan, and quickly placed it on his head to cover his hair. Then as he got the car going again he decided Hal Banks was the cause of his premature aging. There were times when he would have thought a bullet, or a bomb, or hotel and restaurant food, or booze, or cigarettes, or a falling airliner—or maybe a failing heart unable to keep up with his hectic pace—would have killed him. Now he was sure Hal Banks was going to aggravate him to death. And he'd bet anything he'd expire on a goddamn Monday, too. He decided that Hal Banks had fucked up his hair: Hal Banks had fucked up his eyes. Hal had fucked up both his marriages. Hal had fucked up his life in general. Now Hal was fucking up his vacation.

As Ferris slowed to make a right turn into the CIA parking lot, he was forced to jam on his brakes to avoid a collision with a woman driver who had just shot across the street from the opposing traffic and bolted into the lot ahead of him. Then, seeing her whip left and pull into his reserved parking space, he raced into the lot after her and stopped behind her car.

With his fur cap tilted to one side of his head, Ferris lowered the car window and waited for the woman driver to step out of her VW Rabbit. As soon as she had, he growled angrily, "First you cut me off and nearly cause an accident! Then you have the audacity to hop into my parking spot!"

"Sorry. I'm late for an urgent meeting," Trish Darrol said apologetically as she locked her car door.

"You may as well unlock your car and get back in it, 'cause you're not parking in my spot."

Trish Darrol looked around the virtually vacant lot. "Can't you just take someone else's spot? I'm really very late."

"I don't give a damn how late you are. Move it."

"Look, I'm here on official business from Fort Meade," Trish Darrol explained. "I'm with NSA and . . ."

"I don't give a damn who you're with," Ferris retorted. "Maybe you people over in Meade do that sort of thing, but here in D.C. we take our own parking spaces. Not someone else's. Now move it, or I'll have security move it for you. With a tow truck."

"You're impossible!"

"And you're impertinent! Now move it!" Ferris returned, then backed out of her way as she unlocked her car and got in.

"You old grump!" Trish Darrol fired back, then slammed the door and got the car started.

"Old grump?" Ferris repeated. "Old grump, for Christ's sake!" He watched as the VW Rabbit sped backward out of his parking spot with squealing tires, then when it hit a waist-high snow mound the plows had built on the opposite side of the lot, he laughed loudly. "That'll teach you to call me an old grump, you young jerk!" He looked on a moment more, enjoying seeing the VW's tires growling in the deep snow to free themselves.

Then he smoothly pulled into his parking spot and got out of the car. "Serves you right to get stuck!" he shouted. "That's what you get for rushing around." Then he turned his back and headed into the building.

As Ferris pushed the call button for an elevator he could still faintly hear the muffled growling of the VW's tires fighting the snow mound. When the noise stopped, he pushed the call button again, hoping to be on his way up to Hal Banks's office before the insulting female from Fort Meade came into the building. He didn't relish sharing an elevator with her after their little verbal skirmish out in the parking lot. "Come on down, for Christ's sake," he growled to the elevator that seemed to be stuck on the fifth floor.

Trish Darrol left her VW Rabbit in its inclined position on the snow mound, satisfied she had backed it up so far that it would take a tow truck to get her rear wheels back down to level ground again. She hurried across the parking lot swinging her leather briefcase with one hand, while the other hand worked to undo the tie strings to her all-white, knitted wool hat. Then as she entered the building she brought her free hand up to the furry ball that topped her hat and pulled it off. Her silky blond hair immediately fell out of the roll it had been tucked into and reformed into inverted curls that dangled to just above her shoulders. The curls bounced gaily as she dashed for the elevator that had just arrived. "Hold the doors!" she shouted.

Ferris had just pressed the button for the twelfth floor when he heard the insulting female call to him. He ignored her and pushed the button to close the doors. Then as the doors glided toward each other, he waved good-bye.

"You bastard!" Trish Darrol shouted as the doors sealed shut. She knew he had done that deliberately. She held a finger on the call button and watched as the elevator indicator continued to climb the numbers on its dial. "Bastard!" she grumbled.

Hal Banks leaned forward in his executive's swivel armchair and rested both elbows on his large maple desk to support his head as he reread the two dossiers and accompanying field operations report that had brought him to his private office on the twelfth floor of Central Intelligence Agency headquarters at four o'clock in the morning. He was unaware that the picture window behind him was now quickly filling with the light of dawn, bringing out of darkness a wintry panorama of Washington, D.C., after a heavy snowfall. He rarely availed himself of his view anymore: he had spent eighteen of his twenty-four years of service in this private office as director of CIA field operations. He often wished he had turned this position down and stayed the field operations agent he had been for six prior years.

A floor-to-ceiling library of operations manuals and reference books took up the wall to the left of his desk. Two huge world maps, one in Robinson's and one in Mercator's projection, occupied the wall to the right. The books and maps, along with the host of routine field operations reports that flooded his desk constantly, were what kept him occupied most of the time, while on a time-sharing basis he supervised numerous field agents on assignments all over the world. Today the paperwork had little priority now that a particular field problem had progressed from long months of nurturing in its planning stage to the operational phase called Operation Gambit, which he was finally going to get to take action on.

Banks was a narrow-framed man not quite five feet nine, but a favorite pair of brown oxfords with double soles and heels added two comforting inches to his height. He had chestnut hair that was getting thin in back, while his brow had widow's peaks that towered over deepset hazel eyes. He wore reading glasses with 14-karat gold frames. On his last birthday he was fifty-two, but the grueling pace and heavy responsibility of being field operations boss had added ten years to his appearance. Good health and rigid physical maintenance was in his favor, though, and he possessed the vigor of men much younger than he.

He had an even temper and an easy-going disposition, and he was renowned for his tact and wit. He was a Harvard graduate with a degree in law, and he spoke French and German fluently. His credo was devotion to duty, discipline, and professionalism. He regarded respect for authority as vital and forewarned his subordinates that they might at times mistake his kindness for weakness and learn the hard way that an even temper didn't mean a lack of one.

Banks closed the cover of the field report and placed it on top of the two dossiers that a special courier had brought from Kiev. He refilled the large bowl of his curved-stem pipe. As he lit it and puffed, the bowl gleamed cherry red and a steady billow of blue smoke quickly rose and filled the room with the sweet aroma of rum and maple. A glance at his wristwatch told him his expected visitors were late for his special meeting. He pulled himself up from his chair and glanced down at the bustling people and traffic in the street below, then left the window and moved over to the Robinson-projection world map. There he looked at the penciled circle he had made around Kiev, and reflected on the city's importance in Operation Gambit.

CHAPTER TWO

Ferris's nostrils filled with the aroma of freshly brewed coffee as he stepped off the elevator. He quickly crossed the outer office to the L-shaped desk of Peggy Lindsey, Hal Banks's aging private secretary. "Hi, Peg," he called out as he took off his fur cap and unzipped his parka.

Peggy Lindsey looked up from her typewriter and settled her eyes on Ferris's multicolored Polynesian shirt. "Aloha! Did you just get in from Hawaii, Matt?"

"No, Peg. I was just about to leave for Waikiki when Hal called me."

"Well, help yourself to some coffee and go right in. God has been anxiously awaiting your arrival."

"What's he up to?" Ferris asked as he slipped off his parka and draped it over a nearby chair.

"I honestly don't know, Matt. But it's got to be something real big. He's been working right through the weekend."

Ferris filled a paper cup with the piping hot coffee which he took black and without sugar. After taking a sip of it, he moved over to Banks's private office door. "All weekend, you say?" Peg nodded. "It's not like Hal to give up golf all weekend," he commented, then opened the door and stepped inside. "Hi, chief!"

Banks swung around from the world map and immediately locked his eyes on Ferris's shirt. "That's a terrible shirt, Matt. It looks like it was patterned after Christmas wrapping paper."

"I didn't wear it to please you, Hal. What's up? Something wrong with the field report I turned in when I got back from Pakistan last week?"

"Your report was fine, Matt. This has nothing to do with your Pakistan assignment, or the Afghanistan problem, either. But it does have a lot to do with the Soviets. In fact, I'm glad you got here first. I . . ."

"First?"

"Yes. I've been working on this latest Soviet problem with Trish Darrol from the National Security Agency. She and I have been jointly scoping out developments for the past few months. She's coming over from Fort Meade to brief you on how NSA has been affected by this new Soviet gig."

"Fort Meade," Ferris repeated. After a moment of thought he added uncomfortably, "Is this Trish Darrol a good-looking blonde with bright blue eyes, about an inch or two shorter than me?"

"That fits her description," Banks replied. "Do you and Trish know each other?"

"Not formally," Ferris said with a grin. "We sort of met briefly down in the parking lot when I arrived."

"Oh!" Banks exclaimed. "Why didn't Trish come right up with you?"

"She was having some trouble getting her car parked and sort of missed the elevator I came up on," Ferris lied. "Besides, I didn't know who she was when I . . ."

Banks interrupted. "It's just as well that I have a moment with you ahead of her arrival. The President has ordered the CIA to work real close with the National Security Agency on Operation Gambit, and . . ."

"Operation Gambit?"

"That's the code name assigned to this new gig, Matt. And for the sake of the mission's success, CIA and NSA are to develop a rapport. No interdepartmental rivalry, no ego flaunting, no professional jealousies. And especially in Trish's case, no sex discrimination. We will naturally keep a lid on the methods we employ to get things done out in the field."

"Naturally."

"Other than that, it's to be a trusting relationship between us and NSA. For as long as the mission takes, anyway. Therefore, you're to be very cooperative when you meet Trish. You're to try to get along nicely."

"Why must I get along nicely with . . . Trish Darrol, Hal?" Ferris asked.

"Because you're going to command the field operations of the mission, Matt. Except for the administrative aspects which I will oversee, Operation Gambit is going to be your gig."

"Out of professional curiosity, when is this Operation Gambit supposed to take place, Hal?"

"It's already taking place in the form of preparations for your part in it, Matt. You'll begin right after Trish and I brief you on what your part entails."

"Hal, that sounds like a right away kind of commitment to me."

"It is. This gig is urgent and therefore it takes priority over all routine field operations presently taking place."

"I just got back from a priority field operation in the Middle East, remember? And I'm presently on a well-earned and badly needed vacation. In fact, when you called, I was just about to leave for the airport and hop aboard the *Wings of Man* for sunny Waikiki to celebrate my second divorce."

"Sunny Waikiki will have to wait, Matt," Banks said with authority. "We're talking about a possible delay of doomsday with this gig."

"Not that old doomsday crap again, Hal!" Ferris complained. "For Christ's sake, we've been delaying the coming of doomsday so much around here lately that I'm beginning to cross streets recklessly just for a little excitement."

"This is the real thing this time, Matt. It's not just another Soviet scare tactic. We have reason to believe the Russians are playing around with a sneak nuclear attack plan."

"And you're playing around with the hotel reservations I paid for in advance, Hal. That's more like doomsday to me. Hell, I start making alimony payments to my second ex-wife next month. I'm not a rich man. I can't afford to pay out hotel deposits for rooms I'm not going to occupy."

"Put in an expense voucher, Matt. Call it travel reimbursement. I'll slip it through."

"But my vacation entails other arrangements, Hal. I've a T-Bird waiting for me at Waikiki Hertz. And I ordered a case of champagne from Waikiki Beach Liquors. It's going to be delivered to my hotel room today. Then there's this shirt and a few other articles of clothing I purchased just for sunny Waikiki."

"As far as your shirt goes, I'm probably saving your life by canceling your vacation. If you step off the plane in Waikiki wearing that abortion, someone is bound to take a shot at you."

"But I need rest and relaxation, Hal. And I need it bad."

"Screw your needs, Matt. My needs are my only concern right now. And you're what I need for this gig."

"Why shaft me with it?"

"I need an ace tactical operations strategist on this mission, and you're my trump ace at the moment."

"Bullshit, Hal. You've got lots of ace TOS agents on the payroll that aren't on vacation. Send one of them."

"None can be spared from their present field assignments, Matt. You're presently not on assignment, so that makes you my most available ace. Besides, even if you were on assignment in Timbuktu, I'd pull you for this gig. You have just the right set of qualifications for the mission. You speak fluent Russian. You know the Soviet Union and its people like a native. And you're on a first-name basis with the key clandestine operative assigned to set things up for you over there. And that covert agent recommended you for the mission specifically."

"Who is the snake in the grass, Hal? I'll kill the bastard."

"The man you've come to regard as your Russian father."

"Ivan Trotsky?" Ferris asked. Hal nodded. "Why that old son of a bitch. I'll kick him square in the ass for volunteering me. What's he up to, anyway?"

"He's been under my wing on the investigative end of this Soviet business, right along with Trish Darrol. He's . . ." the intercom buzzed and Banks broke off his conversation to cross the room to his desk. "Yes, Peg?"

"Trish Darrol is here, Hal."

"Send her right in, Peg," Banks said, then moved over to the door to open it. "Remember, interdepartmental cooperation is mandatory, Matt."

Ferris faced the door as Banks opened it, and as Banks greeted Trish he said with a devilish grin, "Hello again."

Trish flushed on seeing the man who had been so rude to her. "What are you doing here?" she asked bitterly.

"I work here," Ferris shot back.

"He . . . works here? For you, Hal?"

"Matt is my TOS agent for the mission, Trish," Banks said.

"He's a discourteous, ill-mannered, inconsiderate ass."

"I'm discourteous! I'm ill-mannered!" Ferris protested. "Where was your courtesy when you cut in front of me at the parking lot entrance? Where were your manners when you hopped into my assigned parking space? And where was your consideration when you called me an old grump?"

"What the hell is going on here?" Banks asked sternly.

Glancing at Banks, Ferris said, "She called me an old grump, Hal!" Looking back at Trish, he added, "Hell, I'm only forty-one, for Christ's sake!"

"Well, you sounded like a grump when you balled me out," Trish said. "And you looked like an old man with that silly fur hat on. So I called you an old grump."

"And you looked like a silly schoolgirl wearing that hat with the pom-pom," Ferris retorted.

"Children! Please!" Banks said with raised hands. "You two are supposed to get along. Now, I don't know what happened to get you off on the wrong foot, and frankly I don't really care. But we have serious work to do here and it necessitates that you work together harmoniously." He faced Ferris. "Matt, this is Trish Darrol." Facing Trish, he said, "Trish, this is Matthew Ferris. Now that you know each other formally, let's work toward getting to know each other more intimately, 'cause Operation Gambit needs that kind of rapport. Shake hands and take seats, both of you."

"Sorry, Hal," Trish said without offering the handshake. "I didn't intend to get you mixed up in our little skirmish. I just had no idea that someone like *him* worked for you." She crossed the room to two chairs arranged to face Banks's desk, then placed her briefcase down on one of them.

"I didn't know NSA had fresh little kids working for them," Ferris muttered. Grumbling, he faced the penciled circle Banks had drawn around Kiev and added, "All I know is that I'm supposed to be on vacation. I'm not supposed to be here getting abused." He looked over his shoulder as Trish crossed the room to a coatrack and hung up her down jacket. He appraised the dark-blue designer jeans she was wearing and approved of the way they hugged her thighs sensuously and accentuated her rounded buttocks. He was pleased with her long slim legs. Her light-blue turtleneck sweater outlined her trim waist and small but shapely breasts. Nice, he concluded. If he was a beauty contest judge, he decided, he'd rate her face and figure a solid ten. But he'd give her disposition a fat zero.

Trish plopped down in the chair to the right and quickly took out her notes. Then, seeing that Ferris was still standing over at the world map and mumbling to himself, she said to Banks, "I'm ready to begin any time, Hal."

Banks called out, "Matt, I think you'll be more comfortable if you take a seat through Trish's presentation. It may take some time to cover all the pertinent points."

Ferris strolled over to the empty chair and seated himself, deciding to make an effort to be friendly, through the briefing at least. He removed a pack of Camels from his shirt pocket and offered Trish a cigarette.

Trish looked disapprovingly at the crumpled pack of cigarettes. "No, thanks."

"Just trying to show you that I do have manners," Ferris said. "By the way, is it Miss or Mrs. Darrol?"

"Trish will do nicely."

"Whatever you say, Trish."

"Go on with your presentation, Trish," Banks said, then began pacing the floor behind his desk.

"Do you know anything about what we do over at Fort Meade, Mr. Ferris?" Trish asked.

"Matt will do fine," Ferris said. "I believe your game is the intelligence-gathering business."

"There's a lot more to it than just gathering intelligence information, Matt," Trish said. "Basically, we are in the electronics end of the intelligence service. On a twenty-four-hour-per-day basis, intelligence data are funneled into NSA from every branch of our armed forces and those of NATO. Those data are added to intelligence reports we receive from the CIA, the FBI, and other intelligence and counterintelligence services we work with around the world. Then all the data are correlated with the product of our own data gathering operations at Fort Meade. Therefore, our Black Chambers not only gather data, but verify all the intelligence reports we receive." She smiled at Matt. "Please ask questions if you have any."

"I've heard of Black Chambers, but what are they specifically?"

"That's the name we've given our subterranean computer rooms," Trish explained. "And our computers are often referred to as black boxes."

"Black Chambers filled with black boxes," Ferris said. "Sounds like Fort Meade is a very drab place to work."

"It has its interesting points," Trish said. "For example, do you know how we gather intelligence data at Meade?"

"Not exactly."

"Well, that's the next point I'll be covering. And it has a lot to do with Operation Gambit, so try to stay awake through it."

"I'll give it my best shot." Ferris said.

"As I said before, we primarily employ electronic surveillance apparatus to gather intelligence data, rather than staff NSA with a host of overt and covert agents working on field assignments."

"Ah!" Ferris interrupted. "There's nothing like the personal contact approach." He formed his hands as though placing them around someone's neck. "You know what I mean. The old reliable hands-on method of getting information from human sources." His comment drew a warning look from Banks.

"We only use human sources indirectly," Trish said as she eyed his gesture uncomfortably.

"Oh!" Ferris said. "What does NSA use instead of humans, robots?"

"Principally, yes," Trish said. "We employ surveillance satellites loaded with what we believe to be the most sophisticated computer hardware and software in use anywhere in the world today. While accomplishing routine aerial photo reconnaissance work and radio frequency eavesdropping, our spy satellites also intercept cipher being received and transmitted between enemy aircraft, ships, land-based installations and space stations. They are mobile antennas that pick up coded communications in much the same way that radio and television relay stations pick up signals and send them on to other points around the globe. Our spy satellites of course send their intercepted cipher to Fort Meade, where teams of highly skilled cryptographers use computers to decode the enemy communications. Once the enemy cipher is decoded and correlated with the other intelligence data that I mentioned before, it is recoded and sent out via satellite to our military units and those of NATO."

"Interesting," Ferris said.

Banks stopped pacing and stared out the window at Capitol Hill. "That's why we're here today. The Russians are screwing up our snooping operation, and we can't stop them yet."

"Matt," Trish said, "Hal told me that you are well acquainted with the Soviet Air Force pilot who defected to our side with a MIG-25 about three years ago."

"If you mean Colonel Nikoli Belinsky, yes," Ferris said. Trish nodded. "I was the one who processed him into the United States after he landed his MIG in Japan and handed it over to us. I lived with him through most of his debriefing and indoctrination period. Hell, I even tutored him in English, and at the same time he gave my Russian a good polishing."

Sensing Ferris's pleasure in talking about the former MIG pilot, Trish said, "It sounds like you and Colonel Belinsky became quite close."

"Close like brothers are close," Ferris said. "Why did you bring up Nikoli?"

"Colonel Belinsky's MIG-25 provided our side with invaluable Soviet aircraft and communications technology," Trish said.

"Nikoli's experience as a Foxbat pilot was also most helpful to us," Banks added. "We're still benefiting from his . . . hands-on knowledge of Russian aerial combat tactics and his hints about what to expect from the Soviet Union."

"I know," Ferris said. "Nikoli taught us a great deal about Soviet political and military leadership, and about life in the Russian armed forces in general."

"After our military and civilian aviation specialists had finished probing Colonel Belinsky's MIG-25, his Foxbat was turned over to NSA for the purpose of studying Russian communications techniques," Trish continued. "We scrutinized the aircraft's radio receivers and transmitters, its transponders, and its encoders and decoders. What we came up with was a comprehensive understanding of how the Russians formulated their cipher, and the kind of communications apparatus they employed for cryptography operations. To our surprise we found out that they secretly allocated to military and intelligence services use of the American computer technology we sold them strictly for agricultural implementation. Their military adaption of that technology was in direct violation of an agreement we drafted to govern any future computer sales to them. With the disclosure of American computer technology aboard Colonel Belinsky's Foxbat, and with a few other incidents that divulged such unauthorized use of our technology, we stopped being a supplier of computer hardware and software to the Russians."

"Well, we must have cut them off far too late," Ferris commented. "While I was on my last field assignment in Pakistan, much of the covert intelligence data being gathered on the Afghanistan conflict revealed that the Russians were using a variety of computer-controlled military weapons on the Afghans."

"It was too late to stop military deployment of such computer technology from the very first day we supplied the Russians with the means to do so," Trish returned. "From the outset we knew the Russians would be able to apply their own research and development to American made computer hardware and software, just as other nations we supplied computer technology to had. The computer sales took place anyway."

"Naturally," Ferris grunted bitterly. "Maybe the thinking by our side at the time the sales took place was that the Russians would apply their own research and development techniques merely to having computers process credit cards with speed and accuracy."

"As it actually turned out, the first-generation computer

hardware and software we sold them became a second-generation creation of their own brilliance," Trish said.

"It's pretty damn infuriating, Matt," Banks said angrily.

"I'll say it's infuriating," Ferris said. "It's like getting kicked in the ass with your own foot, for Christ's sake."

"Fortunately, continued research and development efforts worked just as well for our side," Trish said. "We proved that when we got through probing the Soviet-made computer apparatus we found aboard Colonel Belinsky's MIG-25. Using what we'd learned about their hybrid computer cryptograph techniques, we developed a way to intercept and crack their cipher as efficiently and effectively as if we had composed the code ourselves. The cipher interception technique proved so invaluable to our cryptography operation at Fort Meade that we were able to design a computerized spying satellite capable of eavesdropping on their encoding and decoding methods from the fringes of space where the information could be gathered without their knowledge. We named the satellite *Skylark* and disguised its spying objective by announcing to the world that it was a weather forecasting vehicle. In actuality, *Skylark*'s weather forecasting was accomplished by another U.S. weather satellite and transmitted to *Skylark* by remote control. *Skylark*'s sister satellite, which was really the orbiting weatherman, was presumed by the Russians to be our new spy satellite."

"Very tricky," Ferris commented.

"The deception took place about a year ago," Trish explained. "And for about half that time we were enjoying cipher interception marvels each time *Skylark*'s orbital path took it over the Soviet Union. Then, about six months ago, *Skylark*'s eavesdropping suddenly became severely impaired."

"How?" Ferris asked.

"It began experiencing a queer kind of interference," Trish replied. "Not the total and lasting blackout we'd witnessed with other satellites. In those cases we attributed a satellite's complete collapse to a laser attack from a Soviet killer satellite, only we're unable to prove that was the cause. But this weird interference *Skylark* suffers is of short duration, and it occurs only when *Skylark* passes over the Odessa region of the Black Sea. Once *Skylark*'s orbital path takes it beyond that region, the interference stops and normal eavesdropping functions resume."

"Could the interference be related to some freakish atmospheric condition *Skylark* encounters in that precise region?" Ferris asked.

"Adverse weather or atmospheric conditions would usually cause intermittent dead spots in the communications linkup of a satellite," Trish explained. "And there would be static, or a weak signal similar to poor television reception. But *Skylark* becomes completely silent when passing over Odessa."

"Have you ruled out the possibility of electrical or mechanical failure?" Ferris asked.

"If it were an electrical or mechanical breakdown the series of monitoring sensors each system is equipped with would alert us and even locate the problem for us," Trish said. "And even if all of *Skylark*'s monitoring sensors were to fail at once, which is very unlikely, a system would not malfunction, repair itself and resume operation, then fail all over again."

"I don't know about that," Ferris said. "My car suffers all sorts of mechanical problems on Mondays. Come Tuesdays, they seem to have fixed themselves."

"Perhaps your car can cause these rare coincidences without difficulty," Trish replied. "But it is impossible to believe that the same electrical or mechanical failure of the same duration each time, over the same geographical locale, occurring daily, is mere coincidence."

"We've been able to disprove that *Skylark* is experiencing any sort of internal problem, Matt," Banks interjected. "We did so on two separate occasions. First, we altered *Skylark*'s orbit so it missed passing over that precise region of the Soviet Union, and the failure didn't occur. Then we had one of our early warning satellites fly *Skylark*'s orbital path over Odessa. Lo and behold, that satellite blacked out in the same way."

"And what do you believe is causing this, Hal?" Ferris asked.

"A new and highly sophisticated computerized jamming technique," Banks said. "And if the Russians can jam one of our early warning satellites, they may in time be able to jam every damn one we have simultaneously. Just think what that could mean. With all of our early warning satellites blacked out, we'd never be able to detect the Russians launching a nuclear attack on us. A sneak attack would catch most or all of our retaliatory missiles in their silos, and most of our population asleep in their beds. That's why I stated before that this may very well bring on doomsday."

"That all sounds very scary, Hal," Ferris said. "But if the Russians really have such a sneak attack capability, I seriously doubt they'd advertise it by screwing around with one or two of our satellites. And they certainly wouldn't be dumb enough to let us know precisely where in the Soviet Union they are keeping that doomsday power, by using it in such an obvious manner that we can pinpoint its location. They'd keep that kind of clout real hush-hush. Then when they had a mind to, they'd hit us with a repeat of Pearl Harbor."

"What if they had no choice, Matt?" Banks asked. "What if they had to risk messing around with one of our satellites, and they decided the chance was worth taking?"

"Why would they have to take such a risk, Hal?" Ferris asked.

Banks opened a manila folder which contained aerial reconnaissance photos. Handing one of the photos across the desk to Ferris, he said, "This was taken by one of our SR-71 high altitude photo reconnaissance planes. We had the spy plane pilot fly over Odessa shortly after we made our satellite switching experiments. Notice the domed structure in the photo, Matt?"

Ferris nodded. "It looks like the roof of a planetarium to me."

"We thought it was a new Soviet satellite observatory at first," Banks said. "That is until *Skylark*'s blackouts kept taking place over that same area. Now we think the facility houses some new kind of jamming apparatus, and the Russians are obviously using *Skylark* as a test. True, as you pointed out, risk is built into their testing. But like anything that isn't totally perfected yet, test they must."

"Did we complain to the Russians about screwing around with one of our satellites?" Ferris asked.

"We never said a word," Banks said.

"Then how could they know their jamming was ever working?" Ferris asked. "Tests must have results."

"They got their results when they detected that *Skylark* wasn't communicating during their test exercises, Matt," Trish put in. "That was all the verification they needed."

"If they verified it worked, why increase the risk of having their secret new technology exposed by continuing to screw around with *Skylark*? Why not conduct just one test exercise, then leave our satellite alone? That way we'd dismiss the blackout as just a freak of nature or something."

"May I answer that, Hal?" Trish asked.

"Go right ahead, Trish. You did most of the homework on the problem of why they didn't just pull a one-shot gig on *Skylark*."

"Inventing a blackout or jamming technique isn't really a high technology accomplishment, Matt. There are many ways to accomplish electronic blackouts, and many applications for such jamming devices. Jamming air waves, radar impulses, and sonar signals are but a few. Other more sophisticated jamming applications encompass evading heat-noise and metal-seeking missiles. But in most cases the blackout or jamming technique being applied against an enemy becomes a two-way street. For example, using a widespread communications blackout system on the battlefield might not only block an enemy force's communications during a surprise invasion, but it may also cause the invaders to become incommunicado with their own forces. The strategic solution to such a need for a unilateral effect of the jamming is to have the user equipped with an antijamming technique to counter the jamming they are causing enemy forces to suffer."

"I get the picture," Ferris said. "Change the two-way street to a one-way in other words."

"In those words, exactly, Matt," Trish said.

"This antijamming aspect of their new blackout technology is being tested at the same time, Matt," Banks added. He handed a second photo across the desk to Ferris. "In this aerial photo there is some construction taking place near the new domed facility in Odessa. What does it look like they're erecting, Matt?"

"Roadways?" Ferris guessed.

"Runways, Matt," Banks corrected. "And barracks, warehouses, and a few other facilities. All of which markedly resemble the makings of a large air base."

Handing a third photo across the desk, Banks said, "This photo depicts an existing naval installation of comparable size to our own naval facilities in Norfolk, Virginia. Its close proximity to the domed structure in Odessa is worthy of note." After passing a fourth photo to Ferris, he added, "Last, but not at all least, is this photo of a complete Soviet Army ground forces base, with supply depots, a hospital, and what looks to be a fully mechanized armored division ready for immediate deployment on short notice. There are also training facilities at the existing installations, and we have no reason to disbelieve that the new air base being constructed there will also feature a sizable training complex. Together the four installations represent the three armed forces of the Soviet Union, and an aerospace laboratory of some kind. And we think there's a solid reason for the Soviet Air Force, Army, Navy, and Space Administration to be close together in that very interesting part of the Soviet Union."

"Which is to take part in the testing and development of the

Soviet Union's new electronic warfare jamming and antijamming technology," Trish added.

"Wonderful," Ferris said. "Then send one of our nuc subs down the Black Sea and bombard the place with missiles before this jamming and antijamming gig of theirs gets bigger and better."

"I wish it could be that simple, Matt," Banks said. "But we just can't handle it that way."

Ferris glanced at the photos again, then said, "I hope you're not going to suggest I lead a raiding party on that conglomerate of military might and try to sabotage the domed facility under the protective eyes of what very well may be a half a million men armed to the teeth."

"You'd never get a large enough raiding party ashore to even cut a hole in the fence surrounding the domed facility, Matt," Banks said.

"But the idea did enter your mind, though?" Ferris asked.

"It did for a fleeting moment," Banks admitted. "But this last photo gave me a more practical idea." He handed the last photo to Ferris, then added, "It's a shot of an existing small Soviet Air Force base on the outskirts of Kiev. The fighter bomber jets lined up on the apron across the way from the propeller-driven aircraft have been identified by our intelligence people as new Soviet MIG-35 Foxbats."

Ferris nodded as he studied the jet planes in the photo. "News of the new Foxbats reached the Middle East while I was over in Pakistan. We even saw a couple of single-cockpit MIG-35 Foxbats flying sorties over objectives in Afghanistan. They're fierce-looking planes."

"The two dozen Foxbats you see in that photo are the tandem cockpit trainer version of the MIG-35," Banks said. "There's a sixth photo our SR-71 pilot brought back, but it's over at the Pentagon for further study by our air force and naval personnel. It showed six MIG-35 Foxbats flying in formation over Odessa soon after *Skylark* began experiencing blackouts. We have since learned that these particular Kiev-based Foxbats are frequently seen flying missions over that region of the Black Sea. The two events, the new domed facility in Odessa, and the two dozen MIG-35 Foxbats being located in nearby Kiev, prompted me to pull Ivan Trotsky out of Khabarovsk and have him set up in Kiev to study the activities of those Foxbats further."

"Wasn't the air base Nikoli defected from located in Khabarovsk, Hal?" Ferris asked. Banks nodded. "Why did you have Ivan in that part of the world?"

"It was Belinsky's idea," Banks said. "Nikoli said there were members of his former squadron who'd expressed discontent with Soviet military life. He thought Khabarovsk might prove to be a good place for Trotsky to snoop around for potential defectors. As it was, the KGB tightened security measures for the military personnel at that air base right after Nikoli made his freedom flight to Japan from Khabarovsk."

"Did you and Ivan really think lightning would strike twice in the same place, Hal?" Ferris asked.

"I didn't. But Trotsky pressured me into letting him take his best shot. Anyway, Trotsky made up for lost time when I switched him from Khabarovsk to that small air force base on the outskirts of Kiev. He managed to set himself up in Kiev as a farm owner, and with food items in great demand he had plenty of booty to exchange for information. It seems Kievans are more attuned to black market trading than Khabarovskans or even Muscovites."

Ferris smiled. "In the days of Vladimir's court, Kievans accepted Orthodox Christianity," he said. "Perhaps by doing so they became more liberated members of the Russian family."

"No doubt," Banks agreed. "Soon after he got himself established in Kiev, Trotsky befriended a Soviet Air Force flight scheduler based at the Kiev airfield. It seems this flight scheduler had an unquenchable thirst for vodka and not enough rubles to pay for all the drinking he wanted to do. Free drinks freed his tongue on more than one occasion, and Trotsky found out a few interesting things. For openers, it was the flight scheduler's duty to know every squadron based in Kiev. He informed Trotsky that the new MIG-35 Foxbat squadron was an outfit called Advanced Training Wing 3. And that it was his duty to set up regular round robins flown by ATW 3 between Kiev and Odessa. Those training sorties were said to be for the sole purpose of training exercises involving the new domed facility in Odessa. Trotsky also learned that the ATW 3 squadron was slated to make the new air base under construction in Odessa its new home, but construction delays were adversely affecting the training program, so ATW 3 was sent to Kiev in advance of the new base's completion to get the training program started right away."

"I gather this training program has to do with the blackout of *Skylark*?" Ferris asked.

"Right, Matt," Banks replied.

"And what we gathered from Trotsky's Kiev investigation and

the related events taking place in Odessa," Trish put in, "is that the domed facility erected along the banks of that part of the Black Sea is conducting extensive testing of the jamming aspects of Russia's new electronic warfare technology. Working hand in glove with the domed facility, the ATW 3 squadron has to be involved in testing exercises related to the antijamming aspects of *Skylark*'s blackouts."

"Once both aspects of the electronic warfare program reach the Party's desired state of perfection, we will probably be seeing more such domed facilities being erected in other strategic areas of the Soviet Union" Banks said. "Then, when enough domed facilities become operational, and enough of Russia's air, sea and ground forces also reach technological perfection, doomsday will not be far off."

"The Russians will have the tactical capability of widespread jamming with their domed facilities, and at the same time all of their military units can deploy on strategic followup objectives, without fear of becoming incommunicado, by utilizing the antijamming phases of the new electronic warfare technology," Trish pointed out. "Together, the jamming and antijamming apparatus will place their side well ahead of our side during a sneak nuclear attack and accompanying land, sea, and air invasion on targets throughout Asia, Europe, the Middle East, and even our own shores."

"In short," Banks said, "their jamming and antijamming technology is going to become the most powerful tactical weapons system in the world if we allow it to go unchecked. We must stop it now. Trish feels confident we can neutralize the facility if she is given some time with one of the MIG-35 Foxbats."

"I'm sure if I can get to scrutinize whatever antijamming apparatus is aboard the Foxbats belonging to ATW 3, I'll be able to figure out how both the jamming and antijamming technique works. Then, back in our laboratories at Fort Meade, we'll devise a way to overcome the blackouts. At the very least, we should be able to duplicate the antijamming aspects of their electronic warfare technology. And by doing that, we'll send the Russians back to square one. They'll have to modify their existing antijamming techniques. Maybe their jamming techniques as well. At any rate, as I pointed out before, one aspect is no good to them without the other. With only the jamming aspect, they'd black out both sides."

"I think I get the whole picture now," Ferris said with a grin as he looked across the desk at Banks. "You want me to take Trish over to Kiev and sneak her onto the air force base so she can snoop around one of the new Foxbats."

"That'd be just as impossible a task as trying to sneak her into the Odessa facility, Matt," Banks said. "According to Trotsky, the ATW 3 Foxbats are heavily guarded on an around-the-clock basis. Trotsky learned also from the flight scheduler that those particular Foxbats are equipped with some new top secret apparatus that only the high brass and a few well-trusted civilian engineers know anything about. Trish would never get within a mile of those planes."

"And I'd need to spend perhaps twenty-four hours inside their component compartments to really give the top secret apparatus a worthwhile going over," Trish said.

"Don't tell me you're planning to have Ivan and me swipe one of those Foxbats, Hal."

"That'd be no good either, Matt," Banks returned. "Neither you nor Trotsky can fly anything more aerodynamically sophisticated than a kite."

"You're right about that," Ferris agreed. "But swiping one is the plan, right?" Banks nodded. "All you need is a pilot, right?"

"Right again, Matt," Banks said. "And Trotsky seems confident that he has one . . . maybe two Foxbat pilots lined up in Kiev."

"Two?" Ferris asked. "Why two?"

"They come wrapped that way," Banks said. "As I mentioned before, the planes belonging to ATW 3 are all tandem cockpit versions of the new MIG-35. Each plane accommodates a flight instructor and a student pilot. So, in order to get one of ATW 3's flight personnel to fly their new Foxbat over to our side, we have to think double defection, a flight instructor and a student pilot. And Trotsky thinks he has just the duo."

"If Ivan does, he really hit the jackpot in Kiev," Ferris said. "How in hell did he manage to talk two Soviets into defecting?"

"We'll cover that angle next, Matt," Banks said. "There's no need to bore Trish with the details of Trotsky's methods." He smiled at Trish and asked, "Is there anything else you have to cover?"

"Not as far as my briefing is concerned, Hal," Trish said. "Now all I need to know is when and where a Foxbat will be made available to me."

"We're still working out those details of the mission, Trish," Banks said. "I'll let you know as soon as I have a date and place." Regarding Ferris he asked, "Do you have any questions before Trish leaves, Matt?"

Ferris thought for a moment, then said, "Assuming we get you a MIG-35, and also assuming you find the electronic warfare apparatus aboard one of their Foxbats, how can you be sure you'll be able to figure out their jamming and antijamming technology, Trish?"

"There's no guarantee that we will without knowing in advance exactly how their apparatus works," Trish replied. "But we've managed to master computer technology in this country. And as I said before, we pioneered the technology they are using. I seriously doubt the pupils have become smarter than the teachers. All we have to do is figure out how they've modified and perfected our invention."

"Trish means that their jamming and antijamming techniques may be well-camouflaged by unfamiliar apparatus, but the basic computer technology should still be recognizable."

"Do we have a jamming and antijamming technique that works near as well as theirs seems to?" Ferris asked.

"Not as yet," Trish admitted. "They seem to have gotten a little ahead of us on this type of computer application."

"Then maybe the pupil has become smarter than the teacher," Ferris said snidely.

"That's what we hope to find out by probing one of their new Foxbats, Matt," Banks said quietly.

"Trish," Ferris said, "even if we do manage to figure out their new computerized electronic warfare technology, won't the Russians find out we've done so and merely modify their techniques?"

"I'm sure they will," Trish said with a grin. "But all we need to do is study their modifications of our computer hardware technology, and we can within a reasonable amount of time figure out how they access their software programs. By being able to do that, we will have the capability of unveiling their software programs almost as quickly as they compose them. That will keep them busy in the laboratory designing new ways to access programs for perhaps a decade to come."

"You can actually stay on their heels effectively enough to nullify whatever new computer programs they generate?" Ferris asked.

"Just about the same way computer game manufacturers keep up with their competitors," Trish said. "Only in a more sophisticated manner, of course. But we know from past experience with

Russian technology that the Soviets rarely invent their own weapons systems. Rather, they copy the weapons systems of other nations and apply some convincing cosmetics to make them look like original engineering designs. Every once in a while they fool us with a very impressive piece of work. That forces us to examine all their systems more closely. After all, we can never be sure one of their new weapons systems isn't an original masterpiece if we don't check it out carefully."

"And in most cases, once we do scrutinize their newest technology," Banks added, "we learn that it's old technology of ours that our advances in research forced into obsolescence. Yet, with a little dressing up of it, they send us into our laboratories in a frenzy, fearing they've just leaped ahead of us with a new ship, aircraft, or missile guidance system design."

"Whatever they're using now is blacking out *Skylark*," Trish said. "We'd go after them for that reason alone. But this is also a good time to find out what they're up to generally with their warfare computers."

"Any other questions, Matt?" Banks asked.

"Just one last question, Hal."

"Shoot."

"You seem to have figured out what needs to be done, and how to do it. But have you figured out what the Russians are going to do when they find out we got a couple of their MIG-35 pilots to fly one of their new Foxbats over to our side?"

"I'm about to brief you on how we plan to handle that little hitch in the mission, Matt," Banks said. He passed three manila folders across the desk. "These are the dossiers on the two Foxbat pilots Trotsky has lined up for us. His latest field report is with them. Glance through them while I walk Trish out to the elevator."

Ferris got to his feet as Trish stepped over to the coatrack to retrieve her jacket. When she returned to the desk to pick up her briefcase, he extended his hand and said, "It was nice meeting you. Once we got beyond the parking lot, that is."

Trish stared coolly at him as she shook his hand. "Yes . . . once we got beyond that."

Sensing there was still a little unfriendliness between Ferris and Trish, Banks began ushering Trish toward the door. "I can't thank you enough for rushing over here on such short notice, Trish. I'd have given you more time to prepare your presentation, but I didn't receive Ivan Trotsky's latest field report until late Friday night." He opened the door for her and stepped out after her. "That didn't give me very much time to scope things out before setting up this meeting between you and Matt."

At Peggy Lindsey's desk, Trish said, "I didn't mind the rushing around at all, Hal. It's just that in my hurry I managed to get my car stuck in the snow down in the parking lot."

Banks regarded Peggy Lindsey. "Peg, have someone meet Trish in the parking lot and help her get her car unstuck." Peggy nodded.

As Banks and Trish crossed the outer office to the elevator, he asked, "Well, what did you think of Matt?"

"I think he posed a lot of valid questions," Trish replied. Then, remembering how Ferris had held his hands as though choking someone, she added, "And he looks like he's quite suited for his line of work."

"You're very observant, Trish. Clandestine field operations is Matt's forte. He'll keep the mission on course right to the very end. And if I'm any judge of Matt, which I feel confident I am, he'll bring Operation Gambit to a successful end." He rang for the elevator, then asked, "Do you think you and Matt will get along all right?"

"Well, now that you ask, Hal . . . I was wondering if it might be better to have NSA send someone else in my place. I think your ace TOS agent and I sort of clash naturally."

"That's only a first impression, Trish. Matt takes a little while to warm up to new people. Call it a professional quirk of his. He's had to deal with all sorts of weird people in the field. He's just forgotten how to act around nice people. You stay with the mission, Trish. You'll see. Matt's a good man. And since you're the best damn computer analyst NSA has, the mission needs you badly. Okay?" He saw a small smile appear on Trish's face. "That's the ticket."

So that was Matthew Ferris, Trish thought on the elevator ride down to the parking lot. Macho Matt, forty-one, twice divorced, prematurely gray, extremely outspoken, and a killing machine if there was any truth to the reputation CIA covert field agents had. If the rep was accurate, Matt Ferris was perhaps the closest she'd ever come to meeting a mercenary, a soldier of fortune. And judging from the cold and uncaring way he'd treated her, Trish believed that Macho Matt was not exaggerating when he demonstrated he had a preference for the hands-on, chokehold personal contact type of work.

Hal had told her much about Matt Ferris, his ace tactical

operations strategist. They had burned the midnight oil a number of nights, investigating the Soviet blackout technique that had been plaguing NSA's *Skylark* for the past months. The late-night sessions spent planning Operation Gambit as a means of resolving the spy satellite problem had often ended with dinner or a few drinks, with Hal telling her she was going to like his ace TOS agent when she finally got to meet him. According to Hal, Matt wasn't the only TOS agent he could pick for the mission but was the only one who could see Operation Gambit through to the kind of success both NSA and CIA needed.

"What to do?" Trish mumbled to herself as the elevator arrived at the parking lot level.

The two uniformed CIA security guards were already working their shovels under Trish's snowbound car when she stepped outside. She walked over to them, gave them each a warm smile, then thought on about Hal Banks, the mission, and Macho Matt. At the start she had been apprehensive. After all, most of the responsibility would be hers once Matt Ferris got her a Soviet Foxbat. From that moment on, Macho Matt could relax and it would be all up to her to figure out the Soviet technology.

What to do?

Before she'd met Macho Matt, Trish had been all psyched up about making a good impression on the man she was going to spend intimate time with in a far off place. It would be just the two of them, faced with an impossible and dangerous task. She'd hoped he'd like her and she'd like him. But now that they had met, she sensed he didn't like anything about her, and she knew she wasn't too crazy about him.

There was something about him though. She had to admit she had been aroused by his display of love for physical force. She couldn't deny that men who were brutes excited her, mostly when she watched them compete in football, boxing, wrestling, or other physically dangerous and demanding activities. Matt's choking demonstration made her fearful of being alone on the mission with him, but his hands-on technique was also reassuring in a protective way.

What to do?

Go for the gusto, Trish decided. She had already promised Hal she'd go, and NSA was depending upon her. And when she took all things into consideration, Matt's macho was teasingly inviting. So, go she would. But she'd take someone from NSA along, someone who was also a gutsy guy. Just in case Matt got too macho for her to handle alone.

CHAPTER THREE

Ferris had finished digesting the contents of the dossiers and Trotsky's field report when Banks stepped back into the office. He also sensed that Banks was disturbed over his and Trish Darrol's little skirmish. "Nice looking number, that Trish Darrol."

"She is worried about whether you and she will get along on the mission," Banks said. "She even suggested having Fort Meade assign someone else in her place. How do you feel about that, Matt?"

Ferris gave the idea a moment's thought, then said, "Bedroom-wise, I think she'd prove to be the Bionic Woman. Professionally, she seems to know what she's talking about. If she's got the qualifications for the job, I have no objection to her going on the mission. Do you want her to go, Hal?"

"Frankly, yes, I do. If the Russians somehow manage to find out that we commandeered one of their new Foxbats, they'll pour the pressure on to get it back real quick. That will make time extremely short for us, and Trish has an outstanding reputation for being able to work with . . ."

"I know, speed and accuracy," Ferris interrupted. "Just like her computers and satellites."

"Getting back to those dossiers and Ivan Trotsky's field report, Matt. What do you think of the two lovebirds his go-between has come upon in Kiev?"

"Neither of them has been approached about defecting yet. All Trotsky says is that the guesthouse proprietor is excited about having adultery going on under his roof. And everyone's hoping a defection can be worked out through a love angle. But love doesn't have to be the basis for adultery. Maybe Nadia Potgornev merely became a little horny in her husband's absence and decided to get in a little bedroom hanky-panky on the sly."

"Trotsky's go-between is convinced that it's genuine love," Banks said.

"Maybe it is love on Nadia's part. But her flight instructor could be saying he loves her just so he can get into her pants," Ferris countered. "When we get down to the nitty-gritty and mention defection, Senior Lieutenant Viktor Aleksei just might prove to be a notch more loyal to Russia than to an erection. He might feel the idea of defecting sucks. For that matter, Nadia Potgornev might also tell us to go to hell. Even if they are madly in love, defection is a rather drastic way to get out of an existing marriage. Divorce would be far less dramatic, wouldn't you say?"

"There's no way I can verify that Nadia and Viktor love each other from here, Matt. That will be a problem for you to solve once you are in Kiev. I can offer you some helpful hints on what to do if they aren't marriage-minded, but later for that. As far as Nadia and Joseph Potgornev are concerned, I did a lot of homework on them over the weekend. They both come from highly regarded Bolshevik families who believe they exist solely to serve the needs of Russia. They also embrace Old World thinking, which is that members of the family exist solely to serve the family needs. That kind of political and social thinking made it mandatory for Nadia to marry the man her family picked as her husband. And their arranged betrothal was given Soviet sanction. They're intended to have a long life together in service to the Party. That's the kind of hitching up that neither can put asunder without bringing disgrace to both family and country. As a promising Soviet Army major whose sworn duty it is to serve the Party, Joseph's career would end in humiliation if he allowed Nadia to divorce him. The Party would rule that if he was unable to control his own spouse, he was not fit to be trusted with leadership duties. Death would be preferred over divorce for him. In that part of the world it might even be required, just to spare his family the shame. Perhaps divorce would doom Nadia to death as well."

"That's thinking from the Middle Ages, for Christ's sake. Do you really believe Nadia Potgornev would rather risk death than stay married to her husband, Joseph?"

"No, Matt. You missed my point. I think Nadia would rather defect than try divorce as a way into Viktor's arms. And I feel strongly that she'd welcome any way of leaving Joseph for good. For one, Joseph is nearly twice her age. For another, she never picked him as her husband. I'm sure Joseph is quite content with spending the rest of his life with the very young and beautiful woman his parents selected for him. But Nadia doesn't want the man her parents decided would be best for her. I think that after meeting Viktor, Nadia feels her taste in men surpasses her parents' taste. And if you'll take another look at Senior Lieutenant Viktor Aleksei's dossier photograph, I think you'll agree readily that he is far more Nadia's type than balding, homely Joseph, as he's described in our followup reports on him."

Ferris did study again the photograph of the young Foxbat flight instructor. He saw a boyish face which he guessed most women would regard as handsome and quite desirable. To him the face was callous, the bright blue eyes cynical. Under the Foxbat pilot's short-cut blond hair, Matt thought he'd find an impressionable mind, enraptured by an impressive uniform, a glorifying rank, an exciting jet plane to fly, and a promising military career. Swimming around in that mind would be visions of an important place in his country's future. Matt seriously doubted Viktor would chance all that for what might be love.

Ferris finally looked up from the photograph. "Hal, Viktor Aleksei worries me," he said firmly. "Have you considered the possibility that these two lovebirds might be covertly working for the KGB or that their secret rendezvous might be designed to entrap foreign clandestine operatives?"

"Yes, I have, Matt," Banks admitted. "But under the prevailing circumstances it's a risk we're going to have to take. If the guesthouse gig turns out to be a trap, then your standard operating procedure will be to eliminate the opposition and do your best to save our people." Banks paused. "You know what I mean. Apply a little of your famous personal touch to the problem." He studied the concerned look on Ferris's face. "Look at the brighter side, Matt. If it isn't a trap, then we just might have two Soviet MIG pilots who are willing to trade their Foxbat for an instant divorce, a la U.S.A., and a honeymoon in Niagara Falls."

"And if they're not willing to defect?" Ferris asked.

"Persuade them, Matt. I'm sure they'll agree defecting is better than having Nadia Potgornev's adultery brought to the attention of her husband."

"I'm sold on the idea that Nadia Potgornev would rather avoid exposure. But Viktor Aleksei may be more interested in saving his ass than in defecting."

"That's where your good friend Nikoli Belinsky comes in, Matt," Banks said. "These two MIG pilots were formerly stationed at Nikoli's old air base in Khabarovsk, so I checked with Nikoli to see if he knew either of them."

"And what did he say?"

"Nikoli knows nothing about the Potgornevs. But he does know Viktor Aleksei. At the time Nikoli was stationed in Khabarovsk, Aleksei was a junior lieutenant, and on occasion one of Nikoli's student pilots. Nikoli said that Aleksei trusted him enough to reveal antiparty sentiments during a few drinking sessions off the air base. Russian vodka has been known to loosen many a tongue." Banks winked. "But the confidence wasn't mutual. Nikoli didn't share his plans to defect, but he feels he might have been able to trust Aleksei that much. Enough so that he's offered to go along with you, in the belief he might be influential in consummating a willing defection."

"That seems rather presumptuous to me, Hal."

"Not to me. A Russian would be skeptical about any promises you would make. He'd probably think everything you said about the U.S. was propaganda. But if a Russian who has already defected, and whom he remembers, tells him the same great things about this country, he'd be much more likely to believe."

"Hal, am I reading you right? Are you really suggesting that I take Nikoli to Kiev with me?"

"That's the gig, Matt," Banks replied matter-of-factly.

"You can't be serious," Ferris grunted as he got to his feet.

"I'm quite serious. The idea was Nikoli's, and frankly I was against his offer at first. But after weighing the advantages, I'm all for it now."

Mondays, Ferris concluded. They were the screwiest day of the week without doubt. "For Christ's sake, Hal . . . do you have any idea of the risks involved in sending Nikoli back to his homeland? Hell, he left a wife and a three-year-old son over there. Did you forget about that?"

"No, I didn't. But your processing reports when he came into this country said you were convinced he'd forgotten about both of them. Your reports stated that his marriage was all washed up, and that that was one of the deciding factors in his decision to defect. Your reports also stated that he wanted to leave the boy with his mother, rather than confuse him by taking the boy along with him. And you convinced me that you believed he made those decisions freely and firmly. That was three years ago. In all that time he's never indicated a change of heart."

"Maybe as long as he's been over here he's been okay. You know, out of sight, out of mind. But if he goes back to Russia and revisits old familiar places, it might become a case of absence making the heart grow fonder. My reports did mention that he suffered severe guilt feelings about leaving the boy behind."

"Your reports also said that he was overcoming those guilt feelings nicely. By now his guilt should be gone."

'What if the trip back to Russia revives the old feelings of guilt? What if he blows the whole gig once we're over there?"

"If that happens, do whatever you must to get yourself and anyone else adversely affected out of danger. Use your famous hands-on method of resolving problems if you have to. But in spite of what you may feel are unnecessary risks, I want Nikoli to go along. He may be our only hope for consummating a willing defection, and the Hill people prefer that it be willing. Of course the bottom line is that we get Nadia and Viktor to deliver their Foxbat to our side, willing or otherwise."

"Of course," Ferris said.

"Now, I appreciate your caution. It's good to be skeptical," Banks said. "I want you to have every chance of making the mission a success. Go and talk to Nikoli. Get all of your doubts about his going along out in the open. Tell him what you expect of him, ask him if he honestly feels he can handle it, then let him know the consequences for all involved if he does anything to jeopardize the mission. But don't tell him to withdraw his offer to volunteer if he feels confident he can handle himself over there. If I ever find out that you persuaded him to withdraw his offer to go along out of overprotectiveness, you'll be spending the rest of your CIA career in the basement fileroom on one shit detail after another."

Ferris sat down again with a heavy sigh. "Where is Nikoli these days, Hal?"

"You mean where is Nick Baxter these days, Matt," Banks corrected him. "Lieutenant Commander Nick Baxter is presently serving as logistics liaison for the Pentagon at the Naval Air Station for Advanced Jet Pilot Training in Jacksonville, Florida. He's doing quite a job for our side, functioning as a consultant to the navy on Soviet aircraft and Soviet tactical aerial warfare. He's also teaching Russian to several select people."

"It sounds like the navy has its own plans for Nick. Maybe he can't be spared for Kiev."

"The navy will loan him to us," Banks said confidently. "Operation Gambit has priority over Nick's general duties. Leave pulling him from the navy to me."

"Assuming Nick goes along on the mission, when do we leave for Kiev?"

"With or without Nick, you're to leave a week from today, Matt. But keep me happy—see to it that Nick goes with you. It's best for you, too."

"A week from today," Ferris repeated sourly. "That's a Monday."

"Screw you and your complex about Mondays. I've cleared it with the Hill people. A submarine has been assigned to get you into the Black Sea. You'll be put ashore by rubber boat in Odessa. Ivan Trotsky will meet you there and take you to Yuri Velinkov's guesthouse. Set up your base of operations there and work out your plan of attack. We expect the two MIG pilots to show up for another lovemaking session that Friday. When they do, consummate the defection at all costs."

"Have you mapped out a defection route, or are you shafting me with that detail, too?"

"You've been spared that agony, Matt," Banks said as he got up from his desk. Walking around to Ferris's side, he gestured toward the world maps. "Step over here and I'll brief you on the escape route I worked out with the State Department. It has presidential approval, and will be supported by the air force, the navy, and two of our NATO friends." He waited for Ferris to join him at the world map, then as he pointed to Odessa, he added, "After the pilots agree to defect they're to sit until their Kiev-based squadron moves on to their permanent air base in Odessa."

"Hal, from the look of the construction work in your aerial photos, it might be a while before the Odessa base becomes operational."

"It may be as much as a month or two more before the base can handle flight traffic according to what Trotsky learned," Banks said.

"A month or two!" Ferris exclaimed. "Hell, those pilots can't sit around all that time waiting to go. They might change their minds, or try to find their own way out through underground connections."

"I know, Matt," Banks said. "I don't like having them sweat out the time, either. But the only country that's willing to help us by allowing the plane to land is Egypt. And according to our latest intelligence reports, the flying range of the MIG-35 is too short to make a nonstop flight from Kiev to Cairo. The Foxbat would run out of fuel and be forced to ditch in the sea halfway across the Mediterranean. Trish would have to put on diving gear to check out the plane."

Looking at the map, Ferris asked, "Why not have it make a pit stop in Turkey?"

"The Turks don't want to handle a couple of defectors on the ground. However, they've agreed to clear the Foxbat through their airspace. And they're promising they'll deny Soviet chase planes permission to take action against the Foxbat for as long as it remains in their air corridors."

Pointing to the Black Sea region between Odessa and the Turkish shores that face the Soviet Union, Ferris asked, "What about protection during the Black Sea crossing?"

"We can't get them any, Matt. But we plan to have them make their breakout from Odessa in afterburners. The additional speed, plus the element of surprise in their sudden breakout, should get them into Turkey safely. By the time pursuit planes are scrambled to search for them, Viktor and Nadia should be well beyond the southern shores of Turkey and out over the Med. From that point on they'll be on their own. They're to fly as low as possible to avoid radar detection by any Soviet ships or planes operating out in the Mediterranean. Once they reach the halfway point, planes from our Sixth Fleet carrier force will give them as much air cover as they can through the second half of their Med crossing. Then, at a point where they'll be under Egyptian air corridor jurisdiction, the Egyptian Air Force will take a hand off from our navy flyboys and escort them into Cairo." He faced Ferris. "What do you think of the plan so far, Matt?"

"I still don't like waiting till the Odessa air base opens up," Ferris complained. "I don't like having them crossing the Black Sea on their own, either. Not with all that Soviet naval power based in Odessa. And most of all I don't like the first half of the Med crossing without protective cover from the air or sea. They might fly right into some heavy Soviet sea or air patrols off the southern shores of Turkey and get themselves shot down by air-to-air or sea-to-air missiles."

"We've thought of that, Matt. The Sixth Fleet is going to do all it can to lure Soviet ships and aircraft away from that area of the Med. That's about all we can do. But both our navy and the Turkish navy claim the Soviets rarely patrol that quadrant of the Mediterranean because they don't want to rub the Turks the wrong way. They depend heavily on Turkish government cooperation to use the Bosporus as a Black Sea gateway to the Med."

"Assuming the Black Sea and Mediterranean crossings take

place without a hitch, what happens when the Foxbat reaches Cairo?"

"It's going to be tucked away inside a well-guarded Egyptian Air Force hangar and will be at Trish's disposal. We and the Turks are going to give the Russians reason to believe that their missing Foxbat and two MIG pilots were forced to ditch over the Med. If they buy that story, they may never look further than the waters of the Mediterranean for both plane and pilots. Then, when Trish is finished probing the Foxbat, we'll cut it up into little pieces and spread it all over the bottom of the Mediterranean Sea."

"What if your ploy fails, Hal? What if the Russians find out you have one of their prize possessions and come to Egypt to get it back?"

"That's where Trish's ability to work with speed and accuracy will come in handy. We'll naturally have to return their Foxbat to them, just as we did with the Foxbat Belinsky flew into Japan. But we'll use every political trick we can think up to stall the return, so that Trish has as much time as possible before we have to give the Foxbat back."

"And if the Russians run short on patience and decide to get rambunctious, are the Egyptians going to stand up to them?"

"You've been a key TOS agent over in the Middle East for some time now, Matt. You tell me."

"I think the Egyptians will kick ass. But I wonder what an Egyptian and Soviet confrontation will lead to. Egypt has a lot of enemies in the Middle East."

"So does the Soviet Union, lately. And we'll be right there backing up every move the Egyptians make in our behalf."

"All the same, the Cairo end of your gig will be quite interesting if the Russians catch on to it," Ferris said.

"Any questions, Matt?"

"How can I get out of this mess?"

"Resign or die between now and next Monday," Banks said.

"You're the pits, Hal."

"Yeah. Go to N.A.S. Jax and let me get some more work done."

"Mondays," Ferris muttered as he headed for the door. "They really suck."

CHAPTER FOUR

Rather than call ahead and announce he was coming, Ferris caught an early morning flight to Jacksonville the next day. He rented a car, drove to the naval air station and was told Baxter was at nearby Mayport, seeing someone off aboard the U.S.S. *Eisenhower*. Since aircraft carriers were routinely deployed for relief duty in the Mediterranean, he knew he'd run into a host of military dependents saying good-bye to their sailors and marines.

When he arrived in Mayport, the U.S.S. *Kitty Hawk*, the *Eisenhower*'s sister carrier, was already under way to join the Sixth Fleet out in the Med, and a crowd of civilians and military personnel was dispersing from the two-berth pier; finding one familiar face amidst the host of onlookers still gathered around the *Ike*'s side of the pier seemed an impossible task.

Hampering his search even more was his inability to take his eyes off the massive carrier. It towered over the crowd, dwarfing everything around it. The windows of the superstructure mirrored the brilliant sun in the midafternoon sky, and he slipped on his sunglasses. He moved closer to the carrier and looked up. Above him were numerous aircraft tails protruding into midair from the flight deck edge. Then, part of the deck supporting one of the planes suddenly began to descend at the sound of a blaring horn. It stopped at the hangar deck level and the plane was towed off the deck edge elevator by a small yellow tractor, which disappeared inside the belly of the carrier. Except for a few sailors calling last minute good-byes from the catwalks that also edged the flight deck, *Ike*'s personnel moved sharply as they prepared for getting underway. An announcement over the carrier's PA system directed other personnel to prepare to haul in the *Ike*'s gangway. The crowd of navy and marine personnel still lingering along the pier began to move toward the ship.

As a number of sailors and marines hurried up the gangway, Ferris spotted Baxter in the crowd. Wearing his dress white naval officer's uniform, Baxter was embracing a young and very pretty Wave lieutenant who filled her navy whites sensually enough to arouse Ferris's interest at once. The passionate way the Wave and Baxter were kissing made Ferris realize that Nick Baxter had successfully shed the shy personality of Nikoli Belinsky.

When the Wave excitedly joined her shipmates in a dash up the *Ike*'s gangway, Ferris sneaked up behind Baxter. Thrusting his index finger hard into Baxter's back, Ferris whispered in fluent Russian, "So we finally caught up with you, Comrade Belinsky, you traitor!"

Baxter's smile immediately vanished. He shuddered as the adrenaline shot through his veins in response to the Russian-speaking voice, the mention of his former name, and the feeling of a gun in his back. He finally managed to say in fluent English, "Excuse me, but there must be some mistake." He envisioned a callous face, a man wearing a KGB greatcoat standing behind him. Beads of sweat began to form on his forehead. "My name is . . ."

"Shut up, and don't turn around," Ferris snarled. "You may fool others, but you do not fool the KGB. We know quite well who you are, without doubt. Your masquerade is finally over, Comrade Belinsky. I am taking you back to the Soviet Union to face a firing squad. Your only hope of evading your just punishment is to buy your freedom with much vodka."

Baxter sighed with relief at the mention of vodka. And the tautness left his body when he suddenly realized who the Russian speaking voice belonged to. He spun around and said excitedly, "Matt, you son of a bitch! I was getting ready to turn around swinging and deck you. Someday you're going to pull a prank like that when I'm armed! Then it won't be a laughing matter!" He saw the ear-to-ear grin on Ferris's face and couldn't help grinning himself. He embraced Ferris happily and said in Russian, "It has been too long since these eyes have seen your face."

Ferris studied the youthful blue eyes glistening with tears and felt tears begin to fill his own eyes. He blinked, stepped back to appraise Baxter's appearance, and said, "I still think our CIA disguise experts shaved off too much of that big fat Russian nose of yours. They took too much baby fat off your cheeks, too. And I think I liked you better when your hair was blond and crew-cut. You look too American with long black hair. But damn, how you manage to keep from putting on pounds, I'll never know. I know the Soviet Air Force didn't overfeed you, but hell . . . doesn't the navy believe in feeding their people, either?"

"The navy feeds its personnel too well," Baxter said. "I never had to exercise so much in the Russian Air Force to keep from getting midriff bulge. Now I have to jog every morning and exercise every night. And I still have to say no to those fancy desserts they serve us in the wardroom twice a day."

"Well, your efforts are paying off," Ferris commented. "Damn, you haven't aged a day in the past three years. How do I look?"

"Not that much older," Baxter said. "Your hair got grayer and you've added a few more wrinkles to your face, but . . ."

"Thanks, friend!" Ferris interrupted. "I needed you to be honest with me about how decrepit I look. Can't you lie a little once in a while?"

"I was getting to the good part, Matt. I was going to say you managed to stay pretty slim, too, for a guy your age."

"A guy my age," Ferris said sourly. "For Christ's sake, I'm only forty-one. You're the second person this week that took me for an old man."

"Who else thought you old—Hal Banks?" Baxter asked.

"That ancient bastard doesn't have the right to call anyone old," Ferris said. "Anyone except his secretary, Peg Lindsey, that is."

Baxter laughed, remembering how old Banks's secretary had looked to him the first time he'd seen her. "I'm not lying about thinking you're in good shape, Matt. You really look like you lost some weight."

"I have, Nick," Ferris admitted. "The pounds went off me from women worries."

"Hal mentioned you were just going through your second divorce, Matt. He called me from D.C. Saturday morning. Sorry to hear the bad news, but maybe you are meant to be a bachelor."

"Maybe so, Nick. Maybe so," Ferris said as he glanced around at the crowd of people shouting last good-byes to their servicemen aboard the carrier *Eisenhower*. He noticed that the far end of the pier, which stretched out some distance into Mayport harbor, was deserted. Pointing in that direction, he said, "Let's walk down there where we can talk more privately about Hal's phone call." As they started walking in that direction, Ferris added, "Exactly what did Hal say to you, Nick? Besides giving you the news about my second divorce."

"That you were back in the States from your Pakistan assignment for the divorce proceedings, and that your next assignment was to head the field operations of a mission in the Soviet Union." He paused to allow a navy jeep to speed past them noisily, then added, "I was surprised to hear the mission involved Soviet defections."

"Hal was surprised that you knew one of the potential defectors," Ferris shot back. "And I was surprised you wanted to go along and help. Was that Hal's idea or yours, Nick?"

"It was actually Hal's, but . . ."

"Why, that lying bastard!" Ferris exclaimed. "He told me you had volunteered."

"It wasn't exactly a lie, Matt. I told both you and Hal I would be happy to help bring defectors out of the Soviet Union in appreciation for all the two of you have done for me."

"How well do you know the Foxbat pilot in Kiev?"

Baxter pointed over his shoulder at the crowd waving last good-byes to the U.S.S. *Eisenhower* well behind them. "Well enough to pick him out of a crowd as large as the one behind us. Only I don't think he'd recognize me anymore with this disguise the CIA gave me."

"Do you really think you'd be helpful in talking Viktor Aleksei into defecting, Nick?"

"I think I stand a better chance than someone who doesn't know him at all. If he's anything like I was when I was considering defecting, he's entertaining all sorts of doubts about receiving a warm welcome here in America. I think once he sees I have been treated well, much of his fear will go away. And as a former Foxbat pilot myself, I can ease his mind about making a landing at a foreign airfield. In fact, I have offered to be on hand when he arrives to help bring him in. A familiar voice speaking his native language would be most reassuring at that critical moment when he lands on foreign soil."

"Did Hal tell you Aleksei might have another pilot aboard his Foxbat?"

"Yes. Nadia Potgornev. I understand they are secret lovers and have marriage problems."

"Nadia has. Viktor is unmarried," Ferris said.

"Well, I don't know anything at all about the woman. But I think they will both listen to reason if they love each other and desire to continue to do so in freedom. If the KGB catches them committing adultery, they could face a firing squad as military personnel. Especially when the woman's husband is also in the military. A long prison sentence would be the minimum punishment for such a crime against the state."

Arriving at the pier's edge, Ferris asked, "Speaking of women, who was that Wave I saw you kissing when I arrived?"

Glancing back at the departing carrier, Baxter said, "Lieutenant (J.G.) Linda Stewart."

"Have you known her long?"

"We put in a Med cruise together aboard the aircraft carrier *John F. Kennedy* last year."

"I didn't know women served aboard naval ships," Ferris said. "And come to think of it, I didn't know you put in carrier duty."

"This is the new navy, Matt. Although it isn't a widespread practice, more and more female personnel are getting sea billets these days. As for me, I'm a full fledged F-14 pilot now. I managed to get in my carrier landing qualifications aboard the *F.D.R.* Then I went on a short cruise to the Caribbean aboard the *J.F.K.*"

Watching the U.S.S. *Eisenhower* as it moved off from its dockside berth, Ferris asked, "Are the *F.D.R.* and *J.F.K.* as big as the *Ike*?"

"They are the same class carrier and therefore relatively the same size."

"Lots of cubbyholes on a ship that big," Ferris commented. "I'll bet you and Linda managed to find a few of 'em, too, eh?" He nudged Baxter playfully.

"Our relationship isn't like that, Matt," Baxter said, embarrassed.

"Oh! How is it, then?"

"We pulled liberty together in every port we visited in the Med. Then, when we got back stateside, we continued dating regularly, except for my brief Carib duty. As it turned out, we fell in love. Now we are engaged to be married."

Ferris stepped back from Baxter for a moment, then shook him happily. "Hell, that's the best news about you I've heard in a long time. When is the big day?"

"We can't set a definite date until Linda gets back from this Med cruise," Baxter said, waving toward the *Ike* as two tugboats assisted it out of the harbor. "But, now that I am teaching Russian, I will have shore duty for the next two years. So will Linda when she gets back, then we'll set a firm date and send out the invitations." He looked at Matt gravely. "Will you honor me by being my best man, Matt?"

"Hell, it's hard to predict where I'll be at any given time, Nick. Hal Banks keeps me on the move. But, if I'm in town at the time, I'll be the one who is honored to be your best man." He thought about Baxter's getting married to an American woman, even envisioned the wedding ceremony with him and Baxter standing at the altar wearing tuxedos. He imagined Baxter even wearing a formal navy tux for the occasion. It was pleasing to give the matter further thought. For a long time Baxter had suffered through a period of maladjustment, first as a defector who was under suspicion of being a double agent, then as a new citizen of America with no relatives and very few friends to rely upon during his first three years in his newfound homeland.

Baxter noticed the expression of deep concentration on Ferris's face and asked, "Is there something about my plans to marry that troubles you, Matt?"

Snapping out of his daydream, Ferris said, "Not at all, Nick. In fact I'm extremely delighted to hear that you've made such a complete adjustment to your new life. I have to admit there were times I thought you'd . . ."

"Never make it through the first year?" Baxter finished for him.

"At the beginning, I didn't think you'd last a week over here."

"Well, I have you to thank mostly for encouraging me to stick it out long enough to give things a chance to work, Matt," Baxter said as he stared down at the murky water beneath the pier.

Ferris took out his package of cigarettes and offered one to Baxter, who shook his head. Ferris lit one for himself, and as he exhaled and stared out at the harbor, he said, "There are a few things I have to go over with you about your volunteering for the mission, Nick."

"I anticipated that, Matt. In fact, with you knowing me as well as you do, I thought you'd say I must be out of my mind and should forget the crazy notion."

"I do think you're out of your mind," Ferris said. "And I still may tell you to forget the whole idea. Whether I do or not depends on how well you satisfy my doubts about your being able to handle such a mission."

"With my qualifications as a pilot I can be of considerable help to the Foxbat pilots who are to defect," Baxter said. "And as I said before, knowing one of them is surely . . ."

"Your qualifications are all on the plus side, Nick. But there are a few serious disadvantages to taking you along."

"Which are?" Baxter asked as he gazed into Ferris's challenging eyes.

"You still have a wife back there, for one thing."

"And I've just told you I plan to have a wife here. Now, if I failed to convince you that I no longer had any interest in my Soviet wife when I defected and left her behind, my remarrying should take away any lingering doubts."

"That's bigamy, Nick."

"True. But it's either that or never marry again."

"What about the son you also left over there, Nick? Have you given up on him completely, too?"

"I haven't thought about my son for the past two years, Matt. True during my first year in America I missed the boy very much at times. But I have come to accept that I lost him as well by defecting. He will be raised by his mother as a Soviet citizen. Perhaps when he is of age, I might attempt to contact him and ask him to consider living in the United States. But only if Linda would be comfortable about having another woman's child as a stepson."

"Have you had any more nightmares, Nick? Have you been waking up in cold sweats recently?"

"I share a room at the base BOQ with Lieutenant Joe Smith. Ask him, Matt. He and I have been roommates for nearly a year now. And before that I had other roommates, both here at N.A.S. Jax and aboard the carriers *F.D.R.* and *J.F.K.* Check into my sleeping habits. You'll find I am no longer haunted by old memories of the Soviet Union. None at all."

"What about when you revisit old familiar places. Will any of those old fears of being caught by the KGB come back to haunt you? Will you relive those cold sweats and nightmares? Will they gnaw at you until you sink back into Nikoli Belinsky and shed Nick Baxter?"

Baxter gave Ferris's questions serious thought, then said, "I killed Nikoli Belinsky three years ago. It was a struggle to kill him, but I succeeded in doing so. Then I sealed all that Colonel Belinsky ever was in a concrete tomb. No trauma, no matter how severe, will ever raise him from his grave."

"Not even the trauma the KGB could bring into your life as Nick Baxter if someone somehow recognized you as Nikoli Belinsky?"

"Your own CIA experts claim that even my own wife would have difficulty recognizing me now. And I don't intend to look her up. With both my parents dead and no close friends to point me out to the KGB, I think it is highly unlikely that I will be faced with such a trauma as being identified for the KGB as Colonel Nikoli Belinsky, the defector."

"You will have Soviet identity papers while we're in the Soviet

Union. You might routinely have your papers examined by the KGB. How can I be sure you won't panic under the stress of being less than a foot away from a KGB agent as you did when you thought I was one?"

"I assure you I will be able to handle myself in front of the KGB. You'll just have to take my word on that if you want me to go along on the mission."

"What if it becomes necessary to kill a Russian while we're over there, Nick? Will you be able to do that?"

"I have never had occasion to kill anyone in my entire life, Matt. But I have been trained by both the Soviet and the American military to kill if necessary. If the situation is kill or be killed, I don't think it will matter to me what nationality my opponent is. I want to go on living and will kill to do so."

"I have one more point to cover, Nick."

"I'm listening, Matt."

"If you find yourself becoming homesick for the Soviet Union while we're over there and act in any way that will jeopardize the mission or the mission personnel, it is my sworn duty to regard you as an enemy and blow you away."

The idea of being regarded by Ferris as an enemy disturbed Baxter considerably. He had never become personally acquainted with the violent side of his closest American friend, but he had heard from other CIA agents he'd met when he first came to America that Ferris was quite comfortable with violence and had killed more than one person during his CIA career. One of Ferris's CIA partners had boasted that Ferris had killed over a dozen enemy agents, mostly with his bare hands. But Baxter'd known only the warm and friendly side of Ferris and had wanted to keep their relationship that way, so he'd never sought a denial or confirmation of Ferris's killer reputation.

"Did what I just said sink in all the way, Nick?" Ferris asked, after a long silence.

"It did," Baxter finally said. "And the same goes for you."

"What the hell do you mean by that?" Ferris asked.

"I am an American now. And as a member of the United States armed forces, I am sworn to abide by the Uniform Code of Military Justice covering behavior in combat in defense of my country. If you were to become an enemy of the United States it would be my sworn duty to . . . blow you away, too."

That set Ferris thinking. In all the time he'd known Nikoli

Belinsky, he had always felt that for professional reasons he must regard Nick as a foreigner. He had been the first to congratulate Nick when he took the oath of allegiance, yet he'd never really accepted him as an American. He'd continued to think of Nick as a former citizen of a foreign land. He now realized he had been unfair. Nick had every appearance of being as American as apple pie in his navy garb. And he had raised his hand to more than one oath to preserve, protect, and perpetuate the American way of life. Realizing he had been a bigot all this time, Ferris felt embarrassed about having brought up the issue of treason. But as a thorough professional, he could never let himself forget that Nikoli Belinsky had committed treason once already by defecting from the Soviet Union.

"Do you have any remaining doubts about me to clear up, Matt?" Baxter asked, ending the silence.

"In all honesty, I seem to have come up with a few about myself in the process of doubting you, Nick," Ferris said.

"How so?"

"I prefer to keep 'em to myself for now, if you don't mind. But let's just say . . . in view of the fact that you deserted from the Soviet Air Force, there's a remote possibility that you might desert again."

"Need we rehash all the political and personal reasons I had for defecting, Matt?" Baxter said, exasperated.

"Not really. I remember them all quite well."

"Then, do I go along on the mission, or don't I?"

"It's still against my better judgment to say yes, but Hal Banks will shitcan me to the mailroom at headquarters if I refuse you without extremely solid reasons. I don't think you should tempt fate by going back. And that's quite a pretty Wave you'll be giving up if we get ourselves captured or killed. True, you will probably be most useful in helping me consummate willing defections and all that that may entail afterward." Ferris sighed wearily.

"Then I gather I'm going?" Baxter said happily.

"Yeah, but if I regain my sanity between now and next Monday, I just may do you a favor and change my mind."

Speaking Russian, Baxter said, "You will be doing me a favor by not changing your mind, Comrade. This is an opportunity to repay you and my new homeland for the many wonderful things that have been given to me. It will also give me a chance to offer other dissident Russians in the military an opportunity to taste true freedom and happiness. And I will be doing you a favor by using my expertise to help the mission."

"Enough talk about doing each other favors," Ferris said, also in Russian. "Hal Banks is the real beneficiary. If it was up to me I'd be in sunny Waikiki right now instead of talking you into what may be suicide. Let's go have a drink on Banks."

CHAPTER FIVE

There was a rainbow-colored lei around his neck, and Ferris was swaying his hips in perfect rhythm with a petite and beautifully tanned, grass-skirted Polynesian princess with pearl-white teeth. In the night sky above romantic Waikiki Beach, a tremendous full moon glowed, illuminating the slow rolling South Pacific surf. From a coral perch on a cliff that overlooked the white sandy beach a Polynesian woman was singing a Hawaiian love song while a Polynesian man subtly accompanied her on a ukelele. Set before Ferris where he danced with the princess was a long, low-to-the-ground table that abounded with colorful and tantalizing gourmet dishes. Turning slowly over an open spit was a succulent pig, an apple stuck in its mouth, sizzling as it was delicately basted with a Polynesian fruit sauce. As Ferris danced, the singer called out to him, "Aloha! Aloha!" It was the hello kind, a well-earned welcome back from Hal Banks's last gig.

Suddenly, from a huge mountain that overshadowed the luau being held in his honor, came a thunderous roar. A violent tremor stopped the dance, the singer, and the ukulele player. "Aloha! Aloha!" Ferris muttered aloud; it was meant in the good-bye sense this time. He felt his arm being tugged. A voice was calling his name. He finally raised an eyelid. "Aloha?" he mumbled, then realized it was Baxter calling to him as he shook his forearm.

Fully awake now, Ferris remembered boarding the U.S. Military Air Transport Service Hercules C-130 that was loaded with military supplies destined for a NATO liaison depot in Istanbul. He and Baxter were occupying a two-passenger seat, which was arranged to face forward, amid wooden and metal crates behind the partitioned-off cockpit section of the cargo plane. He recalled waving good-bye to Hal Banks from the rounded cabin window when the Hercules taxied away from the MATS terminal at Andrews Air Force Base at 0800 hours. He massaged the sleep from his eyes, then glanced at Baxter. That made him remember why they were aboard the huge, four-engine turboprop Hercules and where it was winging them to. It was still Monday, and he and Baxter were well on their way to meet the submarine that was to put them ashore in Odessa. "What time is it, and where are we?"

"It's fourteen hundred," Baxter said. "The pilot just announced we're about an hour out of Istanbul." He moved away from the cabin window. "Take a look out there, Matt. It's the *Ike* and the *Hawk*, steaming along with their task force armada toward Cyprus."

Ferris slipped on his sunglasses because of the glare of the afternoon sun reflecting off the blue-green waters of the Mediterranean Sea. What he saw, some thirty thousand feet beneath the plane's glittering silver wings, was a thrilling panoramic spectacle. A host of supply and war ships peppered the surface of the sea, trailing arrow-shaped foamy wakes. Centered in the task force and guarded by two heavy cruisers and nearly a dozen escort destroyers were the two angle-deck aircraft carriers he and Baxter had watched leave Mayport a Monday ago. He drew away from the window, removed his sunglasses, and asked, "What the hell are they planning to do with all that sea-going hardware? Invade Cyprus?"

"They're headed there to relieve the task force belonging to the carriers *Forrestal* and *Coral Sea*," Baxter explained. "It's a routine Sixth Fleet task force changeover that takes place about every six months. And Cyprus is the established rendezvous for incoming and departing armadas. There the homebound carriers transfer some of their air group complement to the oncoming flattops, as a way of filling plane and personnel shortages. Believe it or not, Russia does the same thing. In nearly perfect synchronization with our task force changeovers, the Soviet Navy makes its fleet changeover in the vicinity of Crete, just a stone's throw away from our fleet. Then, while both task forces going off duty head for their respective home ports, the relieving Soviet task force goes about its usual shadowing of the new task force we've put on stations out in the Med."

"It all sounds so out in the open to me," Ferris commented. "I'd have thought our task force would use a variety of places to accomplish such changeovers, just to keep the Soviet Navy off their backs."

"It's sort of a cat-and-mouse game," Baxter said matter-of-factly. "By closely shadowing our task force, the Soviets do manage to learn a little about our operations. But in turn we scrutinize their operations, learn interesting particulars about their ships, and in general sort of keep tabs on them."

"In my business we call that overt operations," Ferris said. "We openly have spies spying on spies who know they're being spied upon. And that's done reciprocally." Ferris was enjoying the exchange of information, and twisted in his seat to face Baxter. "We use the technique for about the same reason you navy people do. The opposition will invariably make mistakes, even though they know they're being watched. And sometimes we learn more by accident than on purpose. Of course, our adversaries benefit from our mistakes, too. But overt activities aren't as critical as covert operations where mistakes can be deadly. And our clandestine operatives can never blow their cover. If they do, we assign them to overt duties where a cover isn't a necessity."

"Obviously you prefer the covert end of the spy business," Baxter said.

"Absolutely," Ferris replied. "Overt activities are more for a guy like Hal Banks. I prefer working in the field where the action is. It's a life-or-death, them-or-you life-style that keeps you on your toes, day and night. I find the danger stimulating. I'm not at all suited for the routine, nine-to-five life-style. I'd become a leaper if I had to live like that for any length of time."

"Well, in the navy we don't always have a choice of what kind of duty we draw. BUPERS plays God over what billets are needed where," Baxter said.

"BUPERS?" Ferris asked.

"Bureau of Personnel," Baxter explained. "It is responsible for assigning manpower to ship or shore duty around the world."

"In my outfit, Hal Banks is God when it comes to handing out assignments," Ferris said. "So we're pretty much in the same situation."

Just then the pilot's voice came over the cabin speaker and announced that the aircraft was descending and it was time to fasten seat belts and refrain from smoking.

"For Christ's sake!" Ferris grunted. "And I was just about to light up, too."

"You can squeeze in a few drags, Matt," Baxter said as he gazed out the cabin window. "We're still at about angels twenty."

"I'm not privy to jet jockey jargon, Nick," Ferris said as he hurried to get out his pack of Camels. "What the hell is angels twenty?"

"Twenty thousand feet," Baxter replied. "Each angel equals a thousand feet in altitude."

Ferris got his cigarette lit and after two quick drags said, "I get it! The higher we go, the closer we get to the angels." After one last drag he extinguished his cigarette. "In our situation . . . it seems it should be the other way around."

"How so, Matt?"

"Well, the lower we get, the sooner we land. The sooner we land, the closer we get to danger. And the closer we get to danger, the sooner we might become angels ourselves."

"As a pilot, it's easy for me to look at landings that way. Takeoffs, too. Most people think pilots feel close to the angels when they're soaring in the clouds. Actually, once a pilot is up in the clouds, he feels safest. It's getting off the ground and returning to it that are the hairy parts of flying. Pilots feel closer to the angels than at any other time."

"Have you had any close calls flying jets, Nick?" Ferris asked.

"I've had my share of hard landings making touch and go runs for F.C.L.P. qualifications," Baxter said.

"What's F.C.L.P?"

"Fleet Carrier Landing Practice. We use a runway the length of an aircraft carrier deck to practice landing and to learn when to lower to the deck so we'll engage the flight deck arresting gear cables for the particular type of aircraft we're being trained to fly."

"Nothing more dangerous than a few hard landings ever took place?"

"I had a couple of wave-offs when I first flew out at sea with the fleet, and had to approach the carrier deck again. But I haven't gone through crash landings, ditchings, or midair collisions, fortunately. Except for training purposes, I've never bailed out; I've never had to do it because of a flameout or anything like that." He locked eyes with Ferris. "Is there any particular reason why you're asking, Matt?"

"I just wondered how you'd . . ."

"Face danger?" Baxter finished for Ferris.

"Right."

"The same way I faced it when I made my freedom flight from Khabarovsk to Japan in my Foxbat. Do you know many people who'd be able to do that?"

"No, I can't say that I do, Nick. And . . . I get your point. I just thought I'd bring up the subject of danger once more while there's still time to back out."

"I'm just not the backing-out kind, Matt. You should know that by now."

"Agreed, Nick. And I promise I won't bring the matter up again."

Lieutenant Commander Luke Thatcher, the commanding officer of the U.S.S. *Dolphin*, was on the bridge as soon as his submarine broke surface in the middle of Istanbul harbor. With short-cut chestnut hair and hazel eyes, he was a veteran submarine skipper in his mid-forties, whose baritone voice seemed out of proportion to his frail and rather stunted frame. "Rudders amidships, ahead slow," he said into his headset. "Line handlers fore and aft come topside." He looked at the pier he was to maneuver alongside. It was in the rear of the U.S. Air Force-operated NATO liaison depot, just outside Istanbul. Standing idly along aprons that paralleled the air base's duty runways were a number of tall-tailed Hercules C-130 prop jets. Standing midway along the pier and clad in civilian clothes were the two VIP passengers who'd taken the *Dolphin* away from its routine reconnaissance patrol duties with the Sixth Fleet out in the Mediterranean Sea.

Next to come topside was the *Dolphin*'s executive officer, Lieutenant (J.G.) Lindsey Chase. He was three inches taller than Thatcher, but had no better build, as was obvious when he took his usual position at the forward conning wall next to him. A decade younger than his C.O., Chase was on his first overseas cruise, and he was excited about going on the special mission that would take the *Dolphin* well into Soviet-patrolled waters of the Black Sea. He joined Thatcher in watching the two men waiting to board their submarine, then in his rather squeaky voice he said, "So that's what CIA agents look like."

"According to the general descriptions COMSIX gave me, the taller one is with the CIA," Thatcher said. "The other one with him is a navy airedale, rank of L.C."

"Hell, he looks kind of young to be a lieutenant commander," Chase said enviously, guessing the navy airedale was close to his own age.

"Flattop pilots make promotions a lot faster than ship's company line officers do," Thatcher stated, noticing Chase's look of envy. "Maybe you should consider switching over to airedale duty. The chow is a lot better, and the accommodations for officers aboard carriers are supposed to be rather plush."

"The *Dolphin* suits me fine," Chase said, loyal to the submarine service he'd chosen over other navy duties.

"Take over docking maneuvers, X.O.," Thatcher said. "When our VIPs come aboard, show them to my cabin."

At dockside Ferris and Baxter were joined by four air force enlisted men and an officer in charge who had been waiting inside a shanty that had kept them protected from the chilling winter wind whisking in from Istanbul harbor. As the submarine was maneuvered alongside, the air force personnel received heaving lines that were tossed to them from the *Dolphin*'s rounded bow and stern decks. As soon as the tie lines were secured, a portable gangway was placed just forward of the *Dolphin*'s sleek fin-shaped conning tower for Ferris and Baxter to go aboard.

"Welcome aboard the U.S.S. *Dolphin*," Chase said as Ferris and Baxter arrived at the top of the gangway. He examined their credentials, introduced himself, then gestured toward an open hatch leading below decks. "This way, sirs. The skipper is waiting for you in his cabin."

Inside the conning tower, Ferris climbed down the steep steel ladder after Chase and Baxter. Arriving in the control room he noticed the dozen or more crewmen manning what Chase had indicated as the sub's nerve center. The crew was a composite of the young and middle-aged, all were bearded and lacked the snap so apparent in the carrier sailors Ferris had observed back in Mayport last week. The control room was a maze of panels, gleaming multicolored lights, switches, and control knobs, all of which were crammed into every available square inch of wall and floor space. The room gave Ferris claustrophobia.

The confined feeling intensified as he continued through tubelike corridors that Chase described as passageways. As they continued forward, Ferris wondered what would take place if someone had to pass them in the narrow passageways. They arrived at a section of the bow that an overhead sign marked as officer's country. Then, in what seemed to be only a few feet more of travel, another overhead sign, placed above a closed cabin door, announced they were now in C.O. country.

"We've arrived, sirs," Chase said, then knocked on Thatcher's cabin door. "Skipper, I have our two passengers with me."

"Come in," Thatcher said, and offered his hand to Ferris and Baxter as they entered.

After shaking hands, Ferris gazed around the cabin and decided he had bigger closets in the homes his former wives had gotten from him. There was a single bunk that folded down on one wall. On the opposite wall a stainless steel sink also folded down for use. Adjacent to the miniature sink were two open sliding doors that revealed a toilet and a shower inside. Neither the toilet room nor the shower stall was any bigger than a broom closet, but they seemed to be adequate for someone of Thatcher's puny build. There was a small closet set to the left of the cabin door, and a fold-down desk was in the lowered position to the right of it. Above the desk was a telephone receiver that was locked to its cradle by a metal latch. Next to the wall phone was a framed picture of the *Dolphin*.

"While you were enroute to us, we received a coded communiqué from Gypsy," Thatcher said.

"Gypsy?" Baxter asked.

"That's Ivan Trotsky's clandestine code name," Ferris explained. "Is there anything wrong?"

"Gypsy is in Odessa," Thatcher went on. "He reports there's a large Soviet task force assembling right offshore. Extra patrol boats have been put into the area to safeguard the fleet, and they're checking all small craft entering or leaving Odessa harbor. Gypsy wants to scrub putting you off in a rubber boat. He's coming out in a Soviet fishing trawler with identity papers to get you past the harbor patrols. We've a rendezvous point well out in the Black Sea that will keep us clear of the patrols when we put you over the side."

"That suits me fine," Ferris said to Thatcher. "I wasn't all that enthused about sneaking ashore in a goddamn rubber boat, anyway. Did Gypsy have anything else to report?"

"Only that the task force he's worried about belongs to Fleet Admiral Georgi Stalovich, whose flagship is the Soviet heavy cruiser *Leningrad*. According to Gypsy, the Soviet fleet is expected to be deployed from Odessa in response to the arrival of the carriers *Hawk* and *Ike* out in the Med. But Gypsy said Stalovich's task force might not leave for days, so rather than hold up Operation Gambit he's coming out to meet you."

"I've heard of Stalovich, Matt," Baxter said. "He's been a real threat to our Sixth Fleet carrier operations out in the Med. I think we should alert the *Hawk* and the *Ike* that the old seadog is heading their way."

"Captain Thatcher can see to that after he drops us off," Ferris said. "For now, let's keep in mind that we're going to have those extra harbor patrols to contend with. The less noise we make en route to Odessa, the better."

"Agreed," Thatcher said firmly. "Shall we get underway, then?"

"Affirmative," Ferris said. "I hate tight spaces. Especially when they're going to have tons of water pressing on them. The sooner we get this undersea voyage over, the better I'll feel."

Thatcher regarded his X.O. "Lin, see to making our passengers comfortable. I'll ride the bridge out of Istanbul harbor." Chase acknowledged him, and Thatcher said to Ferris and Baxter, "Although our accommodations are rather cramped, I think you'll find our cook quite proficient. On the ship's menu for evening chow is liver and onions a la the U.S.S. *Dolphin*."

Great, Ferris thought as he followed Thatcher, Chase, and Baxter out of the cabin. He was sure by evening chow he'd have his own liver in his mouth from being seasick. Mondays . . .

CHAPTER SIX

Trotsky's tall, thick frame rocked from side to side with every rolling swell of the Black Sea as he sat on the aft deck of the troller *Sonya*. There were snowflakes dancing down from the dark night sky above, and a biting wind stung his puffy cheeks and nose, but he kept his eyes trained on the surface. It was three o'clock and the sub was now a full hour overdue. The ride back to Odessa, some twenty miles astern of the troller, would take close to three hours. That would have them sailing past Admiral Stalovich's armada under light of dawn instead of under cover of night.

More long minutes passed with only a murmur seeping out of the cabin door to disturb the silence. Trotsky glanced with concern at the occupants in the cabin, sensing that his two compatriots were growing more and more restless as the American submarine became more and more overdue.

They were the two fishermen who owned the troller, and both had reasons for hating the Party. The strongest reason was that they were both Soviet Jews who had had their fill of religious persecution. Only their surnames, Barinov and Yankovsky, were still Russian. They no longer were. They were supporters of freedom, who would give their lives to strike a blow against totalitarianism. But they were also family men who didn't want their families to suffer for what they did. It was because of their families that Trotsky worried for them, even though they'd jumped at the chance to help him bring two American agents into Russia through a back door.

Suddenly, out of the corner of his eye, Trotsky caught a glimpse of something moving on the surface of the sea some fifty yards off the troller's starboard beam. At first it looked like a shark's fin, then the fin rose bringing a black mass up from the chilling depths. In a moment more he had full view of the *Dolphin* with tons of foamy sea water running down its sleek conning tower and rounded sides.

"They are here!" he called out excitedly in Russian as he got to his feet. His voice brought the two fishermen scurrying out of the cabin at once. Pointing to the sub, he said, "Let's get them aboard before a patrol boat or plane comes along."

Heavy surface patrol activity en route had caused the *Dolphin* to arrive late; nevertheless, Thatcher was not going to cast safety aside for speed. His ship's sonar indicated that the troller was alone in the sea, but he rose only to conning depth at first to allow ship's radar a chance to scrutinize the sky above the *Dolphin* as well. Then, to be extra sure, he and two lookouts hastened to the bridge to train their night binoculars in all directions before he ordered the sub to surface fully. Once he had taken all precautions he finally ordered line handlers topside to receive the troller coming alongside. That brought four crewmen up to the bow deck, two of whom were carrying a portable rubber ladder, which they lowered to the troller while their shipmates secured the troller's bow and stern lines.

Next to climb out of the bow hatch were Ferris and Baxter. They had said good-bye to the *Dolphin*'s C.O. and X.O. before surfacing but waved a last time to Thatcher, who was staring down at them from the bridge. Then, assisted by the two crewmen, they descended the rubber ladder to the troller's aft deck.

"Cast us off!" Trotsky called up to the line handlers, in slightly Russian-accented English. Then as the two fishermen with him hauled in the bow and stern lines, he gave Ferris a bear hug. Speaking Russian again, he happily exclaimed, "These old eyes have waited an eternity to see you again, Comrade!"

Ferris felt the wind being forced out of his lungs, but he was too overjoyed to mention it. Also speaking Russian, but finding it hard to muster the breath to speak, he gasped, "Now I am reunited with my adopted father."

"And like a loving father, this old man will kiss his adopted son on both cheeks," Trotsky said gleefully, and did so.

With the *Dolphin* beginning to descend, Ferris gestured to Baxter. "This is my traveling companion, Nick . . ."

"This brave young man needs no introduction," Trotsky interrupted in Russian as he grabbed Baxter's hand. "When you made your successful defection to the West, I wished someday I would have the great honor of shaking your hand. Now my wish has come true. Welcome back to the Soviet Union, Comrade Nikoli Belinsky." Then Trotsky turned back to Ferris. "We have spent as much time as we can afford on reunions. Your late arrival will have us in dawn's first light by the time we reach the shores of Odessa, and Admiral Stalovich has already assembled nearly two dozen ships there."

"Will Admiral Stalovich and his task force be a real threat, Ivan?" Ferris asked as one of the fishermen swung the troller around on a course to the north.

"One never knows what to expect from an unpredictable man like Stalovich," Trotsky replied. "In addition to the task force ships, surface and air patrols have been increased around Odessa now that the domed facility has become fully operational. Therefore, I decided to be cautious. I think I can safely predict that our arrival in Odessa aboard a Soviet troller will draw little or no attention."

"Good. I'm not looking forward to having the Party make an example of me," Baxter said firmly.

"I have very convincing identity papers for you both," Trotsky said as they stepped into the warmth of the cabin. He showed them a set of documents. "These you will use once we get ashore. They declare that you are Soviet agriculturalists. I also brought along Soviet-made attire for you." Displaying a second set of documents, Trotsky went on, "And these will serve to identify you both as Soviet fishermen, just in case we are stopped by a patrol boat before we get ashore."

"As always, Ivan," Ferris commented, "you think of every detail."

"There is no room for oversight in our business, Matt, as you well know," Trotsky said, then pointed to the Soviet-made garments Ferris and Baxter were to slip into. "Hal Banks provided me with your sizes. Learning that you now take a smaller size in trousers, Matt, I gathered that divorce had trimmed your waist as well as your purse."

"You're right," Ferris said. "And speaking of Hal Banks," he went on, "I could have lived without your recommending me to handle this latest gig of his."

"But it was not I who recommended you, Matt," Trotsky said. "Hal Banks said you were available and insisted on sending you."

"I was about to vacation in sunny Waikiki Beach," Ferris said. "That's another lie I've caught that bastard in."

Dawn brought an abrupt end to the snowflakes that had been tormenting them through the night. It also unveiled the sprawling armada commanded by Fleet Admiral Georgi Stalovich, which covered the surface of the Black Sea with broad-beamed, battleship-gray and camouflage-painted ships for as far as the eye could see. There were several tanker and supply ships berthed at piers at the Odessa navy depot. They were taking on fuel and stores for the impending six-month stay with the task force out in the Mediterranean. At anchor out in the harbor were the fleet's escort destroyers, frigates, and cutters. Tied to the port side of a huge tender ship were four dull black nuclear-powered submarines that would protect the fleet from subsurface attack. Also at anchor and circled by warships, was the massive heavy cruiser *Leningrad*. The pride of the Soviet fleet, the *Leningrad*'s superstructure was topped with the flag of the Soviet Union. It fluttered proudly in the early morning wind just above Stalovich's four-star admiral's flag, which announced that the *Leningrad* was the flagship of the Mediterranean-bound fleet.

Ferris joined Baxter and Trotsky on the aft deck to observe the warships the troller was maneuvering its way past. Then, seeing the heavily gunned ship that dwarfed the vessels surrounding it, he asked, "Is that the battleship *Leningrad*, Nick?"

"It's the cruiser *Leningrad*, Matt," Baxter corrected. "But its complement of sixteen-inch cannons and missile launchers makes it comparable in fire power to a dreadnought." He recalled flying over the *Leningrad* in his MIG-25 Foxbat while training student pilots before he defected. He also remembered seeing the Soviet heavy cruiser more recently from the flight deck of the U.S.S. *John F. Kennedy* and from the air as he flew his American F-14 on carrier-borne training exercises. But those two sightings had been from a safe distance.

The heavy cruiser hadn't looked too threatening from the air. Perhaps, he thought, that was because as a pilot he had a higher regard for the destruction capabilities of aircraft than that of ships. Now, as they drew to within fifty yards of the *Leningrad*, it seemed much more awesome. Since he'd defected and enlisted in the American navy, he'd enjoyed a sense of supremacy that he'd never felt as a Soviet military man. But that was because he'd found American aircraft to be superior to Russian. When it came to ships, a subject he knew far less about, he wondered which navy ranked supreme. As an American now, he held the *Leningrad* and its power in contempt. Yet as a former Soviet citizen he was proud of the magnificent ship. The traitorous pride troubled him.

"So that's the renowned Admiral Stalovich's ship," Ferris commented as he appraised the *Leningrad*.

"Matt, that four-star admiral's flag raised atop the main mast means Admiral Stalovich is aboard ship," Baxter explained. "Traditionally, any ship he goes aboard will hoist his flag and become the task force flagship for the duration of his stay. His flag is lowered whenever he goes ashore, and a smaller one accompanies him everywhere he travels."

"Stalovich could prove to be a powerfully troublesome man," Trotsky said. "He will be *your* nemesis if he happens to be in the area of the Mediterranean that the Foxbat pilots will cross on their way to Egypt."

"Hal Banks assured me our Sixth Fleet will have lured the Soviet Navy to the opposite end of the Med on the day the defection takes place," Ferris returned.

"The decoy should work nicely, Matt," Baxter put in. "Any Soviet task force I've ever seen operating out in the Med always followed our super carriers around dependably."

Suddenly, while still a few hundred yards from shore, two MIG-35's thundered overhead, pulling all eyes on the troller skyward. The twin-tailed, dual jet engine Foxbats were in mirrored formation as they flew low over Stalovich's armada.

Baxter studied the two jets, checking every aerodynamic detail of the newest version of the Foxbat. Unlike the MIG-25 Foxbat he'd delivered into American hands, which was a single-place cockpit, the two Foxbats that had streaked overhead were the tandem cockpit trainer version of the MIG-35. But as a former flight instructor, he had flown the two-place MIG-25 Foxbats as well.

Baxter noted a marked improvement in speed, but he couldn't tell if the maneuverability had been improved. Only a hands-on-the-controls testing could establish that.

Noticing Baxter's scrutiny Ferris asked, "How do they rate compared to our aircraft, Nick?"

"They seem pretty fast," Baxter said. "But if they're as awkward to handle as my old MIG-25 was, they're no match for the F-14's I'm flying these days."

Just then, from out of the rising sun, two more MIG-35 Foxbats soared overhead. To Ferris the show of military might, aerial and naval, was unnerving. But he could tell by the gleam in Baxter's eyes that it was too exciting to be unnerving to him. He felt like asking Baxter if he'd like to be at the controls of one of the new Foxbats, but didn't. He knew what Baxter's answer would be. Absolutely. Pilots were pilots, he thought. He turned away from Baxter and looked toward shore.

Trotsky pointed at the domed structure that was adjacent to

the Soviet navy yard in Odessa. "That is the culprit which has necessitated your visit to these shores, Comrade."

"I know," Ferris said. "Hal Banks showed me some aerial photos of the installation. It looks even more impregnable than Hal's reconnaissance photos suggested it was."

"There are guards armed with automatic weapons at ten foot intervals around its circumference, inside and outside," Trotsky said. "All of them are hand-picked KGB personnel sent to Odessa from Moscow."

"They have what looks like a full armored division positioned around the outer perimeter of the domed complex," Baxter said. "I can see light and heavy tanks, halftracks, rubber-wheeled personnel carriers, and a mechanized rocket launcher brigade."

"That's not all," Trotsky said excitedly. "Look at those antiaircraft batteries along the sea wall. And those two concrete bunkers you see are for bombarding any ships that dare to launch an invasion on the facility from the Black Sea."

"It's quite a fortress, just as Hal Banks said," Ferris put in. "Hal also said we'd never get enough of a landing party ashore even to cut a hole in the fence, and he was right about that, too. I'd hate to have to try to knock that concrete commode out of action."

The men watched two helicopters come to life outside the domed facility. They lifted skyward and streaked out toward the anchored Soviet fleet. They stopped over the aft deck of the cruiser *Leningrad*. As the helicopters hovered, waiting for the signal to land, a boatswain's whistle shrilled and brought ranks of Soviet sailors to snappy attention on the flight deck. Turning to Baxter, Ferris asked, "Does that display of protocol take place every time a helicopter lands aboard a navy ship?"

"No, Matt. The red carpet is rolled out like that only for high-ranking military brass or government dignitaries."

Suddenly two loud whistles sounded from another direction. Seeing the approaching harbor patrol boat, the pilot of the troller reduced his speed, then called out to the aft deck from the cabin controls, "Be calm, everyone. It is the harbor police. They are probably going to stop us for a routine check of our identity papers, so be sure you do not speak a word of English in their presence."

As the patrol boat drew closer, Trotsky regarded Ferris and Baxter anxiously. "If they do ask to see your identity papers, make sure you show them the sets that identify you as two Soviet fishermen. And by all means, remember the names on the documents. It is an old KGB trick to collect identification first, then ask your name."

Standing on the aft deck of the twenty-foot police patrol boat, the officer in charge shouted to his pilot, "Be sure to take the troller on her starboard side so our navy comrades can readily see the harbor police conscientiously enforcing tight security measures." He was a tall man with a weather-beaten face and was wearing a black leather surcoat with matching black calf-length boots and a fur cap. The half-dozen men on the aft deck with him were all dressed in white parkas and black fur caps, and all of them had automatic weapons slung from a shoulder strap in front of them.

"They have a Soviet flag atop their mast, Comrade Officer," the boat pilot called out from inside the launch cabin.

"They still could be Turks posing as Russians so they can come into our waters and steal our fish," the boat officer called back.

"That is most doubtful, Comrade Officer," one of the armed men on the aft deck put in. "My brother is with the Party's Black Sea fishing fleet, and he claims fishing has been so bad in our waters that he fears the fish have chosen to make their homes in the waters on the Turkish side of the Black Sea."

"We will soon find out who they are and why they are in our waters," the boat officer said with authority. "Keep your weapons at the ready."

Baxter saw the familiar red star centered on the front of each man's hat as the boat pilot put his launch into neutral to come alongside. The Soviet emblem brought back old unhappy memories, memories of being harassed by the Soviet police, even bullied at times by an arrogant KGB agent who'd had it in for Soviet military personnel. He found that those memories could still anger him.

Doing his best to ignore the threatening automatic weapons, Trotsky forced a friendly smile as the patrol boat came abreast of the troller on starboard. "A very good morning to you all, Comrades," he shouted over to the police launch in a cheery tone. "Is there something we have done wrong?"

Indifferent to the friendly greeting, the boat officer called back with authority, "Heave to for boarding."

"But, of course," Trotsky returned, then regarded his two Jewish fishermen friends. "Comrade Barinov," he shouted to the older man at the troller's helm, "cut your engine so the police can come aboard." To the younger man, he called out, "Yankovsky, get up on the bow to catch their heaving line." Then to

Baxter he said, "Comrade, you catch and secure their stern to the aft cleat." In a whisper, he told Ferris to toy with the fish in the half-full holding tank as though he were displeased with their meager night's catch. When the bow and stern lines were secured to cleats, he offered an assisting hand as the police boat officer stepped across the gunwale to the troller's aft deck.

"Your identity papers, all of you!" He accepted Trotsky's papers first, then Ferris's and Baxter's. He motioned the troller pilot out of the cabin and took his documents, too. Impatiently he shouted to the man on the bow, "Did you not hear me? I said all of you!" When he had that man's papers as well, he studied each set of documents suspiciously, then compared each man's face to the photos on the identity papers as he called out their names one after the other. Satisfied that the photos matched the faces, he asked, "Tell me, Comrade, what village do you live in?"

Baxter was caught off-guard and could only remember that the village listed on his papers was near Odessa. The name of the village escaped him for the moment. Rather than remain silent for too long, he said, "I live just outside of Odessa."

"There are a few villages just outside of Odessa, Comrade. Be more specific."

Finally clearing his mental block, Baxter said, "In Il'ichevsk."

After staring at Baxter steadily the boat officer turned to Ferris. "And you, Comrade?"

"I live right in Odessa," Ferris said.

"And I live in the heart of Odessa as well," Trotsky offered when the boat officer's eyes settled on him.

Not bothering to ask the other two men the names of their villages, the boat officer returned each man's identity papers. Then, he asked Trotsky, "How has the fishing been lately, Comrade?"

Remembering that his fishermen friends had said fishing was bad, Trotsky replied, "Terrible, Comrade Officer." He pointed to the catch-holding tank. "This meager amount of fish is all we have to show for a long night's work. After we give what we must to the Party, there will not be much for the five of us to divvy up."

"You should complain to your party section leader about the poor fishing," the boat officer said. "Perhaps you will be given special permission to go into Turkish waters to steal our fish back."

"We shall do that, and thank you for the good idea," Trotsky said as the boat officer stepped back to the police launch. He waved to the police as the lines were tossed back. When the police launch had pulled away, he faced Ferris and said, "Well, your identity papers passed with flying colors."

Ferris nodded. "Let's all hope they keep passing tests that nicely."

PART TWO

CHAPTER SEVEN

The two government dignitaries stood at attention in their civilian clothes with their hands placed over their hearts until the last note of the Soviet national anthem sounded over the decks of the *Leningrad*. To the Kara class cruiser's portside, a fishing troller that had been stopped by a harbor patrol boat resumed its course for the port of Odessa. It went unnoticed by the Soviet sailors who maintained rigid attention in their dress blue uniforms, even after the music ended. The two helicopters belonging to the *Leningrad* rocked on their wheels as crewmen boarded to service them, and then, with the flight crews moving off to get to their ready rooms below deck, the two dignitaries were escorted over to Fleet Admiral Georgi Stalovich, who was standing at the head of his crewmen waiting to receive his VIP visitors most anxiously.

In his mid sixties, totally bald, short and almost pear-shaped, Stalovich took a few steps toward them and rendered his distinguished countrymen a hand salute. One of them, a man also in his mid sixties and quite short, but much slimmer, was an old World War Two crony and close friend of his. He was Vladimir Kosenoff, the deputy secretary of the navy. The other visitor, a man in his late thirties, nearly six feet tall and quite muscular, was Mikhail Yudalslov. He was the deputy director of Project Threshold, which was the Soviet Union's top secret laser and microwave communications jamming and antijamming project. Their stay aboard Stalovich's flagship, which had been ordered by top Kremlin leaders, was to be brief for the deputy secretary and rather lengthy for the deputy director.

Stalovich had been restless ever since he'd heard that his old friend was paying him a visit. Not knowing in advance what the special envoy was coming to see him about, he'd assumed it was in response to the most recent request he'd made of the deputy secretary, which was to get party approval for a more impressive carrier fleet for the Soviet Navy. In anticipation of some good news from Kosenoff, his spirits were unusually high. He had a cheery gleam in his bright blue eyes and a warming smile on his face as he said in his gravely voice, "It is an honor to welcome you aboard my flagship, Comrade Deputy Secretary." He shook hands heartily with Deputy Secretary Kosenoff as he added, "Is it not over two years since we last saw each other, my old friend?"

"It was just two years ago," Kosenoff replied in his baritone voice. Their last face-to-face meeting had occurred by no coincidence on the very day he'd been appointed to the post of deputy secretary of the navy. Since then the name Stalovich had echoed resoundingly at the Kremlin and had appeared on documents that had crossed his desk without end. All the papers had been requests from Stalovich that he use his political influence to encourage party leaders to add more carrier/cruisers (aircraft carriers) to the two Kiev class carriers that had joined the Soviet fleet a decade ago. At first, out of loyalty to his old friend, he'd made an earnest effort. But with the advent of computer technology, his ideas about conventional warfare had quickly and firmly changed, and he'd become an advocate of electronic warfare. That had forced him to choose between his own convictions and those of his friend. He'd flatly chosen the former but had kept his decision a secret from his friend.

Kosenoff introduced Deputy Director Yudalslov to Stalovich. As they shook hands, he said, "Comrade Yudalslov is second in command of Project Threshold at the Odessa facility."

"I have heard quite a lot about you, Comrade Deputy Director," Stalovich said, his smile fading. "Was it not you who requested that my task force come to Odessa and participate in these electronic war games with the Kiev-based Foxbat squadron?"

"It was," Yudalslov said matter-of-factly. "Our party leaders agreed with me that we should coordinate our electronic warfare training program with the army, navy, and air force on an accelerated basis. We seem to be behind schedule in qualifying laser and microwave operators. Especially in the navy."

"I find it surprising that the navy is lagging in training results, Comrade Deputy Director," Stalovich said defensively. "Speaking for my task force, we are spending more man hours on your newest gimmickry than we are on combat readiness and required routine maintenance."

"I am sure you are doing your very best, Comrade Commandant," Yudalslov said in an appeasing tone. "But our latest efficiency reports indicate that, while we are realizing commendable results from the army and air force units presently equipped with the new laser and microwave apparatus, the navy is lagging behind. Perhaps the problem is lack of enthusiasm because of the newness of it all. At any rate, that is what I am here for. To find out what might be wrong, and correct it."

"Comrade Yudalslov will be going along with you on your Mediterranean deployment, Comrade Stalovich," Kosenoff said.

"Why?" Stalovich asked bitterly.

"To evaluate your training program and the apparatus," Yudalslov interjected coolly.

Looking at Kosenoff, Stalovich said, "But I was told my task force would only be required to participate in the first phase of testing, while we waited for our new deployment orders. Fleet Commandant Mediterranean assured me that once our deployment directive came we would be permitted to resume our badly needed combat readiness exercises out with the American Sixth Fleet."

"We will discuss your deployment orders at greater length in your cabin, Comrade Stalovich," Kosenoff said. "For now, your ship's company awaits my inspection. And Deputy Director Yudalslov is most anxious to inspect the new apparatus in your combat control sector room. Shall we proceed, Comrade Stalovich?"

The inspection of Stalovich's flagship personnel proved to be a farce, with Kosenoff and Yudalslov rushing in and out of the ranks of officers and crewmen as though everyone aboard had the plague. When it was over, and just moments before ship's company was dismissed, the *Leningrad*'s commanding officer accompanied Deputy Director Yudalslov to the flagship's CCS room, while Stalovich and Deputy Secretary Kosenoff went off to the task force commandant's private cabin.

It was his first time aboard Stalovich's flagship, and Kosenoff was immediately taken back by the very plush accommodations the navy provided the task force commandant. The fleet admiral's private cabin was richly decorated with oil paintings of historic Soviet naval sea battles and a select collection of prominent Soviet leaders. A gold-framed painting of the Soviet premier hung on the wall directly behind Stalovich's well-polished Napoleon-era desk. It was flanked by the flag of the Soviet Union and the Soviet naval banner. The rest of the study, as well as the adjoining sleeping nook, was artfully furnished with articles which seemed to be from Napoleon's own palace. The Persian carpet that covered the study and sleeping nook was probably several hundred years old, he guessed by how faded it was.

Kosenoff waited for Stalovich to seat himself behind his antique desk, then said, "I recall, from my own time in naval service, that as senior officers we were privileged with comfortable quarters. But this cabin of yours resembles a stateroom aboard a luxury liner, old friend."

"It is a meager repayment for the many years of deprivation caused by Hitler," Stalovich stated. "Do not our great party leaders permit themselves gracious quarters at the Kremlin?"

Kosenoff smiled. "We will discuss their life-styles over good vodka at another time. At this moment we have your deployment orders to review." He reached inside his suit jacket pocket and took out two cigars. "These are fresh Havanas, compliments of Comrade Castro. The Cuban premier gave me a generous supply of them on his recent visit to the Kremlin." He offered one to Stalovich, then reached across the desk and lit it for him.

Stalovich puffed noisily, sending blue smoke billowing up to the crystal lamp that hung over his desk from a gold-linked ceiling chain. "My compliments to Premier Castro on his taste in cigars, Vladimir," he said, availing himself of the intimacy of his private cabin to address his friend by his first name.

"I will send a supply to you since you approve of them so highly, Georgi," Kosenoff replied.

"It is unusual for a deputy secretary of the navy to hand-deliver routine deployment orders to a task force commandant, Vladimir."

"It is done only on very special occasions, Georgi," Kosenoff replied.

"Could it be, then, that this special occasion has to do with my most recent request for additional carriers for my fleet?" Stalovich asked hopefully.

"I would be delighted if my answer could be yes, Georgi. But that's not why I'm here."

"Then, what is the nature of your visit? Besides telling me that I am expected to turn my task force over to Deputy Director Yudalslov. To use for his electronic warfare games."

"There is no other reason, Georgi," Kosenoff answered. "Our party leaders regard Project Threshold as the most urgent military program presently being undertaken. It is considered by the Kremlin to be *indispensable* to our national defense and has been given highest priority. I have been directed to convey the Party's desire that you cooperate fully with Deputy Director Yudalslov's efforts to improve naval participation in the program."

"As I pointed out to Comrade Deputy Director Yudalslov moments ago, my personnel have been tied in knots trying to learn to operate his newest magical machinery. Then, as quickly as the mysteries can be solved, technological obsolescence sets in. That forces us to repeat the training cycle. And while our personnel are glued to seats in one classroom after another, routine duties which must be performed to maintain combat readiness are totally neglected. Also, we do not have a sufficient number of senior officers to allocate to full-time teaching duties, or of junior officers qualified as technological instructors. And the few technicians we do have available for teaching duties in noncommissioned officer ranks are consumed by efforts to replace prematurely outmoded electronics gear with unending updated versions."

"Leaders of men are expected to overcome obstacles," Kosenoff said flatly. "We are not seeking problems, we are seeking solutions to them. In terms of Project Threshold's short-range application, we are doing quite well. It is the next phase, the long-range implementation of the new jamming and antijamming technology, that is proceeding less satisfactorily. And it is that particular phase of testing that you are to devote your impending Mediterranean deployment to." He reached into his other suit jacket pocket and removed a legal-size manila envelope that had "Top Secret" stenciled in bold red letters across it. Handing it across the desk to Stalovich, he added, "These are your orders. They spell out in detail what is required of you. Your six-month stay in the Mediterranean is expected to serve as an evaluation period for the long-range application of the new laser and microwave apparatus."

"The Party is obsessed with technology and minimizes the importance of conventional warfare. I must have new carriers."

"No," Kosenoff barked. "You will have to rely upon the two carriers our party leaders recently added to our fleets."

"Recently!" Stalovich exclaimed sourly. "The *Kiev* and *Minsk* were added ten years ago. And as tactical vessels they are very limited. Each carrier has a meager complement of nine YAK-36 V/STOL jet aircraft, which are no more impressive than the Harrier jets the British used to reclaim the Falkland Islands from the Argentines. Additionally, the *Kiev* and *Minsk* each have fifteen Kamov KA-25 antisubmarine and missile-targeted helicopters, which are merely general-purpose helicopters, such as the one you and Deputy Director Yudalslov flew out to my flagship in."

"The navy has other priorities, Georgi," Kosenoff insisted. "We have a submarine fleet to maintain."

"Does not the American navy have a submarine fleet to maintain as well, Vladimir?" Stalovich shot back. Not expecting an answer, he went on, "Yet the U.S. Navy manages to maintain an entire carrier-borne air force that is treated as separate from its regular air force. Each American angle-deck carrier has a staggering complement of nearly a hundred assorted fighters, fighter-bombers, and bombers. And without counting their helicopter-support carrier fleet, they have thirteen such super carriers dominating the oceans of the globe. What could our two Kiev class carriers hope to do in a conventional engagement with such a superior force?"

"It has become pointless to debate this ridiculous issue of carrier cruisers with you, Georgi," Kosenoff said impatiently.

"Ridiculous!" Stalovich bellowed. "Is that how our party leaders view my request for carriers? Or is that your own opinion?"

"What do you mean by that remark?"

"Perhaps you were not really sincere in your offer to promote my pleas for a mightier carrier fleet, old friend," Stalovich said. "Perhaps . . . you were merely pacifying me all this time."

"I have done all I could to acquaint our party leaders with your needs," Kosenoff protested. "Always my words fell on deaf ears. In my efforts to support your glorious cause, I exposed myself to ridicule time and again. Finally, I grew weary of the insults and the party's indifference. The Kremlin is no longer concerned about building a carrier fleet. Now, if our friendship must come to an end because I must do what is required of me as deputy secretary of the navy . . . then so be it."

"Could you at least win approval to have either the *Kiev* or the *Minsk* deploy out to the Mediterranean with me in the near future?" Stalovich pleaded. "Perhaps if I were able to demonstrate by maneuvering around the U.S. carrier-borne air force, the tactical advantages of having as many carriers as the opposing fleet, the Kremlin would grant my requests."

"For whatever it proves to be worth to you I will suggest that you have a carrier added to your task force on the next deployment, Georgi," Kosenoff agreed. "But for this deployment, concentrate your efforts on Comrade Deputy Director Yudalslov's needs." Gesturing toward the unopened manila envelope, he added, "I suggest you read your deployment orders now. They direct you to rendezvous with Fleet Admiral Rukniv's off-going task force in the vicinity of Cyprus, instead of the usual meeting place off the island of Crete."

Stalovich opened the envelope and removed the orders, then quickly ran his eyes over the first page of print. "Why this change in procedures, Vladimir?"

"Our latest intelligence reports have established that you will be sharing the waters of the Mediterranean Sea with the U.S. carriers *Kitty Hawk* and *Eisenhower*. They are en route to Cyprus now to relieve the carriers *Forrestal* and *Coral Sea*. You are to deploy your task force at once for the isle of Cyprus, so you will arrive in time to catch the American fleet changeover."

"For what purpose, Vladimir?"

"To begin testing the long-range capabilities of our new jamming and antijamming techniques," Kosenoff said proudly. "The American fleets will be exchanging their usual flow of communications as the incoming task force debriefs the outgoing fleet about any tactics they should expect during their six-month stay in the Mediterranean."

"And my task force will be exchanging the same type of strategic information with Admiral Rukniv's fleet," Stalovich said matter-of-factly.

"Correct," Kosenoff said. "Then, with the aid of the electronic warfare apparatus aboard the ships of your fleet, Yudalslov will supervise a long-range broadcasting of the information you obtain from Admiral Rukniv. He will send it to the domed facility here in Odessa using the antijamming technique, while the jamming technique causes the American fleets to suffer what will appear to them to be a total and uninterrupted blackout of all of their eavesdropping and communications efforts. The application of the technology is therefore the same for the long-range phases of test exercises as it was for the short-range testing your fleet participated in with the domed facility and our Foxbat squadron here in Odessa. We are merely testing the system's ability to perform desirably over greater distances. Its basic performance capability was proven when it jammed the American satellite that passes over Odessa."

"Not being a laser, microwave, and computer technologist, I am still quite confused about how this system works," Stalovich admitted.

"I have instructed Deputy Director Yudalslov to give you at least a layman's understanding, Georgi," Kosenoff said. "But do not feel you must trouble your mind with the more intricate facets of the two techniques for now. Once the electronic warfare project passes all phases of testing, everyone who needs to know more will be instructed and trained. For now, much is being kept top secret."

"The Party's top secret technology will not remain secret very long if it's tested on the ships of the Sixth Fleet. The Americans are sure to become quite upset over having their communications channels interfered with."

"True, Georgi. And they are probably most upset over our causing problems for their satellite as well, even though they have not as yet complained. But knowing we are able to cause them such grief is one thing. Knowing how to stop us is another."

"The Americans are masterminds at making magical machinery, Vladimir. And if we give them cause for concern we may find they are also masterminds at making trouble for us."

"We are aware they are presently engaged in electronic warfare research. But they show no signs of advancing to the stage of testing such technology. That tells us they have not gone beyond the laboratory stages of development. By the time they begin testing their own jamming and antijamming techniques, our technology will have progressed to the full-deployment stage. By then any technological breakthrough the capitalists will have made will be useless to them."

"Perhaps so, Vladimir," Stalovich said. "But how will we fare if the Americans dictate that we fight a conventional war instead?"

"Our technological supremacy will dictate what kind of war will be fought next, Georgi," Kosenoff insisted.

"What if the capitalists decide they will wage war on us before our technology rates supreme? How will our two measly Kiev class carrier cruisers fare against the U.S. Navy's aircraft carrier supremacy?"

"We have already covered this ground thoroughly. Enough," Kosenoff said wearily. He stood up and closed his eyes for a moment. Opening them, he said, "Please see to my return flight to Odessa."

After showing Kosenoff out, Stalovich relit his Havana cigar, then picked up his Napoleon-style desk phone and pressed the button for the bridge. The bridge duty officer answered almost at once and Stalovich ordered, "Prepare one of our helicopters to shuttle the deputy secretary of the navy to Odessa. Then advise the commanding officers of all ships of the task force that we will deploy for the Mediterranean in one hour. Tell them there will be a predeparture briefing aboard the flagship in twenty minutes, and they will be expected to see to all preparations for getting underway before attending."

After returning the phone to its gold-plated cradle, Stalovich sat back in his chair and pondered what it was going to be like spending the next six months in the Mediterranean with the crews of his task force ships bogged down with still more electronic warfare training exercises. It bothered him that combat readiness training would continue to suffer as a result. But what bothered him most was placing the ships and men of his fleet at the disposal of a technologist who knew nothing about combat efficiency and cared to know even less. That, he decided, he would like to do something about. But it seemed highly unlikely that he would get the chance to divert his crews to conventional war games with Yudalslov aboard.

CHAPTER EIGHT

It was nearly noon when Ferris, Baxter, and Trotsky left the fishing troller behind and put their counterfeit identity papers declaring them to be Soviet fishermen to their second test at the port of Odessa checkpoint. From there they relied on their second set of papers which identified them as agriculturists returning to Kiev after attending a farmers' convention in Odessa. Then in Trotsky's four-door Zhiguli, a Soviet version of the Fiat-124, they drove three hundred miles over snow-covered country roads and arrived at Yuri Velinkov's guesthouse just as the sun was setting behind the nearby city of Kiev. A biting wind sent crystals of snow dancing over the tops of drifts as they crunched their way to the front door of the two-story wooden structure. When they were halfway up the front walk, the door opened, suggesting that their arrival had been anticipated by the frail and aging guesthouse proprietor.

"I have the potbellied stove going to warm you, Comrades," Yuri Velinkov called out to his visitors. "And a bottle of vodka to help take the chill of winter out of your bones." When they reached the front door he whispered, "Remember, now. My wife, Yekaterina, has been told nothing about your business with the two young lovers. She is a very sickly old woman and worries over the littlest things, so keep that alarming information from her during your stay."

Trotsky reassured Yuri that his two colleagues wanted to maintain secrecy about their business at his guesthouse as much as he did. He introduced Ferris as Milovan Feliks, and Baxter as Nikita Bakschev, using the names listed in the identity papers. They were names he'd picked from Soviet obituaries, which he'd cleverly matched to their initials to make remembering them easier.

At the potbellied stove, where Yekaterina Velinkov was sitting round-shouldered, Trotsky announced, "Comrades Feliks and Bakschev are agriculturist colleagues of mine. The party leaders have sent them to Kiev to learn my farming techniques."

"And in what part of Russia do you make your homes, Comrades?" Yekaterina asked in a voice thick with phlegm.

"They are from Moscow," Trotsky answered for them.

"Moscow," Yekaterina repeated with a nod. "It is a restless city compared to our peaceful Kiev."

"You have not gone into Kiev for years, old woman," Yuri commented. "You would not find it so peaceful if you did." He regarded his visitors. "Come, Comrades. I will show you to your rooms. With winter being our slow season, you can pick from five of the six rooms we have. Once you are settled, you will all join my wife and me at the kitchen table for some Kiev-style homemade borsch that holds the spoon upright."

"That sounds appetizing to me," Baxter said. He hadn't had real thick borsch since he defected.

"Enough talk about food!" Trotsky said. "Just the mention of borsch puts pounds on me. Come, I will see you to your rooms."

On the way upstairs Yuri explained, "There are two small rooms in the front of the house with windows that face the road you came here on. To the left the road only leads back to the city limits of Kiev, but to the right and just a few hundred yards away it passes through Ivan's very spacious farm. The two rooms in the rear of the house overlook our summer garden, which at the moment the deep snow has made invisible. The other two guestrooms are centrally located on the second floor. They are larger rooms, situated closer to the bathroom that all guests share. For those reasons they earn me additional rubles."

Arriving at the top of the L-shaped staircase, Ferris asked, "In which room will you be putting the two Foxbat pilots if they come here this weekend?"

"They will come," Yuri insisted. "There is no if about that." He pointed to the two front rooms. "And they always pick the front room on the left side of the hall, so they can see who comes along the road from Kiev while they are secretly making love here at my guesthouse."

Walking toward the room Yuri'd pointed out, Ferris asked, "You're quite sure they are in love?"

"I have eyes," Yuri said. "I see it by the way they look at each other." He opened the door to their favorite room. "And I also have ears. This door does not keep in their sounds of love at night. The sounds they made each weekend that has passed tell me they will dependably need to make love again. And they will do so in this very room because they believe their lovemaking will go unnoticed again, as it did each time before."

"What Yuri has said in many words instead of the few that would have sufficed," Trotsky said, "is that our business with the Foxbat pilots can be expected to take place without interruption or delay. No one comes here during the winter months, except them and me."

"That simplifies things nicely," Ferris commented as he inspected the guestroom the potential defectors were in the habit of using. Between the two front windows that offered a view of the country road outside was a double bed that was covered by a multicolored quilt blanket. To only one side, the right, was a night table and a shaded lamp. There was a clean glass ashtray placed on the table next to the lamp. Along the wall to the left of the bed was a wooden chest of drawers, the varnish of which had peeled off almost completely. Adjacent to the chest was a doorless closet that was empty except for a few wire hangers and a spare blanket. Hung by a nail on the opposite wall, across from the bed, was an oil painting of two elderly Ukrainian men playing chess at a table in a Kiev park on a sunny day. Looking at the painting appraisingly, Ferris asked, "Did you paint this?"

"It is my wife's artistic contribution to the guesthouse," Yuri explained. "There are others in each room, things she did during her better years."

Ferris glanced behind the door to his right and saw against the wall a small round wooden table and two armless wooden chairs. Assuming it was a dining area, he asked, "Do you offer room service to your guests?"

"I am usually too busy doing both my and my wife's chores since she took ill," Yuri said. "For that reason we invite our guests to share our meals with us at the kitchen table. For a few rubles per day above the cost of their room, of course. But if you would prefer to eat alone during your stay, I will make an exception for two friends of Ivan's and bring your meals up to you both."

"The kitchen table will be fine," Ferris said, not wanting to be a bother to the old man and woman. He moved over to one of the twin front windows and peered out at the snow-covered road. "Does the room next to this have a view of the road like this one?"

"It is identical both in view and furnishings," Yuri replied. "But the young lovers will not expect to find other guests staying here when they come. And they just might peek into the room next to theirs before getting settled."

"We'll stay in the two back rooms," Ferris said. "We'll keep our things out of sight, too. Just in case they're in the habit of inspecting all your rooms for other guests before they get settled. We want our visit with them to be a total surprise."

"What do you plan to do with them?" Yuri asked. He felt all eyes on him, condemning his inquisitiveness, so he added, "The house is always very quiet at night. Disturbances of any kind might awaken my wife. Then she would ask many questions about . . ."

"I gave you my promise that no harm would come to your guests, and my promise still stands, Yuri," Trotsky said. "There will be no disturbances, that I also promise. What goes on up in their room will be our business. You needn't concern yourself with that."

Yuri nodded submissively, but he had eyes. He had an idea what Trotsky and his friends wanted of two Soviet pilots who flew Russia's newest Foxbats. He had put all the clues together. Trotsky's unusual generosity, his offer of many rubles to have a private meeting with the two young lovers, the questions that had been asked, and so forth. And he read the Soviet newspapers. He knew members of the military were discontented with Mother Russia. It all added up to one thing. Trotsky's friends, especially the young one with the familiar eyes, were going to offer the two young pilots an opportunity to do their lovemaking in freedom. The kind of freedom that exists outside the Soviet Union. He knew of that kind of freedom. He didn't only read communist newspapers. Every once in a while Trotsky gave him pro-western underground newspapers to read, under the condition that he burn them as soon as he had read them. That he always did. He burned them in the potbellied stove, just as he'd promised Trotsky he would. But he kept some of the Soviet newspapers that were of special interest to him. And now that he had seen Trotsky's young friend with the familiar eyes, he was going to look at one particular yellowing clipping from a copy of *Pravda*.

After his inspection of the guestroom the two pilots spent their weekends in, Ferris regarded Yuri. "I also promise you no harm will come to your patrons, and you and your wife will not be disturbed. All you have to do when they arrive is show them up to this room, then go back downstairs and retire for the night."

"I no longer show them to their room," Yuri told them. "Not since their first visit. They just make their own way upstairs now, out of pity for my shortness of breath."

"He lost a lung while serving in the Soviet Army during the Second World War," Trotsky explained.

"Then, you will remain downstairs as you usually do," Ferris said. "And we will want to keep your wife out of the way, just in case we run into a snag with them."

"Yekaterina is usually in bed by the time they walk here from Kiev," Yuri said.

"They always walk here?" Ferris asked.

"From the military bus stop in Kiev," Yuri went on.

"How do you know that?"

"I have overheard them say they make a military bus connection back to their air base. Observing them meet along the road outside the city limits, I assumed they could not afford to chance being seen together by their military comrades in Kiev."

"You watch for them?" Ferris queried.

"From the large guestroom that faces Kiev," Yuri replied. "From there I can see the curve along the road where the man waits for the woman. He always arrives first—she joins him about an hour later. They kiss briefly before coming here."

"Interesting," Ferris commented. He liked the sound of things. It sounded like a genuine love affair, not a pretense staged by the KGB. But he had to make sure of that for himself. "You will not have to watch for them this Friday night, Yuri," he went on. "I plan to be at that military bus stop ahead of their arrival."

"For what reason?" Yuri asked.

"To make sure that is exactly what they do when they arrive in Kiev," Ferris said. "They could be KGB agents posing as two military officers involved in adultery."

"Comrade Feliks is quite right, Yuri," Trotsky said. "The KGB often pose as members of the military."

"And if the young lovers are with the KGB, what will become of us all?" Yuri asked fretfully.

"Leave that worry to us, Yuri," Trotsky insisted. "We are trained to handle such matters. For now, go down to the kitchen and see to your borsch. We have a private matter to discuss." He waited for Yuri to descend the staircase, then regarded Ferris and Baxter. "He is an inquisitive old man, but he will do what he is told to earn his rubles. As for the two young lovers, how do you want to handle things once they are in this room?"

"You and Nick will wait in the kitchen out of sight until I get back from Kiev," Ferris said. "If their behavior is as authentic as the old man described it, I'll let them arrive to do their lovemaking."

"And what if it isn't, Matt?"

"The kiss they exchange along the curve of the road will be their last goddamn kiss if it turns out to be a staged one," Ferris said.

"And if you fail to return?" Trotsky asked coolly.

Ferris gestured toward Baxter. "Get him the hell out of Russia on the next goddamn sub."

"You can be sure I will do that, Matt," Trotsky promised. "But assuming they are not KGB and you allow them to arrive, what is your plan of attack?"

"We'll want to give them time to get comfortable and intimate," Ferris answered. "Naked in bed and wrapped in each other's arms. You'll need a quality Polaroid, Ivan."

"I have such a device at my house," Trotsky said.

"And I'll need a weapon, of course," Ferris added.

"Of course," Trotsky said with a nod.

"When we hear the sounds of their lovemaking through the door, we'll barge in on them. Then, while I hold them at gunpoint, Ivan will take a few snapshots. I'm sure that when we threaten to send the snapshots to Nadia Potgornev's major husband, they'll be most cooperative. Nick will then proceed to convince them their only way out is defection."

"And if we strike out with them?" Baxter asked.

"Then they strike out, too," Ferris replied firmly.

"Of course we will keep the consequences of their refusal from Yuri," Trotsky said.

"Of course," Ferris reassured him. "If they turn us down, we'll be waiting for them along the road when they head back to Kiev."

Baxter shook his head. "I sure hope it doesn't come to that, Matt."

"I hope so, too," Ferris said. Just then he heard Yuri calling up the staircase to announce he was ready to serve his homemade borsch. "Enough talking for now. And let's avoid discussing the finer details around Yuri. He's running a little worried, and that's making me slightly nervous. The next few days are going to seem like a week of back-to-back Mondays. And you both know how Mondays scare me."

Throughout the evening meal Baxter couldn't help notice Yekaterina and Yuri glancing at him hauntingly. Their preoccupation with him left him with such an uncomfortable feeling that he decided to mention their strange behavior to Ferris and Trotsky. When supper was over, and while Yuri was seeing Yekaterina to bed, he gestured for them to follow him out to the potbellied stove. Then he said softly, "Those two old people didn't take their eyes off me all through supper."

"I know," Ferris said. "I was going to mention that, too."

"I was also aware of their staring," Trotsky admitted. "Perhaps I can explain. You see, the Velinkov's son, Petr, died while serving in the Soviet Army. Not because of war, but because of needless neglect. Had their son lived he would have been about your age by now, Nick."

"And I sort of remind them of Petr?" Baxter asked.

"All young men remind them of Petr," Trotsky said.

"Excuse Ivan and me, Nick," Ferris put in. "We are going over to his farm. We have to let Hal Banks know that we are in Kiev and settled at the guesthouse."

"I'd like to tag along," Baxter said, wanting to see what Trotsky's Kiev-based clandestine headquarters looked like. He also wanted to avoid any more staring.

"You can see the farm tomorrow, Nick," Ferris said. "I want one of us to remain in the house with the old man throughout our stay."

"If you are fearful that Yuri would betray us to the KGB, Matt, I assure you he would not," Trotsky said. "Even if he wanted to, he would be unable to do so. Like me, he has no phone in the house. And with one of his lungs missing he can barely walk from his house to mine, much less all the way to KGB headquarters in Kiev."

"I'm not fearful of that," Ferris replied. "But if our two potential defectors just happen to show up ahead of schedule, he might panic if he's alone in the house and scare them away."

"I didn't think of that, Matt," Trotsky admitted. "It is a good idea to save Yuri from any unnecessary worries. His sickly wife causes him enough concern."

Yuri kissed the wrinkled forehead of his wife as he bid her good night. Returning to the front room, he found Trotsky and one of his visitors slipping on their parkas. "Where are you going?" he asked. "I was hoping we could drink some vodka and talk man's talk now that my wife has retired."

"I asked Ivan to show me his farmhouse," Ferris answered.

Yuri glanced at his young visitor seated in front of the potbellied stove. "And you do not wish to see Ivan's elegant farmhouse as well, Comrade Bakschev?" he asked.

"Comrade Bakschev prefers to share your vodka and talk man talk with you," Trotsky said for Baxter.

"I am honored," Yuri said. "Yekaterina is not much of a conversationalist. She usually sleeps while I talk. And Ivan's visits are too few and too brief to make up for her silence. So it will be a precious opportunity to share vodka and talk with someone from the outside world. I will get the vodka at once."

With Yuri out of the room, Ferris said, "I thought you told me the old man didn't know we came from outside Russia, Ivan."

"It is merely a figure of speech," Trotsky said reassuringly. "To Yuri anyone beyond his front door is from the outside world." He regarded Baxter. "Be patient with him as a favor to me, Nick. He is such a lonely old man." Baxter nodded. "Come, Matt. Let us be off."

In the kitchen, Yuri placed two glasses and the bottle of vodka left over from supper on a small tray. Hearing the front door close, he quietly made his way to the master bedroom in the rear of the house. Being careful not to awaken Yekaterina, he removed his newspaper-clipping scrapbook from its hiding place under the clothes in his bottom dresser drawer. All of the clippings he'd saved were about Russians who'd displayed their disapproval for Soviet Communist Party leadership in a most dramatic way. He hadn't had occasion to add any new clippings to the scrapbook for three months. In that time the newspapers that Trotsky had brought to him on an irregular basis had been free of the kind of articles he collected in his scrapbook. None of them had had anything to do with his and Yekaterina's discontent with the Soviet Union because of its indifference to the plight of old and sickly citizens. None could help him plan what to do about their discontent. But the last clipping he'd added to the scrapbook looked very promising. He prayed it would be what he was looking for.

He returned to the kitchen, carrying his scrapbook under one arm. He picked up the tray and went out to the front room to rejoin his young visitor with the alarming eyes. He set the tray down on a round knee-high table that was situated between them, then poured a generous serving of vodka into both glasses. "To good health," he said, raising his glass in a toast.

Baxter raised the other glass. "To good health."

Yuri seated himself, thinking as he did that he should begin their talk casually, then gradually lead into the clippings in his scrapbook. He thought current events would be a good topic to start with, but he knew nothing about such things. He thought of sports next, but he knew nothing about such things, either. He considered the Olympics, feeling that could lead to the scrapbook. But he wanted to discuss another topic ahead of that one, so he decided he'd open the conversation by apologizing for his and Yekaterina's staring at him, which he knew his young visitor had noticed. He took another sip of his vodka to ease his anxiety, then said, "I am afraid my wife and I were rude to you at the supper table, Comrade Bakschev."

"Rude?" Baxter repeated.

"My wife, Yekaterina, was staring at you because she thought you looked a lot like our deceased son, Petr. Petr froze to death somewhere in the rectum of Russia, because the Party did not provide him with proper attire to withstand winter's indifference to human frailty. Petr was even more frail than I am. He was in his mid-twenties and halfway through his required military service hitch when he died."

"Comrade Trotsky mentioned something about your loss," Baxter said in an understanding tone. "I'm sorry for you both."

"Thank you," Yuri said, his voice full of sadness as he reflected on Petr's death. "Unlike Yekaterina, who thinks every young man looks like our Petr, I do not think you resemble our Petr at all. And I regard myself as quite an expert in recognizing faces, especially eyes." He held up his scrapbook stuffed with loose pages. "You might say I am quite a collector of faces in a very special way. It was my interest in faces and eyes that aided me in picking out the young lovers who visit my guesthouse from a host of photographs of young military officers that Ivan showed me."

"I'm sure you are very good at it," Baxter said politely. He detected anxiety in the old man's voice, but assumed Yuri wanted "man talk" so badly that he was awkward in getting things started. He noticed a chess set on a pedestal table across the room and to help make conversation he said, "That's a beautiful chess set. Do you play the game much?"

Yuri shifted his gaze from Baxter to the hand-carved pieces and matching oak playing board and pedestal. Looking at the set affectionately, he said, "Before my wife became ill I used to play fanatically. When she still had her health, Yekaterina and I used to spend every summer Sunday in Kiev. We'd take a picnic basket along with us and attend Mass at a Byzantine church in the city that we are parishioners of. Then after Mass we'd go down to the banks of the Dnieper River and picnic with other parishioners from our church. And while Yekaterina and the other lady parishioners talked woman talk, I would join the men in chess tournaments that were so competitive, each move a player made would be rigidly timed."

"Sounds like a real nice way to spend a summer Sunday," Baxter commented.

"They were wonderful summers," Yuri said fondly. "A highlight of one particular summer was a Kievan-Muscovite Byzantine inter-parish tournament for grand master, which all of Kiev lined the banks of the Dnieper to see. As the Kievan defender who defeated the Muscovite challenger three out of three matches, I won both title of grand master and that chess set," Yuri concluded proudly.

"And I was just about to ask you for a match," Baxter said.

"Do not let my title of grand master scare you off," Yuri replied. "I have not played since that day."

"Why not?"

"Before summer could come again, Yekaterina became crippled with arthritis and rheumatism. There were no walks to Kiev after that. No more Byzantine Masses. And no more chess tournaments, either. I found that I needed to spend summer Sundays the same way I spent every other day, which was making up for the work that Yekaterina could not perform, and being the nurse to her that our meager guesthouse business could not provide. Soon the extra work began reminding the lung that escaped a Nazi sniper's bullet how much it missed the other lung's help. Now a walk up the stairs is a hike for me," he said as he gestured toward the staircase.

Baxter was saddened by Yuri's story, but pleased that the old man would share his sorrow with him. Feeling it would be a good idea to change the mood to a cheerier one, he said, "Well, why don't we play a game and see if you still deserve to keep your grand master title."

Yuri thought about his young visitor's challenge. At any other time he would have jumped at the chance to defend his title. But he had already decided how they would spend the evening while they were still alone. "Perhaps tomorrow after lunch," he said. "I would hate to forfeit my title because of fatiguing late hours of play."

"Tomorrow, then," Baxter agreed.

Returning to the subject he planned to discuss, Yuri said, "As I was mentioning before, you are much too strong a man to look at all like my son. And your eyes are nothing like Petr's. Yet I felt as though I had seen those eyes somewhere before. That is why I also stared at you during supper."

Baxter had already put the incident out of his mind and was surprised that his host had suddenly elected to return to it. He was also a little taken aback by the old man's reference to a prior meeting. He was sure he'd never crossed paths with Yuri. And even if they had met sometime, he no longer looked anything like he had then. Yet the thought of being recognized as Nikoli Belensky while still in Russia hit a nerve. "I'm sure we never met before," he said defensively.

"I didn't say we ever did," Yuri said. "What I said was I felt sure I had seen your eyes somewhere before. In another face, perhaps."

"That's possible," Baxter agreed, feeling less tense about the subject of eyes. "Lots of people have similar eyes."

"Similar, yes," Yuri agreed. "But no one has the same eyes as another. And in looking through my clippings I found your eyes." He opened the scrapbook to the page he had studied earlier. Handing it to Baxter, he added, "These newspaper clippings all pertain to Soviets who managed to somehow flee the choking grip our party leaders keep on Soviet citizens. Some clippings are about civilians who scaled the iron curtain and found political asylum in some part of the free world. Others are of members of the military who, like the two young lovers you and your colleague want to meet, have reasons for needing more freedom than Russia will allow. And the remainder of the clippings are about those who were either captured or killed in their attempt to escape to freedom." Seeing his young visitor studying the photograph of the man in the article he was referring to, he announced, "That young air force officer made one of the most daring of escapes to the West. In case you don't know, he is Nikoli Belinsky. And while your face and his face look different, your eyes and his eyes seem to have a lot to do with each other."

"I don't think so," Baxter said. He wanted to return the scrapbook at once, but a nostalgic response to the photo of himself forced him to continue staring at it. He thought he looked much younger then. He guessed that was because of the boyish-looking crewcut that was such a prominent part of his Soviet military appearance. He looked at the senior lieutenant's uniform—it was the same one he'd worn the day he'd defected. He hadn't seen the uniform since the day he'd shed it for American-made civilian clothes when he'd landed his Foxbat in Japan. Seeing it again on himself, he found it to be far less attractive than his American navy uniform. The longer he stared at the picture the more he found himself reliving old memories. Memories he had suppressed. Some were fond memories.

Others were far less so. A few were disturbing enough to make him finally return the scrapbook. He did so without saying a word.

"Look through the other clippings if you'd like," Yuri suggested. Baxter shook his head. "You do not agree you bear a strong resemblance to the man in the photo?" Yuri asked coyly.

"People in military uniforms often look similar," Baxter stated. "It is the uniform, rather than the person wearing it, that suggests a resemblance to someone else."

"And the eyes? What about the eyes in particular?" Yuri went on.

"It is a black and white photo," Baxter replied. "How can you tell what color the eyes are?"

Yuri examined the photo again, concentrating on the eyes of the man in the clipping. When he raised his head, he stared into Baxter's eyes and said, "I can sense their color. They are the same blue as your eyes are."

Baxter dismissed Yuri's statement with a wave of his hand. "With all due respect to whatever supernatural powers you may feel you are gifted with, I find that hard to believe. Even identification experts can't tell the color of someone's eyes from a black and white photograph. But I guess the only way to know whether Nikoli Belinsky's eyes and mine are the same would be to have both of us in front of you at the same time."

"I feel that I do have both of you in front of me at the same time," Yuri insisted. "This photograph of Nikoli Belinsky as he looked before he defected. And you as Nikoli Belinsky looks now three years after defecting."

"That's preposterous!" Baxter snapped. "I don't look at all like the man in that newspaper clipping."

"The nose and cheekbones look different," Yuri admitted. "But a good plastic surgeon could have altered them. And the fact that you have black hair and Colonel Nikoli Belinsky's hair is yellow is easily explained. A change of hair color is commonly used to disguise someone. And the change of hair color makes you look much older than the Nikoli Belinsky in the photo would look three years later. But some things remain unchanged. Your build. Your lips and ears. And especially your eyes. A KGB description of Nikoli Belinsky accompanied that three-year-old *Pravda* photo. It stated the shade of blue of Belinsky's eyes. Your eyes are the same shade of blue."

Very perceptive, Baxter thought. Especially for an old man who didn't leave his guesthouse because of ill health. As he thought more about Yuri's uncanny ability to point out characteristics identifying him as Nikoli Belinsky, he decided that the ability was near professional. Yet Trotsky hadn't said the old man was a professional at anything other than running a guesthouse. That seemed strange. Trotsky knew very well that it would jeopardize the mission if anyone besides him and Ferris knew he was Nikoli Belinsky while he was in the Soviet Union. Either Trotsky had trusted the old man with that highly privileged information, or Yuri Velinkov was as competent at identifying people through professional disguises as professionals were. That added up to the strong possibility that the guesthouse proprietor might be a pro. But on whose side?

"I gather by the astonished look on your face that you are quite impressed with my ability to know people by their eyes," Yuri said. His statement drew no response from his guesthouse patron, so he added, "And I'm sure you are wondering why I am bringing up such a connection between you and former Soviet Air Force Colonel Nikoli Belinsky." There was still no response. "There is a reason, which I will get to in time. I assure you it has nothing to do with causing you any harm whatsoever. I am not a man of violence. And I have nothing to do with police work of any kind. Please trust me on that and listen without apprehension."

"What is your reason for mentioning a connection?" Baxter asked anxiously.

Yuri quickly turned the pages in his scrapbook until he got to the most recent newspaper clipping. As he offered the book to his young visitor, he pointed to a small inset at the top right corner of a larger accompanying photo. "This inset was reproduced from the larger photo of Colonel Nikoli Belinsky that I first showed you," he said. Pointing to the larger photo, he added with emphasis, "And this is a photo of the wife and son Colonel Nikoli Belinsky left behind when he defected." Leaning back in his chair to allow his young visitor to examine the photo more closely, he said, "In case you are not who I think you are, the woman in the photo is going under her maiden name of Ludmila Zhukeev. And the name of the six-year-old boy she is holding by the hand is Pavlik. The boy's last name was also changed to Zhukeev to protect him from the disgrace the name of Belinsky brought into their lives three years ago." He had deliberately chosen the word *disgrace* to see how his visitor would respond. But Baxter's head remained bowed over the newspaper clipping.

Baxter's hands were trembling as he held the scrapbook. After almost memorizing the photo of his wife and son, he switched his gaze to the caption, then hungrily read the accompanying article. As he did, he kept telling himself that he was reading it merely out of curiosity, to learn what the two people he had once loved so dearly were doing with their lives. He was pained by what he read. He could take all the political ridicule the Party heaped on him. But he didn't appreciate being called a cruel and heartless father as well as a coward and a traitor. The title of traitor belonged to him now, that he couldn't deny. And perhaps he should also be titled a coward for running away from political persecution instead of staying and fighting oppression to his death. He also had to accept that he had deserted both wife and son and while he wasn't proud of that, his wife hadn't wanted to leave with him and his son had been only three, too young to take from his mother. What really hurt him most was what the Party quoted his son as saying about him, which was that he'd left Pavlik fatherless because he'd never loved him from the day he was born. That was just not true. His wife had brainwashed his son into believing that. The party leaders had had a hand in it, too. They were good at turning a lie into the truth and the truth into a lie. He wanted to punish both wife and country for lying to a little boy. Unable to read any more of the vicious things his son was quoted as saying about him, Baxter turned his watery eyes away from the article and settled them on the photo of his son.

Yuri didn't have to ask if his young visitor found the photo and accompanying article of interest. He had eyes. And he had to say more, though he knew it would cause the young man pain. "As the article points out, Colonel Belinsky's wife has been devoutly serving the Party as a gymnastic proctor in Moscow for the past three years, to make up for the treasonous behavior of her husband. And it states that she has served the Party so honorably and loyally that she is now being made head gymnastic director at the School of Olympic Events in Kharkov, which her son will attend as a student of Olympic performances."

Yuri took another sip of his vodka for courage, to help him with his recital of the rest of the degrading points made by the article. "The article also states that Nikoli Belinsky deserted his wife because he was ashamed of the adulterous acts he'd committed. And he deserted the Soviet Air Force out of fear that it would be discovered that he had stolen money and personal property from his comrades. And that he'd sold military secrets to enemy agents. And that he . . ."

"They really make it sound like he was one terrible person," Baxter finally said.

"I would wager that Nikoli Belinsky was not an adulterer," Yuri said quietly. "That he never stole things from his comrades. That he was never a spy, working for enemy agents. And most of all, I would bet my life that he was a good father to his son, and a good husband to his wife. I only wish Nikoli Belinsky would tell me these things himself."

"If he did, would you believe him?" Baxter asked.

"More so than the Party's obvious propagandized version of the man."

"Why would it be important to you to hear his side of the story?" Baxter asked. "Did you ever meet him?"

"No. But I feel as though I know him quite well."

"How is that?"

"Men who would give up their most treasured possessions for true freedom say all that any other man needs to know about them just by doing so."

"And you're convinced that I am such a man?" Baxter asked as he looked again at the face of his son.

"I doubt you continue to look at that photo because the woman's radiant beauty has you spellbound."

"Why, then?"

"Because she is your wife. And the boy is your son. Because . . . you are Nikoli Belinsky."

Handing the scrapbook back to Yuri, Baxter said coolly, "What you suggest is wrong. I am not he. But the woman seems too beautiful for any man to just up and leave. I'm sure leaving her must have been very hard for Belinsky to do. Even for freedom."

"Why then did he?"

"Perhaps he couldn't stay any longer, and she wouldn't leave with him."

"Perhaps," Yuri said. "But what about the boy?"

"Pavlik is six now, so he was three then. Should his father have taken him with him, when leaving the country was so dangerous?"

Yuri smiled sadly. "If those were Belinsky's reasons, then I suppose he did the only thing he could do."

"Yes," Baxter said, and he and Yuri shared a moment of silence. Then Baxter asked, "Why are you keeping newspaper clippings about Nikoli Belinsky and his wife and son?"

"As I said before, I am interested in the stories of all Soviets who flee Russia."

"Why?"

"Because someday I hope to get Yekaterina and myself out of the Soviet Union. I hope to take my wife to a warm place where she will either be well again or go to her death with far less pain than Russia's bitter winters inflict on her. By studying the successes and failures of others who have already dared to flee, I hope to come upon a way out that will work for a winded old man and a crippled old woman."

"Ivan is a close friend of yours, and he has had some success in such matters," Baxter said. "Why don't you ask his help?"

"Because Ivan has told me he can only manage to get Yekaterina and me out of the Soviet Union."

"Isn't that enough?"

"It is only part of the distance we need to go for the sake of my wife's ill health," Yuri replied.

"What is the full distance?" Baxter asked.

"To the United States. To a place like Arizona, where the hot climate will dry up Yekaterina's pain."

"Ivan can't arrange such a relocation for you once you are out of Russia?" Baxter asked.

"Even with whatever influence Ivan has in America, he is still a Russian. And we would need a relative living in America to sponsor our immigration to that country. If we could bring a precious Foxbat along with us, we would be given instant political asylum and much more upon our arrival. Otherwise we would spend endless time waiting at the end of long lines of aliens seeking political asylum in the United States."

"Where did you get that information from?" Baxter asked.

"From a fellow Byzantine parishioner I know who has underground connections."

"Well, whatever you paid this fellow Christian for the information, it was wasted rubles," Baxter said. "The United States government is not that unsympathetic. In hardship cases exceptions are made to immigration laws. Especially in cases of Soviets seeking political asylum."

"But it would still take countless time," Yuri sighed. "And while we wait for an opportunity, the cold winters continue to torment Yekaterina."

"There are other warm places in the world outside the Soviet Union to do your waiting in."

"If I went elsewhere I would be forced to use the rubles I have saved for spending on our old age in the United States," Yuri said. "That is why I took the chance of talking to you so openly. I hoped you would admit that you are Nikoli Belinsky, so I could make you a proposal."

"And if I were Nikoli Belinsky, what would your proposal be?" Baxter queried.

"To offer you half of the rubles I have saved in return for your help in getting Yekaterina and me approval to immigrate to America. As Nikoli Belinsky you did the United States government a great service by delivering your Foxbat to them. Surely the government would show its gratitude and allow you to have your closest relatives join you in America."

"I'm not sure what you mean."

"Nikoli Belinsky's parents are deceased," Yuri explained. "But what is the harm in adopting two living parents like Yekaterina and me to take their places? As long as the wife and boy will not be going, and the real mother and father cannot take advantage of the opportunity, why shouldn't we go? We could make such good use of the opportunity."

Baxter leaned back in his chair. He was astonished by the idea of taking on a set of parents in return for half of the old man's savings. But recalling his own determination to leave the Soviet Union, and the risks he'd taken, he well understood Yuri's desperation. He filled both glasses again and said, "Drink up, Comrade. It took a lot of courage to even suggest such a proposal. Especially when you are not certain I am Nikoli Belinsky."

Yuri raised the drink to his lips, sipped, and said, "Very well, then. Allow me to pretend you are and ask you again. Would you consider what I have proposed?" Before his question could be answered, the front door opened and he whispered to Baxter, "Sleep on my offer at least, Comrade. And please do not mention our conversation to the others. They will deprive me of this wonderful chance to earn still more rubles to spend in America."

Baxter nodded, then looked over at Ferris as he came toward the potbellied stove. Watching him rotate his hands over its warmth, he asked, "How was your visit to Ivan's farm?"

"Terrific," Ferris replied. He noticed a strange look on Baxter's face, and thought he detected a similar look on the old man's. For some reason, they looked guilty. "How did your talk go?" he asked.

"Enjoyably," Yuri answered. "I was telling Comrade Bakschev about the days when I won the title of grand master."

"Grand master of what?" Ferris asked.

"Chess. Do you not play the game?"

"No," Ferris answered.

"Pity," Yuri commented. "It is truly a most relaxing game. Comrade Bakschev and I are planning to have a match after lunch tomorrow. You are welcome to watch if you are interested in learning how to play."

Eyeing the bottle of vodka on the table between Yuri and Baxter, Ferris said, "I'll pass on the chess match for tomorrow, but I'll join you for a nightcap right now if I may."

"Please do," Yuri said. "You will find another glass out in the kitchen." He waited for Ferris to leave the room, then whispered, "Will you at least sleep on my offer, Comrade?"

"And if I were Nikoli Belinsky and declined your offer, how would that affect the business we have with the two Foxbat pilots?"

"One has to do with earning rubles," Yuri replied. "The other has to do with spending them. If I do not perform the earning business satisfactorily, there will be no spending business to perform."

"One more question," Baxter said. "If this is all just a business to you, why were you so worried about what we were going to do with the two Foxbat pilots?"

"If you do not harm them perhaps I can continue earning the rubles they spend to do their lovemaking at my guesthouse."

"Is that the only reason?" Baxter asked.

"There is one more."

"Which is?"

"I would not like to see them harmed merely because they needed each other's love. That would be a thing that only the cruelest of men would do. And I see no such cruelty in your eyes."

"If you trust so much in what you see in a man's eyes, then why did you even ask if we would harm them?"

"Because in Comrade Feliks's eyes I see that ability." He stopped, seeing his other visitor step out of the kitchen. He waited for Ferris to arrive at the archway leading into the front room, then got to his feet and announced, "Take my seat, Comrade Feliks. It is time for me to take my place by Yekaterina's side." He bade them both good night, then with his scrapbook tucked tightly under his arm he shuffled down the hall to the back bedroom.

Ferris filled his glass with vodka and took a large sip, then sat down in the chair Yuri had occupied. "We got the word out to

Hal Banks that things look real good here as far as the layout goes. Told him if things go along as smoothly with the two lovers Friday night, we might be back in D.C. as early as Sunday." He thought about that, then added, "Hell, I might even be on a jet bound for Waikiki on Monday. If so, it'll be the first goddamn Monday that ever brought any sunshine into my life." He noticed Baxter's lack of response. "Hell, you're not one for getting overly excited about good news, are you?"

Baxter was about to comment when a distant howling filled his ears. He perked up in his chair as the noise grew louder and their glasses began to tremble on the table before them. When the thunderous roar was directly above them, Ferris sprang from his seat in alarm. "Relax, Matt," Baxter said with a grin. "It is only a wave of Foxbats flying overhead."

"Flying overhead!" Ferris exclaimed. "They sounded like they were passing through the rooms upstairs." He retook his seat, then said, "They're noisy goddamn planes, aren't they?"

"The way this old wooden house vibrates would make any plane sound louder than it really is," Baxter said.

"Are you suggesting those planes aren't really loud, Nick?"

"Not at all. They're a hell of a lot louder than the Foxbats I used to jockey. It seems this house is right smack in line with one of the duty runways at Viktor and Nadia's air base. And if Trotsky's right about their flying round robins between Kiev and Odessa three times a day, we'll be hearing that clamor six times daily on a five-day-a-week basis."

"As long as they don't make their touchdown on top of us while we're sleeping, I'll put up with their damn noise. And as long as Trish Darrol finds the black boxes that are supposed to be aboard them, they can make all the noise they need to."

"I'll drink to that," Baxter said as he raised his glass to his lips.

"Speaking of drinking to things, I'll drink to that guilty look you and the old man had on your faces when I walked in. What caused that expression?"

"What the hell are you talking about, Matt?" Baxter protested. "I didn't look guilty. I . . ."

"Don't try to fool the old pro. I can read faces better than you can read newspapers, Nick."

"What you saw was a look of sadness, Matt."

"Oh?" Ferris said. "And what brought the shared sadness on, then? And before you answer, I want a poop sheet's worth of convincing, 'cause right now I feel like you're trying to hide something from me. And you know from my days of interrogating you how upset I get when I think I've been left in the dark about something I should be told."

"The old man was telling me all about the trials and tribulations of his and his sickly wife's life here in the Soviet Union. That's all there was to it, Matt."

"Try again, Nick. See if you can come up with an explanation that will fit the look a little better."

"No, Matt. You tell me what you think the look was about."

"I wish I had a clue."

"Well, you must be thinking of something in particular to feel you're being lied to. Tell me, is it the same doubts you expressed about me while we were back in Jacksonville?"

"You have to admit that as a pro I have to consider the fair possibility that those doubts could become realities while we're here, Nick. I can't disregard them just because you say I should. Especially if you do anything to blow this mission that my good sense could have prevented."

"Well, why don't you handcuff me like the good professional cop you are for my entire stay in Russia."

"The thought entered my mind, Nick," Ferris admitted. "But I would rather be convinced by you that such a measure won't be necessary. So get on with giving me that stuff about how this old man and his sickly wife nearly brought tears of sorrow to your eyes."

Baxter decided he could tell Ferris most of the conversation he and Yuri had had. He left in the parts about how the old man had lost one lung in World War Two, how his son, Petr, had died, how his wife was stricken with arthritis and rheumatism, and how he'd had to give up his two favorite pastimes, attending church and playing chess. But he left out the parts about the old man's newspaper clippings and how the old man had perceived he was Nikoli Belinsky. He also left out the part about the old man's request that he adopt him and his wife. In conclusion he said, "So that made me feel bad for the old man and woman."

"That's it in a nutshell?" Ferris asked firmly.

"That's the whole poop sheet's worth, Matt," Baxter insisted. "And that's why I agreed to play chess with the old man tomorrow. To give him a chance to enjoy one of the activities he misses so much."

"Forgive me if I acted overly cautious, Nick. But lies are my Achilles' heel. As a professional, I must be very careful, even if it means hurting someone's feelings. Lies get people killed. So do half-truths."

Baxter extended his arms toward Ferris. "If it'll make you sleep better tonight, put the cuffs on me. I'll understand. Just take them off again when I play chess with the old man tomorrow."

"Wrap those mitts around your glass and sip your drink, Nick," Ferris said. "I'll take your word for it that you're telling me the truth. That there's nothing for me to worry about. But if I catch you in a lie, you won't be wearing handcuffs. You'll be wearing a goddamn body bag."

"Such terrible talk for good friends to use over good vodka," Baxter said with a warm smile. He raised his glass in a toast, then said, "To the success of Operation Gambit, Matt."

"Cheers to that," Ferris returned as he joined Baxter in a hearty swig. As the vodka burned his insides on its way down, he decided he'd keep an eye on Nick anyway.

CHAPTER NINE

The six Foxbats joined up in the night sky over Kiev, then quickly got into a mirror formation and streaked out to the south for the domed facility in Odessa. They were Mikoyan MIG-35 twin-engine jets, with a speed of up to twenty-five hundred miles per hour and a range of twelve hundred miles. Their dual rudders stood vertically on the backs of two swept-back stabilizers that eared out from each side of their glowing red engine exhaust tail cones. Set ahead of the tail section configuration were fixed-overhead, delta-shaped wings, the undersides of which housed thick intake ducts for each engine. The intake ducts straddled the razor-thin wings from the trailing edge to a point beyond their leading edge where the individually sealed tandem cockpits began. From the cockpits forward their fuselage tapered to a birdlike beak. On their tails and wings were bright red stars, the symbol of the Soviet military.

The six Foxbats were headed for night training exercises at the Odessa facility. Each was flown from the rear cockpit by a student pilot of Advanced Training Wing 3, while an instructor monitored the performance from forward cockpit. In the hellhole (electronic components compartment) under the floor of the cockpit, was a new computerized jamming and antijamming apparatus. As a security measure, the pilots—students and instructors alike—had only a functional understanding of the "black boxes" aboard their MIG-35's. Of the ATW 3 engineering personnel responsible for servicing the highly sophisticated laser and microwave equipment, only a few knew the technological aspects of the apparatus that was the key element to Russia's top secret Operation Threshold.

In the front cockpit of Foxbat 114 was Senior Flight Lieutenant Viktor Aleksei. He was a veteran Foxbat pilot and flight instructor whose seniority in the squadron gave him authority over the other five flight instructors participating in the round robin mission to Odessa. As group leader of the six-plane training sortie Viktor was responsible for evaluating the tactical warfare aerial performances of all the student pilots in his group, in addition to appraising the training techniques of their instructors. His Foxbat was flying the "point" (lead) position and maintained radio communication for the group with the mission control sector leader in Odessa.

Viktor had been looking forward to the late-night flight all afternoon, ever since he'd learned that his student pilot and secret lover, Junior Flight Lieutenant Nadia Potgornev, had received disturbing news at that afternoon's mail call. Married to an army officer and on military duty away from her husband, Nadia was always closely watched by her barracks party sector leader, whose duty it was to keep Major Joseph Potgornev informed of her behavior on and off the air force installation. For that reason Viktor and Nadia could never chance having their personal conversations overheard on the base or while on weekend passes in Kiev. And because all aircraft were equipped with a cockpit voice recorder that taped everything they said over their radio and intercom, the same rule applied when they were sharing their Foxbat.

Their secret weekend rendezvous at the country guesthouse outside the city limits of Kiev provided them with a means to converse privately about the week-long activities affecting their lives at the air base. And to get around the lack of privacy while in flight, Viktor had invented a unique form of communication. He and Nadia were separated in the Foxbat by individual canopies that sealed them inside, and a partition that divided the front from the rear cockpit positions. But there was a thick trunk of electrical wires that snaked forward from the aft to the front cockpit, the rubber seal of which could be pulled away from the wall dividing them so a note could be passed through. When a note was being passed, the sender signaled the recipient by applying foot pressure on the dual brake pedals, which were not used while airborne. At the end of each flight, or each session of communication, the rubber seals would be placed back over the trunk of wires on both sides of the partition. The notes would later be flushed down barracks toilets at the air base.

Feeling Nadia's foot pressure on his forward cockpit brake pedals as soon as they reached cruising altitude, Viktor pulled the rubber seal away from his side of the partition and searched around the trunk of wires for a note. Instead he found a letter-size parcel. He pulled it through, and with Nadia at the controls, he took the letter out of the envelope and slowly read every typewritten line:

> My beloved Nadia:
> I have the most wonderful news to pass along to you. News I expect will delight you and brighten up your day. You are no longer married to Major Joseph Potgornev. I
> . . .

Viktor paused, feeling it would delight him and brighten his day if Nadia really was no longer married to Joseph Potgornev. Then he read on:

> . . . have received my long awaited advance in rank, so you are now the wife of Colonel Joseph Potgornev. My promotion requires me to serve on the general staff, HQ in Moscow. It is a Kremlin assignment that grants me considerable fringe benefits. A chauffeur-driven General Staff car. A large and richly furnished apartment close to Army Headquarters in the heart of Moscow, which also happens to be near the Moscow Ballet Theater. Food will now be abundant. I will receive invitations to all of the fancy parties the high brass holds, some of which the Premier himself attends.
> Saving the best news of all for last, I am entitled, as a Colonel of GS-HQ, to have my military wife stationed closer to my place of work, so that you can attend these military and political events with me. You need not do a thing about that, however. I have already sent the required documents to GS-HQ in Moscow. As quickly as administrative channels can process my request, you will be en route to Moscow to take once again your rightful place at my side. I will have some caviar and chilled champagne on hand when you arrive to celebrate our good fortune. Until that time comes, which I am told could be less than two weeks, try and endure the short wait remaining before we are in each other's fond embrace once more.
> Your loving husband,
> Joseph.

Viktor was furious that Nadia's husband had arranged her transfer without consulting her first. His first response was to encourage Nadia to refuse to go. But, reflecting on what Nadia had told him about her arranged marriage to Joseph Potgornev and the political commitments involved, he knew she would never be permitted to deny her husband his wishes. He knew that Nadia's betrothal to Joseph was the result of a promise her parents had made to his family when she was born. He knew that party leaders had given the marriage political sanction. He knew that Joseph Potgornev was nearly twice Nadia's age, and because they were married when she was only seventeen, Joseph was pledged the full support of both families on all matters pertaining to running Nadia's life. He knew that her husband habitually exercised his position as head of the household to dominate her unbearably. He knew that Joseph Potgornev frequently made decisions that would affect Nadia's life, without regard for her feelings or personal preferences. And he knew that because Joseph was such a selfish and inconsiderate man Nadia didn't love him and never would.

Viktor also knew that Nadia had been pushed into a military career so that her husband and her parents would have complete control of her once she reached an age when she could defy their dominance. If she were to go against Joseph's or her parents' wishes, they could use their political influence to have the military constrain her, even punish her for her acts of defiance. Above all, through military and political control over her, they could force her to remain married to Joseph if she ever dared to exercise the rights she had as a legal adult. Viktor was sure Joseph Potgornev would never consent to divorcing Nadia. Her parents would never sanction such a divorce. And the Party would never let Nadia live it down if she demanded one. She would be chastised, humiliated, scorned, and abused for every day remaining of her military service obligation. Then, just before she completed that obligation, the Party would cite her on trumped-up charges of acts against the state that could have her spending the rest of her life in a Soviet prison for women.

Viktor could never chance putting Nadia through such inhuman abuse. He could never ask Nadia to stand up to her husband, her parents, and the state just so he could have her. But he could not stand by and do nothing, either. He well knew that. He also knew that by being named her lover, he could face prison, perhaps even a firing squad for being a party to acts against the state. All seemed hopeless for him and Nadia. Everything they wanted in life—love, happiness, peace of mind—was being denied them by one man. Joseph Potgornev. It seemed to him the only way he and Nadia might be able to continue loving each other was to rid their lives of Joseph Potgornev. But that was no easy matter. And even if Joseph Potgornev were dead, they might be kept apart by Nadia's parents or the Party.

Viktor was well aware that he could not kill everyone who was standing in the way of his and Nadia's uniting. But he was wondering how he might kill Joseph Potgornev. As an army officer who would now be attached to general staff headquarters in Moscow, Colonel Potgornev would be a prime candidate for assassination by political dissidents. It was not uncommon for members of the KGB or the military echelon to be found murdered. And there was no way he would be suspected of murdering him. No one except Nadia's closest friend, Mishka Borken, knew they were in love. There was still the possibility that Nadia would have to submit to the transfer to Moscow, but at least she would no longer have to live with her estranged husband while there. And perhaps not long after Joseph Potgornev was buried, Nadia might be permitted to transfer back to her old squadron here in Kiev, or in Odessa if ATW 3 had moved on to the new air base there by then. Then they could go on loving each other, even if it meant doing so secretly for a while longer. Once an appropriate period of mourning had elapsed, she would be expected, even encouraged, to remarry, as a young and attractive woman of child-bearing age. And the Party would certainly sanction her marriage to another military man. That preference even her family could not disapprove of.

Viktor knew his plans were very long-range and dangerous. He wasn't even sure if Nadia would approve of such a drastic measure as killing her husband. She might not want Joseph harmed, even though she despised him. She would certainly protest over the risk involved for him, but he might be able to convince her he could murder Joseph and get away with doing so, as long as it was also her wish that he kill Joseph. He knew he could murder Joseph without her knowing, but Joseph's death might cause Nadia to become sympathetically repledged to him and she might feel obligated to remain Joseph's widow. That would bring an end to their love affair, just as surely as if Joseph lived on and took Nadia away from him. For that reason he felt he must discuss his plans to murder Joseph with Nadia and allow her to share in the decision.

Viktor felt Nadia applying pressure to his brake pedals. Deciding he would wait until their next meeting at the guesthouse to discuss his dangerous plans with her, he scribbled a note and pushed it toward the rear cockpit along with Nadia's letter from Joseph. As soon as he had, he applied pressure to his brake pedals to signal her.

Nadia dislodged the thick parcel with difficulty, making sure her anxiety didn't cause her to tear its contents into shreds as she pulled it through the tight space. As soon as she'd freed it, she signaled Viktor to acknowledge she had his message, and to cue him to take over the controls while she read his reply. Removing his note from the envelope containing Joseph's letter, she unfolded it, and quickly read the scribbled lines:

Dearest Nadia:
In sharing love with you, I have made all of your wishes my own. Your needs are now my needs. And all of your troubles are mine to share with you and help you resolve. If you were to leave my side and never return, my life would become meaningless. And only my death can take me away from your side. In every way you have shown that you feel the same about me. Therefore, we will remain inseparable for the rest of our lives, just as we promised each other we would.
Give Joseph's letter no further thought until we are once again in each other's embrace this coming weekend. At that time I will reveal to you what I plan to do about your husband's demands.
With unending love,
Viktor.

Nadia felt tears forming, and the instruments before her blurred for long moments. She caressed Viktor's note, wishing he was in her arms at that very moment, when she needed to kiss him so desperately for the heartwarming words he'd written. She was troubled over what Viktor's plans might be, certain they would be drastic. But she was so moved by his promise they would always be together that as long as Viktor's plan caused him no danger and allowed them to go on loving each other, she would risk anything.

She guessed he would ask her to desert the Air Force and go into hiding with him. That she would not hesitate to do. She hated the military. And if they deserted this coming weekend, it would be in time to prevent her being transferred to Moscow, where her husband would be watching her every move closely. She thought that Viktor's long-range plans would include their fleeing the Soviet Union somehow. Perhaps with the help of the underground they might get to a country outside Russia that would allow them to spend the rest of their lives together as husband and wife, without her having to divorce Joseph. She was sure such things were permitted in places like Italy, France, Spain, or even West Germany, where they might welcome Soviets who'd deserted.

Rubles, Nadia thought next. She had some rubles saved up from her military pay. And she could ask her dearest friend, Mishka Borken, to donate whatever rubles she'd saved up, to help her and Viktor escape. Mishka knew of her situation and sympathized, just as most women would who had any idea what it was like to be forced to live and sleep with a man you didn't love at all. She allowed herself to dream about spending the rest of her life with Viktor in a place where they could love each other freely and openly. Then, hearing the mission control center at the domed facility in Odessa calling Viktor over their aircraft radio, she snapped back into the reality of her military surroundings. That brought more tears.

"Mission control, this is wing leader for flight group seven," Viktor called into his radio mike. "Understand we are to commence Threshold test exercises. Will comply, over and out." He keyed off, then keyed back on to address the pilots of the other five Foxbats flying in formation with him. "Flight group seven, from wing leader. Switch communications channeling to Threshold modes one and two and execute practice broadcasting operations as per briefing. Wing leader, out." He waited for acknowledgments from the other Foxbat pilots, then keyed his intercom. "Comrade Potgornev," he said to Nadia in an impersonal tone. "You will participate with the rest of flight group seven's pilots and exchange verbal communications with the Odessa facility during tonight's jamming and antijamming test exercises. I will handle the exchange of cipher communications with mission control myself. It has been some time since I have given my electronic warfare apparatus a good functional check to make sure it is operating properly."

Nadia knew Viktor had volunteered to handle the more intricate phase of their text exercise because he knew how upset she was over her husband's letter. "Whatever you say, Comrade Wing Leader."

Viktor sensed Nadia's gratitude in the tone of her voice. He removed a computer disk from his flight bag and inserted it into the slot labeled "Data Send," on the face of the computer console on his instrument panel. He had to boot up and program the disk with the dummy communications load that that night's preflight briefing introduced before he could access it. A second disk, a blank, for recording, he inserted into the slot labeled "Data Receive." Using a computer keypunch board he typed out the text he was to send to mission control, then accessed it as a saved program for transmitting. He switched on his Foxbat's encoder, which would convert his program into cipher. He flicked a switch that turned on the decoder so it would convert the reply to his transmission from cipher to a typed readout on his cockpit display screen, as well as furnish him with a typed hard copy of mission control's answer to his test program. With everything prepared for transmitting, he pressed the transponder's "Data Send" key, then removed his radio headset and listened to the host of rapid clicks that came faintly through the cockpit flooring from the component compartment located just under his and Nadia's ejection seats.

With lightning speed his transmission was sent out and the hellhole compartment's clicking noises stopped. Then after a brief interval the clicking sounds resumed in unison with a green light that suddenly came on above the transponder's "Data Receive" key. He pressed that key, and mission control's reply began appearing on his display screen, as the same information was being fed out of a slot on teletype ribbon.

When mission control's return transmission ended, Viktor sat back in his contour pilot's seat and looked over the data on the display screen. Being only a dummy communication for test purposes, the ciphered message that his decoder had turned back into words was merely a weather forecast for the immediate area. What was significant about the communication was that no outside monitoring equipment could intercept the cipher, and no eavesdropping stations belonging to Russia's enemies would be able to hear the verbal versions of the same information the other pilots were transmitting.

Viktor could envision how laser blasts might accomplish the jamming of enemy communications. It was how the verbal communications could not be heard by outside monitors unequipped with the antijamming apparatus that puzzled him. He had a vague understanding of how the coded version was slipped past enemy cipher interception apparatus. The cipher was transmitted in segments over a variety of radio frequencies that sent and received the fragments the way a telephone switchboard handled incoming and outgoing calls. But how voices were also segmented with such amazing speed and transmitted over laser hookups to and from various points was still quite baffling to him. He was never allowed anywhere near the electronic component compartment of his Foxbat—such marvels of technological research and development were kept hidden from all but a very select number of military and civilian systems engineers. That didn't really bother him. As far as he was concerned, the Soviet Union could keep its secrets about the new technology, as long as he could keep his and Nadia's love for each other a secret from the Soviet Union.

A second communiqué came over his display screen from mission control, requesting him to resend the last transmission. After a hearty yawn that expressed how boring the test exercises could become in noncombatant situations, he leaned forward to repeat his sending cycle of the dummy transmission.

CHAPTER TEN

Ivan Trotsky sprang from his double bed in response to an urgent pounding on his front door. Still groggy from the deep sleep he'd been pulled from, he had no idea how long the pounding had been going on. It sounded like the kind of commotion the KGB would make if they'd learned of his clandestine activities and come to arrest him. He glanced out the master bedroom window that gave him a view of the road leading to Kiev, half expecting to see Soviet police cars surrounding the house. But there were none in sight, and the roof covering the porch denied him a view of whoever was attacking his front door so unmercifully.

With his heart pounding in his chest almost as loudly as the pounding at the front door, he slipped on his robe and hurried downstairs. He stopped off at his den to slip a .45 automatic into the pocket of his robe. By the time he reached the door the pounding had stopped. Peering out the door's small rounded window he caught a glimpse of Ferris winding up to heave a fire log through the living room window. "Comrade! Wait!" he called out as he hurried to unlock the door. He got it open and stepped out. "No need to break a window. I am here!"

Ferris dropped the fire log onto the pile Trotsky had neatly arranged on his porch. "Sorry! But you took so long to answer that I was starting to think you'd expired overnight!"

"I sleep like a dead man when I drink too much vodka," Trotsky commented. "And last night we drank quite a bit more than I'm accustomed to." He noticed as they stepped into the house that Ferris didn't have a shirt on under his parka. "Looks like you dressed in a big hurry. What is wrong?" he said as he closed and locked the front door behind them.

"We've got real big troubles," Ferris said. "Nick took off during the night."

"That may very well be a disaster, Matt," Trotsky said. As he glanced out the living room picture window, he added, "Unless he has just gone for an early morning stroll in the nearby woods."

"We won't find him out there, Ivan," Ferris said as he took a newspaper clipping out of the deep pocket of his parka. Handing it to Trotsky, he exclaimed angrily, "He's gone for a real long hike on us." He slammed a fist down on a lamp table. "God damn it! I warned Hal Banks this might happen! I told him not to send that kid over here with me!"

Trotsky shook his head in disgust as he looked at the photo and inset of Nikoli Belinsky and his wife and son. After speed-reading the accompanying article, he said, "It seems Banks should have listened to your advice."

"It's my own damn fault this happened," Ferris said, banging his fist on the lamp table again. "I should have had more sense than to trust Nick. But I believed him. He told me nothing was bothering him." He looked Trotsky in the eyes. "He deliberately lied to me, Ivan. And I warned him, if I ever caught him in a lie I'd kill him."

Trotsky looked away from the fire in Ferris's eyes, knowing he was a man who never failed to back up his words with action. Glancing at the newspaper clipping again, he said, "This clipping is nearly three months old. I hate to rub salt into an open wound, Matt . . . but do you suppose Nick has been keeping track of his wife and son with the intention of coming back to the Soviet Union to look them up?"

"I have no way of knowing for sure, but it seems that may have been his reason for wanting to come along on the mission. I mean, he *has* taken off on us."

"If he has been carrying this article around with him since he left the United States, I want to kill him as well. He could have gotten all of us killed if the KGB had ever searched him and found a newspaper clipping of Nikoli Belinsky in his possession . . ."

"The newspaper clipping wasn't Nick's," Ferris interrupted. "I wormed that out of the old man just a few minutes ago."

"You got this clipping from Yuri?" Trotsky asked, surprised.

Ferris nodded. "The old guy has a scrapbook filled with newspaper clippings like that. He's made a hobby of keeping track of all Soviet military and civilian defectors who ever made it out of Russia. And he keeps a separate section in the book on those whose attempts to flee Russia were foiled by the KGB."

"I had no idea that Yuri was doing that. How did you manage to learn about it?"

"With a dash of deduction and a smidgen of scare," Ferris said. "After I left you last night, I found Nick and Yuri heavily engaged in a serious conversation that my arrival interrupted. They both had what I thought were guilty looks on their faces. After the old man shuffled off to bed, I confronted Nick. He told me that he and the old man had taken a walk down memory lane and that the trip had led them to sobsville. Hence their look of sadness, as he called it. When I told him I thought his explanation was crapola, he told me to handcuff him to a bedpost all night if I didn't believe he was telling the truth. And like an idiot, I told him that wouldn't be necessary. Damn it! I should have cuffed his hands and feet, instead of being suckered into a . . ."

"The horse has gone, now," Trotsky said. "It is too late to think about locking the barn door."

"True enough," Ferris said in exasperation. "Anyway, finding him missing when I woke up, I remembered his and the old man's guilty expressions, so I shook the truth out of the old man about what they'd really talked about last night. According to Yuri, he had a hunch Nick was Nikoli Belinsky, and . . ."

"I never even hinted to him who Nick really is," Trotsky insisted.

"Well, maybe the old man is a double agent and he never hinted who he really is to you, either."

"This cannot be," Trotsky insisted. "Yuri has a fondness for rubles, but I'd wager this farm he is not in the spy or counterspy business."

"He claims he has mastered an ability to identify people by their eyes. That he developed the knack by playing a lot of chess and studying the eyes of his opponents for clues to what moves they were planning."

"He was a Kjevan chess master," Trotsky said.

"I know. He told me."

"And it is true that he has shown an uncanny ability for reading eyes. It was by the eyes of the two air force pilots that he picked their faces out of my collection of military dossiers last week. I am confident that was the first time Yuri ever used that ability for anything other than playing chess."

"Well, he just used it for the second time, Ivan. And he said his purpose for wanting to get Nick to admit he was Nikoli Belinsky was to have Nick adopt him and his wife as parents and help them emigrate to the United States."

"Now, that sounds more like the Yuri I know," Trotsky said. "He has been pestering me to help him and his wife relocate to a warmer climate because of his wife's ill health. He even mentioned his preference, which is Arizona. I told him such things take time, and I would do whatever I could to help. But he complained that he feared his wife, Yekaterina, might not live through another of Russia's bitter winters."

"You're pretty sure that's all there was to his probing into Nikoli Belinsky's life?"

"Yes. How did you leave off with him before coming here?"

"I left him scared shitless. Told him he'd better not pry into our affairs again or his wife certainly would not live through this winter. Him either."

"You never confirmed his suspicions about Nick?"

"I didn't take the time to either confirm or deny them. After I shook the truth out of him and he handed this newspaper clipping over to me, I left him standing at his front door begging me to let him still make the rubles you promised him for helping us meet the Foxbat pilots."

"If he is still worried about that, then we do not have to fear he will run off to the KGB and report our business. We can still go on with our plans to consummate the defections. That is, we can if we manage to get Nick back under Yuri's roof before the KGB learns of our affairs from him."

"Well, according to this newspaper clipping, his wife and son are in Kharkov. So at least we know where to start looking."

"My car!" Trotsky said in alarm. "He might have . . ."

"That was the first thing I checked when I came running over here, Ivan. It's still sitting inside your garage."

"There is good and bad to that news," Trotsky said. "The good part is that we will not have to walk to the city to rent a car. The bad news is that Kharkov is roughly two hundred miles from here. To get there Nick would have to hitchhike, or use public transportation. If he hitchhiked, he would be in danger of being picked up by the highway patrol. Therefore, he probably chose public transportation. And since there are no regular bus routes between Kiev and Kharkov, he would have to go by rail. Do you have any idea what time he might have left?"

"We went to bed about two in the morning. And I woke up at six."

"It is six thirty now," Trotsky said as he glanced at his seven-foot tall grandfather clock standing in the front hallway. "If he left soon after retiring, he has close to a four-hours head start."

"Do you know what the train connections are between Kiev and Kharkov, Ivan?"

"As a car owner, I do not keep a train schedule in the house. And as a man involved in the spy business, I do not keep a phone in the house, either. In the Soviet Union phones draw the attention of the KGB. However, we can obtain a schedule from the trainmaster in Kiev on our way to Kharkov."

"That article didn't mention where his wife and son were living in Kharkov," Ferris said. "That means Nick will probably look them up at the Kharkov School of Olympic Events, where his wife works and his son attends classes."

"Most educational institutions in the Soviet Union hold classes between six in the morning and six at night. But a school for gymnastics might have sessions that start as late as eight A.M. If that is the case with the Kharkov School of Olympic Events, it could be another hour and a half before Nick is able to make contact with them. But if we only do the speed limit between here and there, it will take us over twice that amount of time to reach Kharkov."

"Then we'll just have to chance speeding when we can do it without drawing the attention of the highway police."

"You will need a shirt, Matt. It would look suspicious to the KGB if you were in your undershirt during business hours."

Ferris eyed the robe that Trotsky had on, then said, "And you will need to get into pants and shoes as well as a shirt."

"Come with me upstairs. I have a shirt that should fit you."

"Good," Ferris said as he followed Trotsky up the flight of stairs. "I'm also going to need a handgun, Ivan."

"Of course, Matt. I have a very impressive armory hidden behind a wine rack in my basement. You'll find enough weapons there to arm a brigade."

"And, Ivan—"

At the top of the stairs Trotsky faced Ferris. "Yes, Matt?"

"I'm going to need a silencer, too. Just in case it's Nick I have to kill."

Stopping off at the Kiev railroad station, Ferris and Trotsky learned from the trainmaster that normal rail connections between Kiev and Kharkov during weekdays were routinely discontinued at midnight, and service wasn't resumed until five o'clock the next morning. That meant that the earliest train Baxter could have taken out of Kiev was the five o'clock limited, which made three scheduled stops en route and arrived in Kharkov at 8.00 A.M. They also learned that the Kharkov railroad station was in the heart of the city, and that the Kharkov

School of Olympic Events was situated near a large park and playground on the outskirts of town. That told them Baxter might have a half-hour bus ride added to his journey, or at the very least a fifteen-minute ride by taxi. Trotsky estimated that Baxter would not arrive before classes were in session, and that when he did arrive his wife would already be among her colleagues and students and his son would most likely be surrounded by classmates and under the watchful eyes of a party proctor. Still thinking that Baxter might have risked hitchhiking to arrive before school began, Ferris insisted that Trotsky chance exceeding the speed limit, as carefully as possible, to help make up for Baxter's head start.

They had gotten onto the intercity highway at seven thirty and found the road to Kharkov cleared of snow, with only light traffic in either direction. The anxious race against time kept the palms and fingers of Trotsky's chubby hands moist as he held a death lock on the steering wheel. Ferris had stiffened in the passenger's seat next to him through every sharp curve that threatened to send them flying off the hilly country road and down the steep ravines that flanked them. But finding no police cars staked out along the way to catch speeders, Ferris forced himself to endure the scary ride so that Trotsky could keep clipping off the eighty miles per hour he was averaging, which required the car to do a hundred over open stretches.

The pace got them to the outskirts of Kharkov in under three hours instead of the good four hours it would have taken them to cover the two hundred miles if they hadn't exceeded the speed limit. It was nearly ten thirty when they reached the Kharkov School of Olympic Events, which they found to be almost exactly where the Kiev trainmaster had said it would be. It was situated on the unpopulated fringes of Kharkov and was surrounded by playgrounds.

The road they arrived on separated the front lawn of the school from a track and soccer field that was directly across the street from the four-story red brick building. The track field was not in use, but there was a soccer match in progress on the other field. Judging by the sizes of the uniformed players, Ferris guessed they might fit Pavlik's age group. To avoid drawing the attention of the three adult proctors refereeing the match, he told Trotsky to pull over and park next to the unoccupied track field so they could have a look around. Behind both fields was a wooded park that sloped down steeply to a frozen lake on which other youths were skating. As he panned the woods of the park he noticed a figure observing the soccer game from behind a cluster of trees and shrubs.

"Binocs, Ivan! Hurry!"

"You see Nick?"

"Let you know in a minute," Ferris said as he accepted the binoculars and trained them on the figure. Certain the parka the figure was wrapped in was familiar, he focused the zoom on the face, then said, "Now the gun, Ivan."

Handing the silencer-equipped .38 revolver to Ferris, Trotsky asked, "It is definitely him?" Ferris nodded as he returned the binoculars and accepted the gun. "There are so many people around, Matt. On the soccer field and the lake."

"There are also plenty of trees and shrubs to hide behind," Ferris said.

Trotsky aimed the binoculars at the figure and seeing Baxter's familiar face clearly, he said, "He is just standing there, watching the children playing soccer. That suggests he has not dared to approach the boy in front of the party proctors. I think we can also assume he has not made contact with his wife, either. If he had, he would surely be in KGB handcuffs by now."

"I'm not assuming anything, Ivan. I'm going over there to make sure."

"What will you do if he hasn't made contact with either of them?"

"Try to talk some sense into his head if I can," Ferris said.

"And if you can't, then you will . . ."

"Then I will keep my promise, and I'll stash his lying ass in the shrubs until we can haul him back to your car under cover of darkness."

"Would you prefer that I come along and take care of that bit of unpleasantness if need be?"

"He's my responsibility. I'll do my own dirty work, Ivan. But thanks for offering."

"What do you want me to do, then, Matt?"

"You stay right here," Ferris said. "You give me twenty minutes. If I'm not back by then, you get the hell out of here."

"And what are my instructions beyond leaving you behind?"

"Contact Hal Banks," Ferris replied. "Tell him . . . he should have listened to me and kept Nick out of this gig." He placed his fur cap over his silver-gray hair and stepped out of the car. "Twenty minutes, Ivan."

Trotsky watched Ferris cross the track field and head toward the thick of trees along the far side of the soccer court. He could hear the muffled shouts of the children playing soccer. He could also hear occasional shrills from the whistles of the referees. And he could hear faint music being played for the distant ice skaters. He thought about the sounds of life, and about the soundless death that might soon occur. In another moment Ferris was swallowed up by the trees.

With his left hand stretched out to guide him through the cluster of trees, and his right hand on the gun in the pocket of his hooded parka, Ferris clicked the safety catch to the off position as he quietly worked his way to a point behind the tree Baxter was standing next to, with his back turned. When he was within a few feet of Baxter, Ferris wrapped his thumb and three fingers around the handgrip and curled his index finger around the trigger, then called out in Russian, "Enjoying the game, Comrade?"

Baxter turned around with a startled look on his face. He had been standing with his back to the lake ever since he'd arrived and found the children assembling on the soccer field for the match. That was nearly two hours ago, and in all that time he had given no thought to anything going on behind him. Not the surrounding trees, or the skaters at the far end of the frozen lake. And except for an occasional glance at the front entrance of the school across the road from the park, he hadn't really seen much of the foreground of the soccer field, either. All he had kept his eyes on was the young players. Especially one young player in particular, who was unmistakably his son.

"Are you suddenly mute, Comrade?" Ferris asked.

"There is not much to talk about," Baxter finally said in Russian.

"To the contrary, Comrade," Ferris insisted. "I think we have a lot to talk about. At the head of the list of topics is . . . have you communicated with your wife at all?"

"No," Baxter replied.

"Do you plan to?" Ferris asked.

"No," Baxter said firmly.

"Have you communicated with the boy?"

"Not yet." Baxter looked back at the soccer game.

"Not yet," Ferris repeated. "Does that mean you still plan to, Comrade?"

"I am not sure," Baxter answered coolly.

Ferris moved over to Baxter's right side. "Which one is he?" He saw Baxter was about to point his son out. "Tell me. Don't point."

"Pavlik is the one who has just fallen down by the goalie," Baxter said.

Ferris looked toward the frozen lake and spotted a patch of tall thick shrubs pushing up through the frozen water's edge. They were almost totally hidden by the surrounding trees. He faced Baxter again and asked, "Did you have a trip to see your son figured in all along, or did the old man's scrapbook clipping put the idea into your screwy head?"

"What difference does it make? I am here how," Baxter replied. "But something the old man told me encouraged me to do whatever I could to save Pavlik from Russia's choking grip."

"Oh? What was that?"

"I told you last night how his son, Petr, froze to death as an army private guarding the asshole of Russia from . . ."

"And you don't want Russia doing that sort of thing to your kid?" Ferris interrupted. Baxter nodded. Looking back at the lake, Ferris added, "Walk with me to the bank of the lake." He saw Baxter hesitating. "I just want to talk more privately about your boy. You see, I know what you're thinking of doing." With his left arm he took hold of Baxter's right forearm and led him down the slope leading toward the cluster of shrubs by the frozen lake. Seeing Baxter look over his shoulder at the soccer game, he said, "Don't worry. According to the scoreboard the game is only half over. We have time to chit-chat before you can do anything."

"And what is it you think I will do?" Baxter asked as they descended.

Ferris waited until they reached the frozen edge of the lake before answering. Confident they could no longer be seen or heard by the soccer players or the ice skaters, he said angrily and in English, "Don't be coy with me, Nick! For Christ's sake, we know each other too well for that sort of crap. You're planning to shanghai the kid to the States. Right?" His question went unanswered. "You don't have to answer that one. Your silence just did."

Also speaking English, Baxter shot back, "And if I am planning to . . . shanghai my son to America! Are you going to stop me?"

"I'm going to talk you out of the ridiculous notion, you idiot," Ferris snapped.

"What is ridiculous about a father wanting to save his son from possibly being killed needlessly?" Baxter retorted.

"How you're planning to go about saving him is the dumb part," Ferris growled. "First of all, he's being watched closely.

Secondly, there's every chance in hell that he won't believe you're his father. Third, there's also the powerful possibility that even if you manage to convince him you are, he'll probably scream for his mother if you try to take him away from her. And if he does put up a protest how in hell do you plan to move a screaming, struggling kid all the way across the Soviet Union? Tied, gagged, and sealed inside a fucking gunny sack?" He cut off Baxter's attempted reply with an abrupt wave of his left hand, while his right remained curled around the gun in his pocket. "How about getting him out of the country, Nick? Did you bother to give that little hitch any thought?"

"I thought I could take him back to the guesthouse in Kiev. From there Ivan Trotsky could get us to Odessa, where we could make a return connection to the States by sub."

"Your ass!" Ferris grunted. "The United States Navy is not going to be a party to an international kidnapping, you fool! And the United States of America is not a place for abductors to hide out with their victims."

"You make it all sound so sinister, Matt," Baxter protested.

"For Christ's sake, Nick! Abduction is sinister! And being kidnapped by a parent instead of a stranger is no less horrifying to a child of six. You'll scare the crap out of the kid in the attempt. Give him nightmares for the rest of his goddamn life."

"I know what nightmares are, Matt," Baxter retorted. "I have had my share of them since I left Russia."

"Yes, God damn it! You have! And you left willingly! Imagine the kind of nightmares a six-year-old will have who was taken away from his mother against his will!"

"He will have a loving father to embrace him and chase his nightmares away," Baxter replied.

"You're still going to attempt this?"

"I think so."

"All you'll succeed in doing is getting yourself arrested. And by doing so, blow our mission."

"Maybe I can talk the boy into going willingly. Maybe he is unhappy with his mother."

"You can't be serious," Ferris said curtly. "Did you see the ear-to-ear smile on that kid's face? Does that look like the face of sadness? Take him away from his mother. Take him to the United States against his will. And you may never see that kid smile like that again for the rest of his life."

"I am here, Matt. And as long as I am, I feel I must at least try to talk him into going."

Ferris glanced at his wristwatch and saw that half the amount of time he'd allotted to reasoning with Baxter had elapsed. With only ten minutes remaining before Trotsky would leave without him, he decided he might have better luck trying to shame Baxter into returning to Kiev with him. "Just like that?" he snarled. "You're here so you're just going to take selfish advantage of the opportunity? Have you given even the slightest goddamn thought to why you're here in the first place? Don't you feel any obligation to our mission? Have you no feeling of responsibility for Ivan Trotsky or that old man and sickly woman back in Kiev? Do you realize what will happen to them if you are arrested by the KGB and are tortured into exposing them as accomplices to your back door arrival into the Soviet Union?"

"I will not betray them if I am arrested. I promise you that!" Baxter insisted. "No matter what the KGB does to me."

"You goddamn liar!" Ferris grunted as he pushed Baxter into a tree. "You've betrayed my trust by coming here. You've put my life on the goddamn line by sneaking out of the guesthouse on me." He shoved Baxter into the tree again. "If you'd sell me out, you'd sell them out, too, you selfish bastard!"

"I cannot blame you for being furious, Matt," Baxter said. "But you must believe me, I will not mention any of you to the KGB if I am arrested. I would not do that. I pledge my word on that."

Ferris pushed Baxter again. "Your word!" he said mockingly. "The word of a liar? Of a man who betrayed the trust of two countries?"

"I did not betray the Soviet Union," Baxter snapped bitterly. "The Soviet Union betrayed me. And now they are filling my son's head with their vicious lies. Did you see the lies they printed about me in the old man's newspaper clipping, Matt?"

"Yes, I did, but by lying to me, you betrayed me."

"I had no choice. I had to save my son."

"And what about me, you goddamn jackass?" Ferris returned angrily. "I treated you like my brother, just as much as if we had the same blood running through our veins. I poured my heart into this relationship we have. I don't do that for just anybody. And I didn't do it so you could turn on me any time you goddamn well please and break my heart like it's some kind of fucking toy. If you betray me now, that's just what you'll be doing."

Baxter looked into Ferris's eyes sheepishly. "I wish you would not put it that way, Matt. I must do what I can for Pavlik or I will not be able to sleep nights when I return to the United States."

Ferris saw that they were locking horns over something that

Baxter regarded as more important to him than his own life. Baxter was compelled to do what he came to Kharkov for, and Ferris was equally compelled. He felt his heart pounding and his hand trembling as though this would be his first time to kill someone. In a way it would. It would be the first time he'd ever had to kill someone he loved. Forcing his anger to overwhelm his affection so he could do what he had to more easily, he yanked the gun from his pocket and cocked the hammer. Staring at Baxter wild-eyed, he growled, "No, Comrade . . . you will not betray me. I will kill you first."

Baxter looked down at the long barrel of the gun. "I see by the silencer already screwed to the barrel that you planned in advance to do more than just talk to me. Didn't you, Matt?" His question went unanswered, so he gestured with his head to the lake behind him. "And in keeping with your professional skill at murdering people, you've picked a perfect spot to execute me."

"Tell me there's a way out, Nick. Tell me you'll forget the boy for now and no one will have to die."

"I can't, Matt. Especially now. I couldn't live with myself if I walked out on him a second time."

"You could come back to Kiev with me right now. Your kid isn't going anywhere for a long time. We could carry out the mission, then talk about the boy."

"I'm not a fool, Matt. Once the mission is over, you won't care about me and the boy. You . . ."

"I could crown you and take you back to Kiev tied and gagged, Nick."

"If you did that, I'd do everything in my power to run off again, Matt."

"You really are leaving me no choice."

"That's because I feel *I* have no choice, Matt. So go ahead and gun me down. I'd rather be dead than turn away from Pavlik again." He looked at Ferris with tear-filled eyes and added, "What are you waiting for, a brotherly kiss good-bye?"

"Don't give me that brother crap at this stage of the game, you goddamn backstabber," Ferris growled in Russian. "It was your idea to come to Kharkov."

"Just get on with it, Matt," Baxter said also in Russian. "And do it quickly as well as quietly, please. We've talked enough about who is to be blamed."

"What about your Wave fiancée, Linda Stewart? Have you bothered to consider how your recklessness will affect her life?"

"If Linda loves me as much as she says she does, she will understand."

Ferris glanced at his wristwatch and realized there was no time left for talking if he still hoped to find Trotsky waiting for him. *One quick bullet in the head and it'll be over with*, he thought. But he couldn't just gun Baxter down like a mad dog. That seemed too much like murder. He preferred his hands-on method of killing. He was sure he'd feel less remorseful if he forced Baxter to fight for his life. Baxter still wouldn't have much of a chance, but it was better than no chance at all.

Ferris uncocked the hammer and slipped the gun back into the pocket of his parka. "You're going to die, Nick, but it's going to be my way. Come on at me. Let's see if you're a coward as well as a traitor."

"Don't force me to hurt you, Matt."

"Get serious, you idiot," Ferris snapped. "I'm going to kill you, you jerkoff. With my bare hands. Are you just going to stand there and let me, you fucking coward? I'm the only thing standing between you and your son. If you're too much of a goddamn coward to save your own ass, at least put up a fight to save Pavlik. After all, isn't that what you came to Kharkov to do?"

"Why don't you just leave me alone," Baxter said, beginning to shake with anger and frustration.

"Enough talk." Ferris lunged at Baxter and got him in a choke hold that brought them both to the ground.

"Let go of me, Matt," Baxter gasped as he struggled to pull Ferris's hands away from his throat. Ferris increased the pressure.

Gasping and wheezing, Baxter with strength born of terror forced Ferris onto his side and got up on his knees. "You are a madman. I will not let you kill me."

Ferris swung around quickly and got Baxter in a throatlock. "Do something to stop me, then."

With Ferris's forearm locked tightly around his throat from behind him, Baxter swung his hands wildly but was unable to strike him. Feeling his lungs burning and his chest about to explode, he twisted to one side and locked his wrists together, then thrust his right elbow backwards into Ferris's stomach with all the strength he had left. He broke free of the throatlock and sprang to his feet. Seeing Ferris doubled over and on his knees, he rushed over to him and pulled the gun out of Ferris's pocket. Then, with Ferris the one gasping for air he cocked the hammer and pointed the barrel at Ferris's head. "I warned you to leave me alone, goddamn you! I warned you to go away and let me be!"

"Screw you," Ferris said, still wheezing. "You'll have to kill me first."

With the gun trembling in his hand, Baxter sobbed, "I don't want to hurt anyone. Damn you. Leave me alone. Leave me to do what I must for my son, or so help me I will kill you, Matt."

Finally catching his breath, Ferris slowly stood up. "I can't do that, Nick. So go ahead and shoot me."

"Why?" Baxter asked. "Why can't you?"

"I told you why, Nick. You'll be picked up by the KGB within an hour after Pavlik is discovered missing. And the KGB won't need three guesses to figure out who would kidnap the son of Nikoli Belinsky. They'll have all of Russia locked up tighter than a duck's ass, while they're combing the country looking for you. You'll never get out of the Soviet Union alive. And they'll force you to reveal how you got back into Russia. That'll put the screws to us."

"I told you I'd never admit I have been helped by anyone."

"Boy, you really are an asshole, Nick. They'll point a gun at Pavlik's head and threaten to blow his brains out. What will you do then? Let them blow your kid away to save us?" His question went unanswered, but he saw the barrel of the gun lowering. Then, out of the corner of his eye, he saw Trotsky moving toward them with a gun drawn. With Baxter's gun no longer pointed at him, he signaled Trotsky surreptitiously to stay out of sight and do nothing. Putting as much torment into his voice as he could, he said, "The KGB will round all of us up with your help. Then they'll bring that old man and his wife and me and Trotsky to the same prison they're holding you in. And they'll force you to watch them execute all of us before they stand you up in front of a firing squad. By then you'll be so tortured by guilt for betraying all of us that you'll beg them to kill you. And you'll have betrayed us for nothing, Nick. Right after they execute you, Pavlik will be returned to his mother and he'll go right on believing all the lies the Party and his mother told him about his father."

"Then help me, Matt," Baxter pleaded as he lowered the gun to his side. "With your help we can evade the KGB. With your help and Ivan Trotsky's help, I can get Pavlik away."

"I'll help you, Nick. But not this trip," Ferris said firmly. "On this trip the mission takes priority over everything else."

"What if I agree to go back to Kiev with you and help you to consummate the defections? Will you promise to help me take Pavlik back to America with us once our business in Kiev is completed?"

"No, I won't promise that at all, Nick. But I will promise you that when Pavlik becomes old enough to make up his own mind about who he wants to live with and where, then we'll make it a personal mission to come back and offer him a free choice. Not until, though. Not until he has the maturity to choose freely between his mother and you, and between the Soviet Union and the United States. That's the only way something like that has even a prayer of working out in the long run. But if you do it your way and force him to come to the States with you now, he'll run away the first chance he gets. Then Pavlik Belinsky will become the first native Russian to defect to the Soviet Union. And you'll never win his love after that."

Baxter dropped the gun to the ground and fell to his knees, weeping uncontrollably as he buried his head in his hands. "Matt," he sobbed, "I'm sorry. Please forgive me. I just went crazy, I guess. I . . ."

Ferris picked up the gun and returned it to his parka pocket, then helped Baxter to his feet. "Stop the bawling. We'll have the rest of our lives to devote to forgiving each other." He waved to Trotsky who was standing behind the tree with his gun at the ready. "You can come out now, Ivan. And you can put your gun away." He took a handkerchief out of his trouser pocket and handed it to Baxter. "Here, dry those goddamn tears. I hate to see a grown man cry."

Baxter looked at Trotsky with concern when he realized he and Ferris hadn't been there alone. With his tears dried and his composure regained, he said, "I guess I owe you an apology, too, Ivan."

"If there is no harm done, there is no need to apologize. I am glad you decided to listen to Matt."

"Speaking of listening to me, it's well beyond the twenty minutes I told you to give me. Why didn't you take off when the twenty minutes were up?" Ferris asked.

"I . . . couldn't get the car started, Matt," Trotsky said smiling.

"You're another liar," Ferris said, knowing Trotsky had followed when he'd become overdue instead of just driving off and leaving him to fend for himself. Glancing around the area, he added, "Let's get out of here before someone comes along."

CHAPTER ELEVEN

Senior Lieutenant Viktor Aleksei looked out the window of the Air Force bus as it pulled into the military depot in the heart of Kiev. There were thick flakes falling straight down from the night sky to cover the city streets with another white blanket of snow. Unlike his peers and superiors who'd shared the bus with him on its half-hour drive from the air base, he was in no hurry to get off. He sat patiently and watched the others hurry off, their brown uniform greatcoats and garrison caps becoming speckled with white flakes as they quickly blended in with the crowd of Friday night shoppers and threatergoers. When the bus was empty, he got off, his left hand curled around the military .25 automatic pistol that was concealed in the pocket of his greatcoat.

Looking down the main boulevard in the direction of the returning bus, he could see the headlights of the junior officers' bus that was bringing Nadia and Mishka to Kiev. But that didn't rush him either. He knew it would take Nadia close to an hour to go through all the precautionary procedures they implemented to keep their weekend stays at the guesthouse a secret from the KGB. And he was in no hurry to leave the city, because it would take Nadia almost an additional hour to catch up with him along the country road they took to get to Comrade Velinkov's guesthouse.

The handgun tucked inside Viktor's greatcoat pocket was one of the two items he needed to carry out his plan for dealing with Joseph Potgornev. He had managed to remove the handgun from a newly arrived shipment of small arms destined for the base armory. The weapons shipment had arrived along with many other supply replenishment items, and he was sure they wouldn't be inventoried until sometime next week. By the time the gun was discovered missing, there would be a host of other items unaccounted for, which the base procurement officer would attribute to pilferage. Pilfering was a common practice among the military personnel at all Soviet bases, and the military items were traded on the black market for cigarettes, food items, alcoholic beverages, and other hard-to-obtain luxury items. By the time a base search was made for the pilfered articles, he'd have the gun hidden at the guesthouse where the old and sickly proprietor would not happen upon it when he tidied the room after his and Nadia's weekend stay. The other item was a set of travel documents he'd forged the base commandant's name to, so he could travel to Moscow next weekend unchallenged, to put an end to Joseph Potgornev's domination of Nadia. And the return address on her husband's disturbing letter told Viktor just where Joseph Potgornev would be spending his off-duty time next weekend. All that remained was getting Nadia's approval of his plan, which he hoped to have this weekend.

Watching from inside a tobacco store, Ferris watched Senior Flight Lieutenant Viktor Aleksei step off the military bus and enter a liquor store. Moments later Viktor slowly headed out of the city in the direction of the guesthouse road. And as Viktor Aleksei was swallowed up by the crowd of civilian Kievans, out-of-towners, and military personnel walking the snow-covered streets, a second military busload of Soviet Air Force personnel arrived at the depot.

When half the uniformed passengers had disembarked, Ferris caught sight of Nadia. She stood briefly a few feet away from the outside of the store window with her back to him, then joined another female officer in a zigzagging dash through traffic to a ballet theater across the boulevard from the depot. The two female air force officers stopped and faced each other under the ballet theater marquee as though discussing their weekend pass itinerary. He waited for their next move.

"Trust my judgment, Mishka," Nadia Potgornev said. She wanted to skip the usual safeguards.

Mishka frowned. "We always check in at the hotel together as soon as we arrive, Nadia. After that we come here to purchase our tickets for the weekend ballet performances. Then you go off to meet Viktor outside the city. Why do you want to do away with that procedure this weekend?"

"I told you why, Mishka," Nadia said. "Viktor said he has a plan that will keep me from being transferred to Moscow. You do want me to stay here in Kiev with you, do you not?"

"Of course I want that," Mishka said affectionately. "But you will have all weekend to discuss Viktor's plans. Why must you do reckless things to get to him?"

"Because I have waited all week and I will die of anxiety if I do not get to him right away."

"And to do that you will not even check in at the hotel as he expects you to," Mishka said.

"It will take too much time," Nadia complained. "And I have no patience this weekend for the hotel clerk's silly jokes."

"The hotel clerk knows we always come to Kiev together on our weekend passes. What if he asks me where you are?" Mishka said.

"Tell him that I did not get a pass this weekend."

"And what if our party section leader calls the hotel to see if we are both registered there as we promised her we would be? What will our section leader think is going on if the hotel clerk tells her that you did not get the weekend pass you practically begged her to give you?"

"Our section leader has not checked on our moves over all the past weekends you have been covering up for me. Why would she suddenly do so this weekend?"

"Maybe because you are being transferred soon?"

"I just received word about that from my husband, Mishka. In his letter he said it would take at least two weeks for the transfer orders to come through. Therefore, our party section leader knows nothing about Joseph's plans to have me join him in Moscow."

"And what if you are wrong? What if the transfer orders arrive over the weekend while you are here in Kiev?"

"What if they do?"

"Our section leader might feel you would want to know such news at once and call the hotel to let you know."

"I do not think she cares that much about me, one way or the other, Mishka. But if you will feel more at ease, then register us both at the hotel. That way if she calls, the desk clerk will tell her we are staying at the hotel, but we are out somewhere. And she will merely leave a message with him."

"What will I tell her if she calls while I am in my room and the desk clerk puts her call through to me?" Mishka asked.

"You will tell her exactly what we rehearsed. You felt tired and I attended the ballet without you. She knows you only go to the performances with me because I like ballet."

"She would be surprised to learn that it is I who attend the performances without you," Mishka commented.

"She will never know that unless you betray me and tell her."

"I would never do such a thing to you, Nadia. You know I would not. I would die before I would betray you."

"Of course, my dearest friend," Nadia said as she gave Mishka a reassuring hug. "I was only teasing you. I know I can always depend upon you for anything."

"What reason can I give the desk clerk for checking us both in?"

Nadia thought for a moment, then said, "Tell him you are doing so to save us time. I am at the theater getting our tickets for tonight's performance so we can have dinner together before the ballet begins."

"That he might believe," Mishka said. "And if he knows we are in a hurry, he will not bore me with his stupid jokes."

"Yes. And by the time the ballet is over, he will be off duty and you will not see him again until we check out on Sunday afternoon."

"That is true. He is always off on Saturdays," Mishka remembered. "And the desk clerk who takes his place on his day off doesn't know us that well. He always thinks that I am you and you are me."

"So you see, the hardest thing you will have to do is register us both tonight. Then the rest of the weekend will go smoothly. If our party section leader calls and demands to speak to me, you will tell her that you will go out and look for me. Then you will come to the guesthouse to let me know she is checking up on me."

"I will not like lying to her, but I will do it for you."

"It is settled, then. We need not talk about it anymore," Nadia said as she glanced around the theater entrance to see if anyone was watching them. "No one is looking this way, Mishka. Let us switch identity cards and I will be on my way to join Viktor."

Mishka removed hers from her wallet and passed it to Nadia, then slipped Nadia's identity card into her wallet. "I still wish you would check into the hotel with me instead of cutting corners to rush off after Viktor."

"You worry too much, Mishka," Nadia said, then gave Mishka a friendly kiss on the cheek. "I will meet you at the hotel on Sunday. We will have a nice lunch together before going back to the base. And be sure you remember tonight's and Saturday night's performances. You will have to tell me about them in detail, just in case our party section leader quizzes me on them."

"Be sure you use all the precautions Viktor told you to when leaving the city. It is bad enough you are skipping some already."

"I will. And you be sure to enjoy the ballet. Perhaps tonight's performance will occupy your mind enough to stop your worrying about me needlessly."

Mishka watched Nadia walk off, then turned to head for the hotel. She suddenly remembered that she needed her own identity card to check herself and Nadia in. Viktor had stressed the importance of switching identity cards at great length. If Nadia and he were caught sharing the guesthouse room together, her identity card would declare she was a married woman, while Viktor's would state he was unmarried. That would establish them as adulterers, which was a very serious crime against the state. But by having Mishka's card in her possession, Nadia and Viktor would merely appear to be lovers. That was also an offense against the state for military personnel, but a much less serious one. In view of that they could hope to be let off with just a warning, or perhaps be able to bribe their way out of being reported to the squadron commandant for follow up disciplinary action.

While she and Nadia looked like identical twins in their identity photos, the hotel desk clerk knew them well enough to tell them apart easily in person. He would surely question why the air force officer he knew to be Mishka Borken was presenting him with an identity card belonging to Nadia Potgornev. Frantic over the oversight, she chased after Nadia and caught up with her two blocks away from the ballet theater. "Nadia, we overlooked something."

Nadia listened to Mishka's explanation, then, exasperated, she returned Mishka's identity card and took hers back. "There. Now you will have no problems, Mishka."

"Why not just come to the hotel and also register with me as we are supposed to. Then I can give you my identity card and you can be on your way," Mishka pleaded once more.

"I am already on my way, Mishka. And we have already wasted enough time talking about these silly precautionary measures that may never be used again after this weekend, anyway. If I go to the hotel with you now, I will be keeping Viktor standing out in the snow. By the time I do join him he will be frostbitten. Now please go on to the hotel and don't worry about me. I'll be extra careful leaving the city."

"Very well. Have it your way, Nadia. I will see you on Sunday."

"Have a nice weekend, Mishka," Nadia said, then continued her trek toward the outskirts of the city.

Ferris couldn't guess what the two female air force officers had been discussing outside the ballet theater all that time, but he had seen them exchange something which at first he guessed was currency. Then after Nadia Potgornev walked off, and her friend chased after her, the second exchange seemed suspicious to him, and he saw that it had caught the attention of a man wearing a black raincoat who was standing in a shop entrance not far away from them. When the two women went in different directions again, Ferris saw the man in the black raincoat heading after Nadia. He gave them both a good head start, then followed after them.

At frequent intervals along their trek toward the city's outskirts, Ferris observed Nadia pausing to peer into shop windows, then nonchalantly glancing back as though looking at the falling snow. He also observed the man in the raincoat ducking into recessed storefronts each time Nadia made a stop along the way. He was watching a pro trailing his prey, and guessed the pro was with the military police or the KGB.

Nadia arrived at the outskirts of the city where the street she was on intersected with the country road leading to the guesthouse. It was snowing harder, and any tracks Viktor'd made were covered up by the thick falling flakes. There were a dozen assorted shops, half on each side of the street that marked the city limits and the beginning of the vastness of rolling hills along the country road ahead. One was a bookstore that she routinely waited in for ten minutes, to double check that she had not been followed from the military bus depot. She glanced over her shoulder and thought she saw a shadow a few doorways behind her. She paused for a few moments outside the bookstore and looked cautiously down the street leading back to the city. Seeing nothing, she went into the bookstore to wait impatiently through the final precaution.

KGB agent Ovanovich carefully peered out from the recessed doorway he'd ducked into to avoid being seen. He had decided on impulse to follow the female junior flight lieutenant after observing her urgently exchange something with a military comrade. With most military personnel on weekend passes in Kiev, enjoying the nightlife available in the vicinity of the bus depot, he was surprised to find his surveillance of her bringing him to the outskirts of the city. He saw her step inside a bookstore, then waited for five minutes before she emerged. When she did, she crossed the street and paused at one of the storefronts across from the bookstore, then walked off toward a country road leading away from the city. *Intriguing,* he thought.

Ferris watched Nadia begin heading down the road leading to the guesthouse. Moments after she disappeared around a curve in the road, the man in the black raincoat came out of hiding in the storefront several doorways from him, and headed after her. When they had both been swallowed up by the darkness, Ferris left his doorway and followed. He kept his right hand curled around the .38 silencer-equipped revolver in the pocket of his parka, and used extra caution as he proceeded along the dark and winding road. After ten minutes he saw the man in the black raincoat quickly duck behind a tree on the side of the road. Ferris did also. He saw a man standing in the roadway. He watched as Nadia walked up to the man who took her in his arms and kissed her.

"You are earlier than usual," Viktor said, after they'd kissed. "Did you stick to all our procedures for leaving the city?"

"Yes," Nadia lied.

"You checked into the hotel?" Viktor asked. Nadia nodded. "And you exchanged identity cards with Mishka before leaving her at the ballet theater?" Another nod. He didn't have to ask if she'd made the usual stop at the bookstore—that she had was apparent from the magazine she had tucked under one arm. He glanced down the road behind them and asked, "You are certain you were not followed out of the city?"

"Of course." Anxious to hear what news Viktor had for her, she asked, "What have you decided we will do about my transfer, Viktor?"

"We will discuss that in our room," Viktor replied, still scrutinizing the road behind them.

Extremely interesting, Ovanovich thought. He was beginning to see things more clearly. A male senior lieutenant and a female junior lieutenant were having a secret rendezvous on the isolated country road in violation of military regulations governing fraternization between senior and junior officers. It seemed to him that they were heading for the country guesthouse he knew was just ahead. If that was true, he might catch them having sex together. And if they were both single, he could threaten to report them and squeeze a few rubles out of them for their violation of the rules. He was sure he could squeeze them for a small fortune if either of them was married. He smiled as they walked in the direction of the guesthouse.

Ferris smiled also as he watched the behavior of the man in the raincoat. He could have easily killed him at any time. But he'd conceived a sly scheme that included the intruder, so he allowed him to live. When they reached the guesthouse, he saw the man crouch down behind a tree as the two air force officers were admitted by Yuri.

Ovanovich saw an upstairs light go on and spill its yellow glow out onto the snow. He observed another kiss, then saw the window shade being lowered as the female officer began discarding her uniform. It had been some time since he'd last had sex with his wife, and when he saw the woman silhouetted in just panties and bra, his penis began to throb and harden in his pants. When the panties and bra were shed, her lover appeared beside her. They kissed and moved away from the window. The room light switched off, returning the outside of the house to darkness, but he had seen enough. He stepped out from behind the tree and quietly approached the front door.

Ferris watched the man in the black raincoat carefully. The front door had been left unlocked for Ferris so he could enter the guesthouse without alerting the lovers. He shook his head as he envisioned what the surprise entry would mean for Baxter, Trotsky, and Yuri, who were waiting in the kitchen for him. Ferris saw the KGB agent draw a gun and slip inside the house.

Ferris's plan included letting the intruder take everyone inside the house by surprise. He wanted to surprise the agent just as he was about to charge the two lovers with adultery. He thought they'd be more willing to defect if the alternative was being arrested for adultery. He hoped that Trotsky or Baxter didn't foul up his plan by trying to overpower the intruder. He waited anxiously.

Ovanovich listened for a moment at the bottom of the staircase, but there was nothing to be heard. With the downstairs seemingly absent of life he made his way over to the potbellied stove. It was still burning radiantly; either someone was still up to enjoy its warmth, or the guesthouse was operated by a very wasteful proprietor. Seeing three closed doors along the adjoining rear hallway, he moved toward the first one, which was on his left. It was a swinging door, suggesting he would find a kitchen on the other side. He eased it open a crack, and finding three occupants inside, he rushed in. With his service revolver moving threateningly from Trotsky, to Baxter, to Yuri, he said in a whisper, "Everyone remain perfectly still and completely quiet."

"Who are you?" Trotsky asked in alarm. He had his .45 automatic inside his camera tote bag and had been connecting the flash attachment to his Polaroid when the intruder surprised them.

"I am with the KGB. I am here on a police matter," Ovanovich announced in a low voice.

"A police matter!" Yuri exclaimed fretfully.

"You will all keep your voices down and answer my questions," Ovanovich ordered. He gestured to Trotsky. "State your name and reason for being in this house."

"I am Ivan Trotsky. I own the neighboring farm and am here visiting my colleague." He pointed to Baxter.

"Your name and the nature of your business here?" Ovanovich asked Baxter.

"He is . . ."

"He will answer for himself, Comrade Trotsky, if you please," Ovanovich interrupted.

"I am Nikita Bakschev," Baxter answered. "I am an agriculturist, here to study hybrid crop growing under Comrade Trotsky's supervision. I am staying here at the guesthouse."

Turning to Yuri, Ovanovich asked, "And you?"

"I am Yuri Velinkov, the guesthouse proprietor."

"You have two others in your house," Ovanovich went on. Before Yuri could comment, he added, "It would be most foolish to deny that. I followed them here from Kiev."

"What have they done?" Yuri asked defensively.

"Did you bother to check their identity cards, Comrade?"

After hesitating, Yuri replied, "I saw no reason to."

"Doing so is required by all hotel and guesthouse operators," Ovanovich said. "But we will not take up your negligence at this moment. I have reason to believe that your two patrons have dispensed with the customary Soviet marital decrees and are having sex out of wedlock. If so, then, being members of the military and holding different ranks, they are guilty of fraternization. Therefore you will all join me in a quiet march upstairs to be witnesses to their sexual acts against the state." He noticed Trotsky's Polaroid camera and asked, "What are you doing with that device, Comrade?"

"I was showing it to Comrade Bakschev," Trotsky said. "He is from Moscow and hopes to take some pictures of our beloved Kiev before he returns home."

"You will bring your camera along, Comrade Trotsky," Ovanovich demanded. "I may have some pictures I want you to take to serve as evidence." He regarded Yuri next. "Do you have a passkey with you, Comrade?"

"Yes," Yuri answered in a woeful tone.

"Good," Ovanovich said. "Now we will all make our silent

climb upstairs in single file." He saw Trotsky reaching for his tote bag and said, "You will only need your camera, Comrade Trotsky." He envisioned confronting the two air force officers in bed nude before three witnesses. If their identity papers declared them unmarried, he would have the photos taken of them as a scare tactic. Then he would order the witnesses out of the room so he could negotiate financially with the two officers. On his way out he would remind the guesthouse proprietor of his failure to check identity papers. That might earn him a few additional rubles in exchange for not reporting the proprietor's neglect. "Very quietly now," he said as they neared the staircase.

Ferris was pleased that the guesthouse remained quiet after the intruder entered. After a few minutes there were shouts as the upstairs light came on. He quickly crossed the snow-covered grounds, and stepped into the house, and slipped off his shoes. He took a wire hanger out of the hall closet and shaped it into a large loop. With the wire held out in front of him he quietly climbed the staircase.

Ovanovich, his police special trained on the naked air force officers sitting up in bed, ordered, "A picture please, Comrade Trotsky." Trotsky moved over to the front of the bed and took the photo. With his free hand, Ovanovich pulled a small table from behind the door over to the middle of the room. His back was to the open door as he ordered, "Everyone will now place their identity cards on this table, one at a time. Ladies first, of course."

"But I am not wearing anything," Nadia said with embarrassment.

"I disagree," Ovanovich replied. "You are wearing the look of guilt. Now do as you are told." He watched her remove the covers and slowly rise from the bed. Seeing her male companion offering her the quilted blanket to cover herself with, he said, "She will come to the table just as she is, Comrade Officer. Comrade Trotsky still has film left in his camera."

Trotsky caught a glimpse of Ferris out in the hall, but was sure no one else had observed him, especially the KGB agent whose back was still to the open door. He aimed his camera as the woman headed over to the chair she had tossed her uniform over, her nakedness a display of sheer beauty.

"A shot of her behind, Comrade Trotsky," Ovanovich ordered, knowing he was humiliating the woman and enjoying doing so. The flash went off, then as Nadia faced everyone and walked toward the table, he added, "Now the front, Comrade."

Trotsky took the third snapshot, knowing the photo-taking was exactly what Ferris had planned anyway. He was glad, though, that the KGB agent had ordered him to do so at gunpoint. That made him feel a little better about accomplishing the necessary detail.

"You may return to the bed, now, Comrade Officer," Ovanovich said, then picked up her identity card to examine it. He found a coded notation that told him she was a married woman and her husband a military officer. "Let us hope it is your husband that is in bed with you, Comrade Junior Lieutenant Potgornev." He regarded Viktor next. "You will now present your identity card, Comrade Officer. I am most anxious to learn whether you are Comrade Potgornev or someone else." He added, "A photo of him please, Comrade Trotsky. In the nude."

Viktor gave Nadia a reproving glance for lying to him about switching identity cards with Mishka. Because of the KGB agent's intrusion, he was sure she must have been irresponsible about the other precautions, too. He had already told her of his plan to kill her husband, and reluctantly she had agreed to the plan. But now that they had been caught by the KGB, it seemed that Joseph Potgornev's life would definitely be spared. In her husband's place they would face execution, for the KGB agent would certainly report their lovemaking to his headquarters and the KGB would notify Joseph Potgornev of Nadia's adultery. He was tormented by a feeling of hopelessness as he crossed the room to his uniform to get his identity card. But he knew he had one way out of the dilemma. He could reach in his greatcoat pocket for his .25 automatic instead of his identification, and . . . he noticed someone sneaking up on the KGB agent from behind, but quickly looked away to keep the KGB agent from looking in that direction.

Trotsky saw Ferris raise the wire loop high over the KGB agent's head. He aimed the camera at Viktor, then spun around and set the flash off in Ovanovich's eyes.

Blinded for an instant, Ovanovich didn't see the wire loop pass in front of his eyes, but he felt agonizing pain as it dug into his neck and began cutting off his air. He dropped his gun and brought both hands up to pull the wire away from his windpipe, but it was being squeezed so tightly against his neck he couldn't grip it.

Trotsky quickly picked up Ovanovich's service revolver. Seeing Viktor make a dash for his greatcoat, he trained the weapon on him. "Stay where you are, Comrade Aleksei," he ordered.

Surprised that his name was known to anyone in the room but Nadia, Viktor asked, "Who are you?"

"Never mind who I am," Trotsky grunted. He regarded Baxter next. "Quickly, Nick! See what he was so anxious to get from his coat." He kept the revolver trained on Viktor and Nadia, then raised an eyebrow on seeing Baxter remove a gun from the coat pocket. "Return to the bed, Comrade Aleksei. Pull the blanket over yourself and your companion and remain perfectly still," he said. Hearing Yuri cry out in alarm, he said to Baxter, "Keep him quiet or the old woman will wake up."

Wheezing horridly, Ovanovich moved his torso to one side and brought his elbow back hard into the midsection of his attacker, then twisted to face Ferris when the wire slackened momentarily. He quickly felt the tautness of the wire around his neck again and reached down to his assailant's groin and squeezed his testicles fiercely.

Ferris choked down a scream. He kept his grip on the wire loop, but his breath, too, was being forced out of him. Gripping both ends of the wire loop with one hand, he jabbed the thumb of his free hand into Ovanovich's right eye and gouged at it to tear it out of its socket.

The pain was excruciating, but Ovanovich was unable to scream. All that came out was gurgling sounds. He felt himself being raised up from the floor and bounced. His strength drained from his hands and he released his viselike grip on his attacker's testicles. There were brilliant sparks before his eyes, then everything in the room disappeared.

Ferris saw Ovanovich's arms fall limply to his sides. His face had turned a sickly blue. Both his eyes were bulging out of their sockets. One was locked in a lifeless gaze at him. The other, the one he had gouged his thumb into, was staring up at the ceiling. It was mauled and bleeding grotesquely. He released the wire loop and Ovanovich's body slumped to the floor with a deep gash circling his neck. There were reddened deep ridges across the palms of both of Ferris's hands. With all eyes in the room locked on him he felt the pain in his groin suddenly intensify and he sank to his knees with a moan.

"My God!" Yuri cried out in alarm. "You have killed one of the KGB! What will Yekaterina and I do now?"

"Just stay where you are and be quiet," Baxter said. He regarded Trotsky. "Keep your eye on all of them, Ivan," he said, then rushed over to Ferris. "Are you okay, Matt?"

Ferris was in too much pain to get to his feet. Grimacing as he held his groin, he grunted, "Sex isn't a big thing with me, anyway." He tried to get up and sank right back down to his knees. He moaned and said, "Damn, but walking is."

"Don't anyone move or the KGB agent will have company on the floor," Trotsky snapped, then joined Baxter at Ferris's side. "Let us help you to your feet, Matt."

"Don't . . . move me yet," Ferris gasped. "Let me just stay like this for a moment longer."

"I did not want this kind of trouble in my guesthouse," Yuri sobbed fearfully. "You promised me there would be no trouble. What will become of my wife and me now?"

"Yuri has been trustworthy up to now, Matt," Trotsky whispered. "But I am afraid he will panic and become unpredictable now that this has happened."

Ferris nodded, then accepted help from Trotsky and Baxter in getting to his feet. Turning to Yuri, he said, "It looks like you and your wife are going to spend your retirement years in America, after all." He glanced at Trotsky. "Book them on the next sub heading in that direction."

"America!" Yuri said happily. "You are telling me the truth?" Ferris nodded. "This is wonderful news. I must go and tell Yekaterina at once."

"Not so fast," Ferris said. "We have another matter to discuss first. And we have to dispose of our uninvited guest here." He removed his .38 from his parka pocket and trained it on Viktor and Nadia, then regarded Trotsky and Baxter. "Put our friend in the next room and cover him up until we can make his funeral arrangements." As Trotsky and Baxter bent down to pick up the dead KGB agent, Ferris said to Yuri, "Get something to clean up the mess he made on your floor." Yuri rushed off to attend to the cleanup, and Ferris returned his attention to Viktor and Nadia. "Slip into your clothes, both of you." He saw Nadia hesitate. "We've already seen you in the nude, if that's what you are worried about." He looked away as they got up to get their clothes on. "I have a trip to America planned for you two also," he revealed.

"A trip to America?" Viktor asked, while Nadia nervously watched Trotsky and Baxter carry the dead KGB agent out of the room.

"It is either that, or a firing squad," Ferris said. "I just saved you both from being arrested by that KGB agent for adultery. But by killing him right in front of you both, I made you accomplices to murder."

"If we fall into the hands of the police, we will swear it was you who killed the KGB agent," Viktor retorted.

"If you fall into the hands of the police, it will be because we turned the photos that were just taken of you both in the nude over to Joseph Potgornev. I am sure Nadia's husband will see to it that you both are hunted down and stood before a firing squad for making a fool of him with your adulterous behavior."

"How is it you know so much about us?" Viktor asked.

"We did our homework," Ferris replied.

"Who are you and what is it you want?"

"We represent the American government. We are here to offer you a life together in the United States in exchange for a MIG-35 Foxbat."

"You are suggesting we defect to America and add treason to adultery?"

"What is the difference, Viktor?" Nadia put in. "We were planning to add murder to adultery by killing my husband."

"Say nothing more about our business to these spies," Viktor growled as Trotsky and Baxter returned to the room. "They have come here to trap us. How can we trust them with our lives?"

"How can we do otherwise, Viktor?" Nadia looked on as Yuri entered the room with a pail of water and a scrub brush and got down on his knees to clean up the bloodstains on the hard wooden floor. Looking back at Viktor, she added, "If we do not accept their offer, they will report us for sure. But what does that matter? If we remain in the Soviet Union we will never be permitted to love each other freely."

"Nadia makes sense, Viktor," Ferris commented. "Unless you love Russia more than you love her, my offer can solve all of your problems. If you went through with your plan to murder her husband, you would have to leave the Soviet Union anyway and go into hiding for the rest of your lives. Also you face a great risk of being caught or shot in your escape attempt. But if you go out my way, you will have my entire government helping you to make it safely. And you will have a place to go where no one will ever bother you again."

"This man is right," Yuri offered. "I have read about many Soviets whose escape to freedom was foiled by the KGB or the border police. Some paid many rubles to the underground, only to be turned in to the KGB instead of being helped out of the Soviet Union." He glanced over at Baxter and added, "Others of the military who were helped by the United States made their escape to freedom unharmed."

"We thought we could trust you, and you turned us over to these spies, old man," Viktor said bitterly.

"What I did was for your own good, you young fool. I wanted to see you love each other in freedom."

"Yuri speaks the truth about that," Trotsky said. "He had me swear we would cause you no harm before permitting us to meet with you here."

"But you are harming us," Viktor growled. "If we do not defect as you demand, you will use those photos to expose us as adulterers. And if we do as you say, you will no doubt shoot us once you get what you want and have no further need of us."

"That is not true," Baxter said. "You have been made victims of party propaganda by believing you will be killed by the West if you defect. The party leaders fabricate stories of cruel treatment, imprisonment, and execution by the West merely to discourage military personnel from deserting. And I can prove such things are nothing more than lies."

"How?" Viktor asked. "By fabricating stories of your own about how the markets in the West are filled to capacity with a variety of foods, and there are no lines? How practically everyone living in the West owns at least one car, perhaps two or three? I have heard these things and many more ridiculous stories, and I think they are merely western propaganda."

"Would you believe it is not propaganda if a Soviet defector that you know told you such things were the truth?"

"Who might that someone be?"

"Former Soviet Air Force Colonel Nikoli Belinsky," Baxter said.

"Belinsky?" Viktor repeated. "According to what I have been told, Nikoli Belinsky crashed in the Sea of Japan and drowned with his Foxbat in his attempt to defect. He has been talking to the angels if he has been talking to anyone at all for the past three years."

"You are very wrong about that, Viktor," Baxter said. "You are talking to Nikoli Belinsky right now."

"I knew it!" Yuri exclaimed excitedly. "I have eyes. I knew it really was you."

"This old man may be fooled by you," Viktor said. "But I remember the face of Colonel Belinsky quite well, and you look nothing like him."

"The American disguise experts who altered my features would be proud of their artistic abilities if you told them that," Baxter said. "But in spite of the fact that they have done such a thorough job of making sure I would not be recognized by anyone, I can prove who I claim to be quite easily by telling you something that only you and Nikoli Belinsky could know."

"And what is that?"

"You were my student pilot for a time in Khabarovsk. And at the time we flew tandem cockpit MIG-25 Foxbats."

"You have been quite resourceful in learning a number of things about me and Nadia. Perhaps you have had access to our military records. If so, you could have also learned from my records that Colonel Belinsky was my flight instructor in Khabarovsk. And you could have easily found out the type of planes we flew."

"Could anyone but Nikoli Belinsky know that you hinted you wanted to defect during those years you and he were stationed together in Khabarovsk?" Baxter asked. Viktor began to look doubtful. "Could anyone else know that you had a secret gift for forging names, and that on more than one occasion you signed the squadron commandant's name to passes so that you and Belinsky could get off the base to keep dates with two female officers we knew? Galina Glazenov and Mira Skorspekt."

"It is enough," Viktor said. "It must be you. Only Nikoli Belinsky and I knew of such things."

"Of course he is Nikoli Belinsky," Yuri said. "I have eyes. And I would know his eyes anywhere, no matter what the face looks like."

"I give you my word as Nikoli Belinsky that you and Nadia will be treated most generously if you agree to defect." He looked over at Nadia and sensed by her expression that she didn't need any further encouragement. But to give her help with Viktor, he said, "You and Viktor will be free to love each other openly as much as you want to. There will be no need to hide your love from anyone in America. You will both be given new identities, just as I was. And you will be well provided for until you have a chance to get totally settled in your new homeland and begin a new and happy life together."

"Viktor, it is like a dream come true for us," Nadia said softly. "It is the answer to our prayers."

"My wife and I are also going to America, now that this kind man has offered to take us there," Yuri said, gesturing toward Ferris. "We can all visit each other there and talk about happy things once again."

"You will never regret accepting the offer," Trotsky said. "And if you turn it down, there is no hope for you here in Russia."

"What is your decision?" Ferris asked. "A firing squad or at the very least a prison sentence—or freedom in the United States."

"Please, Viktor," Nadia begged. "Say we will choose freedom."

Viktor looked at each person in the room as he gave the matter further thought. Then he settled his eyes on Ferris and asked, "How would I do such a thing? How would I go about exchanging a Foxbat for freedom?"

"Well, it is not the Foxbat itself we are interested in," Ferris said. "Of course we would be delighted to evaluate one of Russia's newest planes, too. But we are primarily concerned with some new kind of electronic warfare apparatus we have reason to believe is aboard your MIG-35."

"You must be referring to the new jamming and antijamming apparatus."

"Precisely," Ferris said. "Do you have a technical understanding of what the jamming and antijamming apparatus is all about?" Viktor was hesitant. "If we are going to become countrymen, you might as well start working for our side right now, Viktor."

"Only high-ranking military officers and a select number of party officials know the technical aspects of Threshold," Viktor said.

"Threshold?"

"That is what the new training program we are involved in is called. All flight instructors and student pilots of our squadron know how to operate the cockpit controls for the new apparatus, but that is the extent of our knowledge."

"But you are quite sure there is such apparatus aboard your Foxbat?"

"Quite sure," Viktor said. "I have never seen it because we are not allowed to get close to it without special party security clearance. But our cockpit controls cause some new devices aboard our Foxbats to communicate with the mission control center in Odessa without enemy interference."

"By mission control center, do you mean the domed facility in Odessa?" Ferris asked. Viktor nodded. "Then we have a definite Foxbat ride to freedom in the making."

"And where is our Foxbat ride going to take us?" Viktor asked. "We would never reach the United States from any part of the Soviet Union on one load of fuel. The flying range of our Foxbat is far too short for that."

"The range of the MIG-35 is approximately twelve hundred miles," Baxter put in.

"At the most," Viktor said.

"That is quite an improvement over the MIG-25 Foxbats we flew out of Khabarovsk together," Baxter commented. Viktor nodded.

"We have a defection route all worked out for you," Ferris said. "You will fly to an Egyptian Air Force base in Cairo from Odessa."

"But we are not yet based in Odessa," Viktor said. "We are based near the city of Kiev."

"I know that," Ferris said. "We are planning to wait until your squadron moves to the new permanent air base in Odessa."

"That will not take place for many weeks," Nadia complained.

"True," Ferris admitted. "It will be something of a wait, but . . ."

"But we cannot wait for many weeks," Nadia protested. "We must go at once."

"I'm happy to hear you're so anxious to go," Ferris commented. "Frankly, I thought I would have a harder time convincing you. But why can't you wait until you get to Odessa? You see . . ."

Nadia reached in her purse and took out the letter her husband had sent her. Handing it to Ferris, she said, "This is why."

Ferris quickly digested the contents of the letter. Then he said, "What if we get you out by submarine ahead of Viktor, then have him join you in America after your squadron relocates to Odessa?"

"We will not go separately," Viktor insisted. "We will go together. We will go from Kiev. And we will go at once, or not at all."

"I'd like nothing better," Ferris admitted. "But it is about fifteen hundred air miles from Kiev to Egypt. You'd run out of fuel some three hundred miles short of Egypt. That would have you ditching your Foxbat in the Mediterranean Sea."

"Then find a country closer to Kiev," Viktor demanded. "Or else we will not go."

"We've approached every nation within flying range of a Foxbat that is friendly to the United States," Ferris said. "Egypt is the only nation willing to take the risk of playing host airport to a MIG-35 with a defector for a pilot."

"Would not the Turkish government allow us to land?" Viktor asked.

"Not a chance," Ferris said. "They're only willing to allow you to cross through their air space."

"They will not even allow us to land for refueling?" Viktor asked.

"No," Ferris said. "All of our NATO friends are afraid you might get caught on the ground by your countrymen and they would be faced with an international crisis as a result."

"How about arranging inflight refueling en route, Matt?" Trotsky asked.

"That will not work unless you can arrange to have a Soviet tanker aircraft do the refueling," Viktor said. "Soviet-made inflight fueling receptacles are not compatible with foreign-made refueling probes. That was done intentionally, to prevent pilots from traveling too far beyond Russia's ability to recapture them with pursuit planes."

"Have you considered Crete or Cyprus, Matt?" Trotsky asked. "Both of those islands are along the way to Egypt."

"Hal Banks has exhausted all other possibilities, Ivan," Ferris said. "It has to be Egypt, and there can be no stopping off on the way to Cairo. I thought my biggest difficulty was going to be consummating a willing defection. Instead I'm faced with an airport problem."

Ending the silence that hung over the room, Baxter said, "Matt, I think I have a plan that will solve your airport problem."

"At this point I am willing to entertain any ideas."

"Give me a little time to share some . . . pilot's talk with Viktor and Nadia before I tell you what I have in mind, Matt," Baxter said.

"Take all the time you need, Nick."

"Let us discuss the matter of our uninvited guest in the meantime, Matt," Trotsky said. "And while we are doing that, Yuri can fetch us all some vodka. I think we could all use a drink to take the edge off things." He led Yuri and Ferris out of the room. As Yuri went down to get the vodka, Trotsky and Ferris stepped into the guestroom where they had placed the KGB agent's body. "I have an old and very deep well that I never use for drinking water in the rear of my farm. It will be a good place to hide the body should his KGB colleagues somehow trace him here."

"No one but us knows he came here, Ivan. I was on to him shadowing Nadia right from the start. He never had time to check in with his headquarters to let them know what he was doing. And no one saw any of us leaving the city. That I'm sure of."

"That is a relief," Trotsky said. "But he will eventually be missed, and a search of Kiev will be made. In view of that, it will be quite risky for Viktor and Nadia to remain here very long. There will be extra KGB agents prowling the city streets. Perhaps the road outside this guesthouse will be patrolled as well."

"I agree. As soon as our business with them is resolved, we'll see to taking them back to the city."

"And if we are unable to resolve the business of their defection to our satisfaction, what then?" Trotsky whispered.

"Then we'll take them to your well instead," Ferris whispered back.

"They are a nice couple. I hope it doesn't come to that."

"So do I, Ivan," Ferris said as he grabbed the dead KGB agent by the shoulders and lifted him. "Grab his feet, Ivan. The sooner were get this over with, the better."

CHAPTER TWELVE

With the KGB agent's body disposed of, Trotsky drove Ferris back to the guesthouse. As they got out of the car and headed up the front walk, he said, "In all the confusion I forgot to ask why you choked the KGB agent to death with the wire hanger, instead of just shooting him."

"I've learned from past experience that a man can still get a shot off unless you hit him in the right spot," Ferris explained. "With five other people in the room, I didn't want to risk getting someone else shot."

They found the others gathered around the kitchen table behaving in a puzzling way. Yuri was on his knees on one side of the table, holding a dinner knife upright against its edge. Kneeling on the opposite side was Nadia, holding a dinner knife in the same manner. Spanning the width of the table between them were several hairnets that had been laced together; the ends of the nets were fastened to both dinner knives.

Baxter was standing on Yuri's side of the table with two soup spoons held out from his sides at arm's length. Baxter was making erratic motions with the spoons as he faced Viktor, who was at the far end of the kitchen, facing him. Viktor was holding a paper airplane out in front of him as he moved slowly toward one end of the table in response to Baxter's verbal commands.

"Would somebody care to explain what this is all about?" Ferris finally asked.

"Just a minute more and I'll explain everything, Matt," Baxter promised, then returned his attention to Viktor. Lowering the spoon in his left hand a little, he said, "Your left wing is a little high, Viktor." He waited for the correction, then added, "Good. Just like that. Now, at this point you would reduce speed, then you would lower your landing gear and bring your flaps down full."

"Reduce speed. Lower gear and full flaps," Viktor repeated as he continued his slow walk toward the table's edge and Baxter.

"Now you should give your Foxbat a slight nose-up attitude, so your main landing gear engages the deck first," Baxter said next.

Viktor adjusted his paper airplane accordingly. "Is that enough attitude?"

Baxter nodded. "Your angle of attack is perfect. Keep your wings level," he added, repeating the command with the spoons which he held straight out from his sides. "Descend," he said, lowering both spoons. "Descend. Descend."

Almost to the end of the table now, Viktor said, "Descending. One hundred feet. Fifty feet."

When Viktor reached the end of the table, Baxter dropped both hands down almost to his sides. "Cut power. Bring your nose down. Okay!" he called out. "At this point your main gear would make contact with the rear of the flight deck. And by bringing your nose down, you'd make your nose wheel touch down. Keep your power off and head straight for the barrier, then brace yourselves and let its arresting capabilities do the rest of the work for you."

Viktor brought his torso over the end of the table as he moved the paper airplane across its surface. Midway along the table's length the paper airplane made contact with the hairnets, and he allowed them to stretch slightly before releasing the paper airplane. The paper airplane remained captured in the hairnets.

"That's all there is to it, Viktor," Baxter said. "You've just made a successful carrier landing." He put down his spoons, reached over to the paper airplane, and removed it from the hairnets. "You and Nadia would be assisted out of your cockpits by plane captains, while the arresting gear crew worked to release your Foxbat from the Davis barrier." He regarded Ferris. "Get the idea now, Matt?"

"Not completely," Ferris said.

Baxter began to pace the floor on his side of the table. He took a moment to regard Yuri and Nadia. "You can get up now. Our little simulated carrier landing is over." Returning his attention to Ferris, he went on, "The range of the Foxbat is twelve hundred miles. The distance from Odessa to Cairo is just a hair under that. But the distance from Kiev to Cairo is nearly fifteen hundred miles."

"I know," said Ferris. "So?"

"If we can arrange to have one of our aircraft carriers meet them three hundred miles out from the Egyptian coastline, we can bring the Foxbat aboard and carry it the rest of the way.

Once the Foxbat is taken aboard, we can move it down to the hangar deck level and keep it out of sight for the three-hundred-mile voyage to the port of Alexandria. From there it can be offloaded and trucked to the Egyptian Air Force base near Cairo."

Ferris envisioned an aircraft carrier like the ones he'd seen in Mayport, Florida. He also envisioned the airplane he'd seen being lowered to the flight deck level aboard the U.S.S. *Eisenhower* when it was at dockside in Mayport. He recalled how the plane had been quickly hidden away in the carrier's huge belly. Then he envisioned a carrier landing, such as those he had seen in war movies, and he smiled. "What you suggest, my good friend, just might allow us to eliminate completely the Egyptian government's participation in the mission. If we can land the Foxbat aboard one of our carriers and keep it out of sight for the twenty-four hours Trish Darrol needs to spend with it, we can keep the defection confined to American hands. Your idea is brillliant, Nick. I'm surprised Hal Banks never thought of using one of our carriers for the defection. I guess he assumed as I did that only specially designed aircraft are capable of landing and taking off from aircraft carriers."

"Your assumption is right, Matt," Baxter said. "Aircraft are specially engineered for carrier-borne service." He picked up the paper airplane and pointed to the underside of the tail section. "All planes require a tail hook to land aboard a carrier. It's a steel arm with a hook affixed to the tip of it." He moved to the end of the table and placed the spoons and knives at intervals across its width. "Let these utensils represent arresting gear cables stretched across the rear of a carrier's flight deck." Holding the plane above the utensils, he went on, "With the tail hook extended, a specific arresting gear cable for a particular aircraft is engaged as the plane touches down. The cable then stretches out from tension wheels to slow the plane's forward motion to a full stop. Then the cable is released and the tail hook retracts until the next carrier landing takes place."

"Wonderful," Ferris commented. "But the Foxbat isn't engineered for that."

"Correct," Baxter agreed. "That's where the Davis barrier comes in."

"The what?" Ferris asked.

"The hairnet," Baxter said as he pointed to the simulated barrier that lay across the table. "It is an emergency device used to land an aircraft with a broken tail hook or a similar landing gear problem such as a gear that is locked in the up position. In such a situation, the arresting gear cables are of no use, so the Davis barrier is rigged to catch the landing aircraft like a baseball."

"You're suggesting that the Davis barrier can be used to bring a Foxbat aboard?"

"A carrier-borne aircraft with a broken or defective tail hook would be in the same situation as a plane attempting a landing aboard a carrier without a tail hook," Baxter said. "Of course the plane attempting such an unorthodox landing would have to be comparable in weight, size, and speed to carrier-borne aircraft, or else it might tear up the flight deck and tear out the Davis barrier."

"Is the Foxbat comparable to our carrier-borne aircraft?" Ferris asked next.

"It's heavier and slightly larger than our fighters and fighter-bombers," Baxter said. "But it's comparable in weight and size to our carrier-borne bombers. However, the speed of the MIG-35 is a problem. According to Viktor and Nadia, the Foxbat has a greater landing speed than our carrier-borne aircraft. We might have to reinforce the Davis barrier because of that, but if we do . . . I think we'll be able to take their Foxbat aboard. We'll need to arrange a few things in advance if we plan to give my idea a try."

"Such as?" Ferris asked.

"A Davis barrier specialist of top quality on hand to assist us with any engineering problems the Foxbat landing might pose."

"We should be able to arrange that," Ferris said. "What else?"

"Viktor and Nadia will have to be furnished with a radio device that operates on our fleet frequencies. And it will have to be small enough to go unnoticed when they return to their air base."

"I can furnish them with a radio receiver-transmitter that will fit inside the shell of a pen," Trotsky said. "And I can fit it with crystals that will operate on your U.S. Navy frequencies. But its size will restrict its range."

"What's the maximum range you can get?" Baxter asked.

"About fifty miles at best," Trotsky replied.

"That will do nicely," Baxter said. Looking at Ferris, he added, "Our carrier-borne aircraft are equipped with computerized control approach apparatus. But in the old days approaches were handled by a landing signal officer, which was what I was demonstrating with those soup spoons. I've been checked out on the paddles, so I'll volunteer for LSO duty. And they'll need someone who speaks Russian on the carrier end of communications, so I'll also serve as their radio approach control operator."

"It will be good to know it is you who will be giving us landing instructions," Viktor said.

"That's settled, then," Ferris said. "I'll arrange to have Trish Darrol aboard. What else do you need, Nick?"

"Just a carrier," Baxter replied. "Think you can get approval from the navy to borrow one for a day or so?"

"If Hal Banks wants a Foxbat bad enough, he'll get approval," Ferris said.

"How soon will we defect?" Nadia asked anxiously.

Ferris studied a calendar on the wall. "We have a couple of carriers out in the Med right now, isn't that right, Nick?"

"We have the *Ike* and the *Hawk* coming on duty, and the *Forrestal* and *Coral Sea* going off," Baxter said. "And all of them will be right along the defection route for the next seventy-two hours."

"If Hal can get approval from the Hill people over the weekend, we could make the carrier landing take place on . . ." He looked sour. "I might have known that would happen."

"What?" Baxter asked.

"Not only might the defection take place on a Monday, but it might be on Monday the thirteenth. To me that means the same as Friday the thirteenth to other people." He regarded Viktor and Nadia. "If we can arrange things fast enough at our end, will you be able to defect as early as this Monday?"

"The sooner the better," Nadia said.

"And you?" Ferris asked Viktor.

"We will be together in a Foxbat on a training sortie over Odessa that morning."

"Good," Ferris said. "That morning, when you think best, break away from the other planes flying over Odessa. Then use your afterburners for crossing the Black Sea, so you can reach the protection of Turkish airspace as quickly as possible. The Turks will do their best to discourage pursuit planes from giving chase through their air corridors, so that you have the best possible chance of making it to the Mediterranean. From that point on you are to fly at the lowest possible altitude so you can avoid Soviet radar detection. We will have a rendezvous point set up for you over the weekend. Then while you're flying due south to meet up with whatever carrier is assigned to take you aboard, the Turks will broadcast a phony Mayday call, stating that you radioed them you were ditching in the sea. If any search planes come after you, they will be concentrating their efforts on the waters off the Turkish southern coastline, while you are miles away from them farther south."

"Once you are about fifty miles from where the carrier is supposed to meet you," Baxter said, "you can use the radio Ivan Trotsky furnishes you with to contact me. We will establish a code name you can use for identification purposes. From that point on, I will be guiding you in for your landing."

"How does all that sound to both of you?" Ferris asked.

"I think it is workable," Viktor said.

"I will have my heart in my mouth all the way," Nadia said. "Especially when it is time to land aboard the American aircraft carrier." She gripped Viktor's arm. "But to be able to spend the rest of my life with Viktor in peace, I would risk any danger."

"That settles it, then," Ferris said. "What I think you both should do now is return to the city and spend the rest of the weekend there. When they discover that one of their agents is missing, the KGB will make life miserable for everyone for miles around. We'll agree on a place to meet before you have to go back to the air base. At that time we will give you the pen-size radio and final instructions for your flight to freedom."

"There is one part of your plan for us that I refuse to go along with," Nadia said, catching Viktor and everyone else by surprise.

"What is that?" Ferris asked.

"I insist that Viktor and I finish our weekend stay here."

"But it is dangerous for you to be here now with a dead KGB agent," Ferris said.

"It will be dangerous in Kiev for the same reason. Here we will be safest. The KGB will not think of looking here right away for a KGB agent's murderer. In the city they will be looking everywhere. And they will be questioning everyone. I would rather avoid being questioned by the KGB so soon after seeing their agent killed."

"She may have a good argument, Matt," Trotsky said. "If the KGB does come here to investigate the whereabouts of their missing agent they will find no trace of him. And we can always hide Viktor and Nadia."

"I have many places to hide them here," Yuri said. "Places they will never be found."

"I also have a number of hiding places at my farm," Trotsky said. "Then on Sunday we can drive them to the city one at a time."

"I will go along with the idea if you both agree to finish out the weekend at Ivan's farm," Ferris said.

"My wife will be away over the entire weekend and it will be nice to have some company," Trotsky said.

"But what about the rubles I was to earn for their stay at my guesthouse?" Yuri asked.

"You will have them anyway," Trotsky said. "Plenty of them."

Turning to Trotsky, Ferris said, "All that's left to do now is get in touch with Hal Banks and tell him what we need." He faced Viktor and Nadia. "You may as well grab your things and move over to Ivan's farm right now."

"I'm coming, too," Baxter said. "I haven't seen Ivan's farm yet."

"You stay here with Yuri and play chess with him to help him calm down from all the excitement, Nick," Ferris said. "You can see Ivan's farm tomorrow."

"Good!" Yuri said. "I will prepare the chessboard at once."

On Saturday morning Trotsky received a reply from Hal Banks. He decoded it and handed it to Ferris. "Good news, Matt."

Ferris read the reply rapidly, then read each line more carefully:

> Operation Gambit renamed Mediterranean Maneuver. Carrier assigned is U.S.S. *Coral Sea*. Will rendezvous with Foxbat two hundred miles due south of Turkish southern coastline at lat. 30 degrees by lon. 35 degrees on December 13. Carrier code name Kangaroo. Foxbat code name Cub. Radio receiver-transmitter communications frequency is channel 13. Backup frequency is channel 25.
>
> Acknowledge need to relocate the Velinkovs and arrangements are made. Transportation ordered. Sub will arrive tonight at point dropped you off. Trish Darrol will meet you in Istanbul with written orders for carrier skipper. Proceed to carrier at once by air force chopper. Sorry it's taking place on a Monday, Matt. Hal Banks.

Ferris handed the deciphered communiqué to Baxter as he asked, "Is the *Coral Sea* one of our new carriers?"

After digesting the communiqué, Baxter answered, "No, it's an old World War Two–vintage flattop."

"This being such a delicate situation, why are they assigning an old carrier to the mission instead of one of the new flattops?" Ferris asked next.

"The *Coral Sea* is slated to be decommissioned and sold for scrap after its present Med cruise is over," Baxter replied. "It is quite risky to land a noncarrier-borne aircraft on a carrier. I guess the navy reasoned that if we're going to chance sinking one of their flattops, it may as well be one that's heading for the scrap pile, instead of one of their elite new carriers."

PART THREE

CHAPTER THIRTEEN

The word came over the U.S.S. *Coral Sea*'s bitchbox just before noon chow on Saturday. At 1330 hours all hands were to interrupt routine ship and air group work to hear a special announcement from the skipper. The crew of the *Coral Sea* were anticipating a return voyage stateside with their sister carrier, the U.S.S. *Forrestal*, now that the carriers *Eisenhower* and *Kitty Hawk* had arrived off the island of Cyprus to relieve them. Everyone aboard the *Coral Sea* knew their flattop was heading stateside to be decommissioned and sold for scrap metal, which suggested there was no urgency to getting the ship back to home port. That made the possibility of an extended Med cruise the most popular rumor circulated at noon chow.

At 1300 hours the host of frigates, destroyers, cruisers, submarines, sub tender ships, tankers, and freighters belonging to the incoming and offgoing Sixth Fleet task forces began to draw closer to the *Coral Sea*. As the biting winter wind blew over the exposed decks and catwalks of both fleets, officers and enlisted men broke from work duties and began to assemble into sub groups by divisions and squadrons.

With the incoming and offgoing Soviet task forces clustered on the horizon behind the Sixth Fleet ships, Captain Tom Redding, the *Coral Sea*'s commanding officer, arrived on the bridge deck to make his announcement. He was a bony man, age forty-nine, who stood just under five feet seven. He had dark brown hair that was combed straight back underneath his navy-blue uniform baseball cap. His light brown eyes were watery as he addressed his executive officer in his baritone voice. "Well, let's get it over with." He glanced at his wristwatch and saw it was now 1:30 P.M.

Lieutenant Commander Kalvin Jones, Redding's X.O., was a hefty black man in his mid-forties with large dark brown eyes that were quick to notice Redding's distress. His bass voice rumbled as he said, "I hate this goddamn detail." Redding nodded. Facing the *Coral Sea*'s leading chief, Jones ordered, "Get all hands at attention, Smitty."

Also wearing a sour look, Leading Chief Wally Smith led Redding and Jones out to the bridge catwalk portside where a P.A. microphone was situated atop a portable stand. In his early fifties, a bald and potbellied man, his deep blue eyes still managed an affectionate twinkle as he gazed down at the ranks and rows of officers and crewmen. He had been aboard the *Coral Sea* since his late teens, and had grown old with Redding, who had also served aboard the *Coral Sea* since he was a teenager. It was a lifetime of friendship, and devotion to the ship they'd called home for so long.

Smitty waited for a boatswain to sound his whistle into the microphone, then replaced him there and ordered, "All hands, attention!" He stepped to one side at attention himself to allow Redding to come to the microphone. "They're all yours, Skipper."

"Stand at ease!" Redding began. "This shouldn't take long." He gave his crew a moment to get more comfortable, then said, "Just before noon chow I received an urgent communiqué from COMSIX. The good news is that our ship is going to escape the cutting torches back in home port, after all." His statement brought cheers from all hands. Raising his hands to curb the cheers and shouts of joy, he added, "The bad news is that in spite of the *Coral Sea*'s extended lease on life, she will no longer be our ship." That disclosure brought growls of discontent from his crew. "An arrangement between our government and the Egyptian government has been worked out, whereby the *Coral Sea* will be given to the Egyptian Navy for use as a floating training base for their helicopter pilots."

"Skipper," one sailor shouted from the ranks manning the flight deck. His voice was loud and clear. "Why don't we all donate our pay and buy the *Coral Sea* ourselves. We could convert her into a museum, just like some of our other old flattops."

"I'm sure we've all thought of doing that," Redding said. "But orders are orders. Apparently the *Coral Sea* is not for sale." He passed his eyes over his crew, sensing by their silence that they regarded the COMSIX decision with contempt. "Think of the brighter side," he said over the silence. "Our Egyptian allies will put our ship to good use. That will give the *Coral Sea* a chance to serve another navy proudly, just as she served our navy."

"Well, they better treat her with respect," another enlisted man called out. His comment drew shouts and cheers from his shipmates.

"There's a great deal of work ahead in getting the *Coral Sea* ready for its transfer of ownership," Redding went on. "And once again, I'm going to need the cooperation of all hands to carry out our orders. We've been given just about twenty-four hours to vacate the ship, and you well know that isn't much time to move all of our personal possessions and naval property to the three flattops out here with us. When we are done stripping her down, only what is necessary to sail the *Coral Sea* safely to Egypt is to remain aboard. By this time tomorrow a BUSHIPS delegation will arrive by chopper to handle the transfer of ownership when we arrive in the port of Alexandria. And by tomorrow, you people are expected to be aboard our sister carrier, the *Forrestal*, or aboard either the *Ike* or the *Hawk*."

"The *Ike* or the *Hawk*!" another sailor called out. "That sounds like some of us are getting shafted with an extended Med cruise."

Redding said, "It's true those of you who will TX to the *Forrestal* are going to get back home a little earlier than those being transferred to the *Ike* or *Hawk*. But those remaining behind will be airlifted stateside from one of our Mediterranean ports of call as quickly as arrangements can be made for MATS or civilian charter flights. So do the best you can to endure the inconvenience and be assured the navy wants to get all of you back home just as much as you want to get there yourselves." He paused for a moment, cleared his throat, and continued. "At this time I wish to say that I feel proud and privileged to have commanded such a fine group of men. The numerous Golden Anchor awards you've won for volunteering to remain aboard the *Coral Sea*, cruise after cruise, expresses the feelings we have for our ship and each other. I know I can count on all of you to carry out these, our last orders, in your usual manner of excellence. If I can ask one more thing of you, it's that you continue the devotion to duty you've exemplified while serving aboard this ship. I thank you one and all, and bid you all goodbye."

Jones joined Redding at the microphone before his C.O. could step away. He called into the microphone, "Ship's company and air group, attention!" He held Redding lightly by the arm as he watched the rows and ranks of officers and enlisted men come to attention with a snap. "Ready . . . hand salute!" With all hands rendering a salute in the direction of the bridge catwalk, Jones said to Redding, "Skipper, would you honor the crew by returning their salute?"

Redding put all the feeling of the past years of naval service into his salute, then quietly stepped away from the microphone.

Turning to the microphone, Jones said, "Ready . . . to!" His command brought the hands of all crewmen back to their sides. With the farewell tribute rendered, he said into the microphone, "Division officers and chiefs, dismiss your men and have them turn to on carrying out evac duties." Joining Redding and Chief Smith inside the bridge, he asked, "Skipper, do you want the Davis barrier gang assembled out of volunteers?"

"No way, Jonesy," Redding replied. "We'll have so many wanting to go along on the voyage to Alexandria that we'll spend the next twenty-four hours just narrowing them down to a select few. As our former arresting gear officer, you head the barrier crew and hand-pick your gang."

"Want the ferrying crew drafted the same way?" Jones asked.

"Yes," Redding said. Then he looked at Chief Smith and said, "But you hand-pick who you want in your ferrying crew, Smitty. And make sure the men you choose are real hustlers. They're going to have to shake their fannies to cover all vital stations while underway to Egypt."

"I know just the guys I want for my gang, Skipper," Smith said.

"Good," Redding said. "Now let's see to getting our ship stripped down to her bare decks."

"Roger that, Skipper," Jones said. "But I hate the idea of running around out here in the Med with all of our firepower taken off. If any of those Russian ships decide to tag along with us on our way to Alexandria, all we'll have to throw at them if they start anything is ship's coffee."

"The way ship's coffee has been tasting lately, that just might be enough of a weapon," Redding commented, then shared a laugh with Jones and Smith as they headed off the bridge deck to assign work details for the evacuation.

CHAPTER FOURTEEN

Aboard the cruiser *Leningrad* Admiral Stalovich had just finished debriefing the flight crews of his two helicopters after their flyby mission to investigate the activities that were taking place aboard the ships of the American task forces. He was told that each ship's crew had been mustered at the unusual time of day when ship's work was normally being carried out. That puzzled him. It seemed to suggest that something very special was about to take place. He wondered if some part of the Mediterranean region had flared up that he hadn't been alerted about as yet. Perhaps there was another skirmish taking place in the Middle East between the Israelis and one of the Arab nations that were friends of the Soviet Union. Whatever the reason, he was sure a directive from the Kremlin to deploy his task force to the troubled region would be forthcoming.

No such directive came. What Stalovich received instead was a coded American communiqué that his cipher sector managed to intercept. In reading the decoded version, his first response was envy. He couldn't believe his enemies were so financially well off that they could afford to just give away one of their angle-deck aircraft carriers to one of their allies. In learning that the Egyptian Navy was to be the recipient of such a generous gift, his next reaction was anger. Furious over what such a weapon could mean in the hands of a nation that had betrayed Mother Russia and had chosen to become an enemy of her Middle East friends, he placed a call over Yudalslov's new "toy telephone system" to Deputy Secretary of the Soviet Navy, Kosenoff, to alert his old friend to the damaging news and what he proposed to do in retaliation. Kosenoff sighed over his request, but agreed to bring the matter to the attention of the premier at once. Then, while he waited for Kosenoff to call back, he summoned his flagship's commanding officer to his private cabin in anticipation of the premier's approval of his plan.

As soon as the senior officer of the *Leningrad* entered his cabin, Stalovich spat out violently, "The reckless capitalists were not satisfied in arming the Jews to the teeth!" His statement drew a puzzled stare from the flagship's C.O. He added, "Now they are daring enough to include the Egyptians in their acts of brazen aggression in the Middle East! They are doing all they can to incite unrest and plunge the nations of that troubled region into an all-out holocaust! And what are we doing about it?" Before the *Leningrad*'s C.O. could offer a guess, he said, "We are playing with our new toy telephones! We are spending countless rubles and endless man hours toying with our newest magical machinery!"

"What has happened, Comrade Commandant?" Captain Boren Garupcheck, the *Leningrad*'s C.O., asked in alarm.

"It is why the ships of the Sixth Fleet are in such a state of unrest," Stalovich began to explain. "They are making a gift of one of their angle-deck carriers to their friends the Egyptians." He handed Garupcheck the decoded communiqué and invited him to read it for himself.

Garupcheck quickly read the communiqué, then looked up at Stalovich and grumbled, "Those who would renounce Soviet friendship and choose the capitalists for their friends are fools."

"Comrade," Stalovich said, "we are fools for permitting the capitalists to arm their allies with weapons they will one day aim at communist nations of the world. We have waited far too long to hold them accountable for their acts of aggression, and the perfect way to put our foot down is to blockade the port of Alexandria and deny the U.S.S. *Coral Sea* entrance."

"But that will be an unprovoked military action that is certain to infuriate both the Egyptian and American governments!" Garupcheck warned.

"It will be an action certain to infuriate them," Stalovich agreed. "But it will not be unprovoked."

"How will such an action not be unprovoked, Comrade Commandant?" Garupcheck questioned in a tone of disbelief.

"Is not an aircraft carrier an offensive weapon, my dear Comrade?" Stalovich asked. He got an agreeing nod from Garupcheck. "And what did the American navy do to our fleet when it attempted to deliver offensive weapons to Comrade Premier Castro in Cuba?" he asked.

"The capitalists blockaded Premier Castro's ports," Garupcheck recited.

"And they ordered our convoy of ships to return to their homeland with their cargoes undelivered," Stalovich added.

"With all due respect, Comrade Commandant," Garupcheck said, "the action taken by the capitalists in that incident was because our offensive weapons were to be located geographically close to their shores and pose a serious threat to their home defenses."

"Cannot an aircraft carrier roam the seas and pose a serious threat to the home defenses of Mother Russia and its bloc nations?" Stalovich argued. "I propose that the Soviet Union force the capitalists to take back their gift of an offensive weapon."

Garupcheck glanced at the deciphered communiqué that Stalovich had given him. "But the Americans are delivering the aircraft carrier to the Egyptians weaponless, according to this message from their chief of naval operations in Washington."

"But of course they are," Stalovich agreed. "They are doing so because they expect we will not take aggressive action against an unarmed ship on international high seas. But the aircraft carrier the Americans are giving to the Egyptians will certainly be fitted with offensive weapons soon after it arrives in the port of Alexandria, will it not?"

"According to the Americans the aircraft carrier is slated to be used as a floating air base to train Egyptian helicopter pilots," Captain Garupcheck said.

"That is precisely what we are being led to believe!" Stalovich barked. "We can no longer trust our former friends, the Egyptians. If a conflict takes place in the Middle East, they will most certainly utilize the American carrier to support their political interests. And we owe it to our allies in that region to prevent their enemies from building up too much military strength."

The phone buzzed and Stalovich picked it up at once. "This is Admiral Stalovich."

"This is Deputy Director Yudalslov, Comrade Commandant," Yudalslov said from his desk in the combat control sector room. "I have a call for you over the scrambler from the deputy secretary of the navy in Moscow." He was acknowledged by Stalovich, then secretly monitored the call.

"How good of you to get back to me so quickly, Comrade Kosenoff," Stalovich began. "Were you able to get a reply to my request from the premier?"

Seated at his large and well-polished desk in his office at the Kremlin, Kosenoff released a sigh of exasperation. "I have just come from a meeting with the premier that took place behind closed doors, Georgi," he grunted. "To say it was an unpleasant experience for me would be a gross understatement."

"Are you about to tell me that the premier has in fact denied my request, Vladimir?" Stalovich asked, his voice edged with anger.

"Most vehemently," Kosenoff returned.

"Vladimir, I am not going to . . ."

"You are not going to humiliate me before the premier anymore, Georgi!" Kosenoff pushed in. "But you are going to carry out your orders explicitly. You are going to deploy your task force in its entirety with the American task force, as your orders spell out. And you are going to commit your personnel and the highly expensive electronics warfare equipment aboard the vessels of your fleet to the advance testing of Project Threshold, as administered by Comrade Deputy Director Yudalslov. You are going to do these things, Georgi . . . or you will no longer have a task force to command."

"Whatever you say, Comrade Deputy Secretary," Stalovich said in a disgruntled tone.

"I gather I have made myself clear, then," Kosenoff said authoritatively. "You are to cease and desist in the matter of the American carrier, U.S.S. *Coral Sea*. Keep your mind on the aircraft carriers that remain in the American navy, not on those being retired from it. And leave the affairs of the Egyptian government to our party leaders, who best know how to deal with such matters!" He slammed down the phone.

Stalovich heard Yudalslov interject that the deputy secretary had terminated the call at the Moscow end. He slowly placed the phone on its cradle and regarded Garupcheck standing across the desk from him with a questioning expression. "It is what we could expect from a bunch of spineless, narrow-minded old fools," he bellowed in a tone of protest. "We have been denied this perfect opportunity to rightfully flex our muscles at our enemies."

"Perhaps our party leaders evaluated the consequences of such a military action and felt the risk of all-out war with the Egyptians and Americans was too great," Garupcheck suggested.

Stalovich gestured to the door. "I wish to be alone now." His voice was absent of its usual bite. "Go and tell Deputy Director Yudalslov that I will do nothing to interfere with his running of my flagship. Tell him the crew of the *Leningrad* and every ship in my task force will remain at the disposal of his electronic warfare program as ordered. Tell him we have even requested the West to please refrain from starting a war, so they will not disturb the progress of Russia's toy telephone project until it finally rings in the demise of the Soviet Union."

Garupcheck saluted limply. Before stepping through the cabin hatch, he faced Stalovich and said, "Perhaps someday our political leaders will put their egos aside and listen to our military leaders."

"Perhaps," Stalovich said sadly as he poured himself a shot of vodka. He acknowledged Garupcheck's supportive comment and downed the vodka.

The sea had remained calm, making easier the work being done aboard the *Coral Sea*, and the next day's sky was painted with dismal winter clouds that stretched from horizon to horizon. Except for two restless hours that he forced himself to spend in his cabin bunk, Captain Redding had somberly endured the past twenty-four hours while his crew diligently carried out the task of moving off their ship.

Dozens of seabags were loaded into cargo nets and carried off by helicopters to the flight decks of either the *Forrestal*, the *Ike*, or the *Hawk*. Metal toolboxes, maintenance service rollaways, and cruise kits (huge trunks and footlockers used to accommodate an assortment of gear belonging to each air group squadron) were brought up to the flight deck and staged by the aviation crane on starboard abaft. These and other heavy objects were also loaded into cargo nets and placed aboard launches that served as lighter barges running between carriers. The launches also ferried crews to their new homes at sea aboard one of the other three flattops of the fleet. The carriers even took aboard excess aviation and ship's fuel, water, and food stores. Everything and anything the *Coral Sea* would no longer need was stripped from her holds and decks and distributed among the other ships, all under Redding's poised gaze.

As the hours expired, so did all that constituted life aboard his ship. In a matter of a day, Redding had seen the *Coral Sea* change from a robust city at sea to a ghost town, with only a hint of life left in the aftermath of the mass exodus that was ordered. In his mind he could still hear the vigorous resounding of activity over the decks. It was a harmonious hum of human happiness; a symphony of man and machinery; an orchestration of laughter and labor; a concert of life and love. It lasted for only a brief moment, then was swallowed up by soundlessness. At times he thought he heard whimpering; that, too, lasted for only a brief moment. He wondered if it was a song of sorrow that his ship was singing as she raised higher out of the sea in response to her continual loss of weight. Her continual loss of all that made her a ship at all. The men could be put off their ship, he mused. But the memories they left behind could not be ordered off. They would walk the quiet decks with him; they would offer comfort through the haunting sadness stowed away in silent crew's lounges, lifeless living compartments, empty shops, and deserted passageways.

The ship's complement of jets and propeller planes had winged off the carrier two and three at a time to make their short flight over to the waiting flattops. And when their cargo-shuttling duties were concluded, the *Coral Sea*'s helicopters took up their residency aboard the *Forrestal*, the *Ike* and the *Hawk*. As the deadline for getting the job done neared, only two F-14 Tomcat jets remained aboard, with a tractor to tow them about. The tractor could stay behind, the jets could not.

Helmeted and sealed inside the single-place cockpits of the two F-14's were the regular air group air boss and the catapult and arresting gear division officer. In keeping with tradition they were to pilot the last two planes leaving the ship. In takeoff position at parallel twin catapults on the forward flight deck, they were busily running through their preflight checklists, which required a functional testing of their instruments and controls before becoming airborne. The exhaust cones of their F-14's were glowing cherry red as their dual jet engines screamed through a preflight runup as well. Upon finishing their preflight procedures, and in voice communication with the carrier that was to take them aboard, they gave a thumbs-up gesture to indicate they were ready to go. When the thumbs-up was returned, they gripped their joysticks for the takeoff.

A qualified air boss and former catapult and arresting gear division officer, Lieutenant Commander Jones was filling the billets the communiqué stipulated for having a checked-out arresting gear and Davis barrier specialist remain aboard. He was wearing ear protectors to shield him from the howling jet engines as he stood between the two F-14's and faced the direction of the takeoff. With columns of steam bellowing up from the twin catapults to signify they were set for the launch, he raised both arms straight up in the air and began making twirling motions with his index fingers to cue the pilots to rev up their engines. After a few moments he thrust both hands out in front of him to signal the planes to go, then dropped down to his knees and curled up into a ball to avoid their jet blasts.

In a thunderous roar the two F-14's bolted down the catapult tracks and left the edge of the flight deck in unison. They dropped down below the flight deck when they cleared it, as though they were going to fall into the slow rolling sea ahead and be run over by their own ship. But it was a momentary lapse of lift caused by the sudden change from solid ground to thin air, and they quickly darted skyward. As they climbed for the clouds they banked to the right simultaneously, then began executing a wide coordinated turn back toward the *Coral Sea*.

Jones got out of his crouch and crossed the flight deck to the port catapult. He joined Leading Chief Wally Smith, who was supervising the crew of arresting gear and Davis barrier technicians who'd been hand-picked by the leading chief to remain aboard. As Jones removed his ear protectors he called out, "Okay, Smitty! That's the end of a beautiful romance between ship and planes. Have your arresting gear crew secure the forward catapults, then stand by to bring the BUSHIPS delegation aboard."

"Aye, aye, sir," Chief Smith said, then regarded his flight deck detail. "All right, you bunch of cable stretchers! Shake your fannies and secure forward cats port and starboard. We have an inbound chopper to receive next."

As Jones crossed the flight deck he noticed that the two F-14's he'd just launched had circled around behind the *Coral Sea* and were now at a low altitude some distance astern of the carrier, as though they were on final approach to land back aboard. It took him only a split second to deduce what the two pilots were up to, and he rushed over to the island and charged up to the bridge deck. Arriving there winded, he gasped, "Skipper, hurry out to the port catwalk. The air boss and his wingman are about to pay you a final tribute, jet jockey-style."

Redding hurried out to the bridge catwalk with Jones right on his heels. He looked down the length of the deserted flight deck as the two F-14's streaked toward the rear of the ship. At what he guessed was an altitude of no more than fifty feet, they flew in tight formation over the flight deck from stern to bow, rocking their wings from side to side in a customary aviator's good-bye salute. As soon as they had passed the island, they soared skyward and executed a corkscrew climbout that had them virtually standing on their tails in the sky. Then, as a second offering of their acrobatic tribute, they separated from each other like peeling sections of a banana skin and executed a spiraling dive that stood them on their noses. When they leveled off above the surface of the sea, they regrouped for a series of wingovers as a finale, then darted off for the carrier that was to be their new home at sea.

Redding highballed a hand salute after the pilots as they whisked off. "Crazy jet jockeys!" he shouted after them. "Have a few ice cold beers waiting for us when we get back home!"

As they headed back into the bridge, Jones asked, "On a scale from one to ten, how would you rate the air show given in your honor, Skipper?"

"I'd rate it worthy of a profound ten," Redding said. "Real Blue Angel quality. But if Admiral Hollingsworth caught the show, he's going to rate it worthy of an ass reaming. Real daredevil quality."

In the CIC room below the bridge, where a host of vital radar, sonar, and plotting stations were normally manned around the clock, just one sonarman and one radarman were on duty as part of the ferrying crew. The radarman had his eyes glued to his yellow-faced scope as he began monitoring a defined blip. He tracked it for bearing, heading, and speed, then keyed his P.A. mike. "Bridge, from CIC. We have a chopper inbound VOR. Bearing, three six zero. Range is fifty miles. Heading one-eight-zero. Speed is eighty knots."

Next, the radio operator called out from the radio shack, "Skipper, I have the inbound chopper on VHF. It's Air Force one three oh out of Istanbul with the BUSHIPS delegation aboard and requesting permission to land."

"Permission granted," Redding returned. "Tell the chopper pilot to look for our flight deck handling crew abreast of the island." He turned to Jones. "Lay down to the flight deck to welcome our distinguished passengers, Jonesy. I'll receive them in my cabin as soon as they are settled aboard."

CHAPTER FIFTEEN

"This must not be so!" Mishka Borken cried out in alarm after listening intently to what Nadia had told her.

"I wish it was all just a horrible nightmare that I could merely awaken from," Nadia returned.

It was Sunday afternoon, and as promised, Nadia had left Viktor at the guesthouse to keep her luncheon meeting with Mishka back in Kiev. But the luncheon plans and their plans to take in that afternoon's ballet performance were now canceled. Instead, Nadia encouraged Mishka to take a stroll with her along the icy banks of the Dnieper River, where they could talk privately. There, under a cloudy afternoon sky with brisk winds swirling in from the chilling waters of the Dnieper, Nadia revealed in detail what had happened to her since she had left to keep her rendezvous with Viktor on Friday night.

"I feel responsible for helping you keep those secret meetings with Viktor," Mishka sobbed. "I feared they would somehow lead to tragedy. Now they have!" She stopped walking to face Nadia. "If I had been a better friend to you, I would have talked you out of this impossible love affair. Then," she sobbed on, "all this would not have happened."

"Do not blame yourself, my Mishka," Nadia insisted. "It would have happened, no matter what you might have done to discourage me. Even in the face of death itself, Viktor and I would have not been discouraged from loving each other."

"But what will you do?" Mishka asked.

"We will go ahead with the defection," Nadia said.

"You will be killed for sure, Nadia," Mishka said woefully. "Either you will be shot down by pursuit planes, or you will crash-land aboard this aircraft carrier of the Americans. Even if you do make it that far, how can you be sure the Americans will not put you before a firing squad once they have no more use for you?"

"Viktor and I face certain death if we do not go," Nadia

reasoned. "By defecting, we at least have a hope that we will land safely aboard the American carrier and be allowed to love each other in peace."

"If you will not change your mind, then I will defect as well," Mishka insisted.

"There is no reason for you to defect, Mishka," Nadia argued. "You have no political grievances to motivate you. And you are not entangled in an otherwise hopeless love affair."

"We have our friendship to protect," Mishka argued back. "If you defect, what will I do without you as my dearest friend?"

Nadia looked out at the river on hearing a chugging sound. It was a tugboat pulling a barge loaded with coal. She blankly stared on as the blunt bow of the tugboat plowed through the chilly water, its smokestack sending billowing columns of black smoke up into the dismal sky as it labored along its course. When it passed abreast of them out in the middle of the Dnieper, she faced Mishka. "You will be strong and go on with your own life, my dear Mishka. It is what you would have had to do if I stayed in the Soviet Union, only to be taken from your side and forced to join my husband in Moscow."

"Somehow that no longer seems as terrible," Mishka said tearfully as she gazed out at the tugboat. "At least I could visit you in Moscow. If you go to America . . . I will never see you again."

"If fate is kind, we will be reunited somehow, my dear Mishka," Nadia said, her eyes filled with tears as well. "If not, we will always be together in our thoughts of each other."

Mishka exchanged a long hug with Nadia, then said, "I will be questioned about your defection because our party leaders know how close we are to each other. But I give you my word, I will die before I will betray you."

"You will not have to fear being questioned, Mishka," Nadia insisted. "I would not put you through such an ordeal. Viktor and I plan to make it appear as though we experienced mechanical difficulty and were forced to ditch in the sea, never to be heard of again. We will even be aided by the Turkish government, which will claim it intercepted Mayday calls from a Soviet Foxbat in distress."

"When do you plan to go?" Mishka asked sadly.

"During tomorrow's training sortie," Nadia replied.

"Tomorrow!" Mishka exclaimed.

"And you can be of immense help this one last time," Nadia said.

"I will do anything for you, of course," Mishka pledged.

"You are such a dear friend, Mishka. How can I stand before you and ask any more of you?" Nadia cried.

"You can because that is what dear friends are for," Mishka said, attempting to regain her composure. She took out a handkerchief and gently blotted the tears rolling down Nadia's cheeks. "Now, what is it you must ask of me this last time?"

Pulling herself together, Nadia said, "We will break away from the others in our group when the turn is being executed over Odessa. Then, as the group heads back for Kiev, we will continue across the Black Sea and head for Turkish airspace in afterburners. When we are out over the Mediterranean, we will broadcast our Mayday call and drop down to the lowest possible altitude so it will appear as though we ditched into the sea. From there we will fly south until we rendezvous with the American aircraft carrier."

"But what is it you wish me to do?" Mishka questioned.

"As wing leader, Viktor is going to order all student pilots to man the controls during the training sortie. And he is going to ensure that your Foxbat flies our wingman position. That way your Foxbat and ours will be the last two planes of the wing group to make the turn for the return flight to Kiev. Without being conspicuous, do your best to keep your right wing banked steeply so that your flight instructor's view of our Foxbat will be obstructed when we go into afterburners and continue on south. Do you think you can do that, Mishka?"

"My flight instructor is a lazy drunk during the week," Mishka said. "Coming back from his weekend pass in Kiev, he will be a sleepy drunk, trying his best to recover from his hangover. If he remains awake at all through our jamming and antijamming exercises with Odessa, he will be so bleary-eyed he will have difficulty seeing the rows of instruments directly in front of him, much less your Foxbat."

"Then we can count on you to cover up our initial breakout from the rest of the group?" Nadia asked. She was given a reassuring nod. "Good. That will add invaluable moments to our escape." She looked into Mishka's watery eyes. "Again, it should appear to any of the other flight instructors and student pilots in the wing that our sudden detachment from the group is due to an unanticipated and uncontrollable mechanical failure. If for any reason we are suspected of defecting, do nothing to suggest you are aiding us. And if you are questioned when you get back to Kiev, deny any knowledge of a planned defection.

Needless to say you must also deny any knowledge of the love affair between Viktor and me. I would hate myself forever if I learned that you were punished for what Viktor and I are responsible for."

"Is there anything else you require of me, Nadia?" Mishka asked in a compassionate tone.

"Only that you swear you will always be my dearest friend, and that you will forgive me for leaving you."

Using their last opportunity, they affectionately hugged and kissed each other good-bye, and Mishka said through more sobbing, "Of course I forgive you. And you promise always to regard me as your dearest friend."

"I promise, Mishka," Nadia cried. "I promise with all my heart."

"Come. We have time for a farewell toast before we catch the bus back to the air base."

They climbed the steps leading up from the banks of the Dnieper, their military boots making crunching noises in the snow. They made their way across a busy boulevard to a nearby inn to numb their heartbreak.

CHAPTER SIXTEEN

Redding stepped out on the bridge catwalk as the air force helicopter lowered from the sky and set down on the *Coral Sea*'s flight deck. He looked on with interest when four, instead of three, members of the BUSHIPS delegation emerged. All of them were wearing one-piece, dark blue regulation air force flight suits that were zippered up to their necks, and bright orange flight helmets that gleamed even under a sunless sky. The puffed-out chest area of one of the flight suits indicated the female member of the delegation. Seeing her remove her flight helmet and toy with her long silky hair, he decided she was not what he had imagined. He had expected some hefty middle-aged woman with a plump face and a double chin. *Very nice*, he thought. *Very*.

What got Redding's attention next—and puzzled him—was the strange looking luggage being offloaded from the helicopter. There were the usual canvas and leather bags that would normally contain clothing and grooming articles, but there were also four shiny aluminium cases that closely resembled the electronic testing equipment kits the air group maintenance personnel had taken away with them earlier that day. It seemed to him to be an odd assortment of gear for a party of administrative civilians to need, just to conduct a transfer of ship's ownership between governments. He shrugged his shoulders at the items, then hurried below to his cabin as the helicopter lifted skyward.

"Welcome aboard the U.S.S. *Coral Sea*, folks," Jones said in greeting the delegation. He exchanged introductions and handshakes, then added, "Ship's skipper is Captain Tom Redding. He'll meet all of you once you're settled aboard."

"We'll have plenty of time to get settled after we meet your skipper," Ferris said. He gestured to the sealed manila envelope he had tucked under one arm. "I'm to hand-deliver these special orders to your C.O. right away."

"Very well," Jones returned. "You'll be quartered in officers' country, which is next to captain's country. We might as well haul your gear along with us." He waved to three enlisted men of his flight deck crew. "Bear a hand in getting this personal gear below to the oh three level, sailors." Gesturing to an open island hatch he added, "The skipper is in his cabin office. Follow me, please."

Baxter felt right at home aboard the flattop as he followed Jones and Ferris down a spiral steel staircase to the level below the flight deck. But he wasn't used to such an absence of life aboard a carrier. With experienced eyes he took note of objects missing from their customary places as they made their way through air group and CPO country to reach officers' and captain's country. Pictures of a squadron's aircraft and personnel were usually hung on the walls of the air group's sleeping compartments and ready (flight briefing) rooms. And there were usually awards proudly on display in showcases, and pilots' helmets and other flight crew garb draped over tables and chairs, or hanging from coatracks. Instead, there was an eerie air of lifelessness everywhere, as though all living things aboard had been destroyed by some plague that had left only the shell of the ship. It was a weird sight, and he disliked it immensely.

To Trish Darrol the lack of noise and activity aboard this, the first aircraft carrier she had ever visited, seemed peaceful and reassuring. The atmosphere was like that of NSA's subterranean computer center at Fort Meade. Except that instead of countless doorways connecting endless corridors there were countless steel hatches connecting endless tube-like tunnels. And there was the same low-pitched murmur of air conditioning. Even the fluorescent lighting was the same: substitute sunlight within windowless walls. She decided she was going to feel at home aboard the carrier. Right down to the last dull detail of the military decor.

Along on the journey to chaperon Trish Darrol and assist her in her impending scrutiny of the MIG-35 Foxbat was Walter Dodge. He was an ambitious computer systems analyst, thirty-five and quite handsome, who found his role as understudy to the top NSA computer specialist to be both educating and enjoyable. He also found Trish to be the top looker of the host of females he came in contact with at Fort Meade daily. He had a secret desire to exchange their professional rapport for a more personal one, but in the two years he had served as her assistant he found that the only music Trish liked to hear was the hum of computer machinery. Accepting that he could learn a great deal from her on the job, but would never get the opportunity to teach her anything in bed, he kept his sexual interest in her a secret. But he continued to sneak glances at her shapely breasts, her round buttocks, and her sexy legs whenever he could. Right now, as he stepped through hatch after hatch behind her, he was gazing hungrily at her rump—camouflaged by her air force flight suit into bulky bumps and puffy pleats. He didn't like the military garb on her at all and was looking forward to seeing her in the Jordache jeans he knew she had brought along as work clothes. The Jordache jeans, he thought, would really do her buttocks justice.

Ferris, too, had been looking forward to seeing Trish in her Jordache jeans. He had had no more than a glimpse of them before she stepped into her flight suit back in Istanbul. That had been a bit of a disappointment, but it was nothing like the disappointment he found her attitude to be. He had hoped to warm up to her during the *Coral Sea* voyage, and if things really went well he might have put her through a meltdown before the cruise was over. The anticipated meltdown was turning out to be a freezeover.

From the very first moment of their being reunited, Trish had given Ferris the cold shoulder. During the flight to the carrier, she'd paid him only a skimpy smile and a chintzy nod as he'd tried to make conversation. And she had done that most begrudgingly. The icy treatment made him recall the sour note they'd left off on back in Hal Banks's office. He thought they had made a truce, but it was now obvious that the truce had been one-sided. He resolved if she was going to continue acting like a childish schoolgirl he wasn't going to let it bother him. He didn't have to get along with her to accomplish the mission—he just preferred to. Now he was going to be just as much of a cold cucumber as she was. Now it was going to be a hands-off relationship instead of hands-on. Now he knew just where he stood with her for the duration of the mission, which Hal Banks had for some reason renamed Operation Mediterranean Maneuver. In thinking about Hal Banks, he decided that his CIA boss and Trish Darrol were two peas in a pod. They were both all business. And like Mondays, they both sucked.

Jones opened Redding's cabin door and stood to one side invitingly. When everyone was inside he introduced them and said, "Mr. Ferris wanted to meet with you before getting settled aboard, Skipper."

Ferris took it from there, revealing everyone's actual identities and their specific purpose for being aboard the carrier. He did so under the stunned eyes and dumbfounded expressions of both Redding and Jones. "These are your written orders from Washington," he concluded as he handed Redding the sealed manila envelope. "They spell out in detail what Operation Mediterranean Maneuver entails, and they authorize you to place your ship at my disposal to carry out the mission."

Redding seated himself at his desk and studied the orders for long moments, then looked up at Ferris and asked in a disapproving tone, "Why my ship? Why not pick one of the newer carriers?"

"As a ship slated to be scrapped anyway, your carrier is the most expendable considering the risk involved in effecting a landing never attempted before," Ferris said.

"Terrific!" Redding said acidly. "The *Coral Sea* is expendable! That's terrific as all hell! Tell me, did the hotshots at BUSHIPS and BUAIR who dreamed up this ludicrous stunt decide my crew is expendable, too?"

"I'm the hotshot that dreamed up the idea, Captain Redding," Baxter volunteered.

Redding switched his stare from Ferris to Baxter. "Did you say your rank in the navy is L.C., Mr. Baxter?" he asked in a challenging tone. He was acknowledged with a nod. "And what duties do you perform as a lieutenant commander that qualify you to make such a proposal?"

"I am presently an F-14 pilot with carrier-borne billets," Baxter returned. "And I was a MIG-25 flight instructor."

"You were what?" Redding asked in surprise.

"He was Soviet Air Force Colonel Nikoli Belinsky," Ferris put in. "He is now also a Russian language instructor for the navy."

"Oh, yes," Redding said through several nods. "I've heard about you. I read your saga in the newspapers at the time of your defection. A most intriguing story. I had no idea you were made a CIA covert operative."

"I wasn't," Baxter corrected. "I'm on temporary assigned duty with the CIA for this mission because of my past Soviet Air Force experience. I talked to the two Soviet pilots who plan to defect and fly aboard your ship tomorrow," he added. "I evaluated the specifications they furnished me on the MIG-35 they fly. Then I took into account my own knowledge of a Foxbat class jet. In adding that information to my experience as a carrier pilot, I believe I can make a qualified judgment about the proposed carrier landing."

"Which is?" Redding probed.

"Aided by the Davis barrier, we feel confident we can bring their Foxbat aboard with marginal risk to ship and crew."

"Marginal risk?"

"That's right, sir," Baxter said. "The mission consultants at both BUAIR and BUSHIPS who were involved in evaluating the feasibility of such a Davis barrier arrested landing concluded that with the major complement of aircraft and personnel taken off the ship, and only a ferrying crew left aboard, the risk to life and property would be minimal."

"Exactly what is at stake?" Redding asked.

"One of our spy satellites at NSA is being tampered with by what we believe to be a highly sophisticated electronics warfare system the Soviets have developed," Trish explained. "If we can't overcome the jamming techniques, our satellite spying activities at Fort Meade will be nullified."

"That's only a small part of the dilemma," Ferris interjected. Trish glared at him for downgrading NSA's importance. "CIA has established that the new Soviet electronic warfare apparatus has also affected one of our early warning missile tracking satellites. With the possibility existing that such a technique could develop into a widespread jamming of our missile tracking satellites, the problem becomes a threat to our national defense. And that takes priority over NSA's problems."

Redding detected a hint of interdepartmental rivalry between two of his visitors and commented, "I hope you'll excuse my intruding on all this NSA and CIA interplay, but aren't the Russians going to be spitting mad if we steal one of their Foxbats?"

Trish shifted her eyes from Ferris to Redding. Speaking confidently she said, "We anticipate that they'll never know we did. I'm certain I can solve the computer hardware and software puzzle we expect to find aboard the MIG-35 that's landing aboard your carrier. And I hope to do so in a matter of twenty-four hours or less. Once I do we will have two options. One, reveal to the Soviets that we have uncovered their new top secret electronics warfare weaponry, and have thus nullified its effectiveness. Two, keep our discovery a secret from them. We could use the antijamming features of the new jamming and antijamming technology to go on spying on their military intelligence communications, but let them continue to believe we no longer have the capability to eavesdrop. They would continue broadcasting their secret armed forces and political communications, thinking they were doing so undetected, thus allowing us to compile and correlate a host of invaluable data on their strategic operations."

"In other words it'll be like having the Russians on *Candid Camera*," Jones offered.

"Something like that," Trish returned proudly. "All I need is time to scrutinize the apparatus aboard the MIG-35."

"And what better place is there to hide one of their Foxbats while the probing of their technology takes place, than aboard an aircraft carrier making a slow voyage to Egypt?" Baxter added.

"If I manage to crack their secrets between here and Egypt, then we can remove whatever black boxes we need for further study, and bury the Foxbat in deep water while en route," Trish offered. "I think we can safely assume the Soviets will presume their missing Foxbat and two pilots perished in a ditching at sea."

"And what if you are unable to crack their new top secret equipment en route?" Redding asked.

"Then we'll cut the Foxbat up into crate-size pieces and offload it in the port of Alexandria," Trish answered. "From there it will be trucked to an Egyptian Air Force base, where a team of computer experts will examine it more leisurely. If all else fails, we'll ship it to the United States and go over every inch of it until we do figure how the new technology works."

"There's a minor detail you've overlooked that may leave us in a very embarrassing way en route," Redding put it. His statement drew all eyes his way. "Per orders I received from COMLANT and COMSIX, I've stripped my ship of all its defenses. That sort of leaves us out here in the Med naked as jaybirds. To put it bluntly, all I have left aboard to fight with are a few M-16's and some .45's. That, in my professional opinion, isn't much of an arsenal to point at the Russian Navy if it should track its MIG-35 to this ship and demand that both Foxbat and defectors be returned, or else."

"That possibility has been carefully weighed by the chief of naval operations, commander Atlantic Fleet, and commander Sixth Fleet," Ferris said. "For one thing, the two defectors have been instructed to fly out to meet you below radar detection altitude. For another, the communiqué you received about transferring the ownership of the *Coral Sea* to the Egyptians was expected to be intercepted by the Soviet task force out here in the Med with your fleet. We anticipate they will have little or no interest in following a stripped-down aircraft carrier when there are two other carriers of more interest to them in the area. Finally, a second communiqué intended for them to intercept will disclose that the carriers *Eisenhower* and *Kitty Hawk* are being deployed to the western end of the Mediterranean to practice some tactical aerial operations with our NATO fleets. We expect the news will lure the Soviet task force to the opposite end of the Med from where your ship will rendezvous with the Foxbat pilots."

"And with the *Ike*, the *Hawk*, and the Soviet task force sailing a course due west of here, and your ship on a heading to the south, it's highly unlikely that you'll need any firepower en route," Baxter added.

"What if the CNO, COMLANT, and COMSIX are wrong and the Soviet fleet doesn't fall for the deception?" Jones asked. "What then?"

"Then we'll just have to give a shout for reinforcements," Baxter said. "But have you ever failed to see the Soviet Navy shadow our major task force around the Med in the past?"

"You have a point there," Jones agreed.

"I must admit, it sounds like the lure might hook the fish," Redding said. "That is, if our fleet does manage to draw the Soviet task force away from us in its entirety. If one single ship tags along with us, that'll deep six your Foxbat landing."

"If I may interject, Skipper," Jones said, "the idea of a Foxbat carrier landing may have to be scrubbed, anyway."

"Why is that?" Ferris asked.

"Not being designed to make landings aboard aircraft carriers, the MIG-35 is probably loaded down with extra armament," Jones said. "In coming aboard it may give our flight deck such a pounding that it'll crash through to the damn hangar deck. And that's just for openers. We may also be faced with a problem of an oversized aircraft as well as an overweight one. All of our carrier-borne aircraft have foldable wings so they can fit into tight places aboard. Their foldable wings also allow them to be accommodated by the deck-edge elevators so they can be taken below to the hangar deck, which is where you'll surely want to accomplish your secret probing of the Foxbat. Finally, a carrier-borne aircraft has a landing speed built into it that is usually much slower than a land-based aircraft. We can't be sure the Davis barrier will stand up to the impact of a jet with a greater landing speed than the barrier is engineered to handle. Were these pertinent factors considered when deciding on a Davis barrier arrested landing?"

"Our communiqué instructed you to keep aboard the most qualified specialist on Davis barrier landing apparatus," Ferris said.

Redding gestured to Jones. "My X.O. *is* the most qualified man for the job. And he just gave you his analysis of what you're up against."

"Well, the consensus of available experts was that the law of probability was in our favor," Baxter said. "As far as the flight deck holding up through the landing is concerned, if it can withstand the pounding of one of our bomber-size aircraft, it should endure the weight of a MIG-35 easily. And as for fitting into tight spaces aboard, the MIG-35 has a delta-wing configuration, just like that of our F-14, only shorter from wing tip to wing tip. To be precise its wingspan is forty-four feet, zero inches. The span of an unswept winged F-14 is sixty-four feet, one and a half inches. Even with its wing tips folded, our F-14's wingspan is greater than a MIG-35 without folding wing tips, so we should have no problem fitting a Foxbat on your deck-edge elevators."

"As you can see, Lieutenant Commander Baxter did his homework before coming aboard," Ferris said.

Baxter winked at Ferris. "The landing speed of a MIG-35 is somewhat faster than any jet aircraft a carrier normally accommodates. But if we could somehow reinforce the Davis barrier to withstand a slightly greater impact, then with a good, strong head wind to also help offset its faster landing speed, we should be able to catch the Foxbat in the barrier nicely."

"Chief Smith and I could try to work out some sort of added reinforcement to the Davis barrier," Jones agreed. "But the prevailing winds for tomorrow will be a matter for the big skipper in the sky. Too bad we had to TX our ship's chaplain, he could have said a few good words for you in that department."

"We'll get the winds we need," Ferris said. "No offense to your ship's chaplain, but my boss is praying his ass off for this gig of his to work. And short of the pope, no one is in tighter with God than Hal Banks."

"What's the E.T.A. of your Foxbat?" Redding asked.

"About noon tomorrow," Ferris said. "The senior pilot aboard the plane was furnished with a short-range radio receiver-transmitter that can operate on our frequencies. He'll be calling in at a point about fifty miles out from our position." He gestured to Baxter, "Nick, you take it from there."

"I also have LSO billets, and I speak fluent Russian. I plan to talk the Foxbat pilots aboard . . . if that meets with your approval, sir."

"I have no one aboard that speaks Russian, anyway," Redding said. "You might as well handle them as a former Russian yourself." He regarded his X.O. "Jonesy, do you think you and Smitty can rig the Davis barrier supports in that amount of time?"

"I'm sure we can if we put every available man on the detail, Skipper."

"Then you do just that," Redding said.

"I'll bear a hand in getting the task accomplished," Baxter offered.

"That's a go," Jones said. "With only a token arresting gear crew left aboard, and our ferrying crew tied up with running the ship, I'll accept all the help I can get."

"We'll all pitch in and help," Ferris promised.

"Good," Redding said. "Now for a course and speed setting."

"We'll need the course to be due south, and at the slowest speed possible until the Foxbat makes radio contact with us," Baxter said. "Then we'll need to come about as sharply into a head wind as we can."

"Very well," Redding said. "Get your gear stowed aboard. We'll have a no-frills chow call in the wardroom in about an hour, then we'll all turn to on rigging the flight deck for the landing." He got up from his desk. Passing his eyes over everyone in the room, he said, "Personally, I think this landing is impossible. But, you've come to a ship that's quite accustomed to doing the impossible."

As Ferris followed the others out of Redding's cabin, he decided that the *Coral Sea*'s commanding officer was his kind of man. A man who thinks no but does the opposite. It seemed to him as he was being shown to a vacant sleeping compartment in officers' country that a carrier landing of a Foxbat was going to prove to be an extremely unorthodox event. A great deal depended upon favorable head winds and the reinforcement job that was to be done on the Davis barrier. Baxter's job as linguist and the man with the paddles were also crucial. But most important was the hands-on performance of the two Foxbat pilots. No matter what anyone did aboard the carrier, they would be the only ones who had any control over the situation once the wheels of their MIG-35 touched down on the flight deck.

Haunting Ferris was the horrifying possibility that the Foxbat pilots might panic and elect to ditch in the sea. There was also a good chance they might misjudge their approach and cream into the stern of the ship, or make a hard enough landing to splatter them and their MIG-35 all over the flight deck. Right now he was pretty damn glad he wasn't facing that hairy hands-on gig. Especially on a goddamn Monday.

CHAPTER SEVENTEEN

Monday morning's electronic warfare exercise with the domed facility in Odessa had never seemed longer, and the time had never passed slower for Viktor. He was in the forward cockpit of Foxbat 104, again serving the six-plane flight training group as wing leader. That gave him freedom to think about what he was to do when Odessa mission control dismissed his group and he ordered the other five Foxbats to return to Kiev. Defecting, and all that it would mean to all he left behind, daunted him. The breakout from the others, which was now only ten minutes away, had the adrenaline running hot through his body. He ran his eyes over the rows and ranks of indicators more meticulously than he ever had before, partly to make sure they had every chance of making it all the way, partly because he was getting the eleventh-hour jitters and was secretly wishing something would give him an excuse to back out before it was too late. He could find no such excuse: all indications suggested that everything was functioning perfectly.

In the cockpit behind Viktor, Nadia divided the slow-passing time between flying the plane and performing the jamming and antijamming functional tests requested of her and the other Foxbats by the mission control sector leader. During the intervals she spent a brief moment looking out her canopy at Mishka, who was flying wingman position off their left wing. Nadia was well aware that the moment to take her last glance at her dear friend was quite near. And she was quite frightened over what she and Viktor faced when that moment did come. But the fearful events ahead of them were somehow distant at the moment, as though she had taken a tranquilizer to put such worries to sleep. She hadn't though. What was causing her to feel indifferent to the impending danger was her sadness. She wanted to defect. Wanted to because it was her only hope of having Viktor. But she was also being haunted by a secret wish that somehow she could have Viktor without losing Mishka. She raised her helmet sun visor for an instant to wipe away a tear. Then she saw Mishka looking over at her, and another tear replaced the first.

The slow-passing time had also been taxing for Mishka. She was at the controls in the rear cockpit of Foxbat 116, while her flight instructor was sleeping off his weekend hangover as she had predicted he would. She, too, was plagued with mixed emotions. As a loving friend she wanted happiness for Nadia, yet her own happiness depended so much on having Nadia around. She saw Nadia face forward inside her cockpit when the mission control sector leader's voice crackled a command over the aircraft radio. She looked forward as well, anticipating what might be the last phase of testing they would be required to perform for the day's exercise. She bit down on her lower lip inside her oxygen mask as she watched the second hand of her cockpit clock close out the final minute of the training flight. The final minute of her cherished friendship with Nadia.

Viktor stiffened in his seat as the order to return to Kiev sounded in his helmet earphones. He acknowledged the mission control sector leader, then keyed his mike again and announced, "Flight group from flight leader. In formations two abreast and in succession execute left turn for home base." His order was acknowledged as the first two Foxbats banked to make their turn to the north. After a brief interval the second two Foxbats reported they were executing their left turn for Kiev. He keyed his mike once more. "Foxbat one one six, on my command execute your left turn."

Her voice unsteady, Mishka acknowledged Viktor. Then, as the command to execute her turn came, she noticed her flight instructor stretching in the front cockpit to shake off his catnap. Without delay and as promised, she put her Foxbat into a steep left bank that sent her right wing pointing up to the sun. Her move caused Foxbat 104 to disappear immediately from view off her right wing. Her instructor keyed his intercom and began reprimanding her for the unnecessarily steep bank, but she kept her Foxbat standing on its left wing for a few precious extra moments as she said under her breath, *Good-bye, Nadia, my dearest friend. Good-bye and good luck.*

Viktor clicked his intercom mike button twice rapidly to alert Nadia he was making his breakout. Then, taking over the controls, he banked sharply to the right and went into afterburners. The sudden action sent their Foxbat bolting away from Foxbat 116 and caused him and Nadia to be thrust back tightly into their shoulder harnesses. In a matter of seconds he was thundering toward the distant northern coastline of Turkey, with Foxbat 116 fading rapidly behind the twin tails of his MIG-35. His next maneuver, which he executed without delay, was to put his nose into a steep dive toward the choppy surface of the Black Sea. He dropped rapidly to an altitude that would put them beneath the floor of radar detection.

The Foxbat's dual engines were gleaming bright red and spilling a trail of black exhaust behind them as they responded in afterburners to Viktor's demands upon them. Then, some hundred feet above the tossing sea, Viktor pulled back fiercely on his joystick to climb out of his dive. That leveling-off maneuver caused the sweptback wings to shudder as they fought the gravitational forces on their surfaces. The Foxbat finally did nose up at less than fifty feet above the tossing Black Sea. It continued its race to the south, picking up the surface of the sea as it skimmed over the whitecaps thunderously. Left in the aftermath of the urgent breakout was a trail of salt spray and exhaust that stood up in a column of commotion behind the Foxbat's dual tails before falling back down to the choppy water.

"You have lost our wing leader's plane, Comrade Borken!" Senior Flight Lieutenant Antonov Borovek growled over the intercom from the front cockpit of Foxbat 116. As he continued to search the sky to his left and right, he said, "We were to make a turn to the left in a coordinated formation position with Foxbat 104. What were you thinking of when you rolled us over and stood us on our left wing?"

"I . . . overreacted to the flight leader's command," Mishka lied. She smiled behind her oxygen mask. There wasn't a sign of Foxbat 104 ahead of them or to either side of them. She envisioned Nadia and Viktor speeding away behind her Foxbat toward freedom and that made the risk she took to give them a head start worth the bawling out her flight instructor was giving her.

Borovek keyed his radio mike. "Flight leader from Foxbat one one six! Where are you, over?" He looked above him, then below his wings. Then he craned to look behind him. Again he keyed his radio mike. "Flight Leader from Foxbat one one six, report your position, over!" He waited for a response from the missing Foxbat. One came from Odessa mission control instead. He was informed that Foxbat 104 had failed to turn left for home and had executed a right turn out over the Black Sea instead. He was then told that Foxbat 104 was last tracked heading due south at an accelerated speed and losing altitude rapidly, before it was suddenly lost on radar.

Borovek radioed ahead to the other four Foxbats of the flight group. "Flight group from Foxbat one one six, we have lost sight of our flight leader's plane! Mission Control alerted us that Foxbat one oh four was last seen heading in the opposite direction of Kiev. I am turning back to investigate its status. All planes are to continue on to home base and report my intentions to the squadron leader. Over and out."

Mishka keyed her intercom. "Comrade Borovek, perhaps Foxbat one oh four experienced mechanical difficulties and had to ditch in the sea."

"Perhaps so, Comrade Borken," Borovek said. "We will go into afterburners in that case. If they have ditched, the sooner we learn of that the quicker we can get a rescue helicopter scrambled to pluck them out of the sea."

"But we may exhaust the fuel we will need to return to home base if we use our afterburners to make a search for Foxbat one oh four," Mishka said. "I suggest we return to base with the rest of our group and order search planes up instead."

Borovek keyed back. "Comrade Borken! Your concern for your own safety at a time when your comrades may be faced with peril disappoints me! As their wingman it is our duty to go after Foxbat one oh four and see if we can lend assistance. I will take full responsibility for that decision, Comrade Borken. And I will take over the controls as well." He gripped his joystick and banked steeply to the left to execute a turn back toward Odessa. As quickly as he got lined up on a southerly pursuit heading, he went into afterburners. Within seconds he passed over the domed facility and ordered Mishka to radio his intentions to mission control as he streaked out over the Black Sea. Mission control advised them that other planes would be scrambled to assist them in the search, but it would be a while before they could arrive in the vicinity where the missing Foxbat was last known to be.

Mishka was gripped by a feeling of helplessness as her flight instructor headed their Foxbat in the direction Viktor and Nadia had gone. She had tried to prevent a pursuit as best she could but had to accept that she could do no more to help. Any further attempt to talk her flight instructor out of his intentions might cause him to become suspicious. She settled back, hands off, behind her controls as Borovek moved them through wing dips from left to right to search the surface of the Black Sea for a downed Foxbat.

Viktor and Nadia had reached the northern coastline of Turkey and had just shut down their afterburners when they overheard Borovek and mission control talking over the aircraft radio about Foxbat 104's sudden disappearance over the Black Sea. On hearing next that Borovek intended to search for them, Viktor elected to go back into afterburners to cross through Turkish airspace as quickly as possible. He was weighing the standing order for all Soviet pilots to avoid entering that country's air corridors without obtaining special clearance from the Soviet high command. And he hoped it was a standing order that Borovek would comply with.

Halfway across the Black Sea and with no sign of a downed Foxbat on its tossing surface, Borovek caught sight of a brilliant burst of light dead ahead of him over the threshold of the northern Turkish shores. The canopy that sealed him soundlessly inside his tandem cockpit shut out any noise that the explosion might have caused, but as a seasoned Foxbat pilot, he only had to see the familiar sudden blast of a jet's afterburners to know what it was.

Borovek keyed his intercom mike excitedly and shouted, "Comrade Borken! I think I have discovered the whereabouts of Foxbat one oh four! Report in to home base and mission control that I have every reason to believe our flight leader and his student pilot have intentions of defecting. Tell base to alert our squadron leader that I intend entering Turkish airspace to give pursuit. Also assure our base commandant I will personally see to it that the defection attempt is foiled. Do so at once, Comrade Borken, while I keep Foxbat one oh four's afterburners in my sights."

Mishka was panic-stricken as she absorbed the gravity of the situation. She knew what Borovek meant when he stressed he would foil the defection. And she knew an all-out scramble would be ordered if she reported that an attempt to defect was in progress. All Soviet planes and ships in the area would join in for the kill, just to be credited for foiling a defection. It was an act of heroism that the party leaders rewarded handsomely.

Again Borovek called back to her and ordered her to radio his suspicions to home base and mission control. At the moment, home base and mission control presumed that the missing Foxbat had ditched in the sea. If she could keep Borovek's suspicions from the homeland, any additional units joining the search would concentrate their efforts in the area of the Black Sea off Odessa. Such a localized search pattern might give

Viktor and Nadia precious extra moments to cross Turkish airspace and execute evasive maneuvers out over the Mediterranean Sea to rid them of Borovek's lone pursuit. Out of desperation she keyed her radio mike button and transmitted their squadron's call sign, but nothing else. Then she held the mike key open so the base's reply couldn't be received. She repeated her ploy several times in the hope that Borovek would be convinced she was earnestly making an attempt to carry out his orders. Still holding the radio mike key open, she keyed her intercom button. "Comrade Borovek, I am getting no reply. Perhaps we are already out of radio range."

At that moment Foxbat 116 entered Turkish airspace and Borovek said back over his intercom, "We may be out of radio range with our base, but we will soon be within shooting range of those two traitors. Arm our heat-seeking missile, Comrade Borken. Foxbat one oh four is just about clear of Turkish airspace. When they are out over the Mediterranean Sea we will fire our rocket and put an end to the chase."

"You are so sure they are defecting that you would shoot them down without confirmation of their intentions?" Mishka protested.

"Even a fool could see that is their intent, Comrade Borken," Borovek insisted. "See if you can raise someone from the Turkish government on your radio. If so, alert them we are attempting to foil a defection and we offer our guarantee that no action will be taken within the boundaries of their shores."

After clearing Turkish airspace Viktor descended to an altitude of fifty feet above the tossing surface of the Mediterranean Sea. He and Nadia had overheard Mishka reciting their squadron's call sign over the air, and they had heard their home base returning Mishka's call. But it was apparent by her repeated call signs that either Mishka was experiencing radio problems, or she was feigning a radio problem for their benefit. It was also apparent that Foxbat 116 was still giving chase, but beyond that nothing was certain. Forced to burn up precious extra fuel by remaining in afterburners, it was now unclear if they would even reach the American carrier after making it to the Mediterranean Sea unscathed.

Borovek heard Mishka calling the Turkish government as he'd ordered her, but a lack of response told him the attempt hadn't succeeded. "Do not bother with the radio any longer, Comrade Borken," he said over his intercom. "If the Turks have made no move to interfere with us by now, they never will. We are almost out over the Mediterranean and clear of their shores. Get ready to fire our heat-seeking missile upon my command."

Mishka moved her hand over to her instrument panel, but she didn't grip the trigger of her missile launcher. She coiled her fingers around one of two pilot ejection levers instead. The one next to her hand was designed to eject her in an emergency. The one her hand was on was to eject the occupant in the front cockpit in the event that the pilot was shot at or wounded in a dog fight, or was otherwise unable to leave the plane unassisted in an emergency.

Foxbat 116 arrived at a point over the Mediterranean that was just clear of the southern Turkish shores. With cold eyes narrowed on the speck in the noon sky that was glittering under the brilliant sun, Borovek dipped the nose of his MIG-35 to enter a shallow dive. Within moments he descended to the altitude he estimated Foxbat 104 was maintaining on its steady southerly heading. Then he pulled his Foxbat's nose up slightly to level off and keyed his intercom. "Now, Comrade Borken! Fire our missile now!"

Staring bitterly at the figure seated in the cockpit in front of her, Mishka yelled, "Never! Never will I kill my dearest friend! I would kill myself first!" She gave the forward ejection lever a firm tug, then gripped the controls.

The suddenness of it all took Borovek by complete surprise. He had expected to see a missile streak out from under the wing of his Foxbat, and race unshakably after the glowing tail cones of Foxbat 104. Instead, his canopy ripped off from its seat with an explosion. And with an immediate second explosion he was hurled skyward. The force tore his radio cable and oxygen feed line out of their flight console connectors. When his upward movement finally stopped, he plummeted toward the chilling surface of the sea like a falling rock, until his parachute was fired open and his plunge was arrested by the chute's white puffy canopy. Descending like a pendulum he eyed the Foxbat he'd been ejected from and took notice of its continued southerly heading. So, it will be three defectors, he thought. He looked down at the choppy sea coming up to meet him and prepared himself for the impending splashdown. "They will pay for their treason!" he grunted. "They will all pay dearly!"

Mishka craned aft in her cockpit and observed her flight instructor's parachute open. She felt she wouldn't have wasted a single tear on the heartless man if it had failed to. She faced forward again and depressed her radio mike. "Nadia! It is me,

Mishka!" she called out. "Wait for me! I had to eject my instructor. He was going to shoot you both out of the sky!"

Nadia keyed her intercom at once on hearing Mishka's voice. "Viktor! Slow down, it is Mishka behind us!" She felt the sudden lag in forward motion as Viktor cut off the afterburners. A few moments later Mishka's Foxbat joined up on their left wing and slowed down to their speed. "Oh, Mishka!" Nadia called out over the radio. "Now you must go with us."

"But of course I will go with you," Mishka said with a hearty wave. "Just tell me what it is that I am to do."

Viktor keyed his radio mike. "You will just fly along with us and maintain radio silence for now. I will give you further instructions when it is time to do so."

Nadia blew Mishka a friendly kiss, which Mishka immediately returned. Then she keyed her intercom. "Will the Americans allow Mishka to land aboard the carrier as well, Viktor!"

Viktor looked out his canopy at the white caps on the surface of the Mediterranean, then keyed his intercom. "The sea is too rough for her to make a safe ditching in. She must be allowed to land aboard the carrier or she might perish." He looked over at Mishka, then added, "If the Americans do refuse to let her land aboard, will we land aboard anyway?"

Without delay, Nadia said, "We will all live through this, or we will all die."

"Then that is the way we will tell the Americans it must be," Viktor said. Thinking on he said next, "It will not be an easy task for Mishka to land aboard if they do permit her to. She does not have the benefit of a radio-receiver-transmitter that operates on their frequencies as we do. That will pose a problem in talking her down onto the carrier's constantly moving flight deck."

"Is there some way to overcome that, Viktor?" Nadia asked anxiously.

After a moment of thought, Viktor answered, "If we have Mishka land ahead of us, by remaining airborne we could serve as a radio relay station for her. We could receive instructions from the carrier over the radio the Americans gave us, then relay them to Mishka over our aircraft radio."

"Oh, Viktor! Can such a thing really work?"

"Can we afford not to try it?" Viktor asked. The silence at Nadia's end was his answer.

Nadia glanced out at Mishka who had no knowledge as yet of what she would be faced with when they reached the American carrier. "I just hope it will work," Nadia said.

Viktor glanced at the elapsed-time clock he'd set in motion when they made their breakout. By correlating his speed and distance with the elapsed time and the position at sea the carrier would be maintaining, he estimated their arrival at the point he was to make radio contact with the U.S.S. *Coral Sea*. "We will soon find out, Nadia," he said in a soft voice over the intercom, then keyed off and fell silent.

CHAPTER EIGHTEEN

The sun was directly over the U.S.S. *Coral Sea* as Baxter took up his position atop the LSO's safety net that was anchored at deck edge on the carrier's port abaft. He connected the electric leads of his khaki jump suit to an electrical outlet; that brought to life the series of tiny green lights that were affixed to the arms, body, and legs of the suit. Then he plugged in the twin paddles, and the matching tiny lights that outlined them gleamed brightly even in peak daylight. The lighted version of the LSO garb was normally used for night operations, but Baxter had decided to furnish the Foxbat pilots with all the visual devices available to aid them in their unorthodox carrier landing. Next, he connected his headset to a jack and keyed the mike with a foot pedal, thus allowing him to keep both hands free for the LSO paddles. "Bridge from LSO for a radio check, over!" he called out.

Redding was on the bridge along with a few of his ferrying crewmen. "I read you loud and clear, Paddles," he replied over his headset mike. He keyed the mike again and called down to the flight deck, "Arresting gear boss, are we ready to receive aircraft?"

"Standby, Skipper," Jones said from his position just forward of the island. He walked beside the network of thick rubber vertical spars and horizonal ribs of the Davis barrier that spanned the width of the flight deck between the port and starboard tension uprights. After completing his final inspection of the emergency landing device, he glanced uneasily at the area of the flight deck behind the barrier that came to an end at the bow. Beyond that leading deck edge was a steep drop to the sea. With his headset extension cord following after him, he returned to his command position and faced the barrier like a conductor addressing his orchestra. "Bridge from flight deck boss! The net is ready to land the catch."

Redding slipped on his hooded parka and baseball cap, then stepped out on the bridge catwalk to join Ferris, Trish, and Walt

Dodge. They were all wearing the regulation navy parkas and baseball caps he had issued them for use during their aboardship stay. "We're as ready as we'll ever be," he said to Ferris. "By the way, didn't I hear you speaking Russian to Baxter?"

"I'm an old language student of his," Ferris said.

Redding handed him a spare headset. "You might as well listen in on the LSO's radio approach handling of the Foxbat. With it all due to take place in Russian, maybe you can serve as my personal interpreter."

"I'll be happy to," Ferris agreed.

Trish glanced down at Baxter as he briefly faced the island. From her perch on the bridge level she thought he looked like a human Christmas tree in his lighted LSO suit. She mused that the garb might someday be favored as a Halloween costume, or as nighttime attire for bike riding and jogging enthusiasts. She eyed the Davis barrier and commented, "That thing looks like a volleyball net to me."

Ferris said, "To me, it looks more like a giant spider web waiting to catch a ferocious fly."

"That's a good analysis," Redding said. "I just hope it works on this fly."

Baxter raised his binoculars and panned the sky. He confirmed what ship's radar had already established; there were no aircraft to be seen in the area. Ship's sonar reported that no surface ships were around, either. But he played his binoculars over the surface of the sea, just to double-check. He let them hang by their neck straps when a Russian-speaking voice came over his headset. He keyed his mike with the pedal and called back in Russian. "Roger, this is Kangaroo! You say you are two Cubs inbound, over?"

"*Two* Foxbats!" Ferris repeated, speaking Russian as well. His expression was a question mark as he passed the news along to Redding in English.

Redding excitedly keyed on and said, "LSO, find out if the other Foxbat is a chase plane."

"I already asked, and that's a negative," Baxter shot back. "There was some sort of snag during the breakout. The second Foxbat had to go along. And according to our Foxbat flight crew, they will not come aboard unless the accompanying Foxbat is also allowed to land."

Trish overheard Ferris discussing the news with Redding and said, "An additional Foxbat could offer us a great advantage, Matt. I could be dealing with the black boxes aboard one while

Walt scrutinizes those aboard the other. By making comparisons between the two aircraft, we might cut our probing of the secret apparatus in half."

Ferris liked the idea of saving time by having a backup Foxbat for comparison. He acknowledged Trish's suggestion with a nod, then faced Redding. "Can the Davis barrier reinforcement withstand two such landings?"

Redding keyed on with his X.O. "Jonesy, I need an evaluation on our chances of having two Foxbats land in your Davis barrier. And I need it on the double."

After a few moments of careful thought, Jones said, "I think the possibility of a second landing depends heavily upon how much damage our support rigging sustains from the first Foxbat."

"And on how quickly we can accomplish some makeshift repairs," Chief Smith added, listening in on the conversation over his headset. "If the major stress points are seriously weakened"—he pointed to the center of the barrier "say around this area where most of the impact will take place, the second Foxbat will have to stay airborne long enough to give us time to reinforce them sufficiently."

Looking right into Ferris's eyes, Redding said, "Jonesy, explain to our mission operations boss what will happen if your makeshift repairs give way to a pounding from a second Foxbat."

Jones gestured to the bow of the ship where the flight deck ended like a cliff edge. "If the second Foxbat tears through the barrier reinforcements and its brakes don't stop it, the damn thing will skid down the flight deck and take a swan dive off the bow."

"And we won't be able to keep the ship from running over both plane and pilots," Redding added. "The Foxbat could rip up our bottom for the length of our hull. That just might sink us. At the very least, it could take out our screws and rudders when the sea spits it out at the stern." He looked away for a moment, then faced Ferris again and said, "I suggest you talk the second Foxbat pilot into ditching or bailing out and spare my ship and crew—and your mission—additional hazard."

Ferris keyed on with Baxter. "Nick, assuming the Davis barrier will hold up to the extra strain, what do you think your chances are of talking both Foxbats aboard?"

Baxter squinted in the direction of the approaching Foxbats. They weren't visible yet, but he envisioned them racing toward the stern of the ship. "I think if they follow my signals diligently we might be okay. We sure as hell can't tell 'em it's no go after we encouraged 'em all the way out here. There's no turning back for 'em now."

"Think you could talk one of them into ditching or bailing out, Nick?" Ferris asked next.

Baxter looked down at the unruly sea passing swiftly under the steel net-like LSO platform he was standing on, then keyed on. "As a pilot myself, I wouldn't let anyone talk me into ditching in those damn whitecaps. Not as long as I had an alternative open to me. There's too much of a chance that the aircraft would flip tail over nose on impact and trap the pilot upside down in the cockpit. That could mean certain drowning for anyone who panics easily."

"What about bailing out, then?" Ferris asked.

"We'd lower a rescue launch," Redding said. "That you could guarantee them."

"Stand by," Baxter said, then radioed the bail-out suggestion to Viktor.

Looking down at the sea, then ahead at the carrier growing larger on the tossing surface ahead of his plane, Viktor keyed his intercom. "They want one of us to bail out. And lacking a receiver-transmitter to avail her of approach control instructions, it would be best if Mishka volunteered."

Nadia silently gazed out at her friend for a long moment, then keyed on with Viktor again. "We will stick to the decision we made before. Either they let both Foxbats land, or we will all bail out and take our chances in the sea together."

Baxter listened to Viktor, then called up to the bridge, "Either you take two Foxbats or none. That seems to be firm, Matt. Viktor intends to remain airborne to relay my approach control instructions to the pilot flying the other MIG-35."

"A radio relay approach?" Redding barked. "This second Foxbat is turning into one hell of a jinx!"

"Today is Monday," Ferris muttered. "We were jinxed from the moment today began."

"All the more reason to forget a second landing," Redding said. "We're taking a terrible chance by trying to bring in a pilot with no prior carrier landing experience as it is. Add the risk of a plane having no direct communication with the LSO, and we're asking for a crash landing that can turn this ship into an inferno. With hardly enough hands aboard to put out a campfire, a fiery crash may force us to abandon ship."

"Matt, Viktor wants your word before the first one lands that you'll take both Foxbats aboard," Baxter said.

In response to Baxter's last message from Viktor, Redding said, "My orders directed me to turn my ship over to you. Along with command of her goes the decision making. All I'm trying to do is protect my ship and your mission from a disastrous outcome."

Ferris took a moment to weigh the possibility of losing all: Foxbats, defectors, carrier, and crew. But realizing his only reason for being aboard the carrier was to give Trish twenty-four hours with a Foxbat, he said with a nod, "Just call me a high roller and get our bow pointed into the wind."

"So be it!" Redding said, then called into the bridge Watch, "All ahead full on a sharp turn to port! Bring us about into the wind and maintain that relative easterly heading until further advised!" He removed a P.A. phone from its cradled mount against the superstructure and announced, "Flight quarters! Flight quarters! All crash crew and fire fighting details man your positions! We are going to receive two incoming aircraft! And we'll treat both as though we were in a down-wind situation! That is all!" His announcement was immediately followed by the shrill sound of the ship's general alarm and a bugle recording that accentuated the order to man flight quarters.

Over the blaring alarm and bugle call, Ferris asked Redding, "What is a down-wind situation?"

"It's a condition where we can't keep the carrier pointed into the wind, which creates havoc for a landing aircraft that depends upon a head wind to help slow its approach. Owing to the fact that your Foxbats land at greater speeds than the aircraft we are accustomed to taking aboard, we'll treat them with the extra precautions taken for a tail wind landing."

"Which are?"

"Doubling the strength of crash crew and fire fighting personnel in light of the double jeopardy involved," Redding said crisply. His aide stepped out to the catwalk and handed him a pair of binoculars as was customary during flight or general quarters. He accepted the binoculars but waved away the battle helmet his aide offered him next out of procedure. He raised the binoculars anxiously to his eyes and trained them in the direction the Foxbats were expected to be approaching from. As the *Coral Sea* turned into the briskly blowing winter wind, he caught sight of the two Soviet planes. They appeared as tiny dots gleaming in the sky as they skimmed the choppy surface of the sea. He lowered his binoculars and keyed his headset mike. "They're inbound at twelve o'clock low."

After taking a last minute glance at the Davis barrier spanning the width of the flight deck behind him, Baxter raised his binoculars and trained them in the direction the two Foxbats were approaching from. They resembled two shining darts racing toward the carrier's port amidships. When they finally turned to get into an approach pattern that would line them up well astern of the carrier, they seemed to be hanging motionless in midair. He pondered the carrier approach demonstration he'd given Viktor and Nadia back in Kiev. All he could hope for now was that they would remember as well. With his LSO paddles at the ready, and his right foot prepared to key his mike pedal, he locked his eyes on the two Foxbats flying a wing-to-wing formation as they banked to the left for their final approach angle of attack.

Holding a close position off Mishka's left wing as they came out of their turn, Viktor was relieved that both Foxbats would be taken aboard. Keying his American band radio mike, he announced, "Kangaroo from Cubs! We are in the slot and ready for final approach instructions, over!"

From the port bridge catwalk, Ferris, Redding, Trish, and Dodge gazed aft hypnotically at the two Foxbats rapidly growing larger astern of the carrier. They watched the flight deck as it rose higher, then dropped lower than the approaching planes in rhythm with the sea's swells. At intervals they glanced over at Baxter as he made a variety of coordinated movements with the LSO paddles he had held out from his left and right sides at arm's length. Mouths open and eyes unflinching they silently stared on.

As well as he could, Ferris translated for Redding the instructions Baxter was giving to Viktor. The exacting responses by the plane on final approach told him the radio relay arrangement was working nicely. He studied Baxter's paddles highlighting the adjustments that were being given verbally; then, relaying the action in English, he said, "The approach is too low!" After a pause, he added, "She got the message all right. She's climbing a little now."

"She?" Redding asked uneasily. Ferris nodded. "Great!" Redding bellowed. "We're making history! We are witnessing the first Foxbat carrier landing, and the first female pilot carrier landing, all in one shot!"

Baxter keyed his radio mike with his pedal and said, "She should lower her landing gear now!" Soon after he gave that command he observed the two main wheels come into view

"Full flaps!" As her flaps were lowered, he made another appraisal of her angle of attack. "Tell her to get her right wing up a little," he said to Viktor, then signaled Mishka with his left paddle to make the desired correction. She was just moments out from the threshold and he wanted her Foxbat straight and level so she'd make the earliest possible contact with the flight deck and have maximum runway.

Flying close by off Mishka's left wing, Viktor had Baxter's lighted paddles ahead and to the right of his aircraft as he relayed to Mishka, "Pick up your right wing just a little. You are forgetting to use your PDI and PHI to judge your axis attitudes."

Holding Baxter's paddle signals ahead and to the left of her cockpit windshield, Mishka acknowledged Viktor, then consulted her pictorial direction and pictorial horizon indicators to gauge the requested correction. She looked out the windshield and was alarmed to discover that the carrier's stern was higher than the nose of her aircraft. Lacking time to ask if she should make a correction, she eased her joystick back and was unnerved when the slight change in her angle of attack gave her excessive lift.

Baxter saw the closing Foxbat suddenly raise higher in the sky. Not wanting the added altitude at the crucial moment of touchdown, he gave Mishka the signal for a wave-off, then keyed his foot mike and urgently called out to Viktor, "Abort! Full throttle! Gear and flaps up! She's way too high! Tell her to circle for another try!"

All eyes watched anxiously from the bridge catwalk as the approaching Foxbat violently increased speed and began to climb skyward again. Its howling engines were ear-piercing as it thundered past the island at eye level, giving all those observing the aborted landing a brief view of the pilot. Then, shifting their gaze forward as though all heads were attached to the darting plane, they stared on wild-eyed as the main landing gear of the Foxbat skimmed the top lateral spar of the Davis barrier. The jet blast vibrated the barrier like a frail tennis net.

"That was too close for my nerves," Redding said.

"For mine, too," Ferris said after exhaling the deep breath he'd held in during the hairy wave-off.

"God! Those planes are huge!" Trish said. She reflected on how the wings of the Foxbat darting past the island seemed to span the width of the ship as though the right wing was going to scrape the wall of the superstructure. "Are you sure they're going to fit aboard?"

"We'll have that answer for you shortly," Ferris said as he eyed the two Foxbats turning to get back into the landing pattern.

"Damage report!" Redding ordered, then watched as Jones and Chief Smith walked the span of the barrier on opposite sides to search for injuries the Foxbat's exhaust blast might have caused.

"None that's apparent," Jones answered for the side facing aft.

"Smitty?"

"Let's just say our reinforcements are blushing a little, thanks to the fanning that Foxbat's jet blast just gave them," Chief Smith commented from the bow side of the barrier.

"Roger that," Redding replied. "LSO, make this next attempt a little less trying on our nerves if you can," he said to Baxter over his headset.

"Affirmative," Baxter replied with a wave of a paddle.

Viktor keyed on with Mishka as they leveled off well behind the carrier for another approach. Sensing Mishka's tenseness, he said, "Nice and easy this time. Make only the moves that are called for. Nothing extra." He gave his fuel indicators a worried glance and their critically low readings made him want to tell Mishka of the importance of her making her landing attempt a success this time. But he knew saying that would only make her more apprehensive and cause more errors in judgment.

"Everything takes place so fast at the end," Mishka complained. "And there is so much to watch . . . so much to do. I don't know if I can make the landing. I might just ruin your chance of getting aboard safely," she sobbed.

Nadia looked out her canopy tearfully at Mishka. She couldn't see her friend's face, but she was sure Mishka was wearing a panic-stricken expression behind her helmet sun visor. She couldn't blame her if she was. After seeing the carrier's flight deck moving up and down in the sea as their Foxbats raced toward the ship's bulky stern, she was glad Viktor was at the controls instead of her. She wished Mishka's fate could be in Viktor's competent hands as well. Keying her radio mike to offer Mishka an encouraging word, she said, "You can do it, Mishka. Just stay calm and do as you are told."

Baxter felt the angle of attack was looking better for a touchdown this time as Mishka brought her Foxbat closer to the threshold. "Gear down!" he said, then saw the landing gear descend. "Full flaps!" He watched the flaps lower. "Down a little!" He waved her down with his paddles. "Now throttle back just a little more."

Beads of sweat were forming across Mishka's forehead as she reduced her speed and lowered her plane. For an instant it looked as though she was going to make contact with the ship below the flight deck and crash into the fantail. But she forced herself to make only the corrections asked for. From well out in the approach pattern the carrier had appeared to be an insanely small object to land on; now as she drew closer to it again, she felt her Foxbat dwarfed by its immense size. That eased a little her earlier ill feelings about making the aircraft carrier landing, even though its flight deck was a far cry from the wide and lengthy runways she was more accustomed to. She judged her landing gear to be at the edge of the ship and locked her eyes on the two paddles guiding her over the threshold.

"Nice! Throttle back!" Baxter called out for Viktor to relay to Mishka. As he did, he brought his paddles down and crossed them in front of him as a cue for Mishka to let her main landing gear make contact with the deck. *The rest is up to her and the barrier*, he thought as he watched the plane touch down.

Speechlessly, Ferris and the others stared as the Foxbat took a bounce just aft of the island. When it touched down again only one main wheel made contact with the flight deck. That caused the plane to pivot to the right and head for the side of the island. He saw the others duck down and take cover behind the bridge wall in anticipation of a collision with the superstructure. But on seeing the other main wheel grab the deck and twist the aircraft away from the island, he relaxed the grip he'd had on the catwalk railing. *Damn Mondays*, he thought.

"Take cover!" Chief Smith shouted when the Foxbat next yawed on its axis toward the angle deck. Then the MIG-35's nose wheel engaged the deck and Mishka brought the plane back on the desired path for the Davis barrier.

"Crash crew, remain at your fire-fighting positions!" Jones yelled. "Here we go!" He looked on as the needle nose of the Foxbat speared into the center of the barrier and applied pressure to the tension uprights. Its speed diminished quickly as the spars and webbing fought to arrest the forward plunge of the plane. Loud noises sang out from the Foxbat as though it were a wild animal fighting to free itself from certain captivity. Then, with half itself wrapped inside the webbing, it surrendered to the Davis barrier's overpowering restraints. Its engines were shut down as crash crewmen charged it with fire extinguishers and wheel chocks. But the chocks were not needed. It stood motionless in the net like a captured beast with all the fight drained out of it.

Chief Smith was unable to move a muscle for a long moment after the plane's forward motion was arrested. He was in a state of shock from seeing Baxter's impossible dream become a reality. *There it was*, he thought. A Soviet MIG had just landed aboard his carrier. That was something for Ripley's "Believe It or Not," he was sure. Seeing the members of his arresting gear crew rush the Foxbat to pluck the pilot out of the cockpit, he shouted, "Crash crew! Secure your fire-fighting gear and bear a hand to push this lead sled out of the barrier! We want to get it below to the hangar deck, on the double!"

Jones tapped one crewman on the shoulder as two others assisted Mishka out of the cockpit. "You ride the brakes, cowboy! They should be no different from any of our own aircraft!" To the tractor driver he ordered, "Get a towline around her nose strut! Stand by to haul her over to number two elevator! We still have another Foxbat to go!"

"Damage report!" Redding shouted into his mike.

Jones joined Chief Smith at the barrier as the Foxbat was being towed off to the deck-edge elevator just forward of the island. "Recoil the barrier," he ordered. When the uprights returned the tension to the webbing he and Smith evaluated the damage. Keying his headset mike, he said, "Damage report is two lateral center spars are spread out of shape, and four vertical ribs at the midway point are torn. We now have a gaping hole smack in the middle."

"Can they be replaced quickly?" Redding asked.

"Negative on replacements," Jones said. "We used what spares we had on the reinforcement job."

"What's the consensus on making repairs, then?" Redding asked as he gazed down at the barrier from the bridge catwalk, eyes searching for the damage.

"Fifteen or twenty minutes if we go like greased lightning, Skipper," Chief Smith answered.

"Mr. Baxter!" Redding said. "Get a fuel status on that remaining Foxbat for me."

Baxter called out to Viktor and the news was bad. "He barely has enough to make this go-around in the landing pattern," he relayed to Redding. "They have to come right in or bail out. And they don't feature doing the latter."

"Tell them they may have no choice open to them if they can't stay airborne for another fifteen minutes, or so," Redding said. "That's how long it's going to take to carry out barrier repairs."

Baxter advised Viktor and Nadia of the problems aboard the carrier, then keyed on with Redding again to pass their intentions along to him. "They are in the slot and are coming aboard, with or without our approval or help. I think we'd better clear them to land. Unassisted, they just may send us all down to Davy Jones's locker."

"Terrific! A couple of headstrong Russians are now running things aboard my ship!" Redding grumbled.

Ferris called down to Jones. "What're our chances of taking the other Foxbat aboard without barrier repairs?"

"On a scale of one to ten I'd reluctantly score it a one," Jones said. He regarded Smith. "What would you give it, Smitty?"

Smith eyed the troubled section of the barrier for a moment, then said, "If we can strengthen the weak spots somehow, I'd say she has a fifty-fifty chance of holding up."

"I'll take those odds," Ferris said. "Do what you can to fill in the gaps, and do it fast. We have no other path open to us, short of shooting the other Foxbat down to stop it from coming aboard."

"Forget shooting them down. We have no weapons aboard to do that, either," Redding reminded him.

"Bear a hand, sailors!" Smith called out. "Let's turn to on making repairs. We've a plane on final approach."

Frantically, the arresting gear crew threw themselves into the repair work under the supervision of Jones and Smith. As they weaved nylon tie-down lines into a makeshift patch to reinforce the tear the first Foxbat had made in the barrier, the second Foxbat closed on the ship.

His back to the repair efforts, Baxter held his paddles out and prepared to guide the fast approaching plane down onto the flight deck. Guide it down was all he would be able to do, now that Viktor insisted he could not afford to take a wave-off. With exhaust trailing out behind the plane like a kite tail, he signaled it lower with his paddles as he keyed his foot mike. "Gear down! Flaps down! Throttle back!"

"That's it! Hit the catwalks!" Jones shouted as the Foxbat neared the stern edge of the flight deck. His command sent crewmen jumping into the deck-edge pits for cover, abandoning the final stages of the hurried repairs.

The last to take his hands off the Davis barrier and rush after the others, Smith called out as he ran for the catwalks, "Crash crew! Man your fire-fighting gear on the double!"

Viktor could see by the position of Baxter's paddles that he was crossing the threshold a little too high. He throttled back and forced his nose down to reduce his lift. The plane bounced hard as it dropped down onto the deck, sending puffs of white smoke out from the tires. The impact jarred the plane and sent an alarming shudder through the fuselage. For an instant his plane was airborne again, just a few feet above the flight deck that was racing past their cockpits. Then, with another pounding, the main landing gear made contact with the deck almost parallel to the island. This time the wheels stayed down long enough to allow the nose wheel to engage the deck as well. Sparks showered out from the wheels as Viktor stood on the brake pedals, but the Foxbat lost forward momentum too slowly.

They smashed into the barrier. They felt as if they'd just flown into the churning arms of an octopus as the barrier wrapped around their tandem cockpits. Their brakes squealed and their Foxbat shrieked as the barrier webbing pulled hard against the metallic surfaces of their fuselage and controls, but the needle nose cockpit and sharp leading edges of the wings gouged the trapping like a grizzly making a fight for its life.

Viktor's eyes were wide open and fixed on the bow edge of the flight deck that was still moving toward them. He decided on a last desperate attempt to get himself and Nadia separated from the plane before their Foxbat tore free of the barrier and darted over the bow to the waiting sea. Keying his intercom he shouted to Nadia, "Brace yourself! We're bailing out!" Then, just as he thrust both hands to his instrument panel to engage his and Nadia's ejection levers, the plane vibrated wildly and drew to a stop just twenty feet short of the edge of the bow.

Jones ordered the crash crew to surround the plane and extinguish the flames climbing the struts from the Foxbat's overheated brakes. Then, as other crewmen scurried up to the cockpits to evacuate the two pilots, he joined Smith in a disbelieving gaze at the barrier. The few strands they had managed to install to fill the gap the previous Foxbat had made were wrapped around the Foxbat's duel vertical tails like a chin strap. The rest of the barrier was stretched out behind the Foxbat like a long and ragged cape. That part was holding nothing of the jet at all, which suggested their last-minute repair strands were all that was.

Baxter ran the length of the flight deck to greet the three Russian Foxbat pilots. They thanked him with sighs of relief, and he shook their hands and said, "This ship is regarded as

American real estate. Therefore, I think it is appropriate to say, welcome to the United States. Home of the free."

As the second Foxbat was being unraveled from the barrier, Ferris regarded Trish. "We'll, you've got your date with a Foxbat. Two, in fact. By way of reminder, they're both probably *hot* aircraft. Don't start your work on them until Baxter and I disarm whatever booby traps the Soviets may have hidden aboard them."

"Don't worry, we won't!" Trish said firmly.

Redding said to his aide, "Pass the word to all hands that those Foxbats may have explosives planted aboard them. No one is to screw around with them without clearance from the mission ops boss."

"Let's go debrief those Foxbat pilots," Ferris said.

"Roger that," Redding returned. "I want to know what went wrong with the one-plane breakout that caused us to play host to a second Foxbat."

Heading for the flight deck Ferris commented, "By the way, Captain . . . you were right."

"Right about what?"

"The *Coral Sea* obviously was the right ship to pick for an impossible task like this. I'd like you to convey my compliments to your X.O. and crew for a job well done."

"Thank you. I'll be sure to do that," Redding said with a proud grin.

PART FOUR

CHAPTER NINETEEN

Twenty-four hours had elapsed since the carriers *Eisenhower* and *Kitty Hawk*, with their armada of escort and support ships, had left the U.S.S. *Coral Sea* to fend for itself at the eastern end of the Mediterranean Sea. In his departure dispatch, the incoming Sixth Fleet task force commander notified the commander of Sixth Fleet operations, the commander of Atlantic fleet operations, and the chief of naval operations in Washington, that an unusual communications blackout was experienced during the rendezvous with the offgoing task force in the vicinity of Cyprus. He thought the Soviet task force shadowing the American fleet was responsible.

In Washington, Hal Banks had been notified by the CNO of Task Force 2's complaint in view of its possible connection with Operation Med Maneuver. The reply the CIA instructed the CNO to pass along to COMLANT, COMSIX, and TF 2's fleet commander was to do nothing about the communications jamming, to expect more of the same for an unspecified duration, and to carry out his deployment orders to the letter.

With the island of Crete rising ahead of their bows and the Soviet fleet shadowing them close from abreast and astern as they continued their trek toward the western end of the Mediterranean, TF 2 would make no further mention of the communications blackout problem if and when the jamming reoccurred, as ordered. And as the deployment orders directed, Task Force 2 commenced the tactical sea and air exercises that were intended to keep all eyes of the Soviet fleet on them and off the activities of the *Coral Sea*.

Captain Redding had also sent a communiqué in cipher to the CNO, which had been relayed in Washington to Hal Banks: "Kangaroo has two cubs in the pouch, and the father of one was given the deep six." The carefully worded explanation of a second Foxbat being taken aboard, and of Mishka's flight instructor being ejected out over the Mediterranean, was acknowledged with "Five by five," which meant it was understood. Redding had left it up to the TF 2 commander to alert the CNO about the intermittent jamming experienced during the transfer of personnel and planes, and he was also advised to take no action if it was repeated en route to Alexandria, unless it posed a threat to ship and crew. With the CIA and NSA teams busily commencing probing activities of the two Foxbats on the hangar deck level, he went below to tell Ferris that Washington was informed of their situation and present progress, and to make mention of his standoff orders pertaining to the Soviet jamming.

Undaunted by Admiral Stalovich's expressed contempt for Project Theshold's long-range phases of testing and training, Project Deputy Director Yudalslov had an air of sheer contentment as he prepared to begin Monday's jamming and antijamming exercises with the admiral's fleet of ships. He had a command center set up on one side of a rectangular map table in the *Leningrad*'s combat control sector room. From a high-back leather swivel armchair, the back of which was stenciled "Project Deputy Director," he looked down on the numerous plastic models of U.S. and Soviet ships meticulously placed on the tabletop map in relation to the flagship's position out in the Mediterranean. At his fingertips was a red-colored desk phone that was labeled "Project Threshold Scrambler." To one side of the phone was a ship's radio with a built-in speaker, the microphone of which was attached to a movable ceiling boom that was just above his head. On the other side of the phone was a teletype machine, and teletype keyboard, and cipher encoder and decoder modules. He ate his meals at the CCS table as he worked, and left his director's chair only to relieve himself and to sleep. Sleep he had taken very little of since he first came aboard the Kara class cruiser in Odessa harbor.

On the opposite side of the map table, Stalovich was seated in the same kind of chair that Yudalslov occupied, which was stenciled "Task Force Commandant." He also had all of the critical communications devices that surrounded Yudalslov. But with the exception of the ship's radio and the scrambler phone, he hadn't used any of them since his task force was ordered to deploy to the Mediterranean. Unlike Yudalslov, he left his chair often: to go to meals, to attend meetings, and to oversee the running of his flagship and task force operations from the bridge deck. And he didn't sacrifice one minute of the eight hours' sleep he was in the habit of taking. If he was to ever skimp on sleep, he told himself, it wouldn't be for the benefit of Yudalslov's electronic war games. It would be for war games of another sort.

Noticing that Stalovich was glancing at him from time to time as he fired up the electronics warfare apparatus, Yudalslov decided it would be a good time to keep the promise he'd made to Deputy Secretary of the Navy Kosenoff and give the fleet admiral at least a layman's understanding of the jamming and antijamming technology. As he actuated toggle switches to bring the devices to life, he said matter-of-factly, "Perhaps you have been wondering how we managed to communicate with mission control in Odessa under the noses of the Sixth Fleet without fear of enemy eavesdropping, Comrade Commandant."

"It was obvious from the way the American spy satellite was unable to listen in on or intercept our air, sea, and ground communications in Odessa that you can cause a blackout of the enemy's communications channels," Stalovich said across the map table. "Is that not so?"

"Yes. But that is only part of the technique. By causing a blackout of enemy communications channels, we cause our own communications to suffer the same disturbing effects as well. Yet, by utilizing the antijamming phase of the new technique, we are able to overcome the blackout, while the enemy, not having access to the antijamming apparatus, is not."

"And how is this wondrous, one-sided form of communications accomplished, Comrade Yudalslov?" Stalovich asked stiffly.

"By using the versatility of computer programming and the velocity of laser and microwave switching," Yudalslov said. "The first thing we do is cause the blackout of all communications channels for both sides. Unable to monitor all of the many communications frequencies that are in existence at one time, our enemies go from one to the other and find no receiving or transmitting channels that seem open for use. Yet all of the various channels are actually usable, if one knows which one to receive or transmit over, and precisely when to do so. At exacting intervals that are computer controlled, the blackout effects are interrupted for split seconds to allow us to receive or transmit communications either verbally in the form of coded sounds, or electronically in the form of cipher signals. And as our computerized programming converts the sounds or signals into fragments of communications, the laser and microwave electronics play them over the widespread communications bands much like a pianist selects keys for a particular musical score, only at lightning speed. At the transmitting end the fragmented composition is gated through an encoder, while at the receiving end the fragments are gated through a decoder. And unless our enemies know exactly when the fragments are being sent or received, and over precisely what channels, they assume a total jamming is taking place that affects both sides of the electronic war."

"Is there not the possibility that the enemy might stumble upon the exact communications channel being opened up at the precise moment we are receiving or transmitting fragments of these sounds or signals over it?" Stalovich probed.

"It is very unlikely when you consider that the fragments of communications are being sent or received faster than the blinking of an eye, and over more communications channels than there are letters in the alphabet and digits from zero to one hundred, my dear Comrade Commandant," Yudalslov said proudly. "It would be more likely for someone to shuffle a deck of cards thoroughly, then throw them into the air and have them land face up with every suit separated from deuce to ace. But even if the enemy happened upon a fragment of the sounds or signals being sent or received, it would take them a lifetime to make any sense of them."

"I can understand how cipher might be fragmented and distributed over a host of communications channels, Comrade Yudalslov," Stalovich said. "But how does this occur when it is voice communications that are being received or transmitted over a host of communications channels? Does one recite fragments of a conversation over one radio frequency after another?"

Yudalslov offered Stalovich an understanding smile. "In the area of voice communications we keep our enemies even more baffled than in cipher communications. In cipher communications our computers access our Soviet alphanumeric system as alphabetical code, alphacoding. This is the signal phasing of the technique. The sound phasing utilizes a computer's ability to access human speech and transpose it into alphabetics or alphabetism. That communications system we call alphabetized phonetics, or alphaphonics. With the aid of laser and microwave truncating and the speed of computer accessing, the alphabet and the voice sounds used to form speech are subdivided into routines that are grouped as fragments. The fragments are all converted into coding and assigned to airwaves, much like calls are directed to switchboard operators who put them through to the desired destinations. The lasers do the jamming and also serve as distributors, much like an automobile distributor sends sparks to a proper sparkplug at a precise moment. The computers handle the compositions of alphacoding and alphaphonics, and the microwave electronics accommodate the truncating requirements. Together they function as a private telephone system that operates like a closed circuit television broadcast. You have to have the right devices hooked up to the programming, or you get nothing when you select the channels that the broadcast is being aired over."

"By causing one of their spy satellites to suffer a blackout over the region of Odessa, then causing their fleet of ships to be plagued by a similar jamming disturbance, are we not revealing to the western world that we are in the process of developing such damaging technological devices?" Stalovich asked.

"The forces of the West will undoubtedly become aware that we are working on some new form of communications system," Yudalslov agreed. "But our party leaders at the Kremlin carefully calculated the risk as one that must be taken in order to test the apparatus realistically and effectively train the air, sea, and ground crews who will operate the devices. Merely to use the techniques on mock targets, or as maneuvers within our own military units, would not produce the desired effect of practical application on our enemies. In the need to proceed rapidly to the full deployment stage, trial and error must be put to the test on actual subjects and under existing adversities to truly perfect the short- and long-range aspects of the program. And until Project Threshold has completed the preliminary stages of testing and training, and a proper evaluation of the desired overall effects on the enemy can be made, expansion of the program cannot proceed. This is the price we must pay for progress."

"But if we continue to expose our electronic warfare activities to our enemies, surely they will do whatever they can to stop our progress," Stalovich said.

"So far they have done nothing," Yudalslov returned.

"That in itself seems quite surprising to me."

"It would not be so surprising to you if you knew the way the Americans think, Comrade Stalovich," Yudalslov said. "They are not in the habit of admitting they are unable to overcome a technological development—they are far too egotistical about their worldly status as pioneers in high technology. To save face they are doing just what we predicted they would do, which is ignore our blackout activities as though they are not troubled by them."

"Perhaps they felt they could safely ignore the blackout plight we caused one of their spy satellites," Stalovich said. "But now that we are plaguing the ships of their navy with communications jamming, they may become alarmed enough to take military action against us."

"We know for a fact that the Americans are heavily committed to electronic warfare research, but we are taking no military action to stop them," Yudalslov argued. "And as long as we do not take military action, they will not do so, either. If they did, all the nations of the communist world and the capitalist world would protest."

"Perhaps they will find out how we accomplish the jamming and antijamming," Stalovich said. "And if they do, what good will our new electronic warfare technology be to the Soviet Union?"

"Our latest intelligence sources have established that the Americans have been unsuccessful in their most recent attempts to be competitive in that field of research and development," Yudalslov informed him. "In view of the fact that we are presently enjoying technological supremacy in that area of warfare, we can expect to reach the full deployment capability long before they manage to move their research out of the laboratory and onto a testing and training field of battle. By then their efforts to compromise our developments will be too late. We will have a sneak nuclear first-strike advantage that will permit communism to dominate capitalism all over the globe."

"And if we are plunged into a conventional war before we are in a position to thrust the western world into a nuclear confrontation, the Americans will find Soviet forces prepared to operate your magical machinery but unprepared for combat," Stalovich insisted. "If that is the outcome of the man hours spent on perfecting the party's new communications system, then the only use we will have for your toy telephone is to privately report our defeat to Moscow. But at that time we will not have to worry about the enemy eavesdropping on our conversation. The western world will already know that they have been victorious over Soviet forces. All they will need to know in addition is, are we willing to have capitalism dominate over communism, or would we rather become an extinct race, obliterated from the face of the earth?"

"You will not see the conventional war you fear so much

Comrade Stalovich," Yudalslov rebuked. "Project Threshold will rid all the battlefields of the western world's contemporary weaponry, then go on to liquidate the homelands of our enemies so no more can be built to take the place of those our arsenal of nuclear missiles wipe out." He flicked a master switch to turn on the scrambler phone, then said, "Now if you will excuse me, it is time to communicate with mission control." He picked up the scrambler phone and found it in use on the other end. Without signing on, he listened in on the urgent conversation transpiring in Odessa. He heard that a MIG-35 had failed to turn back for its home base in Kiev and that a second MIG-35, extending its flight to make a search for the first, was now also missing. He raised a concerned eyebrow when Odessa reported that the Turkish government had announced it monitored a Mayday call from a Soviet pilot in distress somewhere close to its shores. What disturbed him was the possibility that either or both Foxbats might have overflown the Soviet territorial limits of the Black Sea, and landed in Turkish boundaries. If that was the case, the Turks might find the planes and take possession of the electronic warfare apparatus aboard them before the pilots could blow them up. With the Turks friendly with the West, keeping the top secret technology out of their hands would have to be regarded as a Soviet national security priority.

Yudalslov heard that mission control and the home base of the two Foxbats had ordered other Soviet planes and ships to make a search. And with the Black Sea too far away for Stalovich's fleet to get involved in the search efforts, he resolved not to concern himself further over the two missing Foxbats. But hearing the *Leningrad*'s radio operator report that he was monitoring a Mayday signal from what he presumed to be an aviator's emergency distress beacon, he perked up in his director's chair and said, "See if you can track the signal to its origin on your radio direction finder. If you can, I will relay the coordinates to mission control in Odessa over the scrambler so the Turks will not hear the location of the signal and investigate its source."

With his scrambler phone still on its cradle, Stalovich was unaware of the activity in Odessa that Yudalslov had overheard. But he had heard what his flagship's radio operator reported to CCS, and in response to what Yudalslov ordered the radio operator to do, he said, "What is all this about an aviator's Mayday signal? And why must we keep the Turks from hearing of its location?"

Yudalslov explained what he had heard over the scrambler.

"If your ship's radio operator is correct about monitoring an aviator's distress signal, then we can assume it is the missing Foxbat pilots who are sending it," he concluded.

After spending a few moments homing in on the signal with his radio direction finder, the *Leningrad*'s radio operator reported to CCS, "I have bird-dogged the signal to a point fifty miles south of the Turkish Mediterranean coastline, and three hundred miles east of the flagship's present position. The signal shows virtually no movement as I continue homing in on it, which would be the case if the signal was being transmitted by a flight crew that has ditched in the sea."

"How sure are you that the signal is coming from an aviator's emergency distress beacon?" Yudalslov asked.

"It is being broadcast over a frequency internationally established as a Mayday channel, and it is the proper decibel for an emergency beacon."

Stalovich bolted from his commandant's chair. "Two of our Foxbats have ditched in the Mediterranean?" he said over his radio mike.

"If we are missing two Foxbats at the present time, I would say the pilots must be broadcasting this signal, Commandant," the radio operator replied.

To the CCS duty officer, Stalovich said, "Ask our radar and sonar if we have any planes or ships in the vicinity of the bird-dogged signal." To Yudalslov he said, "Report this latest development to Odessa over the scrambler. Tell mission control we are standing by to lend assistance in the event no other Soviet aircraft or ships are in closer proximity."

Within moments the CCS duty officer reported, "There are no other Soviet units nearby, Commandant. But we are monitoring an American navy ship about fifty miles south of the bird-dogged signal."

"Have you established what American ship it is and if it is heading toward the signal?" Stalovich asked.

"Our CCS surface and air activity log establishes it as the U.S.S. *Coral Sea*. It is the aircraft carrier that deployed from the main body of the Sixth Fleet when we departed from Cyprus."

"Yes, I well remember," Stalovich said. "It is the one the Americans are giving to their friends the Egyptians."

"That is correct, Commandant," the duty officer said. "Both radar and sonar report it moving away from the bird-dogged signal on a course due south."

Stalovich glanced across the table at Yudalslov, who was or

the scrambler with Odessa. Regarding the matter of the downed pilots as a reprieve from the electronic warfare training exercises, he ordered, "Advise mission control that my flagship is the only vessel capable of ensuring that the downed pilots will not fall into enemy hands. Therefore, I am interrupting our Project Threshold activities to deploy on a rescue mission. I will send my two Kamov helicopters on flyout ahead of the *Leningrad*, then follow after the air rescue units to shorten their return flight. All other ships of my fleet will remain behind to continue shadowing the American task force, as ordered."

Working on the two MIG-35's parked side by side in the rear of the *Coral Sea*'s hangar bay 3, Ferris found the top secret apparatus to be an electronic nightmare. When they began their search for booby traps, Baxter had mentioned that the belly compartments they were working inside of were called hellholes. The component and accessories compartments were situated under the forward cockpit floor, with access to them gained through an underbelly hatch just behind the nose-wheel-landing gear struts. Not long after climbing atop a waisthigh inspection stand to squeeze into his compartment, he decided a more fitting name for the area would be "torture chamber."

Ferris picked Foxbat 104 to work on. With Baxter out of hearing range in the hellhole of Foxbat 116, they made good use of the walkie-talkie units Redding had lent them. After two tense hours of tracing through electric circuits with oscilloscopes, stroboscopes, and even stethoscopes, they had managed to disarm two large incendiary explosive packs and a half dozen small fragmentary detonator caps. They were sure the two large demolition devices were hooked into the cockpit "panic button," an ordnance system used to destroy the aircraft if the flight crew had to abandon it in enemy territory. The smaller explosive caps seemed to be personnel mines that were fired off at face or chest level when any "top secret" electronics they were wired to were touched, so they would liquidate an intruder without demolishing the aircraft or the device being tampered with. They couldn't know just how many bombs were planted aboard the MIG-35's, but they had only one electric circuit left that hadn't revealed something foreign in its configuration of components, wires, connectors, and relays.

Meticulously confirming every detail of his work with Ferris, Baxter put the steadiness of his hands to the ultimate test as he disarmed the booby traps his former countrymen had him pitted against. He had gained a working knowledge of incendiary bombs and fragmentary detonator caps in the Soviet Air Force. And more recently, the U.S. Navy had given him a crash course on bombs and other high explosives as a routine phase of his flight training. But he didn't have the technical training the CIA had given Ferris. As a TOS agent, whose work comprised both espionage and sabotage, Ferris had the benefit of working with highly sophisticated demolition devices. Ferris had also served as a member of a bomb disposal team while attached to a guerilla warfare unit during the Vietnam war. That's why he was eager to be schooled every step of the way as the disarming detail dragged on.

Redding left the disarming work taking place on the hangar deck, when his ship's radar operator reported that one of the Soviet task force ships had reversed course somewhere along its trek toward the western end of the Mediterranean. He was told the lone ship was believed to be a Kara class cruiser, now heading in the direction of the downed flight instructor that Mishka had ejected from her Foxbat. He was sure that the Soviet cruiser was merely responding to the Mayday signal his ship's radio operator was also monitoring, but he told his radar and sonar operators to alert him if the Soviet ship began heading their way.

At the debriefing of the Soviet defectors, Mishka assured everyone that her flight instructor was never told of the planned aircraft-carrier landing. Redding could only hope that the female student pilot was telling the truth. If so, the Soviet cruiser would only learn from the rescued pilot that the two missing Foxbats had continued south after he was ejected. He prayed that would suggest the pilots had exhausted their fuel in their attempt to defect, and had gone down with their planes. If the Soviets did think that, there was nothing to fear from the Soviet cruiser. *But what if they didn't?* he wondered. Deciding there would be time enough to worry about that if the Soviet cruiser did head after his ship, he put his apprehension aside. For now.

"I think it's safe to say that both Foxbats are no longer *hot*," Ferris said to Trish and Dodge as he climbed out of Foxbat 104's hellhole. He saw Baxter heading over to them. "Do you agree, Nick?"

"We've checked and double-checked every damn circuit in and around those black boxes," Baxter announced. "All of them seem to be disarmed."

Trish had been shown some of the explosive devices planted

among the electronics apparatus she and her colleague Walter Dodge were to probe. They looked horrid and left her with an eerie feeling. From a safe distance she and Dodge stared spellbound as Ferris and Baxter risked their lives to disarm the booby traps. In doing so, she found herself changing her opinion of Hal Banks's ace TOS agent. She recognized Ferris's professionalism and was highly impressed with his courage and coolness in supervising Baxter at the extremely delicate work, while at the same time mastering the intricately located and installed life-threatening demolition devices. She doubted she would have ever had the nerves of steel needed to be face-to-face with sudden death for two tense hours as one bomb after another was disarmed.

Facing Trish, Ferris asked, "Willing to trust in our bomb defusing expertise?"

"I must admit, I'm quite impressed over the manner in which you handled the problem," Trish said, still feeling a little uneasy about acting friendly to Ferris. "Thank you seems like such a small thing to say in return for insuring mine and Walt's safety."

"It's all in a day's work. All part of the job," Ferris said coolly.

"Well, after what you both have just been through, I hate to put anything else on you, but there is more to do before Walt and I can begin the probing."

"Name it and it shall be done," Ferris said cheerfully. He was relieved that the bomb disarming had gone without a hitch; and that was more than enough to lift his spirits after the two hours of torture he had spent in the hellhole of Foxbat 104. But something else was causing his spirits to rise as well. It was the realization that NSA's computer whiz was beginning to thaw. He liked the warming trend and hoped it would continue.

After huddling with Dodge, Trish said to Ferris and Baxter, "The first problem is that we will need the Foxbat pilots to operate their cockpit controls as we probe, and none of them speak English."

"That's an easy hitch to overcome," Ferris said. "Nick and I will serve as interpreters."

"Another problem is that all the electronic components and circuits in the black boxes are labeled in Russian," Trish went on.

Ferris said, "Nick, you work with Walt Dodge and Mishka in Foxbat one one six. I'll work with Trish and Viktor and Nadia in their Foxbat." To Trish, he added, "Nick and I will read the labels for you and relay your instructions to the cockpits. What else will you need?"

"Walt and I can use those two walkie-talkies to confer with each other as we do our probing, just as you and Nick used them during the booby trap defusing," Trish said.

Ferris handed Trish his walkie-talkie, prompting Baxter to turn his over to Dodge. "Will that do it?"

"We'll also need headsets to be in voice communication with the cockpits," Trish said.

"Nick, see if Captain Redding has some headsets that aren't in use," Ferris said.

"Some floodlights also," Trish went on.

"Roger that," Baxter said as he headed for a wall phone.

"We have our own tools," Trish said next. "And we can use the mechanics inspection stands you and Nick worked from to do our probing work."

"How long do you think it will take you to find the key computer module, Trish?" Ferris asked.

"Walt and I counted sixty black boxes in each hellhole, Matt," Trish replied. "And although there's a good possibility that some of the computer modules might be dummy loads just to confuse anyone attempting to scrutinize them, we'll still have to check each and every black box to establish which circuits are cold and which are actually part of the jamming and antijamming systems." She faced Dodge. "Walt, do you think you could handle the circuit tracing on your own once I get you started on what to look for?"

"I think so, Trish," Dodge said. "If the circuit layouts don't vary too much from one black box to the next."

"We won't know if there's a standardized layout scheme to the circuitry until we open a number of the modules and get some of the chips exposed to view, Walt," Trish said. "But unless the Russians are cagier than we anticipated, the schematic groupings of most of the black boxes should prove out to be quite similar in design." She regarded Ferris. "We have two Foxbats and we have two ground and cockpit crews. That will enable us to split into two teams operating independently. My team will cover black boxes one through thirty while Walt's covers thirty-one through sixty."

"By splitting it in half, it seems to me like it shouldn't take very long to probe all sixty black boxes," Ferris commented.

"Don't let the number of modules involved fool you, Matt," Trish warned. "There could be anywhere from ten to a hundred chips and related circuitry elements inside each black box. The ones with less computer components might only take minutes to check out. The complicated ones might take an hour or more to solve. We could get extremely lucky and happen upon the key module that controls the functions of all the others, and in finding the mother load we'd be able to figure out the rest of the circuits without tracing through each one. But don't build your hopes up over finding a shortcut like that any too easily. If the Russians went through such painstaking efforts to install so many booby traps in and around the apparatus, we can rest assured they spent equal time or more to camouflage the master circuit, too. And, if they were foxy enough to complicate the schematic configurations just to confound us, we'll be forced to reduce our probing productivity to a snail's pace and tackle each damn module one at a time on both Foxbats, just to insure we don't overlook a key element in the circuitry."

Baxter returned from the wall phone and said, "Captain Redding is sending some spare headsets down."

"Good deal," Ferris said. "As soon as they arrive, we'll get started."

The two Kamov helicopters lowered from the sky and set down on the *Leningrad*'s flight deck aft. With anxious eyes Stalovich watched the rescued Foxbat pilot stepping down from the open cargo doorway, his flight suit dripping wet. It was obvious the pilot was suffering from exposure to winter's cold winds and the sting of the Mediterranean's salt spray. They had turned his face beet-red. He decided there would be time later for the pilot to thaw out as he anxiously asked, "What of the other pilots and your planes?"

"I was ejected against my will!" Borovek said furiously.

"What happened?" Stalovich asked, as Yudalslov joined him and the Foxbat pilot on the flight deck.

"I was in Foxbat one one six with my student pilot, searching for my wing leader in Foxbat one oh four, whom I lost radio contact with over Odessa. Finding him and his student pilot in afterburners and racing toward the northern coast of Turkey, we gave chase. When the runaway Foxbat crossed through Turkish airspace and continued south over the Mediterranean, it became apparent my wing leader and his female student pilot were defecting. I ordered my student pilot to fire a missile at them and shoot them down. Instead, she ejected me and raced after Foxbat one oh four."

"I must alert mission control at once!" Yudalslov said.

"I agree," Stalovich said. "But first let us attempt to establish where they're defecting to." He regarded the Foxbat pilot again. "Do you have any idea what their destination was?"

"None at all," the pilot replied with a shiver.

"Could it have been Cyprus?" Stalovich asked.

"I do not believe Cyprus has a runway that would be able to accommodate a MIG-35," Borovek replied.

"Not only that," Yudalslov put in, "we have several KGB agents residing on Cyprus. The landing of two Foxbats there would not escape their notice."

"The only other land mass to the south of Turkey is the Middle East," Stalovich said. "Could they have gone there?"

"If the Middle East was their destination, then they are both fools," Borovek barked. "In afterburners, they would exhaust their fuel supply before they got halfway across the Mediterranean."

"Obviously, by your pursuit you caused them to panic," Yudalslov said. "And they overflew their destination, which must have been Turkey. If that is the case, then we can conclude the Foxbats and the traitors flying them have been claimed by the sea, which will hide them from our enemies."

"The Foxbats surely have been claimed by the sea if they exhausted their fuel reserves," Borovek said. "But the three defectors could have been rescued if they ditched nearby a passing ship."

Stalovich recalled checking on the air and sea traffic in the vicinity of the Turkish Mediterranean coastline. His ship's radar and sonar had reported only the aircraft carrier U.S.S. *Coral Sea* to the south of the ejected Foxbat pilot. To be doubly sure, he picked up a wall phone and asked CCS to confirm that the American carrier was the only ship radar and sonar monitored in the path of the Foxbats' southerly heading.

After careful scrutiny of the surface, subsurface, and aerial traffic in that area for the past few hours, the CCS duty officer reported, "No other planes or ships were in that area, Comrade Commandant."

"You are quite sure, Lieutenant?"

"Quite sure, Comrade Commandant," the duty officer said confidently. "We have recorded that the American carrier made some erratic course changes en route to its port of Alexandria destination. But there was no other activity to log."

"Erratic course changes?" Stalovich asked.

"A turn to port on an easterly heading at full speed for approximately half an hour," the duty officer said. "Then i reduced speed to about one-third headway and turned to starboard on a southerly course again. That would have the carrier back on a heading for its original destination, the port of Alexandria, if she does not alter course any more."

Well acquainted with the behavior of ships, especially aircraft carriers, the duty officer's information suggested something to Stalovich that prompted him to ask, "Out of what direction was the wind at the time the American carrier altered course, Lieutenant?"

"One moment, Commandant," the duty officer said. After consulting with the meteorology officer, he replied, "Comrade Commandant, the prevailing winds were out of the east at twenty-two knots."

Stalovich paused for a moment to envision the activity of the carrier in relation to the wind direction, then in an authoritative tone he said, "Get us on an interception heading with that American carrier at once. Advise mission control in Odessa and the senior officer acting as task force commandant in my absence that we are extending our search for the missing Foxbats."

"By your leave, Commandant," the duty officer said. "Did you not mean the missing pilots?"

"Perhaps both," Stalovich said firmly. "Tell Odessa and our fleet that we will report in as soon as we learn more. But say nothing more than that for now." He saw the two helicopter flight crews heading toward him, and hung up the phone. Waving to them, he said, "Comrades, tell the flight deck officer to have your helicopters refueled to capacity. You are to be scrambled on a reconnaissance flyout to an American aircraft carrier as soon as we have the next light of dawn."

Yudalslov overheard Stalovich's orders to the flight crews. In astonishment he asked, "Why are we heading after the American aircraft carrier, Comrade Commandant?"

"I will answer your question with a question, my dear Deputy Director," Stalovich returned smugly. "Why does a carrier usually turn into the wind at accelerated speed?"

"To land aircraft would be my guess," Yudalslov said in a puzzled tone. "Why do you ask that question?"

"Because with our very own eyes we saw this particular carrier transfer its entire air group to other carriers of its fleet, so that it would arrive in Egypt to carry out a transfer of ownership without the costly burden of sending its complement of aircraft and personnel back to their home bases from Alexandria."

"So," Yudalslov said. "That is merely logistics."

"True enough, Comrade Deputy Director," Stalovich agreed. "But with no aircraft aboard, why did this U.S. carrier display all the characteristics of retrieving aircraft at the precise time our two missing Foxbats might have been in the ship's vicinity? Foxbats, I will add, that are now presumed to be piloted by defectors."

"Are you suggesting the missing Foxbats landed aboard the carrier?" Yudalslov asked.

"Based upon the carrier's behavior, it is a logical assumption," Stalovich said.

"With all due respect, Comrade Commandant," Yudalslov said, "a MIG-35 is not designed to make such a landing. It is ludicrous to suggest that a Foxbat pilot would dare to attempt such a task with no aircraft carrier landing experience, and in a plane that has no such capability."

"On the contrary, Comrade Deputy Director," Stalovich fired back. "In a desperate situation, people often do things that are ludicrous."

"Perhaps in a do-or-die situation our three pilots might take such a risk," Yudalslov said. "But that does not mean the American carrier would be willing to subject both vessel and crew to such reckless endangerment."

"Not even for two Foxbats with top secret apparatus?" Stalovich asked.

"I am certain a Foxbat would only be able to crash-land aboard an American carrier," Yudalslov said. "That could destroy both. And what good would the top secret technology do them if they lost both ship and planes?"

"But if the planes and ship did manage to survive the landing, then it would be our loss, wouldn't it?"

"I suggest you consider the loss your retirement plans may suffer if your planned escapade with this American carrier causes Project Threshold to suffer delays in . . ."

"Comrade Yudalslov!" Stalovich bellowed. "You will leave the matter of my retirement to me. I question your shocking lack of responsibility about a matter crucial to Soviet national security. I am surprised that you didn't insist I alter course and investigate the whereabouts of the Foxbats further. Surely I needn't remind you what a loss it will be to your precious Project Threshold if our enemies gain possession of the new technology."

To that Yudalslov had no reply.

"You heard me order my ship on an interception course with

that carrier," Stalovich went on. "Now hear this as well. As long as I am commandant of this task force, I will do all the decision making for it. As commandant, I will also assume total responsibility for the decisions I make. And my decision making will go unquestioned by all military members of my task force, as well as any civilians on deployment with it." He narrowed his eyes, feeling gratified he had established who was king. "I trust I have made myself quite clear, Comrade Yudalslov."

"Quite clear, Comrade Stalovich," Yudalslov said bitterly.

Having made his point with Yudalslov, Stalovich regarded the exhausted pilot. "Are you quite sure the others were defecting, Comrade Borovek?"

"Commandant, they showed no inability to maneuver their Foxbat. That indicated they were not suffering any form of mechnical malfunction which would force them to leave the rest of the group. Instead, they made a breakout from the turn for Kiev in afterburners, which establishes they were in full control of their aircraft and had every intention of heading in the opposite direction from home base. And the fact that my student pilot hindered my efforts to stop them seems to suggest she knew of their plans to defect."

Patting the pilot on the back, Stalovich said, "Come with me, Comrade. We will get you out of these wet clothes and have you fed." As they left the flight deck, he added, "I will advise your superior that you are safe aboard my flagship, and recommend that you be well rewarded for your heroic effort to foil the defection."

CHAPTER TWENTY

Under a star-speckled sky the *Coral Sea* continued on a slow trek across the width of the listless Mediterranean, its destination over two hundred miles away. Absent of life, the flight deck was an ink-black platform, its catwalks and deck-edge limits hidden by the shadows of night. With only running lights and a crimson glow filling the wraparound bridge windows, the island looked like a fire-breathing serpent standing up in the middle of the sea. The three hangar deck elevator doors, one forward and one aft of the island on starboard, and one outboard on portside aft, were drawn tightly shut and would remain sealed throughout the voyage to Alexandria. They concealed the rows and ranks of overhead lights that had been burning without end in hangar bay 3 ever since the two twin-tailed Foxbats had been brought below. Hangar bays 1 and 2 were empty and dimly lit, as were all of the compartments and passageways not in use.

It was 1:00 A.M. Tuesday, and an air of uncertainty loomed over the MIG-35's idly parked in hangar bay 3. In strategically located positions surrounding the two planes were portable fire-fighting apparatus. They'd been kept handy since the bomb disarming had taken place some twelve hours ago. Also facing the aircraft, but with their lamps turned off, were half a dozen portable spotlights at the ready for resumption of work. Standing on opposite sides of the opened inner doors separating hangar bays 2 and 3 were two sailors with hip-holstered .45's who kept a security and fire watch over the winged guests aboard their ship. It was dead quiet, and except for a lone figure seated on the nose wheel of Foxbat 104, all those participating in the probing had taken a recess to recuperate from anxiety and fatigue.

Deep in thought and barely aware of the presence of the two-man watch, Ferris heard the faint clapping sound of footsteps drawing toward him at a brisk pace. He raised his bowed head and stared, as did the two sailors, in the direction of the noise, then saw a shadowy figure wrapped in a parka passing through the void that was hangar bay 2. When the figure reached the glow of hangar bay 3's overhead lights, Ferris noticed the gleaming gold embroidery of a naval officer's uniform cap.

"Attention on deck!" one of the sailors snapped, spotting the familiar face and uniform.

"As you were," Redding said. As he headed over to Ferris, he called out, "Mr. Baxter told me I might find you here, Mr. Ferris."

"Good evening, Captain," Ferris said as he got to his feet.

"Good morning would be more precise."

Ferris reached for his parka, which was draped over an inspection stand. He removed a pack of cigarettes and held it out invitingly when Redding was a few steps away from him. "Care for a smoke?"

"Smoking lamp is out in the hangar bays," Redding said as he pointed to a NO SMOKING sign. "But it's lit out on the fantail," he added, gesturing toward the stern of the ship. "Put on your parka and we'll have a smoke out there." As they headed aft, he asked, "How did the first twelve hours of probing go?"

"Terrible," Ferris answered, slipping into his parka. As they passed by the dark and empty aircraft maintenance shops on both sides of the passageway leading aft, he explained the number of black boxes that were involved in the search to find the main controlling computer module.

"Sounds quite time-consuming," Redding said as they stepped through the fantail hatch. At once the cold night air rushed up their nostrils with a sting, turning their breath vaporous.

Ferris panned the star-studded heavens for a moment, then said, "So far we've burned up half the twenty-four hours allotted, and we've only managed to cover a fourth of the black boxes aboard each Foxbat. Each one is loaded with computer chips that must be inspected."

"At that rate it'll take a lot longer than the twenty-four hours Trish Darrol said she'd need to crack the top secret technology," Redding said. He accepted a cigarette and a light from Ferris.

After lighting his own cigarette, Ferris said, "Well, you did say our sailing time en route would be a good thirty hours in these rather choppy seas. That gives Trish an extra six hours before we get into the port of Alexandria. If she fails to crack the secret to the jamming and antijamming apparatus by then, we'll just have to hope we can keep the whereabouts of the two Foxbats from the Russians long enough for Trish to finish her probing of them when we get into Alexandria."

"We may never reach the port of Alexandria with the two Foxbats," Redding said. "And Trish Darrol might not have any more than a total of six hours left to crack the top secret technology."

"Why is that?" Ferris asked in alarm.

"Because I doubt we're going to be able to keep the whereabouts of their two Foxbats from the Russians any much longer than that," Redding said as he gestured astern of the ship. "Remember the Soviet cruiser that left the main body of its task force to rescue Mishka Borken's flight instructor?"

"What about it?"

"It's been heading our way ever since we tracked the rescue choppers back aboard."

"And you think the rescued Foxbat pilot has something to do with that?"

"Mishka Borken said her flight instructor got wise to the defection in progress, which was why she ejected him. Unless he was unconscious or dead after leaving the plane, he had a bird's-eye view of their direction for some time on his slow parachute ride down to the sea. And if he was plucked out of the sea alive and talkative, that cruiser now knows the missing pilots headed their Foxbats south."

"Okay," Ferris said. "Let's assume that the Soviets now know that much. But Mishka's flight instructor had no knowledge of the planned Foxbat landing aboard the *Coral Sea*. Their destination could have been any of a number of places to the south of where Mishka's flight instructor was found."

"True," Redding agreed. "But her flight instructor was well-acquainted with the flying range of the MIG-35's. By knowing just how far the Foxbats would get on what fuel they had aboard, the Russians could eliminate a lot of destinations right off the bat. They would rule out any airfields and airports that are friendly to the Soviet Union. And they know as well as we do what areas of the Mediterranean region would welcome Soviet defectors. With a little figuring, they'd come up with the same thing we know. There are no airfields to the south friendly to Soviet defectors within flying range of the downed pilot."

After a deep drag on his cigarette, Ferris said, exhaling, "I think the Soviets will conclude that both Foxbats exhausted their fuel in a futile attempt to defect, and were forced to ditch or bail out. I think they now expect to find their three missing pilots floating around in rafts in the sea, hoping to be rescued by friends of the West. And I think they'll assume their missing

MIG's have gone to the bottom of the Mediterranean. The Soviet cruiser could be heading our way merely because we are along the southerly path their search is taking them."

"I wish I could go along with that, Mr. Ferris. But I'm convinced by the cruiser's behavior since it rescued the downed pilot that she's given up looking in the sea in favor of a more probable place for the missing pilots to be."

"Here?"

Redding nodded. "If the Russian ship was conducting a search, we'd be tracking her at about one-third the headway she's making. According to ship's radar and sonar, she's clipping along at nearly flank speed instead. And my people confirm that her two choppers have stayed aboard ship since the cruiser took up her southerly course for us. If the search were still going on, her two choppers would be flying criss-crossing search patterns of the sea ahead of the cruiser. That tells me they might have guessed the missing pilots were already rescued. I'd bet next month's pay that the cruiser plans to catch up with us and look us over."

Ferris looked astern at the pitch-black horizon as though searching for a sign of the Soviet cruiser. "You say she'll catch up to us in six hours?"

Redding pressed the light button on his wristwatch. "At oh seven hundred hours according to our plotting of her. But we can expect she might send her choppers out on a flyover ahead of her. I'd say they'd be scrambled at about oh five thirty hours. They'd want to use the light of dawn to check us for any signs of flight deck damage two Foxbats making a hairy landing might have caused."

"They're not going to see very much," Ferris said. "Your people cleaned up the flight deck nicely after the Foxbats landed. And with the elevator doors closed, they can't get as much as a peek at the hangar deck. Even if they do suspect we might have rescued their missing pilots, there's nothing about our looks to suggest their missing Foxbats are aboard."

"I'm not so sure we look all that innocent to them anymore, Mr. Ferris."

"Why not?"

"Most navies of the world operate on similar standing rules. Crews usually maintain an activity log on the round-the-clock basis. For example, if you wanted to know what air, surface, or subsurface activity we encountered at a particular hour of a day, we would have radar, sonar, radio, and other communications log entries that could be checked."

"Exactly what are you getting at, Captain Redding?" Ferris asked.

"There might be nothing to it. We might have been too far away for them to be concerned. But there's still the possibility that when we turned and headed into the wind yesterday afternoon, the Russian radar and sonar operators aboard that cruiser might have observed us and entered our course and speed deviations in their ship's activity log. I know *my* radar and sonar operators would. Along with the entry would be time of day. The activity log would also have notations about weather conditions, sea currents, and prevailing winds. If we were observed, and if their skipper is earning his pay, he's surely going to wonder why an aircraft carrier with its air group no longer aboard made the exacting maneuvers that would be executed to land aircraft. And at just about the same time their two missing Foxbats could have reached the vicinity of that aircraft carrier."

"If you're telling me all this to worry me, I assure you you're being successful," Ferris commented.

Redding chuckled, then became serious again. "What I'm telling you is that Operation Mediterranean Maneuver was well camouflaged and would probably have been a total success with only one Foxbat involved. When the second one joined the party, it stopped being private. Now there's every reason to fear the Russians are planning to crash our party."

"You think they'll board and search us?"

"I think they'll try."

"Should we make a run for it?"

"After cruising along at a moderate headway, making a sudden change to flank speed at the precise time they're following us would suggest we have something aboard to hide from them for sure. And even at flank speed, we'd never win the long race to the safety of Egyptian waters."

"How about calling for help?"

"I considered that, Ferris. But they've already demonstrated to us that they can cause us to suffer a total communications blackout. They might be jamming us right now, and that'll mean our call for help will never be received by Task Force 2 or anyone else. Besides, if we'd done nothing wrong, we wouldn't send a call out for help just because a Russian ship was following after us. Hell, the Soviet Navy shadows us out here in the Med all the time."

"I see what you mean, Captain. A guilty conscience needs no accuser."

"Exactly. We'd just feed their suspicions and make them more determined to board and search once they caught up with us. Even if we did somehow manage to get a call for help past them, by the time the cavalry came to the rescue the Indians would already be inside the fort. One look at what's inside this fort, and the Indians will have every right to give us a scalping."

"Well, I've had plenty of experience at handling the Russians on land," Ferris said matter-of-factly. "But none at handling them on the high seas. With the sea being your forte, I'll just trust in your expertise. How do you want to handle them when they do catch up with us?"

"We'll act as innocent as a newborn baby," Redding said. "Until wrongdoing can be proven, we are under the protection of maritime laws governing a vessel's free passage on international high seas. We can use that as leverage, maybe even scare them off with a warning of military reprisal for any hostile action taken against us."

"Do you think they'll back down?"

"I won't know what our chances are until I feel out the cruiser's skipper. If he's the kind that doesn't scare easily, he'll probably just laugh his ass off at my threats as his people are coming aboard. But if he shows signs of apprehension, I'll do the laughing. I've heard the Russians get more worried over someone laughing at them than at someone pointing a gun."

"There's some truth in that," Ferris said. "They know exactly what to do about the man with the gun. But when a man laughs down the barrel of a gun, the gutsy recklessness sometimes throws them off balance."

"Well, lacking the kind of firepower I'm used to having aboard to back up my threats, we'll just have to try and act more nervy than they. I'll do my best to play for time topside, while you do all you can to push for progress below. Maybe we'll get lucky and win the probing race. If we do lose it, be prepared to hand over their two Foxbats, with or without cracking their top secret technology. To make a fight of it would be a repeat of the Alamo."

Just then one of the hangar bay watches stepped out on the fantail. "Excuse me, Skipper. Chief Smith wants you to call the bridge right away, sir."

Redding flicked his cigarette into the passing sea. "What now?" he grunted, then stepped just inside the fantail hatch and picked up a wall phone.

Ferris tossed his cigarette over the side and followed fretfully after Redding. *What now, indeed,* he mused. He felt he had all the bad news he could take for one day. He narrowed his eyes on hearing Redding order Chief Smith to make some course changes, taking note as he did of a rather cheery tone in Redding's voice. When Redding hung up the wall phone, the smile on the navy captain's face prompted him to ask, "What were those course changes all about?"

"We got the best kind of play for time we could have," Redding replied happily. "Smitty found a pea soup fogbank blanketing the surface just a little to the east of our present course. If we steer into it, we can add several hours to your probing work without fear of interruption from that Soviet cruiser or its helicopters."

"Sounds good to me," Ferris said, smiling.

"We'll have to reduce speed, of course. But so will the Russians to safely negotiate the fog. And their choppers will be grounded for as long as the fogbank lasts. If your people manage to make a breakthrough before the fog lifts, we can deep six their two Foxbats and stash the defectors in one of more than a million hiding places aboard. Then if they board and search us, we'll make damn fools out of them."

"Let's hope it all turns out that way," Ferris said.

"It just may, Mr. Ferris. It seems we might have a guardian angel after all."

"If we do, its name is probably Hal Banks."

"Who?"

"My boss," Ferris replied. Gesturing to the star-filled sky outside the fantail hatch, he added, "Hal's in pretty tight with the man in charge of miracles."

"He must be if he sent that fogbank our way. It's just the kind of miracle we needed."

Ferris glanced at his wristwatch. "We'd better grab a couple of hours shut-eye. I'm going to want your bugle recording to sound reveille for my probing teams at the crack of dawn. We'll put that miraculous fogbank to good use while it lasts."

CHAPTER TWENTY-ONE

The fog had defied the early morning clearing that the *Leningrad*'s meteorologist had predicted. By late afternoon it was still keeping the flagship's two Kamov helicopters from their airborne mission, and their flight crews tensely at the ready in anticipation of a weather break at any moment. In the elapsed time, the Soviet cruiser had shrunk the distance between itself and the American aircraft carrier. While its presence was detectable only by ship's radar and sonar, Stalovich envisioned the carrier's meaty battleship-gray mass sitting on the smoky surface some five inviting miles ahead of the *Leningrad*'s bow. He had expected the American carrier's captain to utilize the fogbank to make a run for it, which would be an admission of guilt. Yet, in spite of the *Leningrad*'s hounding, the *Coral Sea* continued on a south-southeasterly course that had it heading away from Alexandria at reduced speed. That had disconcerted but not dismayed him. He endured the wait and Deputy Director Yudalslov's pressure to rejoin the task force, certain his patience would be rewarded in due time.

When the flagship's meteorologist finally reported the fog to be lifting, Stalovich and Yudalslov left the CCS room and hurried up to the bridge to get a glimpse of the United States carrier they had followed all through the night and half the next day. Joining the *Leningrad*'s commanding officer, Captain Garupcheck, on the forward catwalk just outside the bridge windows, they squinted at the thick haze that was still drawn around the cruiser like a drape. Within moments the stark gray curtain began to rise ahead of the *Leningrad*'s bow. As the fogbank thinned more and rose higher, the *Coral Sea*'s bulky stern took form in the distance, then the entire ship emerged from the fog like a monstrous ghost emerging from its grave.

Stalovich accepted a pair of binoculars from the *Leningrad*'s C.O. As he trained them on the *Coral Sea*, beams of sunlight speared through the rising mist and bombarded the carrier's starboard bridge windows. The burst of brightness reflected off the windows as though it had bounced off a pot of gold. He continued looking for long silent moments, mesmerized by the sight of the vessel. To him it wasn't just any ship. To him it was a ship that held a special meaning, a ship of magnificent design, a ship that his country's party leaders had denied him. Now such a ship lay off his flagship's bow, perhaps guilty of wrongdoing. Guilty and defenseless.

"Contact is altering course, Commandant," the bridge duty officer relayed from CCS through an open window facing forward. "She is coming about on a new heading to the south. Range, four miles. Speed, ten knots."

"Once again she is back on her course for Alexandria, Commandant," the *Leningrad*'s C.O. announced. "But at the same headway she maintained through the fogbank."

Yudalslov watched the American carrier coming about on the course change to the south as he said, "She must know we have been following after her all this time. Yet all through the night she has made no attempt to run away from us. Not even in the fog. And throughout our chase after her, she has made no effort to call for help from her task force, or even notify her homeland that we are in pursuit. That suggests to me that her captain feels uninhibited by our presence. Would not a man with something to hide show some sign of uneasiness by now?"

"If a thief was still in possession of the property he stole, would he not act cagily if he knew its owners were nearby?" Stalovich asked. His question was ignored. "And would you not say this American carrier captain's strange preference for sailing in the fog hints of a foxy attempt to avoid these property owners, Comrade Deputy Director Yudalslov?"

"Perhaps his sailing into the fog was unrelated to our close proximity," Yudalslov said.

"But of course," Stalovich said sarcastically. "And his course altering of yesterday had nothing to do with our two missing Foxbats either, I suppose? The Americans are merely squeezing in a little sightseeing on their way to the port of Alexandria, perhaps? Yesterday, at the same time our Foxbats became missing, the Americans went out of their way to tour the wind. And in the wee hours of this morning, as it became apparent to them that we were following them, they went out of their way to tour the fog."

"Their course alterations could be coincidental to our missing Foxbats and their pilots," Yudalslov said. "Ships change course for many reasons, do they not?"

Stalovich looked at Yudalslov with contempt. "Perhaps you are fooled by them, but I am not. As I pointed out to you yesterday, an aircraft carrier heads into the wind at accelerated speed either to get out of another ship's way or to launch or land aircraft. We know there were no other ships in this carrier's path when it altered course to face the wind. We also know, for reasons involving the transfer of the carrier's ownership in a port quite distant from her homeland, that there were no aircraft left aboard her to launch. And with the aircraft of the other two American carriers at the opposite end of the Mediterranean, she would not have had occasion to land any American planes. Yet she gained headway into the wind just as if she was landing aircraft. Perhaps she did just that. But the aircraft that landed did not belong aboard."

"That is a wild assumption," Yudalslov protested.

"So is my theory about the American carrier's attachment to the fog," Stalovich argued. "But I know for a fact that ships usually do their best to steer around the fog. Take my word for it as an old sea dog, Comrade Yudalslov. A ship heads into the fog either because the fog is in the path of its destination and cannot be reasonably avoided, or because the ship wants to use the fog as a natural smoke screen. This ship veered from its destination to put the fog in its path. It did not steer away from its destination to avoid the fog. And I suspect it did so in the hope of delaying an anticipated confrontation with the owners of the property it is hiding aboard."

"Comrade Commandant," Yudalslov said, "let us assume that our missing pilots landed their Foxbats aboard the American carrier and surrendered them in exchange for political asylum, just as you seem convinced was the case. And the American carrier now plans to take our two Foxbats to the port of Alexandria, where they will be examined for our top secret technology under the protection of the Egyptian government. If all this is so, what would the carrier captain gain by delaying his arrival in those protective waters?"

"Perhaps, in agreeing to take the Foxbats and defectors aboard yesterday when no other ships or planes of the Soviet Union were on hand to see them land, the American carrier captain felt confident no one would ever suspect he had them aboard his ship. However, our continued pursuit must now suggest to him that we are suspicious and expect to find that our missing pilots and their Foxbats have been taken aboard. In view of our close proximity and in realizing we can sail at greater speeds than his ship can, he knows he will never be able to outrun us to Alexandria, where the Egyptians would protect him. And in view of the great distance he has put between his task force and his ship, he knows his own countrymen would never arrive in time to assist him in a confrontation with the owners of the Foxbats he is hiding aboard. Perhaps, out of panic, he sought the privacy of the fogbank to rid his ship of the incriminating evidence, rather than run the risk of being caught with the stolen property. He could easily hide a few defectors aboard his ship, but not two large aircraft like our Foxbats."

Yudalslov shook his head in a gesture of condemnation for Stalovich's reasoning. "First of all, I doubt two aircraft not designed to make an aircraft carrier landing would manage to do so without crash-landing aboard and busting into small pieces, perhaps even causing the ship to catch fire and sink as well. But let us assume that some miracle took place and not one but two such aircraft actually did make a safe landing aboard. If, as you suggest, the Americans did utilize the cover of the fogbank to hide the evidence of such a landing in the depths of the sea, our Foxbats will no longer be of any use to them by doing so. The salt water will corrode the top secret apparatus aboard the planes, even if the detonators aboard the Foxbats fail to explode."

"What detonators are you referring to?" Stalovich asked with a raised eyebrow.

"I thought you knew of the precautions we took to prevent our enemies from salvaging one of our Foxbats equipped with the new top secret apparatus in the event of a ditching at sea," Yudalslov said matter-of-factly.

"I didn't know," Stalovich returned. "Do enlighten me, Comrade Deputy Director."

"All Foxbats equipped with the electronic warfare technology were also equipped with a densimeter that automatically causes a watertight explosive device to detonate once the plane becomes submerged in water more than fifty feet in depth. The explosion is powerful enough to turn the aircraft and everything aboard it into a heap of metal fragments the size of your eyeballs. Therefore, if the Americans have committed our Foxbats to a watery grave, there is no need for further concern over the planes. They will be spread all over the sea's floor in tiny pieces."

"Now that you have told me of this, we can be sure that if our Foxbats were aboard the American carrier before it entered the fogbank, then they are still aboard at this moment. Otherwise my ship's sonar operator would have reported monitoring a submerged explosion the size you have described."

"If they ever were aboard to begin with, then you might still find our Foxbats aboard the carrier now," Yudalslov repeated emphatically. "But I still doubt they ever were taken aboard."

"We have come this far on the assumption that they are," Stalovich insisted. "Now that we are so close, we may as well take a look aboard the carrier and prove or disprove my suspicions."

"And you expect the Americans to cooperate with your desire to satisfy your suspicions? You expect they will let their enemies tour their military vessel and examine its tactical aspects?"

"The carrier is now a stripped-down platform in the sea," Stalovich said. "With all of its aircraft removed, there should be nothing of a classified nature remaining on the flight deck or in its hangar bays to hide from us. And if there are no aircraft belonging to us aboard either, then they should not object to showing us just those two areas of their ship."

"But what will you do if they do object?" Yudalslov asked.

"I will be more persuasive in that case," Stalovich said.

"You will use force to make a search without knowing for sure if our Foxbats actually are aboard?"

"But of course. How else will I ever know whether they are or not? Take the American carrier captain's word that they are not?"

"It will be . . ."

"It will be most embarrassing to the American carrier captain if our two missing Foxbats are found aboard his ship," Stalovich interrupted. "If they are he will most certainly deny my request to board and make a search of his ship. That will tell me that they are aboard. And it will be a matter of Soviet national security for us to recover the planes. The American captain must know that, and surely so must you. In finding our planes aboard, we will not only get them back, but we will also repatriate for trial the defectors who betrayed their homeland and committed high treason by turning their aircraft over to the Soviet Union's enemies. And as punishment for harboring the defectors and being the receiver of stolen property, we will also seize the American carrier and take it as prize, and hold its captain and crew accountable for espionage."

"But Comrade Commandant," the *Leningrad*'s C.O. said in hearing Stalovich's intentions of seizing the American ship, "the

Americans will put up a fight rather than face a Soviet firing squad for committing espionage."

"It will not be much of a fight if they do refuse to surrender their ship and themselves," Stalovich commented. "They have also stripped their ship of its defenses, just as their superiors had foolishly ordered them to do near the island of Cyprus. We will either overpower them and force them to surrender, or we will sink them instead."

"If you find our Foxbats aboard you can use recrimination as a defense for seizing their ship and crew," Yudalslov pointed out. "And if they refuse to return our Foxbats and repatriate the defectors who ran off with them, you might be able to justify sinking the vessel. Especially if they are guilty of doing so and put up a fight. But if the Foxbats are not found aboard, you will be held accountable for using military force to board and search their ship while on international high seas. That much I know about the international maritime law. I also know it is considered piracy to take a ship by seizure if no wrongdoing has occurred, and war was not declared on the nation whose flag is hoisted to the top of the ship's mast."

"I am not interested in how acquainted you are with international maritime law, Comrade Yudalslov," Stalovich retorted. "I know quite well what laws apply on international high seas, both in peacetime and in time of war. In the case of the Americans, we are always at war with that nation, whether war has actually been declared or not. Why else are you doing all you can to perfect your electronic warfare technology, if not to be used against them some day?" Yudalslov made no response. "And why are the Americans doing all they can to beat you at your own game of magical machinery, if they do not intend to use such devices against the Soviet Union?" There was still no reaction from Yudalslov, which told him the deputy director of Project Threshold had no argument to present on the issue of cold versus hot war conditions.

"Then your orders are that we will seize the American ship if our Foxbats are found aboard, Comrade Commandant?" Captain Garupcheck, the *Leningrad*'s C.O., asked in a nervous tone of voice.

"They are," Stalovich said firmly.

"And we are to sink the vessel if it refuses to surrender?" Garupcheck asked with heightened apprehension.

"That is correct," Stalovich reaffirmed.

Facing Yudalslov, Garupcheck said, "I, too, am familiar with international maritime laws. But I am equally familiar with the military laws of the Soviet Union that compel me to obey the orders of my superiors. In executing Commandant Stalovich's orders, I will be doing my duty to the Soviet Union. But I do not wish to be held accountable for being a party to violating laws governing a captain's behavior on the high seas if our Foxbats are not found aboard."

"If you take part in the forced boarding and your search fails to produce our missing aircraft, you will have to face an international maritime tribunal as master of the vessel carrying out the unlawful assault in international waters," Yudalslov warned. "There will be no escaping that for you or for Commandant Stalovich as the two senior officers aboard the *Leningrad*."

"No one will have to face an international tribunal if our missing Foxbats are not found aboard," Stalovich rebuked.

"But in not finding them aboard we will have no choice but to let the American carrier proceed to the port of Alexandria, where her captain will surely complain of our forced boarding on the high seas," Garupcheck argued.

"In that case," Stalovich said, "we will simply refuse to admit that they were not found aboard. And in that case the American carrier will never be allowed to reach Alexandria. We will claim that the American captain put up a fight when we demanded the return of our property. And we will also claim that in order to defend ourselves against his attack we had to sink his ship, and there were no survivors."

"No one in the western world will believe such claims, Comrade Stalovich," Yudalslov protested. "It is insane to think we could get away with such a deception."

"Who will ever be able to prove otherwise?"

"The American captain will surely report to his countrymen that his ship is under attack when we open fire on him for refusing to heave to," Garupcheck insisted.

"Who will hear him claim he is being assaulted if we utilize the new electronic warfare blackout apparatus to prevent him from communicating with the outside world?" Stalovich responded. He sensed by the surprised look on the faces of Yudalslov and Garupcheck that they had failed to grasp the strategic advantage they had. "Do you not see the great opportunity we have come upon, Comrades? Either we take the ship as prize and add it to our own fleet in finding our Foxbats aboard or we will sink the American carrier and thus keep it from falling into the hands of the Egyptian Navy, who will surely use it someday in the future in combat against the Soviet Union or our Middle East friends."

"Perhaps it could work," Garupcheck felt urged to say.

"But of course it will work," Stalovich said. "As Deputy Director Yudalslov pointed out a few minutes ago, the Foxbats are equipped with demolition devices that automatically detonate once the aircraft are submerged in fifty feet or more of water. All we will have to do is blow her to tiny pieces the size of eyeballs, which will be scattered all over the bottom of the Mediterranean. We will also see to it that no one survives the sinking. We will lower boats to pick off anyone who does flee the ship. Then we can tell the outside world that the Foxbats the carrier captain refused to return to us had detonators planted aboard them, which blew up as the ship was sinking when it lost the battle its captain chose to engage us in. If anyone decides to investigate its sunken hull to establish if our Foxbats actually were aboard, they will find no trace of ship or planes to prove or disprove our claims. We will in effect have gotten away with murder. It will turn out to be the perfect crime."

"You are forgetting something, Comrade Stalovich," Yudalslov said.

"And what might that be?"

"The officers and crew of the *Leningrad* will know the truth. And how can we insure that none of them will ever reveal what really took place?"

"This is where you are wrong, Comrade Yudalslov," Stalovich said. "We will carefully select the men who are to board and search the American carrier. And they will actually board the vessel, even if under fire. If they find nothing of our Foxbats aboard, it will remain a secret that only they and the three of us will share. We will not even include the *Leningrad*'s X.O. in on the secret. And when we claim to the rest of our officers and crew that the Foxbats were found aboard, sinking the American ship will meet with their approval, I am sure."

"Before we left the vicinity of Cyprus to follow after the American fleet, I overheard a conversation you had over the scrambler phone with Deputy Secretary of the Navy Kosenoff," Yudalslov revealed. "During that conversation Comrade Kosenoff expressed his disapproval of your desire to blockade the port of Alexandria and prevent the Egyptians from taking ownership of the American carrier. Comrade Kosenoff pointed out that the Soviet Union might suffer severe political consequences if you took such a drastic military action to intervene in the affairs of the Americans and the Egyptians."

"Comrade Kosenoff has been out of the military and a political servant far too long to appreciate the tactical advantages of such a military action," Stalovich replied.

Ignoring Stalovich's defense of the blockade plan he had tried to sell the party leaders at the Kremlin level with no luck, Yudalslov said, "Comrade Kosenoff also warned that you would face severe consequences if you do anything to jeopardize the progress of Project Threshold. By wanting to use the new jamming technique to play pirate captain of your own private fleet of the Soviet Navy, you are placing the new top secret technology in grave jeopardy of being prematurely tested for its strategic deployment capabilities before it is safe to do so. In view of that, you are demonstrating irresponsibility concerning the secret technology we have been entrusted with. What makes you think I will join you in this irresponsibility and fail to report the incident to your superiors for the reckless act that it is?"

"You will report nothing about what we do with the American carrier to anyone," Stalovich said. "You will not, because you know damn well that your precious Project Threshold will be faced with the severest jeopardy if we do nothing to reclaim the Foxbats in time to keep the top secret technology out of enemy hands. And you know, even though you are unwilling to admit it, that the reckless act I am about to embark upon is the only sure way of truly safeguarding that entrusted top secret technology under the present circumstances. The last time one of our Foxbats was turned over to our enemies by a defector it was not returned until the Americans examined every square inch of it. And if we permit the American carrier to continue on to the port of Alexandria, the same thing will occur again. Our Foxbats will be thoroughly inspected for top secret information, then crated up in small pieces and shipped back to us when the Americans have no further use of them. Is that not so, Comrade Deputy Director?"

"Commandant," the bridge duty officer called out through the open window, "our helicopters are ready to get airborne."

Stalovich looked at the *Leningrad*'s C.O. "Comrade Captain, you are to hand-pick two dozen of the most trusted and qualified men we have aboard the flagship to serve as a commando assault team. Furnish them with automatic weapons and walkie-talkies, then divide them into two squads and have them airlifted by our helicopters over to the American carrier. On my command, one helicopter is to land its assault squad aboard the carrier's flight deck forward of the superstructure, while the other lands its assault squad aboard aft. Once aboard, six men of each squad will remain topside on the flight deck to draw any resistance away from the others. Then, from their positions forward and aft, the other two six-man squads will attempt to reach the carrier's hangar deck level to search for our missing property. Whether our Foxbats are found aboard or not, it is imperative that they get word back to me."

"I think we should inform our party leaders of your intention to land a raiding party aboard the American carrier," Yudalslov said firmly.

"There will be time to use your toy telephone system after our objective has been accomplished, Comrade Yudalslov," Stalovich said. Returning his attention to the *Leningrad*'s C.O., he ordered, "Have both our helicopter flight crews confirm that the carrier's major defenses were removed. Also have them inspect the carrier's flight deck for damages that two Foxbats might have caused. Then have them stand by for my order to execute a forced boarding in the event my request to make a search of the ship is denied." He gazed forward at the *Coral Sea* and added, "That is all, Comrade Captain. See to it that my orders are carried out at once. I am most anxious to learn the American navy captain's answer to my request."

"At once, Comrade Commandant," the *Leningrad*'s C.O. said. Then he hurried aft to the helicopter flight deck.

Turning to Yudalslov, Stalovich said, "You may now occupy your deputy director's throne and put your magical machinery through some real military maneuvers."

His right hand wedged snugly between a black box and an orange one, Walter Dodge shook his head in annoyance over the close proximity of the two avionics components. He was standing next to Baxter atop a five-step metal mechanic's inspection stand that had them elevated from the waist up inside the open hatch of Foxbat 116's hellhole. Surrounding them were the numerous computer black boxes they were probing, amidst a host of other varied colored avionics components and related electronics gear. They had just finished probing black box number forty-eight when Dodge realized the orange box was denying him access to the next module to be inspected. He said to Baxter, "Read the identification tag on this orange unit and tell me what the hell is, Nick."

Training his flashlight on the side of the unit, Baxter translated the Russian printing. "It's the cockpit voice recorder."

Trish and Ferris were sharing a similar mechanic's inspection stand that had them raised inside the hellhole of Foxbat 104, a wingspan away from its twin in hangar bay 3. She had already gotten inside the next black box to be inspected and was forced to wait for Dodge to catch up. Early on in their probing, they had decided to work independently, in the hope of covering the numerous modules twice as fast. But each module had so many circuits they soon decided they could cover ground quicker by working in unison. With her test meter leads already hooked up to black box forty-nine, and no word from Dodge that he was ready to proceed on that module also, she was wondering if they should revert to probing independently. She hissed impatiently as she waited for Baxter's voice to come over Ferris's walkie-talkie and announce that her assistant was also hooked up in Foxbat 116. Instead, she heard the carrier's P.A. system blare an announcement that didn't penetrate the walls of the Foxbat surrounding her like a metal tent. Facing Ferris she asked, "What did they say?"

"Two helicopters are approaching from starboard."

"The Russians?" Trish asked uneasily.

"They're certainly not ours."

"Damn it! We're never going to make it. We still have a dozen black boxes to probe, each with fifty or more circuits inside it." She heard another garbled announcement. "What did they say that time, Matt?"

"I'm wanted on the bridge," Ferris replied.

"What the hell for?" Trish asked, annoyed.

"Captain Redding said he might need me to serve as an interpreter between him and the Russians if they paid us a visit."

"Find out what's holding up Walt before you go."

Ferris keyed his walkie-talkie mike button. "Nick, what's the hold up? Over."

"Walt has a cockpit voice recorder right in the way of black box number forty-nine, Matt," Baxter replied.

Hearing Baxter's reply, Trish looked up at the orange box in her Foxbat that Ferris had identified as an identical unit a few minutes ago. "Tell him we have plenty of room to work around the damn thing. He must, too."

"Where is the cockpit voice recorder located in your Foxbat, Nick?" Ferris asked over the walkie-talkie.

"It's mounted upright and almost against the black box we're trying to get inside of," Baxter replied.

Trish and Ferris looked again at their Foxbat's cockpit voice recorder, and Ferris called back to Baxter, "Ours seems to be installed a little differently, Nick. It's hanging upside down from the compartment ceiling. We've got plenty of clearance."

Hearing that come over Baxter's walkie-talkie, Dodge grunted, "Leave it to the damn Russians to lack consistency." Then, remembering that Baxter was a Russian by birth, he added, "No offense meant."

"None taken," Baxter said.

"Call up to the cockpit and ask Mishka to actuate her jamming system controls again," Dodge said. "Maybe the response we heard before was coming from the black box next to this one. I'd hate to have to pull out that damn cockpit voice recorder to get into number forty-nine if it is just another dummy load."

Baxter slipped on a mechanic's headset that was plugged into the aircraft intercom. Speaking Russian, he relayed Dodge's instructions to Mishka, who was seated in her former flight instructor's canopyless cockpit just above their heads. The black box in question reacted to the cockpit controls with a low pitched hum. "It doesn't sound like a dummy load to me," Baxter said flatly.

"We could skip forty-nine and go on to the next black box," Dodge suggested, not wanting to spend time removing the cockpit voice recorder in his way. "Forty-nine could turn out to be just a secondary tie-in to the main control circuitry of one of the other modules we've yet to cover."

"True," Baxter agreed. "But it could also turn out to be the key black box. And with Soviet choppers overhead, this would be a nice time to hit the mother lode."

Dodge gestured for the walkie-talkie, then keyed on. "Trish, I'm going to need time out to remove our cockpit voice recorder so I can get inside number forty-nine."

Taking the walkie-talkie from Ferris, Trish keyed on and asked, "Are you sure forty-nine is part of the system in your Foxbat, Walt?"

"Yeah, we're sure," Dodge called back. "We double-checked it with the cockpit controls."

Ferris heard the P.A. paging him to the bridge again. He picked up his mechanic's headset and keyed on with Viktor and Nadia. Speaking Russian, he said, "Viktor, I have to leave for a few minutes. If you hear two clicks over the intercom, actuate your jamming controls. When three clicks follow, shut them down again." He turned to Trish. "Use the mike-clicking signal to get around the language barrier while I'm gone."

"Okay, Matt," Trish said with a nod.

"Might as well have Walt remove the obstacle he's hung up by," Ferris said. "And do the best you can to go on checking your black box in the meantime. I'll get back here as soon as I can be spared from the bridge."

It was the first time since they'd departed from the main body of the task force that Yudalslov had fired up the *Leningrad*'s electronic warfare apparatus. On doing so, he heard signals coming over the jamming and antijamming equipment as though the system had been operating on its own in his absence. He actuated a number of switches to make a functional test check of his apparatus, thinking at first that some sort of internal feedback malfunction was causing the new electronics to operate. His test served to establish that the signals were external, coming in over his apparatus from some unidentifiable source. And the signals had no defined meaning to him, rather they were just pulses that seemed to be occurring randomly. Guessing that one of the task force ships had left their electronic warfare apparatus on accidentally, he picked up the phone at his station and pressed the bridge button. It was quickly answered by the bridge duty officer. "This is Deputy Director Yudalslov. I must speak to the Commandant at once." He was told to hold on.

Stalovich stepped inside the bridge and accepted the phone. "What is the difficulty, Comrade Yudalslov?"

Yudalslov explained the problem and said, "I wish to contact the main body of our task force. Perhaps one of the ships of our fleet has accidentally left its jamming apparatus on."

Stalovich pondered Yudalslov's request for a moment, then asked, "Will these outside signals you're encountering prevent you from jamming the American carrier's communications channels?"

"Not at all," Yudalslov answered. "One has nothing to do with the other. But I would like to verify the source of the interference, anyway. These electronics are very delicate, and replacement parts are quite scarce. It is wasteful to subject them to unnecessary use."

Stalovich shook his head impatiently. "Kindly concentrate your efforts on carrying out my order to jam the American carrier's communications channels for now, Comrade Yudalslov. When my military objective has been completed, you can see to your problems of waste."

Yudalslov eyed the light on his control module that was blinking in unison with the signals. He shook his head in annoyance over Stalovich's stubbornness, then said, "Very well, Comrade Commandant. I will do it your way. But it is my duty to . . ."

"It is my duty to oversee the military maneuver I am executing at this moment," Stalovich growled. "We will discuss your duties later." He hung up the phone bitterly, then faced the bridge duty officer and said, "I do not wish to be interrupted while our assault team is engaged in carrying out their objective."

"I will see to it, Commandant," the bridge duty officer said.

Dusk was falling off port. Off starboard, the sun was a huge crimson ball that was being swallowed by the sea. Stalovich returned to the forward bridge catwalk, thinking of how the fog had delayed his awaited encounter with the American carrier. It had him feeling ambivalent about evening's darkness. Night would make it harder for his helicopter flight crews to search for signs of proof that the Foxbats were aboard. But it would also serve to create confusion when the *Leningrad*'s helicopters landed aboard. He was wondering if perhaps he should order the assault team to wait for the last traces of daylight to disappear. He raised his binoculars to observe the aerial activity of the two Kamov helicopters as they arrived above the American carrier. As long as they were already in position and the American carrier captain had done nothing as yet to chase them off, he decided to let the raid take place right away.

Garupcheck arrived back on the bridge level. Joining Stalovich on the forward catwalk, he asked, "Has the American carrier captain responded to your request to board and search his ship?"

"I have elected not to ask him," Stalovich returned. "He will surely refuse to grant permission. Besides, I have already ordered Comrade Yudalslov to commence the blackout of the carrier's communications. With the American captain incommunicado, we will not need to be invited aboard. He can do very little to stop our visit." He slipped on his headset and adjusted the mike bar in preparation for giving his two helicopters the order to land aboard the carrier.

Garupcheck felt uneasy about the *Leningrad*'s helicopters' forced landing aboard the American ship, but he made no mention of his feelings to Stalovich for fear of a reprimand. He just quietly watched the activity through his binoculars.

CHAPTER TWENTY-TWO

Redding was out on the port bridge catwalk, watching the two Soviet helicopters, when Ferris joined him. "So far they've given us a flyby well above our flight deck," he said. "And they've made a flyaround of my ship at hangar deck level. That tells me they're searching for their two Foxbats and suspect we have them aboard."

"They can't know that for sure," Ferris said. "All we have to do is keep them from landing aboard to take a look below decks."

Redding gestured to the flight deck below them. "I have my X.O. and leading chief on hand with a ten-man welcoming committee, just in case they try to come aboard. The rifle team's ten M-16's should stand off the two choppers nicely, but they won't even put a dent in the hull of that Kara class cruiser off our stern." He gestured in the direction of the *Leningrad* growing larger on the surface some four miles behind the *Coral Sea*. "Without our topside defenses and with no aircraft or escort ships to support us, we are going to be asking for a real ass-kicking from that bullying bastard if we have to put up a fight."

Ferris eyed the helmeted rifle team standing in a single-file rank beneath the bridge catwalk. He noticed the military .45's holstered on the right hips of Jones and Smith as they stood in front of the welcoming committee. After looking uneasily astern at the menacing cruiser, he decided that putting up a fight without help was suicidal. "I think we'd better break radio silence and get word out to our task force that we might need some muscle at this end of the Med."

"I've already thought of that," Redding said. "But it seems the Russians want to keep us incommunicado. All of our channels of communications are on a total blackout, just like they were back in Cyprus for a time."

"They must be using the same jamming and antijamming technology on us that's fouling up our surveillance satellites," Ferris said.

"Now I can see why your NSA team is trying so hard to crack the new technology aboard those Foxbats," Redding commented. "I can't even raise that Soviet cruiser or its choppers on ship's radio, and they're close enough to spit at." He raised the P.A. mike he was holding limply in one hand. "I resorted to using this in the hope of chasing them away, but so far they've ignored my threats. Either they don't speak English, or they don't scare easily. And I want you to establish which is the case. Tell them in Russian that their proximity to our ship is an unlawful encroachment. That their intrusion violates maritime laws guaranteeing a vessel's right to free passage through international high seas. That we regard their presence as an unprovoked hostile action. That our ship's defenses are at the ready and we can legally use armed resistance to put an end to their aggressive behavior. Then tell them, if they persist, we will exercise our right to do just that."

Ferris eyed the two helicopters lining up one behind the other just ahead of the *Coral Sea*. He estimated their altitude to be about fifty feet above the flight deck as they arrived overhead of the bow. Accepting the P.A. mike, he keyed on and announced Redding's warnings in fluent Russian, his voice resounding over the flight deck and out over the slowly rolling sea. Still the two Kamov helicopters continued their slow airborne march toward the superstructure as though they had every intention of making a landing aboard. Their rotors sent vibrations crashing down to the flight deck and turned the area beneath their whirling blades into a windstorm. Ferris repeated the warnings loudly to make sure he was being heard.

Redding looked on with approval as Ferris spat out angry Russian words. Seeing the helicopters were still paying no heed, he bellowed, "They're really itching for a fight."

"Those rotors are pretty damn noisy," Ferris said. "Maybe they can't hear me over the P.A."

"They heard you all right," Redding insisted. "We've used the P.A. to bring choppers aboard many times before. And there's no language barrier to use as an excuse now, either. They're just pretty damn nervy." He gestured for the mike, then keyed on. "Jonesy, on the count of three, have your rifle team fire a five-second warning burst into the air off port. If that doesn't take the wind out of their sails, then your next volley will take the wind out of their rotors."

Facing the rifle team lined up just outside an open island hatch, Jones drew his .45 and ordered, "Squad, cock and aim your weapons." His command brought ten M-16 rifle barrels pointing skyward with the clicking sound of cocked breeches. It also encouraged Chief Smith to unholster his weapon. Using a megaphone held in his free hand, Jones called up to the bridge catwalk, "We're at the ready, and waiting for your count, Skipper."

Ferris looked toward the *Leningrad* as the setting sun splashed the cruiser with a last spray of rays. The glitter it caused astern of the *Coral Sea* had him envisioning ominously large cannon muzzles being pointed in their direction by obedient turret crews. He reached for the P.A. mike. "They're closer to the P.A. speakers now. Let me make one last attempt before we start shooting. Cut off from the outside world and out here like sitting ducks, I'd like to avoid getting that cruiser mad enough to pounce on us just because we fired a warning volley."

With the two helicopters still advancing on the island at a speed that was slightly faster than a hover, Redding ordered, "Hold your fire, Jonesy. But stay at the ready." Handing the P.A. mike to Ferris again, he added, "They're close enough now to hear you without the damn P.A. system. If they ignore you this time it's because they want to."

As the first helicopter dropped even lower in the sky, Ferris tried once more. Again the warning was ignored, forcing him to face the reality that the helicopters were going to land and search for their MIG-35's, even if they had to fight their way aboard. Again he shouted a warning in Russian, this time threatening to open fire on them. Even that failed to scare them off. Gripped with a feeling of hopelessness, he returned the P.A. mike. "Go ahead and try your warning volley," he said to Redding. "It's all we can do now."

Keying the mike, Redding shouted, "Rifle team! I am starting my count. If the warning burst goes unheeded, my next order will be to open fire on the two choppers." He hoped that someone aboard either helicopter understood English and hearing his yelled orders would do something to prevent a fight. But both helicopters continued their brazen descent to his flight deck. With ten M-16 rifle barrels aimed at the quickly darkening sky to port, he keyed the mike again. "One." His voice echoed over the flight deck. "Two . . ."

Suddenly an explosion erupted that sent both of the Soviet helicopters in a sharp bank away from the ship and climbing for altitude. The pilots and their crews, astonished by the unexpected clamor, hovered over the sea well off the carrier's portside and looked on in disbelief as thick black smoke gushed out of the stern of the American ship from the hangar deck level.

Unsure of what had happened, the pilot at the controls of the second helicopter quickly raised the pilot of the lead helicopter. "Did you cause that explosion, Comrade Flight Leader?" he asked anxiously.

"We did nothing," the helicopter flight leader said excitedly. The assault team leader aboard his helicopter was also questioning him, while the dozen armed commandos filling the cargo compartment of the vibrating helicopter looked out the round cabin windows to eye the column of thick smoke billowing up to meet their aircraft. Fearful that the armed sailors lining the carrier's flight deck were eyeing him accusingly, the lead pilot keyed his radio mike and ordered, "Return to the flagship at once."

Frantic over the suddenness of the thunderous burst, Jones, Chief Smith, and the rifle team indecisively aimed their weapons after the fleeing helicopters, not certain whether or not they had somehow caused the explosion.

Hearing a blaring fire alarm immediately follow the explosion, Redding shouted, "Damage report!"

Answering a call from a hangar deck watch, the bridge duty officer called out in alarm, "Sir, it's in hangar bay three! One of the Soviet Foxbats just blew up! The watch on duty there says the plane's a fireball."

Charging into the bridge, Redding snapped, "Have every man that can be spared lay down to hangar bay three to man fire-fighting stations." He was nearly in tears over the news of a shipboard fire. When he stepped back out on the catwalk, he noticed that Ferris was gone. Seeing the two Soviet helicopters streaking back to their ship, he picked up the P.A. mike and called down to the flight deck, "Jonesy, take half your rifle squad below to hangar bay three and have them bear a hand with the fire-fighting requirements. Get a damage and casualty report to me as soon as you possibly can." Jones and five sailors scrambled for catwalks to get below decks, and Redding turned to Chief Smith. "Smitty, you keep the remainder of the welcoming committee topside, just in case those Soviet choppers return."

With the news that one of the Foxbats had blown up still reverberating in his mind, Ferris sped down staircases, taking the steel steps two and three at a time to get to the troubled area. He arrived at the hangar deck level amidships, and found bays one and two filled with a smoky haze. Seeing flames rising to the ceiling in bay 3, he raced toward them. A dozen or more crewmen walled the front of the fire as they frantically trained fire extinguishers and fire hoses on the flames. Other crewmen were climbing up stationary wall ladders to get to the high capacity foam nozzles mounted on rotatable platforms on both sides of bay 3. More were charging after Foxbat 104 to assist the tractor driver in towing it away from its burning twin.

What Ferris first saw when he pushed his way to the front of the fire fighters sickened him. The open cockpit of Foxbat 116 had turned into an inferno while he was away. Still seated inside it was a human form that he knew was Mishka. She was enveloped in flames and making no attempt to get out. What he saw next was mind-shattering. Lying in a twisted heap atop the inspection stand under Foxbat 116's hellhole were two more forms engulfed in fire and barely recognizable as human. They were making no effort to escape from the flames either. He charged the Foxbat without regard for his own safety. "Nick! No!" he screamed. "Not you! Not you!"

Jones had arrived just as Ferris was rushing toward the burning Foxbat. He gestured for two of his crewmen to follow him as he raced after Ferris. "Grab hold of him!" he shouted as he wrapped his arms around Ferris's waist.

"Let me go! I've got to help Nick! Let me go!" Ferris yelled as he fought Jones and the two crewmen.

"You can't be of any help to them now," Jones said as he and the crewmen forced Ferris backwards away from the flaming MIG-35.

Ferris continued to struggle. "Get him out of there!" he begged tearfully as he looked at Baxter's burning body. "Please! Get him out!"

Jones felt the fight draining out of Ferris. He released Ferris's torso and gestured for his crewmen to let go of Ferris's arms. He saw a crewman wearing a hooded asbestos fire suit and summoned him over. "Get those bodies removed as soon as the fire is under control." The face behind the silver asbestos hood nodded and walked off toward the burning plane.

Viktor had witnessed Ferris's futile attempt to free Baxter from the blanketing fire; he well knew that hopeless feeling. He and Nadia had instinctively abandoned their cockpits when the explosion had occurred. Moments before Ferris had rushed Foxbat 116 to save his close friend, Viktor had tried to rescue Mishka. But the intense heat and leaping flames had driven him back, and all he could do now was keep Nadia wrapped in his arms to shield her from the horrifying sight of her dearest friend's fiery death.

The explosion had knocked the mechanic's inspection stand out from under Trish's legs and sent her crashing to the hangar deck. The test meter she had hooked up to black box number forty-nine was dangling out of the hellhole by its leads when she got to her feet. It was still swinging back and forth like a pendulum as Foxbat 104 was being hurriedly towed off to the safety of bay 2. She had been plunged into shock by the sight of Foxbat 116's forward cockpit and hellhole turning into a furnace just moments after she'd told Walt Dodge to proceed with removing the cockpit voice recorder. Shock kept her insensible to the bodies burning just a few yards away from her. It wasn't until she saw Viktor beaten back by flames while attempting to rescue Mishka that she realized the explosion had claimed the lives of everyone working on her Foxbat's twin. When she saw Ferris being dragged back from Foxbat 116's flaming hellhole soon after Viktor's failed rescue attempt, she became aware that she might have been burned alive, too, if she had been working on that aircraft instead of Foxbat 104. "My God!" she exclaimed, as she gazed at the charred bodies in horror.

For long moments Trish stood to one side of the fire-fighting activity, alone and stunned by grief. Her eyes were helplessly pulled to the black figure still seated in the forward cockpit of Foxbat 116. *Mishka, the pretty Soviet MIG pilot*, she thought dolefully. Unwillingly, but compulsively, she dropped her eyes to the two forms the fire had fused together atop the mechanic's inspection stand. "Walt," she sighed. He'd been alive just moments ago. Now he was burned to a crisp. And Matt's navy friend, Nick Baxter. He was dead, too. She looked over at Ferris, and seeing the grief in his eyes, she felt herself being drawn to his side. She surrendered to the impulse and crossed the hangar deck to join him. Touching him lightly on the forearm, she said, "Oh, Matt . . . it all happened so fast. I . . ."

Ferris turned to Trish and seeing her tears, he pulled her into his arms. "Go ahead. Let it out," he said compassionately, wishing he could cry away his torment as well. He was crying, though. Deep down inside.

Trish allowed herself to release the emotions shock had kept locked inside her. "My God!" she sobbed. "It's horrible. I had just talked to Walt on the walkie-talkie. Then this." She wept, her sorrow deep and agonizing.

Ferris knew an incendiary bomb had caused the fiery explosion, and when Trish had finally cried herself out, he said, "We disarmed every damn booby trap connected to every damn black box in both Foxbats. How could this happen?"

"It must have been the cockpit voice recorder, Matt," Trish sighed. "That's what Walt was working on when the explosion occurred."

Ferris moved over to the parked tow tractor and slammed a closed fist on its steel fender. "Damn!" he grunted. "Viktor told me he and Nadia had to fear saying anything incriminating to each other in their cockpits because their conversations were monitored by their party leaders. I should have known an eavesdropping device like the cockpit voice recorder would also be booby-trapped to prevent pilots from erasing damaging cockpit dialogue."

Astonished by what Ferris had said, Trish replied, "I can't believe the Russians would blow up people just to prevent them from having a little privacy."

"You don't know the Russians like I do," Ferris said bitterly. "Privacy promotes secrecy and subterfuge in their eyes. Communism can't afford privacy for the people." He saw Jones hurrying by and waved him over to them. "Better let your people know the other Foxbat may still be *hot*. My people were removing the aircraft's cockpit voice recorder when the explosion took place. That's one damn unit I failed to search for booby traps," he admitted painfully.

"I'm calling in a damage and casualty report to the skipper now," Jones said. "I'll have him pass the word to all hands over the bitchbox."

Gesturing to the fire, Ferris asked in a worried tone, "What's our situation?"

Jones looked over his shoulder at the two cannonlike high-capacity nozzles bombarding Foxbat 116 with steady streams of foam from both sides of hangar bay 3. The gooey white liquid was splattering off the fuselage and wings and accumulating into a mound of oozing suds under the MIG-35. The rest of the firefighting detail were keeping their fire hoses and extinguishers raining on the cockpit and hellhole to drown the base of the fire. "It must have been a personnel mine that erupted into a fireball," Jones said. "Luckily, all of the avionics gear crammed inside the hellhole walled the blast. That kept the flames concentrated in an upward and downward direction, instead of an outward spread that might have ignited the fuel tanks. If the tanks had exploded, the other Foxbat might have been touched off, too, and we'd all be abandoning ship right now."

"You'll be able to get the fire out, then?" Trish asked anxiously.

"All fires need oxygen to burn. With the kind of smothering we're giving this one, I don't see how it can go on breathing for much longer," Jones said confidently.

With Jones rushing off for a wall phone to call in his damage and casualty report to Redding, Trish asked, "Once the fire is out, what do we do, Matt?"

Watching the fire-fighting efforts, Ferris said firmly, "We go on with the probing."

"Matt, I don't think I can go back into the hellhole again after this."

"Then I will," Ferris said. "All you have to do is tell me what to look for."

"There's too much involved in the probing to explain it all just like that, Matt," Trish said.

Ferris stared into her eyes. "You'll just have to find a way, Trish. You'll have to find a way for me to do it, or you'll have to help me do it. One way or another, Operation Mediterranean Maneuver has to succeed. Now more than ever." He looked at the foam-drenched Foxbat. "Those people gave their lives for this mission. And I'm not going to let them die for nothing."

Shortly after the explosion erupted aboard the aircraft carrier, Stalovich summoned Yudalslov to the bridge. He denied his two helicopters permission to land aboard his flagship and kept them hovering over the sea just ahead of the *Leningrad* while he reevaluated how the situation aboard the American ship might affect his commando assault team's mission. When Yudalslov joined him on the forward bridge catwalk, he looked at the thick column of black smoke billowing up from the aircraft carrier's hangar deck level aft, and said, "You told me before you went below that all Foxbats equipped with the new jamming technology are also equipped with demolition devices to destroy them in the event they are inadvertently lost at sea."

"That is correct, Comrade Commandant," Yudalslov said. "Depth-sensitive demolition charges, to be precise."

"Might there also be touch-sensitive demolition charges installed elsewhere aboard such equipped Foxbats?" Stalovich asked.

"But of course," Yudalslov replied. "There are numerous

booby traps strategically placed in and around the many electronic warfare system components to safeguard the new technology from being tampered with."

"And if by chance our two missing Foxbats were aboard the American ship and their electronic warfare apparatus was being tampered with, might one of these detonated booby traps explain the recent explosion?"

Yudalslov stared at the column of smoke climbing up to the twilight sky, then said, "It would also explain the source of the strange signals I reported monitoring over the electronic warfare apparatus. When did the explosion occur?"

"Just a few minutes ago," Stalovich said.

"It was just a few minutes ago that these strange signals suddenly ceased," Yudalslov said. He added, "They could have been caused by someone actuating the electronic warfare apparatus with little or no knowledge of the new technology. That would also explain why the signal patterns made no sense." He looked at Stalovich and their eyes met. "Comrade Commandant, you must send your helicopters back to the American carrier at once and have them investigate this fire."

"Then you now agree we might find our two missing Foxbats aboard," Stalovich said, smiling triumphantly.

"If the explosion was caused by our booby traps, you will find only charred pieces of our Foxbats remaining," Yudalslov said. "And with the Americans busily fighting the shipboard fire, your assault teams should meet little resistance when they land aboard."

"I can keep those who are not fighting the fire busy as well by diverting their attention away from the helicopters," Stalovich said. He ordered the two helicopters to carry out their forced boarding and search, then summoned the flagship's signalman.

Redding eyed the returning helicopters uneasily as they came abreast of the *Coral Sea* from well off port. He glanced down at Chief Smith and the five-man M-16 rifle team that had been released from the fire-fighting efforts to defend the flight deck. Smith had his men clustered around an open island hatch below him, and Redding was about to give his leading chief a shout over the P.A. to have him spread his reception committee out to positions forward and aft, when the bridge O.O.D. signaled him. "What is it?" he asked impatiently, fearful it might be bad news about the fire-fighting efforts below decks. "Skipper, that Soviet cruiser is communicating with us over a signaling light."

"What do they want?" Redding asked as he glanced aft at the light flashes coming from the huge ship astern.

"Our signalman says they recognize we are in distress and are prepared to lend us assistance," the duty officer relayed.

Redding said crisply, "Have our signalman tell them thanks, but we can handle things without their help." When he returned his attention to the helicopters, he saw they were moving in on his ship from two directions. He quickly grabbed the P.A. mike and shouted, "Smitty, spread your men out and wave those two choppers off."

Chief Smith scrambled three riflemen forward to deal with the helicopter coming in from the bow. With the two remaining riflemen he rushed aft to stop the second helicopter's descent from the sky astern. "Stand off!" he shouted over his megaphone, brandishing his .45 as he did. When his warning was ignored, he fired a shot over his head, but still the helicopter lowered to the flight deck. "Okay, sailors! Let 'em have it," he ordered.

From his perch on the bridge catwalk, Redding looked on in disbelief as the helicopter astern returned Chief Smith's shot with a burst of machine gun fire that sent Smith and his two crewmen crashing backwards to the deck before they could fire another shot. He looked forward when he heard shots ring out from the bow end of the flight deck. He saw the three crewmen deployed in that direction scurrying for the deck-edge catwalks to take cover as they were fired upon. "You bastards! You dirty bastards!" he bellowed. "Sound G.Q.," he growled to the bridge O.O.D. "We're under attack!"

As soon as the wheels of the helicopter astern touched down, twelve Soviet commandos jumped out onto the flight deck. Armed with automatic rifles, six of them took up defensive positions around their helicopter, while the other six dashed off for the catwalks to gain access to the stairwells leading below. While making their descent they encountered four American sailors heading topside to man their battle stations. A quick burst of machine gun fire dropped the sailors to the steps and cleared their path to the hangar deck hatch on port abaft.

The fire was nearly under control as Jones responded to the G.Q. alarm. "We're under attack! Those of you with weapons, follow me. The rest of you make sure the fire is put out!" Ferris, racing forward with Jones and six armed sailors to get topside, quickly drew his service revolver from inside his coveralls when he saw a half dozen Soviet sailors emerge on the hangar deck just across from where he and Trish were standing. "Everyone take cover!" he called out. His shouts sent the fire fighters scrambling for things to hide behind, and he pulled Trish down behind the parked tow tractor. Using the heavy metal-clad vehicle as a shield, he fired a volley of shots in the direction of the Soviet commandos, sending them back inside the stairwell for cover as well.

Viktor was quick to draw Nadia behind the partly shut fire doors separating bays 2 and 3 when the six Soviet commandos returned Ferris's fire. The two defectors were joined by one of the hangar bay security watches, who drew his .45 and got off two rounds in the direction of the Soviet assault team before a machine gun burst slammed into him. The watch pitched forward with a grimace and Viktor quickly took possession of the military .45 that fell from his hand. Aware he had his own countrymen in the sights of the American-made handgun, he discharged the entire ammo clip. He lowered the empty gun when two of the Soviet commandos collapsed to the deck with a grunt just outside the stairwell hatch.

"Thanks, Vick," Ferris called out in Russian. He heard one of the Soviet commandos order those with him to withdraw. At that moment there were six others moving in on him, Viktor, and Nadia from the direction of hangar bay 1, to pin them down from behind. But before he could fire a shot at them, they also broke off their approach and retraced their steps forward. Their sudden retreat didn't have Ferris puzzled. He knew they had found what they were searching for and were fleeing to get word of the find back to their ship. "Everyone! Get back to fighting that fire!" he called out. As the fire fighters came out of hiding, Ferris raced after the fleeing commandos.

Feeling useless staring down at Chief Smith's motionless body, Redding had relieved the bridge O.O.D. of his .45 and raced down to the flight deck. Hugging the open island hatchway, he fired four rounds at the Soviet assault team positioned around the helicopter aft of the island. He noticed that Jones had arrived at a vantage point on port and was engaging the assault team forward of the island. He saw four Soviet commandos emerge from the port catwalks abaft and make a dash for the waiting helicopter aft of the island. Certain they had seen the Foxbats on the hangar deck level and were evacuating to report the news to their ship, he chanced leaving the protection of the open island hatch to stop them. Firing a volley of shots at them, he heard return fire whistle close over his head and ricochet off the steel wall of the island behind him. Accompanying the pinging sounds of bouncing bullets was a burning sting at his left temple. Dizziness overcame him, and he staggered a few feet toward the helicopter. Then his legs folded under him.

Jones saw Redding fall to the deck; it made him furious. "Skipper!" he cried out as he climbed out of the catwalk and rushed toward Redding. As he did he spotted six Soviet commandos rushing topside from the forward catwalks on starboard to make a dash for their waiting helicopter. In a rage he raced back to his men and grabbed an M-16 rifle out of the hands of one of them. The helicopter assault team was back aboard and the helicopter was climbing skyward as he and his rifle team fired a long barrage of shots at the craft. When the helicopter banked out over the sea, a return volley strafed the catwalks and flight deck, forcing the men manning the catwalks to cease their fire and duck for cover.

But Jones was out in the open and a burst of shots tore into his chest. He dropped to his knees with a cry of anguish, but he kept his M-16 pointed skyward at the fleeing helicopter. As he began to sink into eternal darkness he fired one last spurt and his short burst slammed into the rotors and engine housing. The volley of shots nicked the rotor blades and pierced a fuel feed line that began leaking the combustible fluid onto the hot engine manifold in a deluge. The helicopter's engine coughed and sputtered from the rotor blade that was knocked out of balance, and from being starved of fuel by the ruptured feed line. Within moments the fuel was ignited by the hot manifold and the fire spread rapidly to the fuel tank, causing it to explode and turn the entire aircraft into a ball of flames. It plummeted into the sea like a flaming meteor with everyone aboard enveloped in fire and screaming in agony.

Just before his eyes closed, Jones had seen the fireball he had made of the Soviet helicopter. With a smile on his face he crashed to the deck facedown.

Ferris arrived on the flight deck aft as the second helicopter was lifting off, and he quickly discharged the rounds left in his service revolver. Two of his shots struck the stabilizing rotor and caused the helicopter to fishtail violently.

Unable to keep his helicopter under control, the pilot keyed his radio mike, "This is Flight Group Leader! The Foxbats are aboard!" he reported excitedly. "We are going to ditch."

Ferris watched the second helicopter corkscrew down to the sea. Life rafts were immediately tossed out of the craft and were automatically inflated as crewmen dived out after them. He turned his back on the downed helicopter as it began to sink into the sea, then caught sight of Redding struggling to get to his feet, and raced down the flight deck to assist him. Grabbing hold of him, he examined the side of his head. Blood was running down his face and neck.

"How bad?" Redding asked.

Ferris tore the front of Redding's shirt off and used it to blot the wound dry. Redding's grimacing response to the dabbing told him the pain was severe, but in clearing away the blood he saw that it was only a flesh wound. "It's just a nick," he finally said. He placed Redding's hand over the bloodstained piece of cloth. "Keep this on as a compress."

"Smitty?"

Ferris had seen Chief Smith on the flight deck aft lying face up, his eyes wide open and staring skyward. He shook his head, and the returning color drained from Redding's face.

"Jonesy?" Redding asked next, almost pleadingly.

Ferris looked forward at Jones. He was lying on his chin in a pool of blood. His arm was queerly twisted under his torso. Four sailors had knelt beside him. One was calling his name aloud as he shook him. Jones remained motionless. The sailor rolled him over on his back and folded his arms on his chest, then closed his eyes. Looking aft, Ferris saw a half dozen sailors attending to Chief Smith's lifeless body, and to the two enlisted shipmates who had fallen beside him in combat. He said somberly, "We took a hell of a beating all around."

Redding accepted Ferris's supporting arm as they made their way over to the open island hatch. He noticed the machine gun bullet holes above the hatchway and siding it. "I have a feeling the beating isn't over with, Matt," he said, grimacing. "If the skipper of that cruiser hasn't already gotten word that we have their Foxbats, the survivors of that downed chopper will tell him for sure."

Ferris nodded. "As a skipper yourself, what do you think the skipper of that cruiser will do now that he does know?"

"I'd demand my property back," Redding said. "And the defectors, too, since I was in a position of strength."

Aiding Redding up a staircase leading to the bridge, Ferris asked, "And if we gave them what they demanded, what then?"

"If it were me, before I'd let anyone go home, I'd have to be sure they didn't take my top secret technology along with them," Redding answered.

"And if you couldn't be sure?"

Redding looked into his eyes. "I couldn't risk being wrong. I'd have to be sure, or . . ."

"Or no one goes home," Ferris finished for him.

Nodding painfully, Redding said, "In view of that, what do you want to do now?"

As they arrived on the bridge, Ferris replied, "Keep heading for Alexandria and do our best to stall for time. Once we're overdue, a search will be made for us. Hopefully, we'll be found before time runs out on us."

"Now that there is no longer any doubt as to the whereabouts of our missing property, we can proceed with the rest of my plans for the American carrier," Stalovich said happily. "See to picking up the survivors of our downed helicopters," he said to the bridge duty officer. "Then bring us to firing range ahead of the American ship."

"You must sink the American carrier without delay." Yudalslov insisted.

"Now you are anxious for me to do so," Stalovich said. "Before you were squeamish about the idea."

"Before I was not sure that it was the right thing to do," Yudalslov said. "But now that they have caused one of our Foxbats to blow up, we can conclude they were probing the electronic warfare apparatus aboard them ever since they landed on the American carrier. In view of the possibility that they have learned our top secret technology, we must not allow them to pass the information along to their homeland or allies."

"I assure you they will not, Comrade Deputy Director," Stalovich promised. "But I will give them an opportunity to be spared death by surrendering their ship to me, along with our remaining Foxbat and the traitors they are harboring."

"You mentioned the ultimatum you would give the American carrier captain before, and at the time I paid the notion very little attention in thinking our Foxbats were not actually aboard," Yudalslov said. "But now that we know they are, and you still intend to take the ship as prize, I must protest."

"For what reason?" Stalovich asked.

"Such a thing is too risky," Yudalslov said. "It is a long voyage from here to a Soviet port. We might never arrive. The American ship is expected in Alexandria. When it fails to arrive there on time, the Americans, and perhaps the Egyptians as well, will search the Mediterranean Sea for the aircraft carrier.

When they find us with it, they will surely put up a fight to free it from our seizure. And if we also put up a fight to keep the American ship, the skirmish could lead to a large-scale military confrontation at sea between both the American and Egyptian navies, and our navy. Perhaps the navies of the entire world will become involved in an all-out conventional war."

"But you yourself reassured me we will never be faced with a conventional war," Stalovich said in a condemning tone. "You were trying to convince me that your magical machinery will compromise our enemies."

"I also said it is premature to rely upon the strategic deployment capabilities of Project Threshold," Yudalslov growled. "But enough with arguing among ourselves. You must sink the American carrier here and now while you can. Your stubborn idea to commandeer the American ship will not work. It cannot be done your way."

"It can and will be done my way, Comrade Yudalslov," Stalovich said harshly. He gazed out at the *Coral Sea* and added confidently, "Your reasons for protesting my intent to take the American ship as prize are not strong enough to change my mind. To begin with, the American Navy would not risk a large-scale military conflict with the Soviet Navy over a stripped-down ship that is to be given away. No other nation of the free world would do so, either. And the Egyptian Navy is too weak to stand up to our mighty naval forces. Therefore, no one will stop me from escorting the seized American ship to a Soviet port. I will succeed at arriving in homeland waters with it, and it will be added to the Soviet Navy instead of the Egyptian Navy as a just consequence for the failed attempt the Americans have made to learn the top secret technology."

"You will only succeed in getting us all killed," Yudalslov said. "But perhaps the American carrier captain will save us all by turning down your foolish ultimatum and force you to sink his ship, just as you should."

"We will use your toy telephone system to issue my ultimatum to the American carrier captain and see if he chooses life or death for himself and his crew," Stalovich said. "We will use the new electronic warfare communications system to raise the American captain over the aircraft radio aboard the Foxbat that survived the explosion. And we will have my flagship standing in his path to Alexandria with our cannons trained on his ship. Perhaps that will have us see a white flag replace the American national ensign atop the *Coral Sea*'s mast."

CHAPTER TWENTY-THREE

The fire was out and Foxbat 116 looked like a snow-topped mountain, set before a half dozen sailors who were using long-handled squeegees to push the oozy flood of foam over to hangar deck drains. Outlined by the black of night, the deck-edge elevator on starboard abaft was bringing down the last two bodies from the flight deck. The others who had fallen victim to either the fire or the fight were placed in the rear of bay 3 and were covered with tarpaulin. The fire doors separating bays 2 and 3 had been drawn almost fully closed, so that the probing work could be resumed without viewing the awesome sight of Foxbat 104's charred twin and the corpses being gathered for future burial.

But the probing work had not resumed yet. Viktor and Nadia were about to climb the wing of Foxbat 104 to man their probing positions, and Ferris and Trish were ready to climb the mechanic's inspection stand and continue their scrutiny of black box number forty-nine, when a loud beeping sound suddenly filled the tandem cockpits of the MIG-35. It drew the attention of everyone in bay 2 at once.

Responding instinctively to the unfamiliar urgent beeping, Ferris grabbed Trish by the arm, and as he quickly withdrew from the side of the aircraft, he shouted, "Everyone! Get back! Quick!" His warning sent the half dozen sailors standing around Foxbat 104 with fire extinguishers scrambling for cover.

Viktor, like Nadia, was puzzled about the sudden panic the beeping had caused. Then realizing the Americans didn't know what it meant, he called out to Ferris in Russian, "Do not be alarmed! It is only the Foxbat's standby radio receiver!"

Ferris had just tossed Trish behind the safety of the steel tow tractor, and he was about to duck down behind it after her, when he heard Viktor's shouted explanation. He went back to the Foxbat.

Nadia added to Viktor's explanation. "When the aircraft radio is turned off, the beeping signal alerts the pilots that someone is trying to communicate with them over the jamming and antijamming scrambler phone system."

"You mean, it was only an electronic paging device?"

"But of course," Nadia said calmly.

"I thought it was a warning that a time delay bomb was about to go off," Ferris said.

"I think the call is from the cruiser that has been hounding us," Viktor said. "The beeping signal is too loud to be coming from any great distance."

"Take the call, Viktor," Ferris said. "Do not answer any questions. Just find out what is on the caller's mind."

Viktor climbed the left wing and reached into his forward cockpit for the aircraft radio mike. After turning on the radio, he said simply, "Who is transmitting and what is the nature of your communication?" He listened to the caller, then said, "Please stand by." Looking gloomy, he called down to Ferris. "It could not be worse. The caller is Soviet Fleet Admiral Georgi Stalovich, commandant of the cruiser *Leningrad* and of Soviet Task Force Mediterranean. He is known in the Soviet Union as the Tyrant of Tymlat, the region of Kamchatka that is his birthplace."

Ferris searched his mental archives for a connection to the name, but he had no data on the Soviet admiral. He did have information about the admiral's flagship, the *Leningrad*, though. He remembered it was the cruiser Ivan Trotsky had pointed out to him soon after he and Baxter had arrived by submarine in the Black Sea. Hs recalled passing abreast of the warship and would never forget the fierce physical characteristics of the Soviet cruiser. He decided that, if the Soviet admiral aboard the *Leningrad* was as feisty as Viktor claimed he was, the combination of cruiser and commandant could mean serious trouble. "And what does the Tyrant of Tymlat want?" he asked.

"He demands to speak with the commandant of the aircraft carrier U.S.S. *Coral Sea* at once," Viktor said.

"Get to a phone," Ferris said to Trish. "Tell Captain Redding what's going on, and that we need him down here on the double." Trish rushed off, and Ferris climbed up the wing to join Viktor. "Advise Admiral Stalovich that U.S. Navy Captain Thomas Redding is being summoned, but he does not speak Russian. Let him know that an interpreter will have to translate any conversation between them. Then show me how to use this . . ."

"Electronic warfare system scrambler phone," Viktor finished. He relayed Ferris's instructions to Stalovich, then after a quick indoctrination, he handed the radio mike over to Ferris. "Once the new jamming and antijamming apparatus is turned on, the scrambler phone part of the system works like any conventional aircraft radio."

"Could we call out to anyone at all over this . . . scrambler phone?" Ferris asked hopefully.

"Only to someone also equipped with the new system," Viktor said. "That is what keeps it secure from enemy eavesdropping."

"I see," Ferris said, disappointed.

"And, as you have already learned," Viktor went on, "the system can also be used as a communications blackout device. But we of lesser ranks in the military are not trusted with such technical aspects of the apparatus, as I mentioned to you back in Kiev."

When Redding arrived he climbed right up on the wing with Ferris and Viktor, leaving Trish and Nadia standing idly by beside the plane. "What's on his mind?" he asked.

Ferris keyed on the scrambler line. "Soviet Fleet Admiral Stalovich. Are you there?"

Seated confidently in Yudalslov's project director's chair, Stalovich said cagily, "This is not the same voice that spoke Russian to me a few moments ago. That voice had the tones of a native of the Soviet Union. Your voice hints of capitalist culture."

"I am the ship's linguist," Ferris replied. "The man you spoke to before is not good at interpreting."

"Could it be he is not good at patriotism, either?" Stalovich said bitterly, guessing the other Russian-speaking voice might belong to one of the Foxbat pilots who'd deserted.

Ferris continued: "The captain of the U.S.S. *Coral Sea* is ready to listen."

"What I have to say concerns the remaining MIG-35. It also concerns the traitors who placed our property in your hands. And since you are harboring both illegally, what I have to say concerns the captain of your ship and every man in his command. You are to inform him that I . . ."

After relaying Stalovich's ultimatum to Redding, Ferris said, "I seriously doubt he's just making idle threats."

"Oh, I'm quite convinced he means what he says," Redding replied. "His cruiser has moved up ahead of us. It's now holding a blockade position across our path to Alexandria at about a mile off our bow. It's a nice safe firing range that'll allow him to send us to the bottom without endangering his own ship. He'd suffer the consequences of such an act, but we'd be dead."

"Well, surrendering your ship to him will mean death for all or most of us, anyway," Ferris commented.

"I'd scuttle the *Coral Sea* before I'd turn her over to the Russians," Redding said.

"I guess that's our only hope," Ferris replied. "We can try to get away in life rafts under cover of darkness."

"It's a long paddle to Alexandria from here," Redding commented. "But, with both of their helicopters out of action, they'll have to lower small boats to make a search. And it could be daylight before they spot us."

"That won't be hard to take," Ferris said. "We'll be way overdue in Alexandria by daylight. Maybe Egyptian search planes will find us before the Russians do."

"That's if the Egyptian Air Force even bothers to come out and look for us," Redding said doubtfully.

"He's waiting for an answer," Ferris reminded as the beeper resounded in the forward and aft cockpits.

"Tell him we need some time to make up our minds," Redding suggested. "That'll give us a chance to pull the scuttle plugs on the ship, and hopefully get the hell over the side before he becomes suspicious."

As Ferris got back on the scrambler line with the *Leningrad*, Trish noticed her test meter dangling by its cords from inside the Foxbat's hellhole. She'd heard the decision to abandon ship, and thought she might as well remove the device now that the probing was to be aborted. As she gripped the test meter, she noticed its needle dancing up and down its measuring scale in unison with the conversation going on over the scrambler. Her professional curiosity got the best of her, and although she was nervous about the orange-colored cockpit voice recorder inside the hellhole, she forced herself up the mechanic's inspection stand and listened intently to the electronic hums emanating from the black box her meter was monitoring. Each module involved in the scrambler communications between the Soviet cruiser and Foxbat 104 was in concert with black box number forty-nine, the module they'd been about to check when the explosion interrupted them. That told her beyond a doubt that black box forty-nine was the key module to the entire jamming and antijamming system aboard the MIG-35. Elated by her discovery, she bumped her head in a rush to get out of the hellhole. Rubbing her sore forehead with one hand, she waved vigorously to get Ferris's notice.

Ferris noticed immediately the gleam in Trish's eyes, and as the Soviet fleet admiral was pondering the request for time to think his ultimatum over, he quickly keyed off and asked, "What is it, Trish?"

"I got it, Matt! I can't believe it, but I found the key unit to the system!" Trish said excitedly.

Ferris rushed off the wing and joined her. "You're sure?"

Pointing to her test meter, she said, "We'd have found the key black box right away if we had thought of turning the scrambler system on and transmitting communications between the two Foxbats! During your conversation with the admiral, the module my test meter is hooked up to was serving as a virtual switchboard between all the other black boxes being used to receive and transmit the communication."

"Good girl!" Ferris said, rejoicing. "At least we won't go home with empty pockets now."

"That's if we get to go home at all," Redding called down from the wing as the paging beeper came alive again.

"Will taking that one unit with us help solve the secret of their new technology, Trish?" Ferris asked, doing his best to ignore the demanding beeper for a moment longer.

"Absolutely, Matt," Trish said confidently. "It will reveal the mystery of their computer programming procedures by enlightening us on how all the components involved in the jamming and antijamming technology get accessed through the master module. Then, back at Fort Meade, we will be able to duplicate virtually every binary function of the aircraft radio-telephone system's receiver-transmitter circuitry. By constructing components that will function in harmony with black box number forty-nine, we can make the jamming and antijamming facets of the technology work the same for us in the lab as they do aboard the aircraft right now. As I said, we won't need the rest of the system. We'll design our own to work with the key unit and . . ."

Ferris cut Trish's explanation short as he charged up the wing and keyed on with the Soviet admiral again. "It is apparent that your ultimatum leaves us very little choice but to surrender our ship to you. The captain wishes, however, to allow his crew to vote on whether to live or die."

Stalovich asked in disbelief, "Do not the captains of American ships decide what is best for their crews?"

"Normally, yes," Ferris replied. "But in a case as unusual as this, Captain Redding is offering a democratic polling about the choice we must make. It is the American way," he added, sensing the Soviet admiral's astonishment.

"It is no wonder you Americans take forever to get things done," Stalovich commented. "You allow the lowest level of your military to interfere with those in command."

"Good thinking, Matt," Redding whispered. "Push for that point."

"Captain Redding hopes you will allow him to grant his crew permission to choose for themselves between life in a Soviet prison and death here aboard their carrier."

"And what does he expect the outcome of the vote to be?" Stalovich asked.

Pretending to ask, Ferris keyed off for a moment, then answered, "Captain Redding is sure most of his crew will choose life over death."

"And what is Captain Redding's preference?"

Ferris replied, "The captain is a very brave man. He would choose death. That is why he is giving his crew the chance to make the choice."

"He is brave. And foolish as well," Stalovich said bitingly. "And how long will the voting take?"

"An hour to poll. Another to count the votes." Ferris hoped to drag things out long enough for them to abandon ship and get well away from the carrier in life rafts.

"No, you have already detained me from my duties too long."

"An hour, then," Ferris pleaded. "We will hurry things along."

"You will have half that time," Stalovich shot back.

"But a half hour is an impossible amount of time in which to accomplish the polling," Ferris argued.

"This is absurd!" Yudalslov bellowed across the map table from Stalovich's commandant's chair. "We must sink the American carrier before it is too late."

"You will keep out of this military matter, Deputy Director Yudalslov," Stalovich growled in front of the open mike.

Ferris heard the voice in the background arguing with the Soviet admiral. Covering his mike, he said to Redding, "Someone with the title of deputy director is in favor of sinking us now. He must be a civilian because the Soviet admiral told him it's a military matter and to butt out."

"Thirty minutes!" Stalovich said firmly. "Inform Captain Redding that he is to heave to at once. If he fails to surrender to me after the thirty minutes has expired, I will order my batteries to open fire on his carrier. And my guns will not cease their bombardment until his ship and crew have been sent to the bottom of the sea." He saw Yudalslov picking up the scrambler phone and called out in front of the open mike, "What are you doing, Comrade Yudalslov?"

"I am going to inform Moscow of your ridiculous notion to take the American ship as prize. Perhaps our party leaders will end your ludicrous obsession to play buccaneer captain of your private pirate navy."

"Remove the deputy director from the CCS room at once," Stalovich shouted angrily.

"You will come with me, Comrade Deputy Director!" the *Leningrad*'s commanding officer demanded. He had been standing silently at his commandant's side during the conversation with the American carrier. And while he also preferred sinking the American ship to escorting it to a Soviet port, he responded obediently to Stalovich's order out of fear of disciplinary action for insubordination.

As Garupcheck was escorting Yudalslov out of the room, Stalovich barked, "Confine him to his quarters under guard until my business with the Americans has been concluded."

Ferris had heard the commotion, and with the mike button off, he said to Redding, "The admiral just confined this deputy director to quarters because he interfered with his decision making. It seems Admiral Stalovich is real bullish on taking your ship as prize."

"He is, is he?" Redding said with a smile.

"More so than sinking us, from what I gather," Ferris added.

For long moments Redding silently pondered the dispute taking place aboard the *Leningrad*. It seemed to him that the admiral's preference for capturing rather than sinking the *Coral Sea* could work to their advantage. All he had to do was find a way to keep the admiral's attention diverted from their escape. A half hour wasn't much time to draft a workable plan, he mused. But being stopped in the sea would help to get things done more quickly, he was sure. After a moment's more thought, he settled on a plan that just might fool the prize-hungry admiral. Facing Ferris he said, "Tell him we accept the half-hour limit, and we're heaving to. Tell him that if the majority rules in favor of surrendering, we'll be back on the line with him within the allotted time. Then sign off. We've got work to do."

CHAPTER TWENTY-FOUR

Stalovich paced the floor of the CCS room anxiously as the half-hour he'd allotted the Americans neared its end. He feared he was going to be deprived of the unique opportunity to seize the American ship. While he was waiting out the slow passing time, he envisioned escorting the huge angle-deck carrier into a Soviet port, where his party leaders would be waiting to cheer him. He pondered what such a rich prize could mean for him: he would be honored for recovering one of the Foxbats intact; he would be decorated for rescuing the new top secret technology from enemy hands; he would be rewarded handsomely for repatriating the three deserters for execution; he would be praised for delivering prisoners to the KGB for trial as spies; he would be commended for denying the Egyptians ownership of the American carrier. And surely, the party leaders would rename the ship he had captured after him, in tribute to its commission into the Soviet Navy. Best of all he would use the American ship to prove to the party leaders that more such monstrous angle-deck carriers should be added to the Soviet carrier cruiser fleet.

Stalovich's face lit up like a child's on Christmas morning when the scrambler phone suddenly began to beep. He seated himself in his commandant's chair and picked it up at once. "This is Commandant Stalovich." As he listened to the American-accented Russian, his elation intensified and he sprang to his feet. "It is wise to choose life over death," he said finally. "I compliment the good judgment the crew has displayed. And I assure you they will be repatriated to their homeland in due time. Now, you will instruct Captain Redding to get under way again. He is to come about to port on a northerly heading and expect further course corrections once we are en route to the Soviet Union. Remind him that the *Leningrad* will remain astern of his carrier, always within firing range. If he fails to follow my directives to the letter, I will open fire on his carrier without further discussion." He was acknowledged, then, seeing the

Leningrad's C.O. step into the room, he said happily, "We have scored a handsome victory over the Americans, Comrade Garupcheck. The American carrier captain has humbly accepted my terms of surrender."

"I will ferry a piloting crew over to the American ship at once, Commandant," the *Leningrad*'s C.O. said.

"Do not bother," Stalovich said. "They would probably be taken hostage. Besides, if any of their countrymen head our way to intervene, I will sink the American carrier after all."

"Shall I get the flagship underway now?"

"Not just yet," Stalovich decided. "We will wait until the American carrier captain has come about on the heading to the north that I ordered. It is quite dark out. Too dark to chance having both ships coming about at the same time. Besides, I want to bring up the rear so we can keep the American ship nicely in our gun sights."

"And Deputy Director Yudalslov? Shall I release him from confinement now that the matter with the Americans has been resolved?"

Stalovich thought for a moment, then replied with a smirk, "We will do so in time. For now, let him experience a taste of punishment for his insubordination. Perhaps he will be less eager to defy my orders in the future."

Cloaked by the pitch blackness of night, the *Coral Sea* began to whip up the surface of the sea with her propellers; behind her broad-backed fantail a frenzy of foamy white water splashed up like spurts of bubbly lava. Her running lights were off and her decks were dead quiet, giving her an eerie air as she moved off her heaved-to position a mile away from the Soviet cruiser. On the bridge deck the telegraphic annunciator was set in its full forward position, and bells from the engine room dutifully gave answer to the demand for all ahead full. Across the bridge from the annunciator at the captain's command console, green lights that had been burning steadily instantly flickered in response to the ship's forward motion. They brought twin indicators, mounted on the console next to them, to life. The twin indicators then caused the helm—an upright silver-spoked wheel in the center of the bridge—to spin automatically slightly to port. The helm caused the twin rudders, submerged in the sea well astern of the bridge deck, to point toward port in the precise degrees that their monitoring meters called for. The movement of the rudders caused the bow of the carrier to swing slowly in robot response to the left turn setting that had been programmed.

An elapsed-time clock in the center of the command console had begun to tick off the passing seconds and minutes from the moment the ship began making headway. In unison with the clock, a mileage meter was monitoring the distance the ship had traversed from the point where it had gotten under way again. At a precise point of convergence between travel and time, the noiseless alarm of the clock would set off a group of sensors and call for course corrections.

The *Leningrad*'s sonar operator listened alertly to the sound of the American carrier's propellers drumming into his ears. "The American ship continues to make headway at full speed, Commandant," he called across the CCS room to Stalovich.

"It is a large ship," Stalovich explained. "It must have full headway to execute a coming about on the course to the north."

The radar operator added, "But the Americans have covered a half mile already. And the ship's turn still remains only slight to port. If they do not increase their angle of attack through the sea soon, they will not come about until they reach the shores of the Middle East."

Stalovich envisioned the slight degree of turn the radar operator had described. Calculating the ship's position in reference to his own, he decided it wasn't a problem yet. But recalling the other course changes the American ship had made, it seemed to him the carrier had displayed marked maneuverability then. He dismissed the sluggish response to coming about that the American ship was demonstrating as being the American captain's use of caution in maneuvering through the darkness in a somewhat choppy sea. "She will come about in the next few minutes, I am sure," he said confidently.

Also thinking about the sluggish movements of the American carrier, the *Leningrad*'s C.O. said, "Could it be this American carrier captain and his crew has abandoned ship under cover of night and left his carrier to sail in automatic pilot to cover up their escape?"

Stalovich gave that idea considerable thought, then said, "It would be foolish of him to try and trick us. Abandoning ship and setting his carrier to steer on autopilot would gain him nothing. We would learn of the deception soon enough and go after them."

"It would be most difficult to find them in the sea at night without our two helicopters," Garupcheck said.

"True," Stalovich returned. "But in this choppy sea it will also be difficult for them to get very far away from us. If they have abandoned ship and left it to sail at full speed in autopilot, we will be forced to sink the *Coral Sea*. Then we will search the sea for them under first light of dawn and send them to the bottom after their ship."

Inside the lifeless bridge of the *Coral Sea*, the noiseless elapsed-time clock alarm triggered the sensors as it had been ordered to. Soundlessly, the green lights flickered. The twin knobs switched smoothly from left to right. Touchlessly, the helm turned hard to starboard. Faultlessly, the rudders swung into action to change their direction. Fearlessly, the bow of the *Coral Sea* pointed at the Soviet cruiser less than half a mile away. The flight deck was now a steel ramming rod.

"Commandant!" the radar operator called out woefully. "The American ship has changed course!"

"But of course," Stalovich said cheerfully. "It is as I said before. The American ship is quite large. It requires considerable headway and room to . . ."

"It has shifted to starboard, Commandant!" the radar operator interrupted in alarm. "It is now heading toward the flagship."

"And it still maintains flank headway, Commandant!" the sonar operator shouted.

Stalovich faced the *Leningrad*'s C.O. and ordered, "Get on the deputy director's toy telephone and demand that the Americans alter their course to the north as I ordered. Inform the carrier captain that I will open fire if he does not comply at once. I will be on the bridge to supervise fire control. Advise me immediately of the American captain's explanation for his defiance."

On the bridge and looking out at the towering black mass heading toward the *Leningrad*, the duty officer saw Stalovich arrive topside. "Commandant! The carrier is on collision course with the flagship!"

"Order our forward turret to fire a warning shot in front of the carrier's bow," Stalovich shouted, seeing the *Coral Sea* closer than he'd envisioned.

The forward gun turret swung around to face the ship approaching off port. The turret crew was uneasy about attacking an American ship, and they ignored the battery officer's first command to fire.

Furious, the battery officer growled, "That is an order from ou commandant!" He drew his holstered automatic. "I will shoot anyone who disobeys that order again! Fire!"

Stalovich was angered by the slow response to his order. He assumed that the turret crew's delay in taking aim was because Yudalslov's electronic warfare program had forced him to cut back on badly needed action station drills. When the forward turret cannons finally thundered, his eyes followed the projectiles as they screamed across the night sky. Both projectiles exploded a few yards ahead of the carrier's bow, and water rained on its flight deck. But still the American ship continued toward the *Leningrad*. Stalovich picked up the bridge phone and called down to CCS. "Has the American carrier captain given an explanation for his madness, Comrade Garupcheck?" he bellowed.

Holding the scrambler phone to one ear and the CCS phone connecting him with the bridge to the other, the *Leningrad*'s C.O. replied, "No one answers aboard the carrier, Commandant. I think they have all abandoned ship as we suspected."

"That cannot be," Stalovich insisted. "He knows he and his crew would never reach Alexandria before we realized what he has done. And he knows we would only find him and his crew in the sea and gun them down. I think he is still aboard and hopes to scare the *Leningrad* out of his way in a desperate attempt to make a run for it to Alexandria."

"But he must also know an attempt to sail his ship to Alexandria would be futile. Even if he forced the flagship to give up its blockading position across his path, our cannons would have their projectiles chasing after him and blow him out of the sea, Commandant."

"Then perhaps he *is* a foolishly brave man and has chosen to go down with his ship after all," Stalovich reasoned. He slammed the phone on its cradle angrily and said to the bridge duty officer standing by nervously, "Order both turrets forward and aft to fire directly on the carrier this time. I want the American captain and his ship sunk at once."

"But, Commandant!" the duty officer protested. "The ship is too close for us to stop it now. We must get the flagship out of its way immediately."

"Do as I ordered!" Stalovich snapped, then ran out to the port bridge catwalk to view the bombardment he'd just ordered. Within moments both forward and aft turrets resounded thunderously, sending their projectiles howling through the sky. They reached their target and exploded, peeling the *Coral Sea*'s flight deck back like a banana skin, and digging a crater into the forward section of the hull that began to spew seawater up into the air like a geyser. In spite of the rupture the carrier's momentum pushed it through the sea relentlessly.

"All ahead full!" the bridge duty officer cried out in panic, seeing that the last bombardment had failed to change anything. "We must get out of the way or we will be rammed."

"I gave no order to make headway!" Stalovich growled. "Have both batteries fire again!"

The duty officer stared at Stalovich in indecision for a brief moment, then, feeling the flagship moving, he said, "What good will it do to sink the American ship if it takes us to the bottom with it?"

In response to the cruiser's forward motion, the *Leningrad*'s C.O. charged up to the bridge. When he arrived there, he looked at the fast approaching carrier. He quickly assessed the threat the American ship posed and saw that his ship was moving toward, instead of away from, the danger. "You fool!" he blared at the duty officer. "You are bringing us right into its path." He picked up the P.A. mike and urgently ordered, "Reverse engines! Reverse engines, at once!"

The sea tossed up wildly behind the cruiser as it was sent into a frenzy by the propeller's sudden change of direction. The ship was stationary for long anxious moments before it finally started to back up slowly.

Too slowly, the *Leningrad*'s C.O. was forced to admit as he eyed the carrier. "Commandant, we are doomed! We must abandon ship at once!"

Stalovich stared blankly at the hell-bent ship, unable to think. Even move. He was deaf to the repeated warnings as he muttered to himself, "It is my carrier now! I will not be cheated out of my rightful prize!"

The *Leningrad*'s C.O. looked away from Stalovich in disgust. He paid a last anxious glance at the advancing ship. Its bow was lower in the sea, but still its flight deck dwarfed the *Leningrad*'s bridge. Exasperated, he keyed the P.A. mike. "This is the captain! Man the lifeboats! Abandon ship!"

Freed from confinement by the guards posted outside his private cabin, Yudalslov joined the frantic rush for the topside decks as the abandon-ship alarm reverberated on all lower levels of the cruiser. Crewmen were climbing over shipmates who had fallen to the decks in their panicky race to escape. Yudalslov was punched and slapped by others when he tried to maintain an orderly evacuation. In his own desperation to flee the ship, he also resorted to physical violence to beat off those hindering his escape from certain death.

When he arrived topside, Yudalslov saw Stalovich, on the bridge catwalk overhang just above him, staring at the closing American ship. He shook an accusing fist up at him and shouted hoarsely, "You wanted a great aircraft carrier! Now you have one! Sail it down to the hell it has come to take you to!" Seeing that his shouts went unnoticed, he left Stalovich in his trancelike state and hurried over to a lifeboat that was about to be lowered. He caught sight of the *Leningrad*'s C.O. and X.O. waving him on, then everything suddenly went dark as fierce pain exploded in his head.

Callously, the crewman who had just struck Yudalslov on the back of the head with the butt of a military pistol stepped on his collapsed body to get over the starboard deck railing, then leaped into the descending lifeboat to take Yudalslov's place.

Oblivious to the crewmen piling into the remaining lifeboats and leaping into the sea from the starboard deck edges, Stalovich remained on the port catwalk, paralyzed. He looked at the carrier, but not at its flaming and battered bow towering above him. Instead, he gazed at the bridge windows of the carrier's superstructure. Two hideous green eyes were staring back at him hypnotically from behind the bridge windows, refusing to let him leave. There was tormenting laughter echoing in his ears that he was sure the giant green eyes were causing. Was it the American carrier captain humiliating him? he wondered. "Why?" he cried out in anguish. "Why did you choose death for your great ship?" Tears filled his eyes and streamed down his cheeks. "Why are you staring at me accusingly?" he screamed. "It is you who are the guilty one! Not I! Why are you denying me what is rightfully mine?"

In the bridge deck of the *Coral Sea* the large green lights on the captain's command console were switched off by the mileage meter as its digital display reached zero. The reflection they'd made in the forward bridge windows disappeared just as the bow of the carrier knifed through the *Leningrad*'s midships at maximum headway, cutting the ship in half. The impact caused the two halves of the cruiser to burst into flames that sent debris rocketing up to the heavens, turning the pitch-black night into the brilliance of day. More volcanolike eruptions occurred as the bow and stern ends of the *Leningrad* lifted skyward just off the port and starboard sides of the U.S.S. *Coral Sea*. The concussion also turned the carrier's hangar deck into an inferno that caused Foxbat 104 to explode in a fireball.

For what seemed an unending time, the fires burned, despite the rising sea, aboard the carrier and both halves of the cruiser. When the *Coral Sea*'s forward motion finally ended, the huge ship was pulled down bow first under the sea. Briefly, the carrier stood up in the sea with its stern pointing to the sky and its four propellers spinning wildly, then it slid slowly beneath the surface. Its suction turned the fiery surface into a violent whirlpool that drew both burning halves of the *Leningrad* down to the depths with the carrier. In a matter of moments, both ships were gone and their fires extinguished. Bobbing atop the swells, the survivors of the disastrous ramming were plunged into total darkness as they fought to stay alive. Some, who were fortunate enough to be aboard one of the lifeboats, were helping those who were hanging to the sides to keep from slipping away. Others who missed the lowered boats were on their own with only life jackets to keep them afloat. The least fortunate were those who got off too late to get into lifeboats or even draw life jackets. They were depending upon their swimming ability, and hoping the flares and emergency radio beacons on the boats would bring rescuers before their tiring arms and legs would give in to the cold of winter. If help didn't arrive in time, they were doomed to join their mother ship at the bottom of the Mediterranean.

EPILOGUE

The sea was stained yellow by die markers leaking their chemical powder around the two rafts floating atop the slow-rolling surface. Both rafts were tied together by a lifeline as the currents carried them at a crawl toward the south. The occupants, fifteen in each raft, were huddled close together to ward off the chill of the long wintry night they had shared in silence. They barely steered as their tired eyes peeked out from under heavy lids to see the first bursts of dawn climbing over the eastern horizon. The spread of rays resembled the long fingers of a Titan reaching up from the depths of the blue-green Mediterranean. And the fiery red ball that followed its brilliant beams skyward appeared as a bloom of hope to all.

Snuggled between Ferris and Redding, Trish had a death grip on black box forty-nine, a grip that had worn grooves in the palm of her hand. But the cold lessened the pain her grip was causing. And the value of the possession she gripped so tightly helped to ease the aches in the rest of her body. She still could see in her mind the fiery end both ships had met last night, and she'd never be able to erase from her memory the horrors she'd lived through aboard the U.S.S. *Coral Sea*. Operation Mediterranean Maneuver was going to haunt her for the rest of her life, she was sure. But for now she would concentrate on the thought of rescue. They had shot off flares, and gotten the emergency radio beacon in the raft transmitting a call for help, as soon as they'd seen the carrier and Soviet cruiser sink. But in the long hours that had slowly passed since, there had been no sign of a search plane or ship responding to their SOS. She raised her head to the new dawn and searched the sky for a hint that rescuers were near. She saw only the rising sun and the endless sea.

"Autopilot," Ferris mumbled, breaking the long and heavy silence in both rafts.

Redding blinked his eyes rapidly to chase the sleep from them. "That's what did it," he said through a hearty yawn. "That, and the speed and course settings I programmed into the computer which runs the autopilot."

"I guess I'd better become computer-minded," Ferris said with a yawn and a stretch. "It seems the hands-on, personal touch is quickly becoming obsolete." He tapped his head with an index finger as he added through another yawn, "So is the gray stuff up here, now that computers are doing our thinking for us."

"Computers will never do all the thinking for us, I'm certain," Redding said as he also stretched the cramps out of his body. "I had to use the gray matter to calculate for the human factor. I had no way of knowing for sure if my ship would meet up with the Soviet cruiser. That's why I had the scuttle cocks opened to the sea. Just in case the *Coral Sea* missed its target. You see, the *Leningrad*'s commanding officer could have either moved forward or backward when it became apparent my ship was set to ram his."

"Which way did you figure him for?" Ferris asked. His question drew stares from the bridge O.O.D., and most of the surviving crewmen, who listened with interest.

"I couldn't make up my mind, so I calculated a ram in her stern if the *Leningrad* moved forward off its heaved-to position. That way, if she moved backward instead, I'd catch her square in the midships. In either case, she'd be hit bad enough to either sink with the *Coral Sea* or just flounder around on the surface with her ass end hanging off for the whole world to see."

"That Soviet fleet admiral would have had some big explaining to do if his flagship hadn't sunk," Ferris said.

"If there's a God," Trish put in, "the admiral's going to have some explaining to do in hell."

Redding cupped a hand over one ear and leaned to the south. "Listen," he said. "I think I hear the pretty popping sounds of approaching choppers."

Within a few anxious minutes, six Egyptian Air Force helicopters were over the two rafts. Without delay, pulleys fed cables down to the rafts with rescue harnesses, while helicopter crewmen, wearing rubber "poopy" (skin-tight and neck-to-boot-fitting antiexposure) suits, jumped into the sea to help the survivors get into the harnesses. In twenty minutes both rafts were emptied. The helicopters banked, then streaked to the south, heading for Alexandria.

Trish was surprised to find Hal Banks aboard the helicopter she was raised up to. When she saw Ferris come aboard and act as though he wasn't equally surprised, she said, "Don't tell me you expected Hal to come and rescue us?"

Ferris winked at her. "Not exactly. All I did was pray . . . and God showed up."

Banks joined them in a hearty laugh, then said, "God had a little hint that you needed rescuing. Our Sixth Fleet task force commander was alert enough to tip me off that the Soviet cruiser *Leningrad* had slipped away from its fleet to rescue a downed pilot. Admiral Walters aboard the U.S.S. *Eisenhower* was going to hightail it after you if the *Leningrad* failed to rejoin its task force in what he figured was a reasonable amount of time. But I told him not to, fearing that the presence of the *Ike* might do you more harm than good. So, just in case the *Leningrad* got wise to my little gig, I hopped a special MATS jet to Alexandria so I could be close by if you were overdue in making your Med Crossing."

"And you waited till we cued you with our SOS before sending the cavalry to our rescue?" Ferris asked curtly.

"I feared if I arrived with help too soon, I might also screw up your efforts to get what we were after," Banks explained. He gestured to the black box Trish was holding lovingly. "I gather from that little jewel, that Operation Mediterranean Maneuver was a success."

"A complete success," Trish stated proudly.

"But we were a hair away from seeing the mission fail completely," Ferris commented. "And all of us get blown away."

Banks listened sadly as Ferris and Redding filled him in on the number of casualties and the circumstances. For a long moment, as though he were offering a silent prayer, he stared up at the cabin ceiling. When he looked across the narrow cabin aisle at Ferris and Trish, he said somberly, "Nick and Walt Dodge will be properly commended for their valor." He glanced at Redding seated next to them. "I conferred with the Hill people on a suitable expression of appreciation for everyone's devotion to the mission, once we got your coded communiqué. It took a little figuring out to realize what you meant about the kangaroo having two cubs in the pouch, and about the father of one being given the deep six. I gathered a second Foxbat had to be included in the defection for unavoidable reasons, and that one of the pilots involved had to be gotten rid of."

"It was because of the second Foxbat that we ran into a snag," Redding said. "When the cruiser *Leningrad* rescued the ejected pilot of the second Foxbat, a stubborn old salt by the name of Stalovich grew suspicious of us."

"That almost put the kibosh on your Operation Med Maneuver gig," Ferris said.

Banks nodded. "You can give me a full report on the incident when we get back to CIA headquarters, Matt," he said, then returned his attention to Redding. "Those of your crew who perished aboard the U.S.S. *Coral Sea* will be awarded posthumous commendations for their valor. Those who survived the ordeal will be decorated by the President of the United States. The President also has a couple of ribbons to pin on you. And there's a promotion to rear admiral by congressional decree." Glancing over at Viktor and Nadia, he said in choppy Russian, "We will all mourn the loss of Junior Lieutenant Mishka Borken and honor the sacrifice she made in your behalf. I'll see to it that both of you are made quite comfortable in your newly adopted homeland."

"Speaking of adoptions," Ferris said, "whatever happened to that old man and his wife that we snuck out of Kiev by sub?"

"Yuri and Yekaterina Velinkov are going to be spending the rest of their lives in Arizona, where the weather and some good American medical attention will help to ease the old woman's arthritis and rheumatism pains."

"And Ivan?" Ferris asked.

"Trotsky and his wife are in Turkey," Banks said. "He's turning over his Soviet connections to a younger operative. He decided it's time for his old bones to retire from the spying business."

"While we're holding muster," Redding said quietly, "I forgot to mention that there are a bunch of Soviet sailors swimming around in the sea where their cruiser went down."

"They're being looked after," Banks assured him. "Only when they see who is coming to rescue them, I don't think they're going to be overjoyed." He pointed to the surface of the sea at two destroyers that were steaming for the area where the Soviet cruiser had sunk.

Ferris, Trish, and Redding looked out the cabin window at the two warships. Seeing the Star of David on the masts of the ships, he laughed aloud. "I think they're going to wish they'd gone straight to hell when their ship went down when the Israeli intelligence interrogators get through with them."

"Trish," Banks said with a smile, "NSA has a nice surprise waiting for you when you get back to Fort Meade."

"I hate surprises," Trish said. "Tell me what it is."

"For openers, you're getting a month off to spend anywhere you want, with all expenses paid," Banks said with a grin.

"What about me?" Ferris grumbled. "Doesn't the CIA have a nice surprise waiting for their ace TOS agent?"

"How does a month in Waikiki Beach with all expenses paid sound?" Banks asked.

"Not bad," Ferris replied. "For openers."

"What else did you have in mind?"

"A new car," Ferris said. "One with a heater that works."

"You got it," Banks promised him. "Compliments of the Hill people."

Facing Trish, Ferris asked, "Where do you plan to spend your month-long vacation, Trish?"

"I always wanted to tour Europe," Trish said, teasingly. She saw Ferris frown. "Or maybe the Orient." Then, looking into his eyes affectionately, she added, "But I also have a passion for Polynesian cooking in a romantic setting."

Ferris took Trish's hand in his. "I know this place in Waikiki Beach that is world-renowned for the best romantically set luau and . . .

IS VIETNAM STILL HIDING AMERICAN POWs?

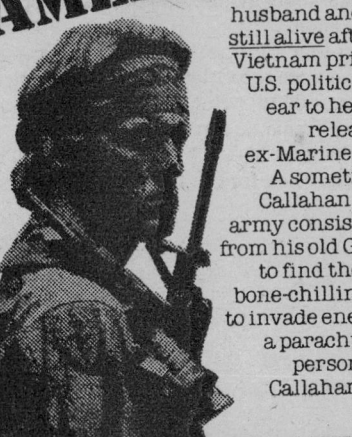

One woman is certain her husband and other men are _still alive_ after 12 years in a Vietnam prison cage. When U.S. politicians turn a deaf ear to her pleas for their release, she turns to ex-Marine, Jack Callahan. A sometime mercenary, Callahan forms a bastard army consisting of four men from his old Green Beret unit to find the POWs. Against bone-chilling odds, he plans to invade enemy territory in a parachute drop no _sane_ person could imagine. Callahan calls the secret escape plan

MISSION M.I.A.
a novel by J.C. Pollock • $3.50

At your local bookstore or use this handy coupon for ordering:

Dell

DELL BOOKS
P.O. BOX 1000, PINE BROOK, N.J. 07058-1000

Mission M.I.A.   15819-2-18 $3.50

B233A

Please send me the above title. I am enclosing $_____ (please add 75¢ per copy to cover postage and handling). Send check or money order—no cash or C.O.D.'s. Please allow up to 8 weeks for shipment.

Mr./Mrs./Miss _____

Address _____

City _____ State/Zip _____